T0208906

PAX BRITANNICA
THE GOLDEN ANVIL

PAUL DALZELL

authorHOUSE®

AuthorHouse™
1663 Liberty Drive
Bloomington, IN 47403
www.authorhouse.com
Phone: 1 (800) 839-8640

Published by AuthorHouse 04/17/2019

ISBN: 978-1-7283-0869-2 (sc)
ISBN: 978-1-7283-0868-5 (e)

Library of Congress Control Number: 2019904517

Chapter 1

"What did you say your occupation was, sir?"

"I didn't say."

"Oh, well, would you care to enlighten me then, sir?"

"Missionary."

"What?"

"I'm a missionary."

"Your passport says soldier."

"I'm a soldier of God."

"Think we're a comedian, do we, sir?"

"No. I was in a missionary position night and day about a week ago," said Doyle.

Instead of questioning Doyle further, the customs officer began a thorough search of his bags. He scrutinized Doyle's suitcase, feeling inside and out and tapping the surfaces with a flat-bladed screwdriver.

Doyle froze as the official ran his hands over the inner surface of the suitcase lid. He inserted the screwdriver blade into the space between the suitcase lid's inner surface and the rim.

Nothing happened.

Doyle hoped that the catches would continue to hold. The customs officer was not easily defeated and kept probing the lid. There was a click, and then one corner of the suitcase's inner surface detached. He looked up at Doyle with a grim smile. He levered the screwdriver in the gap, forcing another catch to pop, and the entire panel flopped open.

Three passports fell out, followed by sheets of opium in Indian government wrapping paper. The customs officer looked again at Doyle, who said nothing.

Doyle wished, for the millionth time, he had kept his dumb Irish mouth shut.

The officer was still smiling when one of his colleagues marched over. His colleague bent close and whispered into his ear, showing him some form of official document. The second customs officer was gesturing at a smartly dressed woman in the doorway of the Heathrow Airport customs office. The customs official with Doyle's luggage looked shocked and angry. He said, "What? You mean he can go free, just like that? Look at this: narcotics and forged passports." He rummaged around and found rolls of gold sovereigns wrapped in Indian Bank paper.

The custom officer's colleague looked sympathetic and glared at Doyle, who was now feeling a sense of relief.

"He's with the Imperial Secret Service. Orders came down from the head office. Look at this memo from the Home Secretary; it says that he be admitted to England with his luggage not to be subject to a customs search," the second customs official whispered harshly.

"I'll be on my way then," said Doyle, trying hard not to smirk.

He took the passports, opium, and sovereigns from the customs officer, who was too shocked to resist, and tossed them into the suitcase. Doyle closed the suitcase and tut-tutted over the damage to the false lid. He would have to take it to Kemal in Rotherhithe. The Egyptian was the best smuggler in London.

Four days from Jodhpur on a plane had taken its toll on Doyle's patience. His back ached, and all he wanted was a hot bath, accompanied by a very large whiskey, into which he would drop a ball of opium. Without waiting for a dismissal, he slung the leather grip over his shoulder and picked up his trench coat, suitcase, and briefcase. He strolled past the examination table to the woman waiting for him in the customs office doorway.

Doyle could see the woman was young and pretty in an English way: flawless skin, a slender nose, and little makeup but rouged lips. Her long hair was scooped up into a bun behind her head. She wore the uniform of civil service women: a charcoal-gray twinset but with a pencil skirt. Her dark shoes had six-inch stiletto heels, which Doyle thought might be pushing the dress code, even at the UK's Imperial Secret Service (ISS).

She gazed at Doyle as he approached.

Doyle said, "I'd shake, but my hands are full. The suitcase might fall apart after what that clown did. I suppose you're the welcoming committee."

"Pleased to meet you, Mr. Doyle. Sorry about all that unpleasantness with customs. Morning rush hour traffic delayed us getting out of London. I am sorry. I do go on. I'm Alexandra McCall, but please call me Alex. Sir Anthony sent me to collect you."

"Good. I need a bath and to get my head down for some serious sleep."

"Oh dear, I'm sorry. We do have a room reserved for you at the Union Jack Club, but I'm to take you straight to see Sir Anthony. There's a terrible flap on, and your presence is required."

Doyle's felt his face flush in anger, and then he saw Alex wince at his expression. Doyle sighed and composed himself.

He said, "Sorry. Force of habit. Let's get out of here. Did you say you were called Alex, Miss McCall?"

"Yes. Just follow me. I have a car and driver waiting close by."

Alex led Doyle through the Heathrow customs office to a rear door. They walked across a car park in which was parked a large

3

Bentley with a uniformed driver. The driver stubbed out a cigarette and came toward Doyle, offering to help with his bags.

Doyle held onto his briefcase as Alex instructed the driver where to go. They drove out of the car park, stopping at a guardhouse, where Alex showed her official government pass.

Once clear of the airport, Doyle made a closer inspection of Alex. Her accent was pure Home Counties, but her hair was dark red—almost copper colored—making him suspect she was originally Scottish.

"Are you from north of the border, Miss McCall?"

"I'm an English girl through and through. My mother is from Norfolk, but my father is from Perth, where we have an estate. We do holiday in the Highlands though. Well, I should say we used to when I was a girl. My parents still take their holidays there."

Doyle knew that the ISS recruited only the best and brightest. He decided to not rush to judgment on Alex McCall.

"Do you know what all this pandemonium is about?" asked Doyle.

"Yes, but I'm under strict instructions to deliver you to Sir Anthony and keep mum about what's going on."

"Well, it must be something big enough to make King Tony drag my weary arse across half the world, and then send the prettiest girl in the office to make sure I came straight from the airport."

Alex laughed. "Oh really? Is it that transparent? And anyway, I'm not the prettiest girl in the office."

"Well, you're not some old boiler though, are you? The customs men were jumping smartly, so good looks and confidence—just the sort of girl I'd ask out for a drink later, if you're free."

"I thought you wanted to sleep. They warned me about you, Mr. Doyle. Said you're only interested in women for one thing and that the streets of the empire are littered with your castoffs."

"A terrible exaggeration, Alex."

"Oh? What were you doing in Kashmir with Mrs. Venkatamaran? She's one of the most notorious brothel madams in Delhi."

"Is that any way to talk about one of the most important ISS officers in India?"

"Hmm. Is she indeed? So you and Mrs. Venkatamaran were doing what? Brushing up on your cipher skills?"

"Something like that—in between bouts of meditation and yoga."

"Now you're bragging."

"I'm serious. Ikshana is a very devout lady, and she shared her devotions with me. So how about that drink?"

"Sorry. I'm going out tonight with my fiancée."

"You're not wearing an engagement ring."

Alex pulled out a gold chain around her neck and lifted a diamond ring from beneath the collar of her blouse.

"We're keeping it a secret for now. Sir Anthony doesn't want me wearing a ring when I go into the field, but I think I can let you in on the secret."

"You're a field agent?"

"Newly minted, I'm afraid, so I've never been anywhere exotic."

"We're heading west," said Doyle, looking at the road signs.

"Yes, I'm not taking you into Vauxhall Cross. Sir Anthony wants to see you at his Windsor house."

"Did he give a reason?"

"I'm sure he has one, but I am too low on the totem pole."

"Low and lovely," said Doyle with a smile.

He felt irritable, and his eyes were gritty from lack of sleep. However, there were worse things than motoring across the Home Counties in spring with a beautiful young woman.

Doyle sighed, thinking of his interrupted holiday. He had been with

Ikshana Venkatamaran and her daughters in a houseboat on a Kashmir lake. Ikshana had invited Doyle to join her, after rescuing her youngest niece from a Delhi gang. She and her daughters cooked spectacular feasts, told stories, sang songs, and treated Doyle like a raja.

His occasional employer, the ISS, interrupted Doyle's reverie in what felt like paradise. A military escort delivered a telegram demanding his presence in London. The telegram specified the trains and flight he was to catch. He journeyed by rail from Srinagar to Jodhpur to catch a commercial flight to London.

Doyle gazed out of the window and watched the world outside pass by—a world from which he felt alienated. *God, it is lovely,* he thought as they passed through Wraysbury and Old Windsor. *There is no green like England's leafy suburbs.*

"You look rather wistful, Mr. Doyle."

"Just enjoying the view, Alex. I'm not often in England."

"Why do you call Sir Anthony, King Tony?"

"Just my private joke. Bartholomew Anthony Raja. Raja means 'king' in Hindi. I thought a smart girl like you would have worked that out."

"Don't be sarcastic. I thought as much. How long have you known him?"

"Since he was a cadet in the Indian Civil Service and I was a lieutenant in the Indian Army."

"There's a rumor that you saved his life all those years ago."

Doyle exaggerated his Irish brogue, saying, "Faith and *begorrah, à* colleen; 'twas nothing."

"That's not what I heard. But why does he not use his first name of Bartholomew?"

"Why don't you ask him?"

"Spoilsport, I—"

A fireball enveloped the front of the Bentley.

Chapter 2

The car lurched violently sideways into oncoming traffic. Doyle and Alex were thrown around the rear of the vehicle. Doyle saw the head of the driver smash into the glass partition of the car. Another blow struck the car. A bus had rammed into the vehicle. The car rolled off the road into a field and lay on its side.

Alex McCall groaned beneath Doyle. He did a quick inspection of his own body and then looked at Alex to see if she was seriously injured. He found no evidence of major trauma, just cuts and bruises like him. Doyle slid the glass partition open and looked at the driver, who lay unconscious, with blood trickling down his head from his ears and nose. The windscreen was still intact, as were the other windows of the Bentley. Doyle realized that the Bentley had bulletproof glass and was armored to survive an attack.

Doyle pushed the door open. He was about to climb out but paused, thinking that whoever had attacked them might still be out there, ready to pick off survivors. There was a series of thuds against the roof of the car. Doyle silently thanked Sir Anthony for sending the armored vehicle to pick him up. More bullets slammed into the car, but the armor kept them safe. Doyle thought the shooter might be trying to get the petrol tank to ignite. He wished he could shoot back, but his guns were in his bags in the trunk.

The car had rolled into a field, but looking out of the front window,

Doyle could see there were houses nearby. He thought they must be just outside Windsor.

Doyle could see people running toward the wrecked Bentley. Whoever had attacked the Bentley might blend in with innocent rescuers and try to finish the job. He looked in Alex's handbag for a weapon but found nothing. Normally he would have had a knife on him, but he had been cautious coming back into England. Doyle's knives, like his guns, were in his luggage. On a hunch, he reached under Alex's dress and ran his hands up both her legs.

"What the ruddy hell?" said Alex.

Doyle pulled his hands out from beneath her skirt. He had found a thigh holster holding a small automatic pistol. Before he could explain, a head peered over the open door of the Bentley.

"Are you all right?"

Doyle could not see clearly and kept the gun hidden behind his back. More people gathered around the wreck; Doyle could see their legs out of the rear window. Another head appeared above the open door, and Doyle recognized a policeman's helmet. One of the people around the car addressed him as Constable Owen. Doyle felt secure enough to stand up, carefully slipping the gun into his trouser pocket. He allowed hands to pull him out of the car and lower him gently onto the grass.

"Are you all right, sir?" asked the constable.

"I'm okay. Please look after Miss McCall. I don't think she's seriously injured, but just in case. The driver is badly hurt. Did anyone call for an ambulance?

"Not yet, sir, I was on my way home on my bike," said the policeman.

"I'll call for an ambulance, Mr. Owen. I can phone from our house."

A schoolboy ran toward a house across the road from the field.

"Good lad, Billy," said Owen, calling after him.

Doyle got to his feet but kept his head below the upturned side of the Bentley. He looked left and right for anyone or anything suspicious. A small crowd of people was assembling around the car. There was a bus on the road, with its front caved in from the impact; Doyle could see a body that he guessed was the driver.

Passengers were dismounting, several with bloodstains and one woman cradling an arm bent at an odd angle. Doyle took several deep breaths to clear his head and calm his heart. He looked again above the side of the car, taking a risk to take a long look at the scene in front of him. He searched for anybody who was just watching or for vehicles that were driving away from the accident.

Doyle saw Billy emerge from his house, pointing to the accident and pulling a woman Doyle guessed was his mother. The next-door house had a "For sale" sign outside, and it looked unoccupied. Doyle looked at the upstairs windows. One was open. Doyle looked hard at the dark interior beyond the windowpane, looking for movement.

Alex was helped out of the car by Constable Owen. Doyle looked carefully as her back was exposed. Doyle thought he saw some movement and ducked his head below the edge of the car. Alex saw his caution and pulled herself forward, landing and somersaulting on the ground. She joined Doyle, following his line of sight.

Constable Owen said, "My goodness, miss, you are nimble."

"Thank you, Constable, but please would you see to the driver."

Alex moved close to Doyle. She said, "Is someone up there?"

"Can't be sure, especially after a shake-up like that."

There was the snarl of a motorcycle, and a rider with a passenger in a sidecar emerged from the side of the vacant house. Both were dressed in leather with crash helmets and goggles. As they rode away, the occupant of the sidecar looked directly to where Doyle and Alex were standing behind the wrecked Bentley.

"Didn't think there was anyone staying in the Robinson's house," said Owen. "Funny that they didn't come down to help. No accounting for people, I suppose."

Doyle and Alex emerged from behind the wreck, looking along the road at the disappearing motorcycle and sidecar.

Chapter 3

The next few hours passed in a blur. Doyle was tired from his long journey and the car crash had shaken him up. He, Alex, and the driver were treated at the King Charles V Hospital in Windsor.

Doyle and Alex had their cuts and contusions cleaned and bandaged in the hospital emergency room. A medical triage team rushed the driver to surgery. The police approached Alex and Doyle for questioning. Alex produced a leather wallet that contained a gold badge on one side, and on the other side was an identity card with a photograph. She removed the card and showed it to a detective inspector, saying, "I think you've seen one of these before?"

The detective did a double take, looking at the card and then Alex. His attitude became more deferential.

Alex said in a polite tone, "Inspector, you see the phone number listed on the back of the card? Please have one of your men call it immediately and ask for the raja. They'll know what who you mean."

"Who'll know?" said a uniformed senior policeman, who pulled back the screen around Alex and Doyle.

Doyle watched Alex look at the newcomer. She took her card from the inspector and passed it to the senior police officer. Doyle guessed he was a chief superintendent or maybe a deputy chief constable. Doyle saw the wind went out of his sails, and senior officer looked at Alex with a mixture of respect and fear.

Despite the circumstances, Doyle chuckled to himself; no

institution in human history was as ruthless as the British Empire in the exercise of power. The instrument of that power was the ISS.

Doyle looked at his watch, finding it hard to believe it was only lunchtime. The attack must have been about half past eight, as children were on their way to school. He lay back on the pillow. The next thing he remembered was being woken up. His vision swam into focus, and there was a nurse looking down at him. Doyle could see the ISS chief, Sir Anthony Raja, looking through the gap in the bed screens.

Doyle swung his legs over the bed and said, "Nice of you to come and see me, King Tony. Did you bring me any grapes?"

"I see your recent escapades haven't improved your manners or your wit, Doyle."

"It's good to see you too. Now what? It seems whatever skullduggery you had planned for me has been blown."

"Perhaps. Are you able to make a short journey into Windsor?"

Doyle nodded, seeing the strain on Sir Anthony's imperturbable face. Whatever was going on had to be very big indeed. Doyle knew that, like many public servants, Sir Anthony had a grace and favor apartment gifted from the monarchy. His apartment laid within the walls the Windsor Castle Upper Ward, a mark of highest esteem in the most favored royal residence.

"Your bags have been transferred to my car. I'm glad that I sent the armored Bentley to pick you up. Otherwise I'd probably be supervising your funeral arrangements and expressing my regrets to Miss McCall's parents and fiancée."

"Is her fiancée in the Service?"

"None of your business—but no, since you asked."

Doyle knew that the ISS staff had rigorously assessed the young man's background and security risk.

"She's a nice girl. How is she? What about the driver of the Bentley?"

"Miss McCall suffered a few cuts and bruises, like you. The driver was not so lucky—several fractured bones, including the skull, and some internal bleeding. They had to remove his spleen apparently. He's unconscious from the operating theater, so we have had no chance to question him."

"Nasty. Do you think he leaked my arrival?"

"No."

"You're very certain about that."

"Yes. Come along; let's go to my house. There's someone I want you to meet."

Doyle followed Sir Anthony out of the emergency room and to a Rolls Royce drawn up at the hospital entrance. Doyle could see Alex sitting in the front. A driver dressed in the same livery as the injured driver held the door of the Rolls open.

Doyle thought that Sir Anthony would continue their conversation, but he sat upright, a dignified Indian Brahmin in a tailored, black Saville Row suit. Sir Anthony's pale brown skin reflected his mixed parentage of an English aristocrat and an Indian prince. Doyle knew he was the second son of that lineage, so he would not inherit the Principality of Sajiristan.

Sir Anthony Raja had a brilliant and meteoric career in the Indian and Imperial Civil Services. For the past decade had been at the helm of the ISS, restoring its reputation after a series of spy scandals had left the Service and the British Empire dangerously exposed.

A heavy police motorcycle escort accompanied the Rolls. Sir Anthony was taking no chances, even on the short drive into Windsor. The procession of vehicles turned into the main gate of Windsor Castle and the large courtyard, with its series of houses.

The motorcycles and other cars peeled off to let the Rolls proceed alone to the Upper Ward. Doyle, Alex, and Sir Anthony stepped out of the Rolls Royce.

The day was warm and sunny, a perfect May afternoon. Doyle saw the Union Jack flag flying above the castle. The King was in residence. There was a lively crowd of visitors streaming in and out of the castle: people of all colors, costumes, and races, reflecting the huge ethnic diversity of the empire. Children were running, jumping, and climbing on everything and being chased off by the security staff.

"I suppose the café and gift shops are doing a brisk trade," Doyle said to Alex, while Sir Anthony spoke to his driver.

"Next year will be the real moneymaker: four hundred years of the House of Stuart on the throne. Rehearsals have already begun for next year's 2007 Jubilee."

"Is that why I'm here, to help organize the celebrations?"

Alex smiled and then asked in a serious tone, "What hit the Bentley on the drive here?"

"Probably an anti-tank weapon, a rocket propelled grenade of some sort. Luckily, it hit front of the car. It's a shape charge designed to punch a jet of molten metal into the innards of a tank. Well, you can guess how that tends to react with flesh and blood."

"Charming. The Bentley's being retrieved by the Armory Division to look over."

"Old Man Sykes will love that, assuming he's still in charge."

"Yes, he's still there. Lookout—Sir Anthony wants us to follow him."

Doyle turned to see the Rolls departing down the hill and Sir Anthony motioning to his front door, held open by a small, tough-looking Asian. Doyle knew that the man was a Gurkha, probably the bravest soldiers anywhere on Earth. Doyle had been in some tough scrapes where Gurkhas had saved his skin. A platoon of Gurkhas had fought their way to free Doyle from an Afghanistan jail. They succeed in rescuing him and losing half their men in the breakout, one of whom dived onto a grenade to smother the blast.

As he passed the little man, Doyle said, *"Jai Mahakali, Ayo Gorkhali,"*[1] at which the man drew himself even straighter and drew his arm up in a *bada salamme*.[2]

"At ease, Gurung," said Sir Anthony. "This is Michael Doyle, whom I've told you about; he's the one your nephew rescued a few years ago."

"Indeed, sir," said Gurung. "It is a great pleasure. I hope my nephew looked after you well."

"I'm here now because of him." Doyle said, feeling inadequate.

"Your other guest is here, sir. I put him in the drawing room, as you requested."

Sir Anthony looked at the closed door and said, "Very well, thank you, Gurung. Could you bring us in some tea?"

Sir Anthony opened the drawing room door and gestured for Doyle and Alex to step through. Inside the room, the lights were on, the curtains were half closed, and a middle-aged man dressed in casual clothes sat in a chair by the unlit fireplace, reading the contents of a cardboard folder.

As they stepped through, the man looked up from the folder and stood. The man's face was instantly familiar, though Doyle had never met him. He had seen that face on stamps, coins, bank notes, and posters across the empire. He could hear Alex give a quick intake of breath as she recognized the man.

---

[1] "Victory to Goddess Mahakali, the Gurkhas are coming."

[2] Great salute.

Sir Anthony said to the man, "May I introduce Mr. Michael Doyle and Miss Alexandra McCall." He then turned to Doyle and Alex and said, "This is His Majesty, King James the Fifth."

The king said, "It's 'Your Majesty' to begin with and then just 'Sir.'" Since Tony has done the majesty bit, lets advance to just 'Sir.'"

Alex continued to gawk. Doyle absorbed his surprise, bowed from the neck, and shook hands with the monarch. Alex recovered and shook hands, while executing a graceful curtsey.

"Please, everybody, let's just sit down. Did Tony tell you we were at school together?"

"No, sir, he did not," said Doyle.

There was a knock at the door, and Gurung strode in with a tea tray, which he put on a coffee table.

"Ah, wonderful, tea. Now, Mr. Doyle, I imagine you'd like to know what you're doing here," said the king.

"I think I'm a stalking horse, if I may be blunt, sir," said Doyle.

There was a pregnant silence.

The king said, "Well, he is as smart as you said, Tony. It says here that you received a degree from Oxford in geography and gained a master's degree in anthropology from Harvard."

Alex McCall looked over to Doyle, who shrugged and said, "I take it that's my folder you're looking at, sir?"

"Quite. Very interesting reading—says your great-grandfather was a member of the Irish Republican Brotherhood but was betrayed to the Irish police by one its members."

"It's how we got into this trade, sir. My great-granddad was left with less than fraternal feelings for the IRB; he found out the betrayal came from the very top, from Éamon de Valera himself."

"Good Lord, really?" The king looked at Sir Anthony.

"Apparently the IRB was split on whether to aim for outright

Irish independence or become a dominion, like Canada and America. Doyle's great-grandfather was in favor of the latter and had swayed the Brotherhood, including Michael Collins. De Valera wanted total independence and so arranged for Miles Doyle to be caught by the police in Dublin," said Sir Anthony.

"What about your stalking horse notion, Mr. Doyle?" asked the king.

Doyle said, "Not too hard to figure out, sir. If Sir Anthony had really wanted me back in England in secret, he would have sent a discreet summons, and I'd be bundled on a military airship or plane. Instead, I'm escorted out of Srinagar by an elite squad of Sikh soldiers and put on a regular Imperial Airways flight back to England—pretty hard to miss if someone was paying attention."

"And why would I want a stalking horse, Doyle?" asked Sir Anthony.

"Well now, that's anyone's guess. What do you think Alex?" said Doyle.

"Oh, gosh, well a stalking horse is a screen behind which a hunter can stay concealed when tracking prey, so I imagine that Sir Anthony guessed that whoever is behind the Anvil conspiracy would reveal their hand."

"Anvil?" asked Doyle, arching an eyebrow at Sir Anthony.

"It's the code word assigned to this operation. Sir, do I have your permission to carry on?"

"Of course, Tony, it's why we are all here."

"Yes, sir. Miss McCall, could I prevail on you to serve us all tea? Mr. Doyle, open this envelope."

Chapter 4

Sir Anthony gave Doyle a large buff envelope that had been sitting on the coffee table in front of the king. There was a heavy wax seal on the envelope flap on the back, and on the front a label said, "Anvil, Top Secret, Eyes Only by Permission of AR." Doyle knew that he would have to read and memorize the information in the envelope and that it would be returned to Sir Anthony. Doyle wondered what had happened that Sir Anthony wanted to emphasize the severity by including an audience with the monarch. He split the wax seal, and as he did so, the king spoke.

"I take it you are familiar with our nuclear weapons program, Mr. Doyle?"

"Excuse me, Sir Anthony, should I leave?" Alex said, breaking into the conversation.

"No, Miss McCall, I need someone to liaise with Doyle, so you need to hear this too," Sir Anthony said.

The king said, "The military has had atomic bombs at its disposal for about thirty-five years, with bombs increasing in explosive power over time."

"Yes, sir, as I understand, the empire has maintained a sole monopoly on atomic weaponry, although I know rival powers have been developing their own nuclear programs."

"What's the biggest explosion you've seen?" asked the king.

"Aerial bombing or artillery barrages, I suppose."

"You've seen the results of aerial bombing?"

"Yes, during the Indian border wars with China, when the Chinese bombed towns in India. That's also where I saw our artillery devastate a massed charge of Chinese infantry."

"I'm a navy man myself; the largest explosions I've seen were against the German fleet, when I was midshipman, just commissioned when we slugged it out with the Germans at Jutland. My cousin, Adolphus, the kaiser, claims the whole invasion of Britain plan was nothing to do with his father or the German monarchy."

"What do you think, sir?" asked Sir Anthony.

"I think that very little happens in Germany without the express permission of the kaiser. But, let's not dwell on that little episode; it turned out right for us after all."

Doyle knew that the settlement terms had included the dismantlement of Germany's overseas possessions, which were divided up between the British Empire and its dominions.

"Could we have some more tea, Miss McCall? Now, where was I?"

"Yes, sir, you were talking about our atomic bombs and nuclear programs," said Alex as she poured fresh tea in everyone's cups.

"Sir Anthony, why don't you take over? It's your bailiwick after all," said the king.

"Very well, sir. Even a relatively small atom bomb can level a whole city. I presume you have seen the newsreels after they were used on Germany. We were careful with how much information we released to the public, but I do not think the average person has any real idea of just how powerful these bombs are. From the blast center to a radius of about two miles, virtually every building is razed to the ground.

"The heat and radiation from the bomb vaporize any living being

19

within this radius, and anyone exposed for several miles beyond suffers terrible burns. The casualty figure for the bombs used on each German city was about 50,000 people, dead or severely burned. The bombs were detonated in the air, and the radioactive fallout was limited. A ground detonation would mean the area would be contaminated by radioactivity for decades afterward."

Doyle thought for a second and then said, "That's all very well if the empire is the only country with such a weapon. What about other countries, I mean? The physics and science of atomic power are not the sole preserve of the empire. What about other European countries? You mentioned Germany, but what about Austria-Hungary and France? There's Russia and China, and let's not forget powerful and wealthy South American countries like Brazil and Argentina, especially Argentina."

The king gave a rueful smile and said, "I gather from your file that you were involved in some shenanigans down there, when Argentina threatened our South Atlantic possessions."

"Yes, my shoulder still aches at the memory of that little episode."

The king continued, saying, "To answer your question, yes, we realize that an Imperial monopoly on atomic weapons is unlikely to last. After the German bombings, we thought that if countries acquired nuclear weapons, they would be reluctant to use them, since they would also be wiped out. Some of our mathematical types have run various scenarios and have come up with the concept of mutually assured destruction. Quite apt would you agree, em ay, dee, MAD."

Doyle knew that the king was referring to the top-secret establishment of Bletchley Park north of London, which worked on codes, ciphers, and strategic analysis. Doyle had been there on several occasions, once to root out a spy, and found the place to be like a university junior common room.

Finding the spy who was working for the Germans was relatively straightforward. He was the only man not behaving like an overgrown schoolboy, especially around the younger female staff. He was undone by his taciturn diligence.

Sir Anthony took up the thread and said, "Of course, we know other countries are trying to manufacture similar weapons, but it's an enormous undertaking, requiring a huge industrial base and electrical power. Much of the work was conducted in North America, both in Canada and in the North American Confederation.

"I don't need to explain the security resources needed to keep all of this a secret. Whole towns were quarantined during the research and manufacturing process. New technologies were developed like special high-speed centrifuges to separate the radioactive isotopes for the bombs."

Doyle said, "And the reason I'm here is because something has gone missing."

Sir Anthony looked over at the king, who nodded. Sir Anthony said, "Five bombs have been stolen."

"I've received a ransom note," said the king.

"How was it received?" asked Doyle.

"In the mail. The monarchy receives thousands of letters every day. My staff thought it was some crank letter, but there is a standing order for any type of threatening correspondence to be passed on to the security services."

"How long after the theft and disappearance did you receive the letter?" asked Doyle.

"The bombs went missing two weeks ago," said Sir Anthony.

"Where from?" asked Doyle.

"In transit from Aldermarston to the Royal Air Force base at Northholt. Government policy is to have atom bomb stockpiles on each continent throughout the empire. These five were due to be transported for our Australian stockpile," said Sir Anthony.

"And you'd like me to get them back, five bombs that can bring down Armageddon."

"Yes," said Sir Anthony.

"Just wanted to check that I'd got the parameters of my mission correct," said Doyle.

"That's why I had you brought here, Doyle," said the king. "I wanted to make sure you understood the severity of the situation."

"I don't think it could be any worse than it is now."

The king stood, so everyone else rose.

The king said, "Please stay seated. I just wanted to get to my feet; it helps me think."

Doyle, Sir Anthony, and Alex sat ill at ease in the presence of the king on his feet. The king walked over to the window and looked out to the Windsor Castle courtyard. A phone rang in the hall and was answered. Doyle guessed Gurung was hovering just outside the drawing room.

"This castle has stood here for a one thousand years, built by William the Conqueror, not all that long after the Dark Ages. Some historians still count this as part of the Dark Ages." The king paused and then went on. "What do you think of the empire, Doyle?"

"The empire—not sure what you mean, sir. I don't know that I feel anything about it. It just is, the empire I mean."

"Come now, Doyle, you're an Irishman, even though you've little love for the Irish independence movement. You're a scholar as well as a soldier; you must realize that the empire is a living embodiment of inequality. I'm king and emperor only because I'm descended from a lineage that goes back four hundred years for the English throne and longer for Scotland."

"You've been well trained, sir—the navy and then the army," said Doyle.

"You're too kind, Doyle. But please tell me what you think about the empire."

Doyle drew a deep breath and said, "Well, sir, since you ask, I would suggest that the empire will not endure. All empires fall. Ireland is quiet for the moment, apart from the usual grumblings of the Protestants who think that the local government discriminates against them. I'm descended from both Catholic and Protestant landed gentry, but I tend to be sympathetic to the Protestant minority.

"There are always independence movements stirring under the surface in the Confederated States of America, but the Civil War put paid to domination from the northern states,. Viceroys from the southern states and a northern Prime Minister seem to have worked as the best compromise.

"In Canada, Quebec continues to be a source of irritation, though the French speakers are no longer a majority in the province. In South Africa, the Afrikaners are probably not going to rise again, not since the chief minister and the cabinet is largely Afrikaner.

"Where else? India, of course, though the border war with China rather subdued the independence movement for a while, but its growing again. We're always going to have to deal with Muslim and Hindu animosity. The dream of an Indian Muslim homeland is still alive."

Doyle sipped some tea. He felt dehydrated from the long trip.

"Speaking of the Muslims, the Muslim Brotherhood in Egypt has still not been wiped out and continues to foment discontent. If we were not in charge in the Sudan, there would be a civil war there between the Muslim north and Christian south. Elsewhere in Africa, like Nigeria and Kenya, we have a rising educated middle class that chafes against rule from London, even though these are now largely self-governing like other empire dominions.

"Our possessions in Southeast Asia are a hodgepodge of different ethnic groups, mainly because we moved people around like pawns on a chessboard for plantation agriculture and mining. These are several potential flash points, since the newcomers have voting rights like the local folks and are involved in politics, same in Africa, the Caribbean, and the Pacific Islands," Doyle said.

"My goodness, Sir Anthony, it sounds like we have a professional revolutionary in our midst. Are you sure he's safe?" the king said.

"Safe enough, sir. I'd stake my life on him."

"Well, in that case, turn him loose. Now if you do not mind, I had better get back to the castle. My retinue will be getting a little nervous, wondering where I am."

All rose as the king readied to leave, and Sir Anthony's servant entered. There was the opening and closing of doors in the house, but the king did not emerge from the front of the house. On a hunch, Doyle said, "Secret passage to the castle?"

Chapter 5

Sir Anthony said nothing, picked up the folder, and passed it to Doyle.

"Read this. Make what notes you need. I do not hold with this nonsense of committing everything to memory. I have a bedroom prepared for you upstairs; Gurung took up your luggage. I imagine you will want to disappear tomorrow into your usual London haunts. Miss McCall, my driver will take you home."

"Won't that be dangerous, sir?" she asked.

"What, going home?" said Doyle.

Alex flushed and said, "You know what I mean. Whoever attacked Mr. Doyle this morning will likely try again."

"I'm counting on it," said Sir Anthony.

"Thanks, thought as much," said Doyle.

Alex continued to look anxious.

Doyle said, "Just feeling this folder; it's clear there's not much in it. I'll wager there's a photostat of the ransom letter and some briefing documents on the atomic bombs."

"What about the two people who blew up the car?" asked Alex.

Sir Anthony looked bleak and said, "Dead—the police caught them and put them in a holding cell in Reading. They had cyanide capsules in false teeth. Gurung slipped me this note as the king was leaving."

Doyle took Gurung's scribbled note. He remembered hearing the phone call earlier.

"It says there was a man and a woman; the man's a European, but the woman looks Asian. Is this all there is?" asked Doyle.

"Yes, for now. We'll photograph and fingerprint them, of course, and look them over for any identification. I suspect we will find very little to work with. But it tells us we're up against a formidable enemy, to command that level of obedience."

Doyle felt weariness overcome him, and he stifled a yawn.

"Come along, Doyle; you'd better get off to bed. You've had a long day—you too, Miss McCall. Gurung, please draw a bath for Mr. Doyle."

Doyle shaved after a soak in the bath. In the mirror, his deeply tanned face made his pale blue eyes shine. There were a few nicks and contusions on his cheeks, with more serious scarring on his torso, where he had been shot, stabbed, and tortured.

His black hair was cropped a conventional buzz cut. There were boxing scars above his eyebrows, and his nose showed it had been broken once or twice. His ears lay flat against his skull and had escaped punishment. It was a classic Irish face, thought Doyle, not a big spud like a Navvie but handsome enough—probably a bit of French Spanish blood in there.

Doyle laid his luggage out on the bed in Sir Anthony's guest room. He saw a bottle of Johnny Walker Red Label whiskey and a soda siphon. He pinched off a small ball of opium, dropped it into a tumbler, filled the tumbler halfway with whiskey, and added a splash of soda. He looked at the battered suitcase, opening the lid and then manipulating the secret release that let the hidden compartment flop open. The catches were working, but he could see the nicks and scratches from the screwdriver wielded by the customs officer. It would be a good time to retire the suitcase and order a new one.

26

Doyle removed piles of clothing to expose the base of the suitcase, which also had a false bottom. Opening this revealed Doyle's pistols: a small Beretta automatic; a broom handle C-96 Mauser with full 10, 20, and 30 round magazines, and a Browning Hi-Power with two spare magazines. The Browning had a modified hammer, so it would not snag on clothing when pulled from a shoulder holster, which was also stowed in the suitcase compartment.

Doyle picked up the Mauser and sighted along the barrel. He loved this nineteenth-century gun, despite its odd configuration. His Mauser was a Chinese 712 model with a detachable magazine and a full automatic setting. Doyle smiled when he remembered trying out this feature at a pistol range. He peppered the back wall with bullets, none of which landed on the paper target. Still, having what sounded like a machine gun sometimes came in handy in a tight spot. The thirty-round magazine was not standard issue, and it was made by a Kabul gunsmith. The gunsmith had also made a telescoping skeleton stock for the gun. Doyle pulled back the slide to ensure that no bullet was in the chamber.

The bath and whiskey made Doyle feel sleepy, but he still wanted to look through the Anvil file. Doyle sipped his opium-charged whiskey and looked over the information in the file. Meanwhile, the police had photographed and fingerprinted the man and woman, and he would be sending the images through wireless and telephone facsimile machines throughout the empire and to police and intelligence contacts in foreign countries.

The file included a summary about the head of the imperial nuclear weapons program. Professor Royston Rogers, an interesting character, thought Doyle. Rogers was a a boy from the Australian bush, whose education included Cambridge and Princeton. Doyle wondered if he was connected with whatever agency had stolen the bombs. Further reading suggested he was a loyal son of the empire. He had not been involved in student politics at Cambridge or Princeton, where there were small but vocal anti-imperial and anti-monarchist societies.

Possession of five atom bombs by an enemy country or organization was a frightening prospect. Wiping out the five of the principal capital cities of London, Philadelphia, Ottawa, Canberra, and Cape Town could bring the empire to its knees, though Doyle knew more than most about imperial resilience.

He read the Photostat copy of the letter sent to the king, demanding a ransom for the five missing atomic bombs.

To His Majesty, James V.

Our enterprise has taken two of your atomic weapons. Their Defense Ministry Identification Numbers are: MOW/ce/765/MkVI, MOW/ce/766/MkVI, MOW/ce/767/MkVI, MOW/ce/768/MkVI, and MOW/ce/769/MkVI.

In exchange for their return, we demand ten billion pounds in Imperial bearer bonds. We will contact you with when and where to deliver the money.

We understand that you will no doubt try to discover who we are and recover your property. You will fail, and the blood of your agents will be on your hands. We will also raise two of your cities to the ground.

Raptor

Doyle read the spare prose twice. Whoever this was sounded supremely confident. Moreover, what about the signature, Raptor—the descriptive term for birds of prey, confident with a romantic streak?

Despite the long day and fatigue, Doyle wanted to talk with Sir Anthony. He slipped off the towel, which he was wearing sarong-like around his waist, and pulled on a T-shirt and blue denim work pants. He slipped his feet into well-worn but comfortable plaited Indian leather sandals.

Doyle reassembled the contents of the folder, picked up his drink, and wandered downstairs. Gurung was taking a tray out of the room next to the drawing room, which Doyle guessed was the study.

"Is Sir Anthony in there?"

"Yes, sir. He asked not to be disturbed—much work to be done."

"I think he'll see me. I'll tell him you warned me off."

Gurung smiled and walked down the hall to the kitchen.

Chapter 6

Doyle knocked on the door and walked in. Sir Anthony was sitting at a desk in front of the room's fireplace. The room was sparsely furnished. The only other items in the room apart from the desk were a chair in front of the desk, a filing cabinet, and a sideboard, on which there were a selection of drinks and mixes. The room curtains were drawn even thought it was still light outside. Doyle assumed this was a security precaution.

Sir Anthony was reading a document illuminated in a pool of light by an angle-poise lamp. The room lights were switched off, with the desk lamp casting shadows on the room walls.

"Gurung said you weren't to be disturbed, but I took a chance you might want to talk to me," said Doyle.

"Very presumptuous of you, Doyle. Is that one of your special cocktails?"

"Yes, scotch and soda spiked with a ball of Uttar Pradesh's finest, from the Ghazipur factory."

"Well, now you're here, why not fix me a brandy and soda? I'll take it without the additional ingredient. I assume you want to talk about the Anvil case."

"Yes. Who the hell is this Raptor—is it a person, an organization?"

"We think it's a criminal organization. There are plenty of those within and outside the empire, but this one is different. We believe that whoever is the head of Raptor is a genius, or at least a very clever and meticulous person."

"Raptor doesn't seem to be in a great hurry to collect their ransom."

"No—what does that tell you? They must know the whole empire would be looking for the bombs," Sir Anthony said.

"My guess is that they have a very secure base. I doubt they will explode the bombs or at least not until they have taken one of them apart to copy the design. I read the specifications about the bombs; you would need a big aircraft to carry them."

"Yes, regular large propeller driven bombers were converted to carry single bombs, but we've recently introduced jet-powered bombers that can carry several atom bombs. They are built at the Avro works in Lancaster and at the Boeing plant in Seattle."

"I thought jet aircraft were still experimental," Doyle said.

"Yes and no—they are slowly being phased into the military, but the bomber program was given an accelerated program. There's a payoff that we can use the bomber design for civilian use, which greatly reduces travel times."

"I imagine there'll be resistance from the steamer and airship companies. Could an atom bomb be carried by an airship?"

"Yes, but not as a delivery vehicle—an airship wouldn't be able to get clear from the blast. However, it could be transported by an airship. We think that Raptor may have used a commercial cargo airship to get the bombs out of England."

"How was the bomb convoy ambushed?" Doyle asked.

"It was taking country backroads to Northholt to avoid creating traffic jams on the major highways. Of course, in hindsight we were setting ourselves up for an ambush. It was after the convoy had skirted Reading that it was struck. A truck drove out of a farm gate and blocked the road. Another truck blocked the road behind to prevent anyone escaping. Machine guns, probably Gatlings, just blew everybody to bits and pieces. The radio operator in the army trucks did not even get a chance to radio for help. Machine gun bullets will just bounce off an atom bomb casing, and the detonators are kept in bullet- and bomb-proof cases."

"How many men were killed?" asked Doyle.

"About fifty in total—an entire platoon plus all the bomb technicians and RAF personnel," said Sir Anthony.

"And then just whisked away?"

"Airships are too big just to put down anywhere. We checked schedules and there was a cargo airship bound for America from Bristol. It had two stops: New York and San Francisco. It's our working theory that the bombs were offloaded there, probably labelled machine parts or something like that and put on a vessel."

"Where do you think it went?"

"I'm coming to that. As you said, the analysts think the Raptor people will dismantle one of the bombs to see how they are built. Reverse engineering it's called by the boffins. They could smuggle the bombs into capital cities—London obviously but also Philadelphia. Or they might target a major provincial city like Madras or Durban."

"Did you have any luck with the two would-be assassins?"

"Actually, we did. Somebody in the Australian federal police had been to school with the woman. She's a Chinese mixed-race woman from our New Guinea territory," said Sir Anthony.

"That's a stroke of luck."

"My staff told me that there was no identification on the man and woman. Even the labels in their clothing had been removed. The serial numbers on the motorcycle and sidecar combination appear to have been eroded with acid."

"You could disassemble the bike; the pair would not have been able to erase every serial number on each component." Doyle realized he was preaching to the choir. Gathering his wits, he said, "Christ, New Guinea, that's a rough old place. But now that I think about it, a good place to get lost, if you know what I mean."

"The woman's name was Elaine Chan. Her mother's from a place called New Hanover. Chan was from Kavieng, the main town on nearby New Ireland."

"And the man?"

"Still searching—we're focusing our efforts on New Guinea. Chan had a position in the personnel department at a gold mine on Lihir Island, a mine owned by a large German conglomerate."

"So although we took the territory on after the botched German invasion in '66, we didn't kick all the Germans out?"

"No, the German administration was replaced by the Imperial Civil Service, mainly recruited from Australia and New Zealand, but we didn't oust the entire German civilian population. Among other decisions, we let the Germans continue mining at Lihir. It was deemed more cost effective to maintain the status quo and have the tax revenues continue to flow to the territorial government," Sir Anthony said.

"What do we know about the Lihir gold mine?" Doyle asked.

Sir Anthony went to the filing cabinet and retrieved a map that he unfolded on the table. It read "British Territory of Papua and New Guinea." He smoothed the map and pointed to the long, thin island of New Ireland. He indicated an island off the eastern coast.

"This is Lihir Island. It has the largest gold deposit on Earth, discovered to date, larger even than the South African deposits. The whole island seems to be one giant gold nugget. The company Lihir Goldbergwerksgesellschaft, or Lihir Gold Mining Company, was operating there for about a decade before the British acquired New Guinea. Apparently, Chan was a recent recruit, a clerical officer for the company, responsible for making sure there were no problems with the locals on Lihir."

"Is there a government presence on the island?"

"Not much—the whole place is privately owned by the company, a bit like other privately owned islands, like Niihau in Hawaii and the Cocos Keeling Islands in the Indian Ocean. The local people deeded the whole island to the company in lieu of a share of the island profits. The company pays a percentage of the profits in tax to the provincial government, actually millions of New Guinea Dollars a year. It is so much that the New Ireland Province draws virtually no revenues from the New Guinea Government. It's held up as a model of economic development that we should apply elsewhere in the empire."

"Who's the senior man in the company?" Doyle asked.

"A German national, Gustave Jäger—he's been in charge for about ten years."

"Jäger? German word for hunter, but a common enough surname. Could we find out if the male assassin was employed at the Lihir mine?"

"We're already doing that; we have inquiries being conducted in Southeast Asia and the Pacific Islands. Miss McCall has been in contact with the provincial administrator, Frank Gardiner. If the dead man was working there, you will definitely be on your way to New Guinea."

"Unless anyone has a better lead."

"Here, you'd better sign this. It's a standard ISS contract with the usual terms and conditions; plus I've upped the allowances and the daily rate. You will have an impress account at Coutts. Set up a password with the manager of the Strand Branch. I know you are an accomplished smuggler, but we will ship weapons and materials through the diplomatic bag to Port Moresby."

Sir Anthony opened his briefcase on his desk and took out a small pile of business cards, putting them on top of the contract. Doyle was leaning against the sideboard. He freshened his drink and then sat in the office chair facing Sir Anthony's desk. He signed the contract and then pocketed the business cards, which were blank except for a string of numbers on one side.

Doyle leaned back and said, "So, now, King Tony, tell me how many agents ISS has lost to date on the Anvil case."

Chapter 7

"Don't be impertinent, Doyle. You've just signed an ISS contract, and I'm now your employer." Sir Anthony countersigned the contract, picked up his drink, and took a mouthful, leaning back into his chair, his face in the half-light staring at Doyle.

"I've recently had to write a dozen or so condolence letters to the families of ISS operatives, not all of them field agents. I know that all staff take our training course at Chartwell, but most end up in desk jobs, not out in the field. Their defensive skills are, shall we say, rusty."

Doyle knew Chartwell was the house gifted to the nation after the death of the great twentieth-century prime minister, Winston Churchill. Its cover was a government archive repository, but its purpose was to train ISS staff, either newcomers or veterans in need of a refresher course in the tradecraft of espionage.

"Were these deaths contrived to look like accidents or outright murders—you know, for example, killings of which the Russians and Chinese are so fond?" Doyle asked.

"The former, but all suspicious, and all people working on Anvil. I don't think it was random either. Hundreds of people are working on the Anvil case, but we think these were targeted at people who may have come up with some discovery or even just a working hypothesis. One of the unfortunates worked at GCHQ in Cheltenham. She was working on the sources of finance for an operation the scale of Anvil.

She took some work home with her, and a coal wagon ran her down. The wagon kept going and was found abandoned. In the immediate aftermath of the accident, no one was looking at her briefcase, which disappeared. We know a little of what she was working on. She was in daily contact with one of the Bletchley Park staff, a specialist in business codes and financial transactions. Luckily, we were able to debrief him the next day," Sir Anthony said.

"Luckily?"

"That night he slipped in the bathroom and broke his neck."

"Christ! Has ISS become so penetrated with double agents? I thought that you'd weeded them out."

"It's more devious that that. We haven't been able to find a single genuine traitor. The GCHQ and Bletchley operatives were both single with no immediate relatives. It turns out that teams like the man and woman who attacked the Bentley were taking hostages of the families of ISS staff, to coerce them into passing on documents, providing cipher schedules, and planting listening devices and taps on supposedly secure lines. They were killed once they had served their function, including their entire families. It has paralyzed the entire bloody service—hence, my cri de coeur for our noble paladin and the intercession of the king."

"How did you find all of this out? I mean, if people were betraying their colleagues and then being liquidated ... how?"

"A stroke of luck, gruesome nonetheless. The family members of a cipher clerk were all shot after she'd passed on cipher schedules for the secure telefacsimile machines. The assassins shot everybody in the house, in an upstairs bedroom. We think the family dog attacked the assassins, as there were bloodstains that did not match those of the dead. It's also why we think that the assassins took off before checking that everyone was dead."

"Someone survived?"

"Yes, a 14-year-old boy—all were shot in the head at close range, and he sustained a nasty wound, but in his case nonfatal. The bullet didn't break up. The barking dog and hasty departure of the assassins alerted some neighbors. They went to the house, found the door open, and the dog still barking, despite also being shot. I'm sad to say it died later."

Typical sentimentality about animals, thought Doyle. "How long was it before the lad could tell you what happened?"

"The next day, actually. The medics did wonders and even extracted the bullet while he was conscious. ISS staff were in the theater questioning him as the bullet was removed. It did not go down too well with the doctors I'm afraid, and we had to do a lot of arm twisting. We put the hospital under martial law and made the surgeons operate at gunpoint, and then we put the fear of God into them under the Official Secrets Act."

"I suppose they wouldn't be able to imagine how important this lad was to national security since they wouldn't know about Anvil or Raptor."

"Yes, quite. The boy told us that three people broke into their house at night. They forced their mother to do as instructed. They kept the other family members at home. The guards were two men and a woman who matches the description of Elaine Chan; we think one of the men was Chan's accomplice who just committed suicide on being apprehended.

I mobilized police and military units to visit every ISS employee in Britain and had every ISS facility swept clean of taps and listening devices. The Bletchley boffins devised new cipher schedules sent around the world by the fastest military aircraft. We only just have these in place and have begun functioning again. Incidentally, I ordered the same military exercise for ISS staff throughout the empire and more discreetly for our people in foreign countries. It seems that this operation was confined to Britain and here in the south, where all the main ISS facilities are located."

"Did you catch anymore of the bastards?" Doyle asked.

"Not alive—two families were being held against their will, and before we could negotiate their release, they were shot and the assassins committed suicide," said Sir Anthony.

"My God, these people have the ruthlessness of the Chinese triads, the cunning of Russian chess players, and the fanaticism of Japanese soldiers."

"Now you know how desperate we are and why I needed my old, if somewhat shop-soiled, friend back in harness."

"Shop-soiled is it? God, I hope I don't let you down. Anymore thoughts on who this could be?"

"If there is a German connection, I wouldn't be surprised. Germany has never recovered from the humiliations it suffered in 1914, 1940, and 1966. Each time we took a bit more of their overseas territories and reduced their territory in Europe. They are a vengeful lot, not content on just running their own country. You mentioned Japanese fanaticism a moment ago; well the Germans can be just as fanatical. And I think there are forces that are itching to avenge those humiliations."

"I remember my granddad telling me that in 1914 the French were out for revenge after the Franco-Prussian War. The Germans were stupid enough to open a war on two fronts by attacking the Russians. The 1940 clash in retaliation for 1914 was just bloody stupid; the Germans went up against the Maginot Line, thinking they could get through. OK, some did get through, but then they ran straight into the British Expeditionary Forces. And they overstretched themselves trying to launch simultaneous operations to capture Norway and the Balkans and North Africa."

"And what's your conclusions about 1966?" Sir Anthony asked.

"Are you familiar with that version of rugby football they play in America?"

"Yes, although I confine my admiration for the proper game."

"They have an expression: a 'Hail Mary' play refers to a very long forward pass made in desperation, with only a small chance of success, especially at or near the end of a game. The Battle of Gettysburg is a good example. Lee's victory and the march on Philadelphia allowed Jefferson Davis to negotiate a settlement with Viceroy Lincoln—a good result for us since the imperial government could clip Lincoln's wings.

"I think the German invasion fleet was never intended to take over the whole country, just land a sufficiently large force in or around the capitol to shake imperial confidence and renegotiate the 1914 and 1940s surrender terms, or we would face a protracted and bloody campaign in England's heartland," Doyle said.

"Yes, I've heard that interpretation. Can't say whether I put much faith in it—Germans at you throat or at your feet. I think if they had got an army in place in the south, there would have been a real chance to take over the heart of the empire. Thankfully, we knew enough of their plans sufficiently to lay a trap and annihilate their military once and for all."

"I was ten at the time and remember the newsreels."

"It was a massacre. Atom bombs dropped on Hamburg and Willemshaven destroyed their troops as they massed for embarkation. The Royal Air Force and Fleet Air Arm blew the grand fleet apart with conventional bombs after the Battle of Jutland. Personally, I would have thought an atomic bomb on Kiel could have accomplished this without the heavy losses our pilots endured, but there was a lot of concern about the proximity of Denmark. Nearly a quarter of a million soldiers and one hundred thousand sailors and pilots, all in one day, the greatest single loss in recorded history—although the Chinese dispute this, saying more were lost in some of their ancient battles. Still, it is motivation enough for revenge."

"I've heard rumors that there were voices in Cabinet who wanted to atom bomb Germany back to the Stone Age. Is that true?"

"Yes, I've read the Cabinet papers. Some of the more hawkish members of government proposed that line of action, though it was a minority."

"Since ISS is up and functioning again, have there been any signals to indicate that Germany has a hand in this? We must have spies in Germany and their ally, Austria-Hungary."

"Yes, and all I can report is that nothing has shown signals, or at least signals we can read. They still use the Enigma machine to encode their signals."

"I thought the Bletchley boys and girls had broken the Enigma code years ago."

"Yes, Bletchley had, in the old three-rotor machine. Unfortunately, the Germans added two more rotors, on the suspicion that we were indeed reading their intelligence. We are still able to read some traffic and even obtain metadata from signals we can't read. When it's the kaiser's birthday, all their military units send him a happy birthday message. Just knowing this has allowed us insight into more recent Enigma ciphers," said Sir Anthony.

"Thank God for totalitarian autocracies. Can you imagine British troops doing that?" Doyle said.

"No, but don't scoff. His Majesty's forces in places like India and Fiji do something similar, though thankfully we have a standing order that all birthday greetings to the monarch are passed in clear on commercial channels, or they just buy him a decent birthday card."

Doyle smiled and yawned, saying, "Sorry, alcohol and opium kicking in."

"Please, I don't wish to know about your damned drug taking. It's bad enough that I am harboring a drug fiend on royal grounds. Go to bed, and I'll take you into London tomorrow."

Chapter 8

Doyle checked into the Union Jack Club. He left his bags in his room and made his way to Rotherhithe. It was a fine spring day and just over a mile to Rotherhithe. Doyle decided to walk. He checked if anyone was following him, taking great care to scrutinize passersby and using shop windows and doorways to look for a tail. He ducked in and out of shop doors, to see if anyone stopped behind and ahead of him. If professionals were shadowing him, they would be very good, but so was he.

Doyle's only concern, apart from spotting surveillance, was his inability to contact Kemal. Someone always answered the phone, regardless of the time or day. He carried his Browning Hi-Power in his shoulder holster and tapped it beneath his jacket for reassurance. The holster was a Berns-Martin Triple-draw on the left, balanced on the right of the harness by two extra magazines and a sleeve for a Brausch silencer.

London was flowing all around him; the imperial capitol was prospering. Its population exceeded fifteen million and drew a massive number of visitors. He remembered a statistic that nearly half the people in the capital were born outside of England. Imperial government and commerce drew people from across the empire and beyond. The favorable business climate and access to huge markets meant that there were about three hundred thousand French living and working in London. They entered on business visas, which the imperial government was happy to grant. Doyle knew losing tax revenues to England greatly annoyed the French government.

He arrived on the western side of Rotherhithe, making his way to the near side of Greenland Dock. The day darkened as storm clouds gathered. Doyle looked at the sky and shrugged. *London weather*, he thought, *never predictable*. He passed a motorcycle and sidecar on the street and thought about the events of yesterday.

The warehouse on Worgan Street was now in sight. The funnels and masts of ships moored in Greenland Dock hung over the roofs. Nothing looked out of place, but it was far too quiet. Kemal's place on the left corner of the dock buildings should have been a hive of activity. There were dockworkers and other people walking to and from the wharf through a brick tunnel in the warehouse building. People should have been coming and going to the shop, and Kemal's children would normally be ducking in and of the shop to go to adjacent warehouses.

Taking his time, Doyle looked very carefully at Kemal's shop. As he neared, he saw a "We Are Closed Sign" in the windowpane of the front door. Kemal would have been open seven days a week, twenty-four hours a day if the law allowed. Looking up, the closed curtains of the apartment gave a slight twitch as Doyle drew near. Doyle faced the front door, with its closed sign. The interior lights were off, and he could see the shop was empty. He tried the door; it was open.

The shop was silent. The counter displays and shelves were full of ship chandlery supplies: knives, tools, clothing, soaps, medical kits, samples of ropes, cables, fabrics, and examples of canned goods to be bought wholesale. The place smelled of leather, salt, carbolic, and the faint aroma of spices.

Doyle made his way to the back and to Kemal's office, passing the stairs to the first floor. The door was halfway open, and Doyle pushed it slowly with his finger. Kemal sat across the room from him, holding a gun in a trembling hand.

"Mick, I'm sorry. They have my family upstairs. They will kill them unless I kill you."

Doyle said nothing but took in the scene of Kemal's office with its shelves of file boxes, out-of-date calendars, and fading photographs of ships and docks. Kemal sat behind a big oak desk, his face streaked with tears, his olive skin gray, looking shrunken and ancient. Kemal cocked the gun and tried to aim along the quivering barrel. Doyle could see the blood flow out of Kemal's finger as it tightened on the trigger. Doyle sidestepped behind the doorframe, taking away his fingers so the door swung back.

Kemal fired and the bullet passed through the top of the door. The gun fired repeatedly, but shots passed harmlessly through the door. There was a clunk. Doyle knew Kemal had dropped the pistol on the desk. Doyle opened the door, and in one motion, he reached the Egyptian. He scooped up the gun, putting it to one side of the desk. Doyle pressed a finger to his lips to quiet any response from Kemal, who was staring at him. Kemal's face was a mass of conflicting emotions.

Doyle took out his Browning from his shoulder holster; he pulled out the silencer and screwed it on to the barrel. Doyle put his head close to Kemal and asked, "How many?"

"Uh, what? Oh, two, a man and a woman. They have my wife and all the kids in our bedroom."

Doyle made the silence sign again and tiptoed across the floor to the left-hand side of the door. He heard the faint sounds of someone descending the stairs and pausing behind the door. The door creaked opened, followed by an arm holding a gun that resolved into a man wearing overalls, a woolen pullover, and sea boots. He looked exactly like any seaman or dockworker in Rotherhithe.

The man focused on the Egyptian as he entered the room. Hiding and pressed hard against the wall, Doyle shot the man in the temple. There was only a cough from Doyle's gun and a spatter of blood and brain on the door. Doyle grabbed the man and lowered his corpse to the ground. Kemal sat rigid in shock. Doyle moved back to Kemal's desk.

"Kemal, Kemal, come on; snap out of it. Are the stairs out there the only way upstairs?" said Doyle in a whisper

"What ... no, there's a separate staircase from the warehouse behind me. We left it as a fire escape when we converted part of the warehouse into an apartment."

Kemal rummaged in his pockets, pulling out a set of keys, selecting one.

"Here, go through the door behind my desk. It opens into the warehouse. There is an iron staircase to your left. Go up this, and unlock the door. It opens into a corridor. Our main bedroom is the second door on the left."

Doyle took the keys and walked through the door into the cavernous warehouse. He saw the stairs and ran up them, knowing that the clock was ticking for Kemal's family. Kemal was coerced into murdering Doyle in return for the freedom of his family—an empty promise. The couple would kill everyone. There was probably some twisted logic to this scenario, but right now Doyle wanted to stop the slaughter. He also wanted to capture the woman before she could kill herself with a cyanide-filled tooth.

Holding his pistol in his left hand, Doyle inserted the key. It slowly revolved as he felt the teeth mesh with the tumblers. He hoped it would revolve in silence, or at least without a loud click. As it passed the apex, there was a faint mechanical tick and then silence as the key completed its revolution. He grasped the door handle, hoping it wasn't stuck from underuse. The handle depressed, and the door swung inward. The floor in the apartment was covered in linoleum, not noise-dampening carpet.

Kemal, you cheap bastard, thought Doyle. The light from the second room to the left spilled out onto the landing. Doyle kept perfectly still, listening for any sound. He became aware of sobbing and hushed whispering from the bedroom.

"Silence, keep still, or you will all die."

Doyle heard the woman's voice, which sounded Australian with Chinese inflections. He guessed she was probably in a far corner of the room, where she could see all of Kemal's family. He knew she would have heard the shots and noise from the room below. She was expecting her partner to finish off Kemal and join her to kill the wife and children. Kemal had many children, some grown and moved out but several younger ones at home.

Doyle kept silent; this was probably the best strategy. The time elapsed without anyone reappearing had to be creating anxiety for the woman assassin. The linoleum floor would convey every slide and creak, so Doyle resolved to remain where he was.

"No one move. If I see a twitch, I'll kill the little girl."

There was a cry, and Doyle guessed the woman was going to use Kemal's small child as security. There was a whimper and then footsteps. Doyle switched his gun to his right hand and pocketed the keys. A small girl, probably three or four years old, emerged through the door, with a hand fastened on the scruff of her neck. Doyle froze, thinking the little girl would look in his direction and give the game away, making for a desperate shoot-out.

The little girl turned, wriggling with her captor, and shouted, "Dolly, dolly, I want my dolly."

There was a scream of Chinese invective. Doyle knew that to the unwary, a small child could exert a lot of force if upset. Doyle tensed, hoping that the woman would not simply kill the girl. The woman said in English, "Get your doll!"

He heard the child clatter across the floor of the bedroom and then run past the woman and out onto the landing. The woman gave an exasperated shout and walked out. Doyle's gun popped twice. Doyle knew it was a reckless gamble. He had kept his gun low and pointed away from the little girl, aiming for the woman's ankles and shins. The heavy caliber bullets whipped the woman's legs from under her.

Chapter 9

Doyle bounded forward. The little girl had backed away as the woman emerged from the room. The woman careened into the opposite wall of the landing, and her gun flew from her hands. She fell to the ground, screaming because of the wounds in her right leg. Doyle drew his leg back and kicked the woman as hard as could on the temple. This stunned her and he kicked her again, making sure to avoid her jaw. A third kick yielded her unconscious.

Doyle shouted, "Kemal, get up here—now!"

There was movement in the bedroom. Kemal's wife ran out, scooping up her child and unleashing a torrent of Egyptian. The other children began to emerge, realizing their ordeal was over. Kemal came running up the stairs, making an inventory of his wife and children crowding onto the corridor when he got to the top.

"Kemal … Kemal," said Doyle, "Get me rags to stuff into this woman's mouth and rope to tie her up. Come on—I know you are in shock. Is anyone dead?" he asked a boy in his early teens.

"No, sir, we're all alive."

"Okay, Kemal, come on! I really need your help to keep this prisoner alive; we can celebrate and take stock later."

"I … tried to kill you."

"Yes, and you failed, so you owe me. Now please help."

Kemal said, "Simeon, Mikhael, go down to the store; get sash cord off the shelves and rags from the rag box. Go, hurry."

"Where's the gun you used?"

"On my desk—shall I fetch it?"

"No, leave it there. Go phone this number." Doyle pulled a business card from his pocket. "Say the Irish man sends his regards to the rajah. Tell them you are the Egyptian in Rotherhithe. They know who you are. Say you need a cleanup team. They'll just keep saying you've reached a wrong number. Don't worry; they know what to do. And tell your bloody wife to calm down. I can't hear myself think."

Mrs. Kemal keened and made supplications to God and the saints of the Coptic pantheon. She dressed in traditional Coptic clothes, a plain black dress over pantaloons, with a headscarf tied behind the neck. Kemal embraced her and managed to reduce her distress to sobbing. The four youngest children all huddled with their parents.

The teenage boys appeared bearing what Doyle needed. Thinking they were probably more use than the remainder of the Kemal family, he spoke to them.

"Lads, I need your help. This woman's got a cyanide capsule in one of her teeth. We need to gag her mouth with rags to stop her from biting down. We have to tie her up, so she can't move and can't bang her head to try and break the cyanide tooth."

The woman's eyes were flickering. Doyle pulled her mouth open and jammed in a handful of rags. He hoped she had no nasal impairment that would stop her breathing. The three of them rolled the woman onto her stomach, tied her hand behind her back, bound her feet, and hog-tied her. Doyle laid her on one side and asked the boys to bring a couple of pillows. He slipped these under her head, so she couldn't bang her head on the floor, made a pressure bandage out of more rags, and tied those to her wounded ankle and shin.

Kemal untangled himself from his wife and went downstairs to make the phone call. It did not matter where in the world Doyle was;

the phone number on the business card would always get through to an ISS switchboard. Numbers given out to agents, even an occasional like Doyle, were unique and identified the caller. Doyle had once asked Sir Anthony how it worked. "A great deal of complicated mathematics and electronic wizardry," Sir Anthony replied.

Kemal reappeared and said, "Wrong number."

"Yeah, thought so. You need verbal codes to get past the switchboard. But they'll be scurrying all the same."

Doyle began to relax a little. It felt as if blinkers were coming off his eyes, and he could take in more of his surroundings.

"I need a new suitcase. Some halfwit at Heathrow airport forced open the lid compartment. The catch is damaged, though it still closes. Can you make a better one?"

"Of course, I have a better design, much more robust. Sorry again for shooting at you. Thank God you came when you did though."

"That was a bloody big caliber revolver, a thirty-eight. Even a nonfatal wound would have put me out of action for weeks—months probably. Missy here might lose her leg. It's pretty mashed up."

Doyle looked at the way the woman's foot was hanging despite the hog-tie. Doyle sat down level with the woman. She was Chinese, but from where? Her skin was pale brown, light ochre. She was young and late twenties or early thirties. Her outfit was not very different from her dead partner's. These days it was usual to have women on the dock engaged in engineering or technical work. There was so much commerce coming through the London docks that labor was recruited where it could be found, although ancient prejudices died hard in this most-masculine environment.

There was a loud banging at Kemal's front door. The cleanup squad had arrived.

Chapter 10

Alex McCall led the cleanup crew, including Colonel Jeffrey Sykes, the chief armorer, and Dr. Mishak Tambo, the Service's chief medical officer. Doyle saw Sykes was still spry, though walking with a cane. Tambo had been one of the first African doctors to work for the service, where his skill, especially with trauma injuries, had seen him rise to the top of the ISS medical hierarchy.

"Here's your patient, Doctor. One of her teeth is fake, with a hollowed out cavity full of cyanide, probably in gel form."

Doyle still sat, the two Kemal boys keeping him company. The Chinese woman stirred to life. Her face looked to show a mix of great pain and rage. Tambo summed up the situation immediately and prepared a syringe from a drug bottle extracted from his bag. He crouched down.

"Doyle, please would you keep her head still?"

Doyle grabbed a handful of hair, which secured her head. Tambo located the jugular vein and inserted the syringe, noting with satisfaction the jet of blood into the syringe barrel. He depressed the plunger. Standing up he said, "Morphine—that'll keep the pain under control and keep her sedated."

"Will she live?" asked Doyle.

"Oh, yes, not to worry. Given her robust vigor, despite the bullet wounds and whatever you did to her, she'll survive. Now I need to get that tooth out."

Sykes looked down at Doyle with disapproval.

"Aye, the prodigal son returns," he said with a refined Scots accent. "I've no doubt you have been up to your usual knavish tricks, Doyle." He looked at the two boys. "Are you Christians lads?"

Simeon said, "Yes, sir, we are, sir. We're Copts."

"Hmm, well that's better than some heathen religion, but it's not the proper kirk in my opinion, but that's by the by. Yon's a bad man, boys."

He gestured at Doyle, with his cane. Simeon and Mikhail looked at Doyle with renewed interest. Sykes was preaching to the choir.

Tambo was on his knees, looking at the Chinese woman's teeth, examining their color and tapping them with the blunt end of a probe.

"Shouldn't you let a dentist do that, Doc?" said Doyle.

Without looking up Tambo said, "I hold a dental degree among my other qualifications, Doyle. Ah, here it is."

Tambo pulled a cylindrical device from his bag and maneuvered it over the tooth in the woman's lower jaw. There was a hiss of gas and the tooth was plucked like a weed from a flowerbed.

"Very neat," said Doyle.

"Colonel Sykes's division came up with it," said Tambo.

"Aye, well, it's just simple mechanics," said Sykes.

"Is this the men's club?" asked Alex McCall, coming up the stairs and advancing on the group clustered around the Chinese woman. "Who are these two fine-looking boys?"

Simeon and Mikhail stared at Alex.

"Close your mouths, lads. You look like a pair of startled chimps. Go on down to your mum and dad, and thanks again for all your help."

The pair looked pleased and ducked past Alex.

"Is Kemal downstairs?" asked Doyle.

53

"Yes, he answered the door when we arrived. He showed us the gun, and we told the family to stay in his office. They said their two eldest boys were helping you."

"You don't need to read the riot act to them. I'm sure Kemal's knows I have an ISS connection, and besides which, he's a smuggler who knows how to keep his mouth shut. Better give him a background story though for the neighbors—police raid or some other nonsense."

Doyle knew that there would be a fleet of official vehicles on Worgan Street.

Chapter 11

Doyle stood up, feeling giddy and tired after an eventful morning. He glanced at his watch; it was barely afternoon, but it felt like a lifetime had passed. Around him, the ISS personnel secured the Chinese woman to ensure she could not injure herself. Apart from being immobilized, she was also fitted with a specialized mask to prevent her biting her tongue and bleeding to death.

"Are you all right, Mr. Doyle?" asked Alex.

"Yes, thanks—an invigorating morning," said Doyle.

"You took what I presume is an Anvil operative alive, Mr. Doyle."

"I wonder where she's from—you know, mainland China or from elsewhere? Oh, before I forget; there's a motorcycle and sidecar parked at the opening of Worgon Street. It might be a coincidence."

"Yes, we saw it. We phoned the registration to the police, which came back as false, so it's coming with us."

"There must be quite a crowd out there?"

"There is, but the police have cleared the immediate surroundings. People are not happy. Kemal's a popular fellow."

"You've never met the old rogue?" Doyle asked

"No, read about him of course."

"I don't want any charges brought about the gun and shooting, though I suppose it's not up to me. Please pass that on to Sir Anthony."

"Sir Anthony? You're suddenly being polite."

"He reminded me the other night I'm working for him now. Anyway, don't want to undercut his authority."

55

Alex put her hand to her mouth as she giggled.

"I need a new suitcase, so let's leave him be after the debriefing. That'll be tough enough anyway." Doyle knew the ISS inquisitors would be exhaustive in their questioning of all of Kemal's family. "Do you know the little girl's name?" Doyle asked.

"Sofia."

"Be very nice to her; buy her a new doll. I'll pay for it. She helped me put the Chinese woman on the ground."

"How did you incapacitate her after you had shot her?" Alex asked.

"Kept kicking her in the temple till she stopped moving."

"Charming."

"Doyle, get yourself downstairs. Sir Anthony wants to talk to you on the phone," said Sykes in a loud voice.

"Better go. Not sure who scares me more: Sykes or Sir Anthony."

"And I don't?" said Alex, making a little moue.

"You most of all."

Doyle hurried down the stairs as Kemal and his family lined up to be taken away. Kemal broke ranks and walked up to Doyle.

"Mick, Mick, thank you, thank you. May God bless you!"

"I'll see you soon, Kemal—suitcase, remember?"

"Of course, of course."

Doyle marched into the back room and picked up the phone. "Doyle," he said.

"Wait a second, sir. I'll put you through to Sir Anthony."

There was a click and a voice said, "Is that you Doyle?"

"Yes, sir."

"Good work—we'll see what we can make of a live Anvil operative."

"She's Chinese—not sure if from China itself or New Guinea like

Chan. Good luck getting her to talk. She looks like a tough nut. Doc Tambo got the cyanide tooth, but she should be searched inside and out for other playthings."

"Agreed, these Anvil operatives are very different to the usual espionage fodder."

"They are more like a cult, not spies. That's how I'd view it as an anthropologist."

"Yes, I forget you are a well-educated ruffian, despite behaving like an Irish hooligan."

"Ha! Do you still want me to go to New Guinea?"

"Yes, we've had a possible match for Elaine Chan's partner. One of our men in Dutch Batavia says a native shipping clerk saw a man of his description board a coastal steamer six months ago."

"Are we sure? I mean six months ago, can we—"

"I asked the same question; apparently the clerk remembers the man's appalling manners. There was slight delay in getting the man's luggage collected and put aboard. The man called the clerk, among other things, a 'filthy, shirking, groveling monkey.'"

"Aye, well, that would stick in the memory."

"The steamer called at ports on the way to Fiji, including Port Moresby. His name on the manifest was Kurt Lutz; he gave his occupation as mining engineer, as required by Dutch East Indies law. He alighted from the vessel in Moresby. Better check your kit."

"I need a new suitcase. It's why I was in Rotherhithe."

"Kemal can build your new suitcase with Sykes. Sykes has always wanted to compare notes with the Egyptian. I'll have him debriefed first then put in Sykes's care. There will be no charges brought against Kemal. The family will go to Chartwell for a week for the interviews and a bit of sea air. Kemal's older sons can run the business ... and other activities.

"Any thoughts on what was behind the attempt to have me killed by Kemal?" Doyle asked.

"I think they wanted a scandal that would greatly embarrass the imperial government and the ISS. Egyptian smuggler kills ISS man and then turns gun on himself and family. The press and broadcasters would have a field day before we could implement a media blackout. There would be a Parliamentary enquiry, possibly a commission. The ISS would be thrown off-balance. There would be calls for me to resign. You know the routine."

"Thank God he's a lousy shot. They gave him a great big revolver. A smaller caliber pistol would have worked better, but even so, the untrained are usually lousy shots. That's why we train so hard in the army. To be honest, it's a relief in a way."

"Relief?" Sir Anthony said.

"Yes, it suggests that there's room for incompetence in all this slick planning and execution—excuse the pun."

"I agree. What are your plans for this evening?"

"Nothing right now."

"Good—come for dinner at my Kensington house. Lady Sonia will be pleased to see you. I'll send my car. It'll be there at six thirty."

"Thank you. Will it be formal?"

"No, lounge suit will be fine."

Chapter 12

Doyle reported for work at the ISS headquarters building at Vauxhall Cross on the south shore of the Thames. Doyle thought the building was far from subtle: a naked manifestation of imperial power. Still, he believed it was a damn site better than the old building at Cambridge Circus, with its shabby corridors and peeling walls. Sir Anthony had bullied the government into building the new headquarters. He had told a Parliamentary committee that if the British wanted to maintain the empire, the ISS needed more than a place that resembled a down-at-heel lending library.

The Cambridge Circus facility had not closed. It was where the ISS sent exiled staff and operatives. This included the alcoholics and those fond of opium and other drugs. It was where men and women went after contracting venereal diseases more than once. This was the terminal posting for operatives who had made unforgiveable mistakes: the wrong building bombed, the wrong person assassinated, the wrong thing said and hundreds dead in ensuing riots. The older filing queens were among those exiled to the Circus, cursing the advent of computers and digitized records.

Doyle knew the people at the Circus, known dismissively in Vauxhall Cross as the "clowns," still possessed a formidable knowledge of their operational areas. He had on occasion bought them drinks or dinner, to pick their brains before missions. They were grateful to be able to draw on their expertise and to receive any gossip about the ISS.

Looking north across the river, Doyle could see Thames House, the home of the domestic intelligence service, MI5. There was no love lost between the two security branches; the ISS called them the "odd job men," and MI5 returned the compliment, referring to the ISS as the "gigolos." Doyle knew MI5 always felt it was shortchanged, with more cash and facilities given to the ISS. It was true, thought Doyle, but then the ISS had a much bigger patch than MI5. Still, they had their uses, even if it was just to pick up the bullet casings after an ISS domestic operation.

The front door of the ISS building was accessible on foot. There were checkpoints on either side within fifty yards from the entrance staffed by heavily armed police. Doyle approached a checkpoint, giving his name and showing an Indian driving license. The policeman checked a list on a clipboard and contacted someone using his walkie-talkie radio. The radio was a new model, much smaller that the cumbersome, brick-sized models with which Doyle was familiar. *Everything's getting smaller,* thought Doyle. Transistors were a marvel when they were developed in the 1970s, but now printed circuits were set to replace them. The ISS, as usual, was ahead of the game.

"Mr. Doyle, one of my colleagues will escort you to the front door."

Doyle walked into a spacious atrium lit by daylight in the roof and concealed lighting. Within this large space sat a receptionist behind a desk. On the desk were several phones of different colors and a large switchboard. There was an ornamental pen set and a typewriter to the right hand side of the receptionist. Above the desk on the back wall was a huge world map, with clocks embedded, showing the empire's principal cities and local times.

The receptionist regarded Doyle with interest. She had a

symmetrical almond face, olive skin, and dark hair, with a slender elegant nose and large liquid eyes.

"Mr. Doyle, I was told to expect you. Please would you wait a few moments?"

Her voice sounded English, but Doyle perceived a lilt suggesting she was from somewhere in South Asia. Doyle guessed an Indian Parsi.

"It was hard work getting in here, but nobody searched me. I could be carrying a gun," said Doyle.

"You might, but the doorframe contains a metal detector, so I know if someone is coming in with something that might be a gun or knife."

"And if I did?"

"Then you would be dead by now."

He looked behind him; the armed policeman was still there.

There was a ping, and a door slid open in a pillar to the left of the desk.

Alex McCall stepped out and said, "Thanks, Persis, I'll take custody of Mr. Doyle."

"Very well, Alex, I'll call ahead and let them know to expect you."

"Good day to you, à colleen. I was betting with myself that Persis here was a Parsi."

"Well done, Mr. Doyle, Persis is also one of my best friends, so I hope you haven't been a nuisance. Come on; you are expected upstairs."

Before he could say anything, Alex ushered Doyle into the elevator, but not before Persis had given him a sidelong glance and the ghost of a smile.

"Stop flirting with the ISS staff, Mr. Doyle."

"Flirting—I've hardly had time to draw breath."

"Hmm, well, Persis seemed taken with you."

"Hardly said a word to her. Must be my winning personality."

"No, just gossip in the ladies lavatory," Alex said.

Doyle chuckled and said, "I'd heard about the security breaches that go on in the ladies loo. So much for the vaunted ISS discipline. I'm surprised the techies haven't bugged the toilets."

"Oh, they'd love to do that, but it would be found out, and then every lady in the ISS would walk out in disgust."

The lift slowed and pinged. "Here we are; they're in Sir Anthony's conference room."

Doyle and Alex stepped out of the lift, but before they went through the door opposite, Doyle said, "They?"

"Sir Anthony, Colonel Sykes, Dr. Tambo, Dr. Hilborn, and—"

"Hilborn? Isn't he the tame shrink?"

"What a way to describe one of the world's most renowned psychologists."

"Who else?"

"Royston Rogers—it's hard to get him out of Aldermarston, but Sir Anthony insisted."

"I should think so. Who's taking minutes? Is that your job?"

"Cheeky devil! I'm also sitting in, but Sir Anthony's secretary will provide meeting support. It's recorded anyway, but Sir Anthony always wants Jane up to speed on any new operations."

Jane, Doyle knew, was Lady Jane Wellesley, a direct descendent of the Duke of Wellington, the national hero who had defeated Bonaparte in Europe and again in America, after he had escaped from Saint Helena.

Alex opened the door and introduced Doyle, before taking a seat beside him at the table. The conference room was a nondescript room, with oak-paneled walls and no windows, a deliberate security precaution. A world map behind Sir Anthony was the only break in the monotony of the wood paneling.

Doyle scanned the faces and looked beyond Sir Anthony to the woman sitting straight-backed to the left of the ISS chief. She ran her eye over Doyle, with an air of disapproval. *An "aristo" to the core,* he thought, even though they both had Irish ancestry. There were many legends about Lady Jane, some of them probably true. She grew up in the military outposts of the empire and had been a field operative herself. When Sir Anthony had taken over the helm of the ISS a decade earlier, one of his first decisions was to promote her to being his personal assistant. Doyle knew that Lady Jane's daughter took after her mother. She was a soldier in the Greenfinches, an elite, all-female, special forces unit of the Royal Irish Regiment.

"Very well, ladies and gentlemen, this is Michael Doyle, one of our best operatives when we can lure him in. Doyle, do you know everyone here?

"Mostly, sir. I know of Dr. Hilborn, but we've never met, and the same for Dr. Rogers.

Hilborn nodded at Doyle, as did Rogers. Doyle thought Rogers looked like an Aussie, with a square chin and broad chest. His face had a creased, weather-beaten look from being outside in the Australian sun as a youngster. His eyes were dark and piercing, though he looked like a man with a sense of humor. All Aussies had a touch of the larrikin about them, which cocked a snook at authority.

"Let's review where we are with Operation Anvil. Dr. Tambo, Dr. Hilborn, what progress have you made with the Chinese woman Doyle captured in Rotherhithe?"

Tambo said, "We X-rayed her body, initially to see where the bullets lay for an operation but also as a precaution. Something showed up on her thigh: an artificial skinlike membrane under which there was a fine wire, which we think is a garrote. It has a loop at each end for handles; a couple of stout twigs will do. We found other membrane skin patches on her other leg and ribcage. Her vagina contained a capsule that could be fashioned into a stiletto. Nasty piece of work, tipped with blowfish poison. There was another capsule in her rectum with a set of lock-picks."

"What was beneath the other two skin patches?" asked Sir Anthony.

"Beneath the one on her leg was a fine tungsten saw blade. The other had nothing, but on the reverse side of the patch was a set of alphanumeric codes. Our cypher teams are looking at it now."

"Doyle, thoughts?" said Sir Anthony.

"It all adds up to an escape kit, in case she cannot use the poison tooth. The patch with the codes is probably a form of identification. What are the skin membranes made from?"

"Shark collagen, but it's commonly called 'shark skin.' It's used to help burn victims grow new skin, but Raptor has found a new use for it."

Hilborn said, "She's a tough nut. She's been talking under interrogation when we've pumped her full of our most potent drug cocktails. But she's undergone hours if not days of hypnotic treatments. If we get near to anything like her identity, who she works for, she goes into a fugue. It was very hard to break through."

"Do I want to know how you did it?" Sir Anthony asked.

"Nothing too brutal, at least not physically," said Hilborn.

"A fugue?' said Doyle

"It's a psychiatric disorder characterized by amnesia for identity, memories, and other identifying characteristics," said Hilborn.

"Jesus wept—what are we up against?" said Doyle.

Sir Anthony said, "More than just the usual espionage. This I believe is an attack at the foundations of the empire. The five missing atom bombs could do immense damage. Destroying our key cities and resources would shake the very fundamentals of the empire, reducing the world to chaos, ready for some power to step in and assume control, not just of the empire but of the world itself."

There was a moment of silence as the assembled ISS personnel contemplated the gravity of the situation.

"Dr. Rogers, what's the likelihood of whoever stole the bombs replicating them?"

Rogers sat up straighter in his chair and looked around the room as he spoke.

"Dismantling the bomb to reverse engineer a new device will take time, even if they are from a country with advanced nuclear programs. Much of the technology to produce the nuclear fuel for the bombs is still top secret. We should keep an eye out for anyone manufacturing high-speed centrifuges or the metallurgy to construct the centrifuges."

"Anything else, Dr. Rogers?"

"Watch out for any outbreaks of unusual poisonings or inexplicable medical conditions. Our atom bombs have gravitated to using plutonium from the original uranium design. Plutonium is nasty stuff, incredibly toxic if inhaled or digested. It's also very dangerous to handle. The critical mass of plutonium is about 25 pounds when it starts to emit deadly amounts of radioactivity."

"Why the hell use it then?" asked Doyle.

"Because it takes about half the plutonium to give the same explosive yield as uranium," said Rogers. "And there's another reason."

Rogers broke off, staring at Sir Anthony.

Sir Anthony gave a slight nod.

"If you have plutonium, then you can develop another type of nuclear device. We call it the hydrogen bomb, as it uses isotopes of hydrogen as part of the explosive formula. The H-bomb is at least five hundred times more powerful than our existing atom bomb arsenal."

Sykes said, "You said 'is' not 'could be.'"

Rogers looked again at Sir Anthony, who said, "Please go ahead, Dr. Rogers. Everyone here is an ISS employee. We all know about secrecy and discretion."

Rogers said, "Yes, we have conducted several tests, every one of them successful. In practical terms, we now have the ability to wipe out whole nations, not just cities."

Chapter 13

"Christ," said Doyle, "Why would we need something this powerful? Atom bombs would surely make any country surrender."

"Yes," said Sir Anthony, "but other countries are catching up with their nuclear research. It seems one or more of them want to speed the process up with this bomb theft. We've always known that the day would come when others would have nuclear weapons, so our scientists have upped the ante, so to speak—our hydrogen bombs trump your atom bombs."

"What about the MAD scenario?" asked Doyle.

"It still applies, but we still want to have a bigger stick. Otherwise we may as well give up the empire, if we're not going to defend it by any means possible."

"Am I still going to New Guinea? Has the Chinese woman given anything away?"

"Not much," said Hilborn, "but when we listened to the recordings of the interrogations, we noticed that she would lapse into Cantonese from time to time and then what we thought was gibberish. It bothered me we were missing something, so I asked our technical staff to isolate the periods when she muttered in gibberish.

"As you know, we have staff from all over the empire in this place, so I had the tapes played for some of our staff from Africa, the Middle East, India, and the South Pacific. Most did not recognize the words; one fellow from the British Solomon Islands thought she might be speaking pidgin. It's a creole language spoken in the Melanesian Islands from New Guinea to the New Hebrides."

"Could you cut to the chase, Dr. Hilborn?" said Sir Anthony.

"Yes, of course. We brought in a lady from Bletchley, who is from what was German New Guinea. She's a cipher clerk, her father is a German-speaking Slovak, and her mother is from one of the Duke of York Islands. She listened to the tapes and confirmed the Chinese woman was indeed speaking pidgin. The language changes between island groups but is most complex in New Guinea.

"There's one more thing: our Bletchley lady said that the woman was also speaking in what they call ples-tok, a local language. She could not understand most of the words, but she said that it was well known that children raised by house girls would often learn the local language as well as pidgin."

"So, Doyle, I want you in New Guinea as soon as possible," said Sir Anthony. "Dr. Tambo, please equip Doyle with antimalarial drugs and anything else he needs for New Guinea. Colonel Sykes, I understand that Kemal has fabricated a new suitcase for Doyle; please furnish this and other equipment he should use. Dr. Rogers, please brief Doyle on the technical specifications of our atom bombs."

"How do I get there? It's a hell of journey, even by plane, with ten days to get to Sydney. No faster by airship, but maybe a bit more comfortable," said Doyle.

"You'll fly on a military plane. We can cut the journey time in half, and you'll fly directly into Port Moresby. It is one of several key military airports in the region, so a Royal Airforce flight landing should not arouse suspicions. We'll have the flight set up with relief pilots along the way at fuel stops. I'm told we have accommodation modules that can be inserted for top brass and VIPs, so you'll have a bunk and somewhere decent to go to the bathroom."

"Good job about the bathroom," said Doyle.

Dr. Tambo said, "Mr. Doyle, please be aware that everything in New Guinea will be trying to kill you, never mind the enemy. I'm from West Africa, from the Gold Coast, which is about a bad as New Guinea, and it's not called the white man's grave for nothing."

"Beware men of the Bight of Benin; there's one comes out for ten goes in," said Doyle.

"Quite—we must get you on antimalarial tablets today, one a day without fail. They are not 100 percent effective; there are resistant strains of malaria. If you do fall ill, and it persists, you can take quinine. I will also include some for you. Treat every scratch, especially below the knee, as a serious wound. Clean, disinfect, and cover. Even in remote areas you can usually find bleach, so use a dilute solution to clean wounds in the absence of surgical spirit."

Sir Anthony said, "Thank you, Dr. Tambo. Please continue this briefing with Doyle after the meeting." He turned to Doyle. "You will do the rounds of the various departments that need to kit you out. I assume you've got your own favorite weapons. Are you lugging that antique broom-handle Mauser around with you?"

Before he could answer, Sykes said, "I've tried to get that piece of nineteenth-century pig iron off him, but he'll not give it up. Have you got your Browning Hi-Power?"

Doyle nodded and Sykes went on.

"Good, bring it in for servicing and your silencer. I hate the damn things, but I know you need them. I'll give you the best ammunition we've tested."

There was a pause, as if Sir Anthony was going to conclude the meeting, and then he said, "Miss McCall, I want you to accompany Doyle on this mission. You will fly as far as Port Moresby and be Doyle's principle contact at our ISS mission in the high commission.

We have a very efficient operative there by the name of Mayflower Pilgrim."

Doyle was about to comment, when Alex said, "Sir Anthony, are you sure you want me to go? I've never operated abroad, let alone New Guinea."

"I'm aware of that, Miss McCall, but we need to keep this operation limited to as few people as possible. You will be in a liaison position in Moresby. I do not expect you to go traipsing about in the jungle, but you will travel in-country as you see fit. Miss Pilgrim will be the lead to undertake any field activities with Doyle. I want to have lines of communication at all times, so you will be the lynchpin. If there's any diplomatic staff nonsense with the high commission or the governor general, I expect you to deal with it. The king will give you plenipotentiary powers to do so. I will give you the decree when it is received from Buckingham Palace later today.

"Anything else?" said Sir Anthony.

"The man I shot yesterday, any ideas who he is?" Doyle asked.

"Not yet, but we are pursuing this and will contact you and Miss McCall with his identity when known.

"Very well. Miss Wellesley, please prepare the meeting minutes and an Anvil action memorandum—eyes only for the people in this room. Miss McCall, please escort and coordinate Mr. Doyle through his various appointments today. See he goes to our personnel department. You will travel on your British passport, Doyle—you too, Miss McCall. Miss Pilgrim will see you are admitted as diplomatic staff. Please carry on."

Chapter 14

Doyle brought all his weaponry into the ISS headquarters on the following day. Getting past security with three guns and associated paraphernalia in his grip was a task in itself. Every gun and magazine was registered to ensure they contained no ammunition. The guards wrote down all the serial numbers of the guns and magazines. His grip was searched to ensure nothing harmful was being admitted into the building. Doyle contrasted this with the Circus, where he could show up with his military identification and gain entry to the building.

At the reception desk, Persis favored Doyle with a cool smile and came around her desk to clip a visitor's badge on his lapel. Doyle noted that she seemed to float rather then walk. Alex appeared just as Persis was smoothing Doyle's lapel. Alex glared at them both and then seized Doyle's arm, practically frog marching him to the elevator. Doyle noticed that Alex was unhappy, but he doubted a bit of flirting with her colleague was the cause.

Colonel Sykes had Doyle's guns stripped and cleaned, including the Mauser. Despite his comments about the C-96, he too had a soft spot for the gun and produced two additional twenty round magazines for the weapon.

"Where did you get these?" asked Doyle.

"Aye well," said Sykes, "I know a few fellows off the books, as you do."

Doyle completed his rounds of the ISS offices, finishing up at Colonel Sykes domain to retrieve the guns, fresh ammunition, and his new suitcase.

Sykes said, "The Mauser is a wee bit warm. The younger boys all wanted to try it out, so I let them shoot out a few magazines at the range. They've stripped and cleaned it again though. The ammunition is the best we can give you, but it's one thing keeping it in the climate-controlled conditions of my workshop and another entirely in the jungle."

On the flight out from England Alex had been on the verge of tears as they flew to Greece and then onward to Cairo. After Cairo, there was a long leg to Calcutta, with a short refueling stop in Bombay. Doyle had noticed Alex touching her gold necklace and guessed it was lacking her engagement ring. He had the choice of ignoring her or asking and being rebuffed. Doyle decided on the latter, feeling that they were heading into a nest of vipers and needed Alex fully alert, not mooning over a romantic setback.

They were cruising over India, and they had eaten lunch, provided by two flight attendants. The attendants were Indian girls in blue air force uniforms, both very pretty. One of them had a large diamond engagement ring. Alex was sitting in a window seat, Doyle next to her. She let out a little sigh, and Doyle could tell from the way she held her head and shoulders that she was sobbing gently.

Doyle went up to the galley and picked up some paper napkins. The two flight attendants had just finished eating and were admiring the one's engagement ring. Doyle told them to relax when he saw they were about to jump to their feet. He returned to his seat and tapped Alex on the shoulder, passing her the napkins.

"Oh, dear, I'm sorry, Mr. Doyle. It's just—"

"Do you want to talk about it? Is it about your fiancé?"

"Yes, it's all over."

"What happened?"

"This assignment—all I could tell Robert was that the trip was totally unexpected, and I couldn't say how long I'd be away. It was the straw that broke the camel's back."

"Yeah, I know, I know—the ISS is a harsh mistress. What did Robert know about your job?"

"I'd always been vague about my career with the ISS. I told Robert that I was a civil servant but security reasons meant I could not be more specific. It did not matter much when we were first courting. Robert proposed after nine months. I was a bit overwhelmed, but I said yes and then informed Sir Anthony."

"I expect he advised you to be cautious," Doyle said.

"Yes, he was full of congratulations, but he counseled me that marriages to people outside the ISS do not have a great track record. The dire need for secrecy and the unusual demands of the job put great strains on relationships. I am not naïve; I have heard about several marriages that have come unglued. Robert is a rising star in a merchant bank. He worked long hours and would often be abroad on bank business, so I thought it would be a good fit, at least until we decided to have a family." Alex wiped her eyes and blew her nose.

"Robert expected me to quit my job and become a full-time wife. Continuing to work for the ISS had already undermined our relationship. He said I could work for his bank until we were married. I declined; I wanted to have a career as well as being a wife. The vagueness of this assignment caused an almighty row, with Robert calling off the wedding, asking for his ring back."

"I'm sorry. I don't have any words of wisdom except to say it is better now than later. You are unhappy now, but think of a lifetime of unhappiness if you'd gotten married and it wasn't a good fit," said Doyle.

Alex rallied, smiled, and said, "It's what my mother said. Do you know where we are?"

Doyle looked at his watch and pulled a small compass from his shirt pocket.

"We're still heading southeast, and it's been three hours since we left Calcutta, so we're probably over the Andaman Sea."

"Have you been here, I mean the Andaman Islands?"

"Yes, not for very long—I had to fix a limpet mine to a nosy German spy ship poking around in the Andamans."

"Goodness me, what were the Germans doing here?

"These islands and the Nicobars are off-limits to anyone except resident natives, imperial officials, and military. It is where the empire sends its most intractable political prisoners. Have you never heard of the infamous Port Blair Cellular Jail?"

Alex shook her head and blinked her eyes, forcing herself awake.

"Yes, of course, silly of me. It's included on the ISS training course," she said.

"Several of the residents of the Cellular Jail were sent there by me," said Doyle. "The whole incident with the spy ship was a hell of a flap. I was a civilian again, putting my talents to earning some filthy lucre, not a government pittance."

"Who were you working for?"

"I was working as a security consultant for the Anglo-Burma Oil Company, polite fiction for a hired thug."

"Now I think you are over egging the pudding," Alex said.

Doyle laughed and then his smile vanished. He said, "No, Alex, it's what I do best."

Alex looked solemn and said in a quiet voice, "What happened?

"There were some bloody Australian Catholic missionaries in the oil fields northwest of Rangoon. They were infecting the local villagers on the oil fields with bizarre notions of government accountability and the sudden disappearances of local political agitators."

"Not wise."

"Not wise in Burma or sensitive spots where the empire has a boot on the neck of the populace. One of the missionary ladies—I remember her name, Cecily Dignan—called me a hired brute, a gangster in uniform, when we shut their mission down."

"What did you do?" Alex asked.

"I was tempted to hit her; she was beating on my arm. I said I was not wearing a uniform, just my regular khakis for the hot climate. I was a civilian representative to ensure there was no damage to ABO facilities. We got chapter and verse on how the mission was not just saving souls but helping with schooling and health, helping improve hygiene and infant survival."

"Probably true, at least the schooling and health. How did you respond to such an impassioned plea?"

"I said she would be rewarded by God in Heaven and recompensed by the Burmese administration. As this was happening, the soldiers were rounding up all the missionaries and their local employees and loading them onto trucks. We took everything on paper, all the filing and contents of desks."

"Did the locals get annoyed?"

"A few Burmese showed up at the gates—more out of curiosity than bothered by the mission closure. Cecily, the missionary lady, had another go at me, saying I was everything wrong with the bloody empire."

Alex laughed and said, "She had a point. So what did you say?"

"As I recall, I said something like, 'The empire survives because of people like me. The empire puts on a benevolent face, but it's a police state and I'm one of the police. So, please, enough … you could have stayed here saving souls and teaching people to wipe their bottoms, but you began meddling in local politics, in things that don't concern you.'"

"Crikey!"

"I think that was when the missionary lady began to realize just how much trouble she was in," Doyle said.

"I presume you came up with some more mots justes?"

"I told her she would be deported back to Australia, passports confiscated, and be under house arrest at His Majesty's pleasure. I added she would never be allowed to travel again outside her hometown, anywhere. I think my parting shot was, 'Take a good look; this will be the last time you see anything except the bottom of your street.'"

Chapter 15

"Do you mean that about the empire being a police state?" Alex asked.

"Yes, all empires are. It doesn't matter how nice you are, all the good you do. In the end you're telling people you know what's best for them. If they don't like it, here's a jail cell," Doyle said.

"That's a very bleak view. I've always thought the world would be a darker more dangerous place without the empire."

"Yes, but I think most people can probably govern themselves without King James looking over their shoulder."

"Most places are dominions, self-government in all but name."

"Aye, I suppose so. There are some places where I'd hate to go without a British presence. It is a higgledy-piggledy patchwork though—places like America, where puritans went because they could not persecute other people, or India, where we went to trade and next thing we had taken over the country. Usually it's the same story wherever we planted our flag: some poor trusting credulous bastards found themselves dispossessed and dying from measles or venereal disease."

Alex laughed and said, "You sound like the anti-imperialists when I was at university."

"They tried to recruit me when I was at Harvard, thinking I'd be a dead cert, being Irish. They were most offended when I turned out to be a loyal subject. They got very unpleasant, but nothing a lad like me could not handle. Other than politics, our family had always had a fancy for boxing, and I boxed for Oxford and Harvard. I was also an officer cadet at both colleges; I went from Harvard more or less straight into the Indian Army officer program."

"Tell me about the German vessel in the Andamans. Were you sent there from Burma?"

"Yes, a German naval vessel, a destroyer—it had been observed by local fishermen, sneaking into the islands at night and leaving for the high seas in the daytime. We do not allow the Germans much of a navy, but they have destroyers that are oceangoing vessels. The Andaman governor was concerned that the Germans may be mounting an attempt at freeing some of the Port Blair prisoners. So, of course, there was an almighty flap—what my Ulster grandmother would call 'a right stramash.' There were no suitable ISS operatives to hand, plenty of placemen but no ugly types who liked getting their hands dirty."

"So they recalled you to active service?" Alex asked.

"I think dragged kicking and screaming out of a Rangoon bar would be the best way to put it, right after the mission burning. I was three sheets to the wind, so I couldn't put up much of a struggle. A sergeant in the Burmese police tapped me on the head, and I was flung onto a plane. Next thing I knew I was woken by dawn coming up over the Andaman Sea. Bit like the Kipling poem," Doyle said.

"'On the road to Mandalay, where the flyin' fishes play, an' the dawn comes up like thunder outer China 'cross the bay,'" said Alex, with a cockney lilt.

"Something like that. The governor was wringing a handkerchief around his finger. He briefed me on landing. His patrol vessel was down in the Nicobar Islands chasing pirates. He had about one hundred local troops and police, but a German navy vessel could set the cat among the canaries by bombarding Port Blair, especially at night, and slipping in a landing party to attack the jail. There are no big artillery pieces, so the town would be helpless. Even if the patrol boat was there, it would be no match for a destroyer."

"Who do you think they were after, in the jail I mean?"

"Oh, they'd be spoiled for choice. Most of the jail population is from India and Burma, but we've also consigned some of the most intractable Africans there. It's imperial policy to bury folks who raise their heads above the parapet as deep as possible."

"I have no sympathies to be honest. I come from a long line of imperial civil servants. I have lost relatives in government service, some killed in uprisings and others by bandits. I suppose I've always preferred not to think about how brutal the empire can be," Alex said.

"Most people prefer to think about the empire's civilizing mission and not its bloody history. The destruction of the German destroyer was brutal. The governor had requisitioned a trading schooner to get me out to sea in a hurry. We towed a fishing vessel with sail and motor power. The schooner dropped me, a limpet mine, and two fishermen at the last known position of the destroyer, between South Andaman and North Sentinel Island. After the schooner left, we just bobbed around, setting gillnets, which I'd never done much, to delight of the two fishermen."

"Were they dragooned into the mission too?"

"Pretty much, but the governor also waved a few high denomination rupee notes in their direction. They also spoke passable English. I think they may have entertained ideas about just slitting my throat and buggering off, so I tossed them both off the boat during a set, which was a bit cruel," Doyle said.

"My goodness, that's rather drastic. What did they do?"

"Splashed around a lot. They were terrified of sharks. So I pulled them back on board and told them to behave themselves."

"Do you speak any Hindi?"

"Not much, just a few commands, I'm not a great one for languages. I don't even speak Gaelic, despite several fluent relatives. The fishermen knew a lunatic when they saw one, so we got on fine from then on. Anyway, I was beginning to despair that we had come up empty when we heard the throb of marine diesels and saw the phosphorescent wake of the destroyer. Large vessels have to be very careful in Andaman coastal waters. The admiralty and naval hydrographers have only mapped the approaches to Port Blair and surrounding reefs."

"Did the vessel head to Port Blair?" asked Alex.

"No, we thought at first it was heading there, but then it hove south. There was a half moon, so we could just about read the charts. A destroyer coming close to shore has to avoid shallows and reefs. The only place we could determine it might get close to a beach was on the south coast of Rutland Island. It's the next big island south of South Andaman."

"Were you able to follow it in a small fishing vessel?"

"Barely, there was a southerly breeze, so we had to tack and turn. We just kept heading south, with Rutland to our west, until we had to turn west ourselves. All guesswork really, but the southern shore of Rutland Island was a good place for a large vessel to make a safe approach to the coast. It's twelve miles to the north coast, through mountainous jungle, so my guess was that someone else would retrieve whomever they dropped off."

"Was that ever found out, I mean with whom the Germans were working?"

"Yes, the ISS sent in some of its best and brightest from Delhi and a Gurkha platoon that went through the place like a firestorm. As you'd guess, there was a nest of independence vipers fomenting trouble."

"Why do they bother? I mean India is pretty much self-governing as a dominion."

"Same reason some of my countrymen keep blowing things up in Ireland. I suppose people want to have the illusion that everything will be paradise once free from the iron grip of the empire. We hugged the south coast of Rutland, keeping an eye out for any lights, even smelling the air for diesel fumes. I was beginning to despair again when we saw a faint glow ahead, which we realized was not on land. I wondered if there was a name for the bay, but there was nothing on the chart."

"It probably has a local name."

"Yes, but I wasn't hanging around to find out. It was about three o'clock when we downed the sail and paddled in toward the destroyer. I was worried we would be caught in the dawn if we did not get a move on. I had to swim the mine over to the destroyer. The damn thing weighed fifteen pounds, but it was supported in a cork ring. The current was slight as the tide was not yet on the turn; otherwise rip currents can be murderous. I swam over to the vessel using a snorkel, no aqualung or rebreather set being available in Port Blair," Doyle said.

"How did you navigate in the dark? In our training we had to do this sort of exercise; I just took a bearing and hoped for the best." Alex laughed at the memory.

"Pretty much what I did. I couldn't use a luminescent compass, as it might be detected by the watch on the destroyer. Luckily, someone was a smoker, probably taking a secret smoke break. There was no flare, so I suspect the sailor lit his ciggie inside and then stepped out and cupped it in his hand. Luckily, he took a drag now and then, so I was able to follow the intermittent glow right in under the destroyer."

"No one spotted you? What about when the mine clanged against the hull? When we did our practice runs, it sounded like a giant bell when the magnets caught and seized the mine."

"I know, so I wasn't looking forward to it. I was treading water, getting ready to free the mine, when I saw some light on the beach and then something began to move. A longboat paddled out to the ship. This was good and bad news."

"How?"

"I might be discovered bobbing about in the water with a longboat crew that had eyes accustomed to the dark. I had to huddle into the stern, above the propeller and up against the rudder. They were a very disciplined crew—well, they were German after all. Even so I could see little flashes of light, probably dynamo torches, the same as the Dutch-made torches that the ISS issues as field kit. The noise of the longboat retrieval was a bonus, as it could well disguise the moment when I attached the mine to the German ship."

"Which I assume you did successfully?" Alex asked.

"Yes. I won't bore you, but it was a bloody awful struggle getting that mine attached to the hull. It made a noise like the doomsday bell. Thankfully, the longboat retrieval covered the clang, so I set the fuse, which gives you half an hour, and took off into the dark. As I swam back to where I thought the fishing boat should be, I had a nasty thought that my two comrades may have buggered off. They could simply report to the governor that I had not come back, eaten by a shark or swept out to sea."

"Since you're here, you lived to tell the tale."

"Aye, but I was getting pretty desperate, and my legs and feet were cramping, making it hard to swim. I was exhausted as the tide had turned, and I was battling the current head on. I thought I might just swim for the coast, but I was worried about being close to the destroyer when the mine exploded. The shock wave would pummel my insides, possibly lethally, and then bodies in the water would create a shark and barracuda feeding frenzy. I was really all in when I was grabbed by my arms and dragged him onto the fishing vessel. I gave the lads a little bonus when we got back to Port Blair."

"And the destroyer went up in smoke?"

"Yeah, though there was an odd ending to the tale. A life raft from the German vessel was spotted on the shore of North Sentinel Island a few days later. It's inhabited by native Andamese who are left alone, due to their extreme ferocity to outsiders. I've seen close-up photographs of them taken from ships and aerial surveys. They look like the folks in New Guinea."

Chapter 16

The plane landed in the early afternoon at Port Moresby airport. The plane came to a stop outside a hanger. Doyle could see a cluster of people with a tall, slender native woman in their midst.

The stairs were brought to the aircraft door, and Doyle and Alex stepped down on to the tarmac apron. They met their welcoming party. The men were wearing either tropical linen suits or short-sleeve shirts and shorts with long white socks.

"Hello, Mr. Doyle, Miss McCall. I am High Commissioner Geoffrey Brown-Walcott. These are various members of my staff. Rather than introduce them all in this heat, we would like to invite to a reception by the governor general at the high commission tonight. The GG sends his regards, but we have a delegation from the Dutch East Indies that arrived today."

Doyle wondered what sins this man had committed to end up in this backwater. Brown-Walcott was gray-haired, gray-skinned and had a slight stoop—a slow horse with a few years left in him.

Doyle looked at the native girl, who was tall and elegant, with straight hair plaited and coiled on her head, accentuating her fine cheekbones. She wore a white blouse and a gray pleated skirt. Her legs were smooth and shined like polished ebony; her arms were slender, with fine long fingers and manicured fingernails. There were two ornamental sticks in her hair, making her look more Southeast Asian than Melanesian.

The high commissioner said, "The one person you do want to meet straight away is Miss Pilgrim, she's … the ISS contact attached to the high commission." Brown-Walcott lowered his voice as he said this, as though a crowd of watchers surrounded them.

"Hello, Mr. Doyle, Miss McCall, please call me May. I'll take care of you now. You have rooms reserved in the Ela Beach Hotel. It's in downtown Moresby."

May led them to a large saloon car, with the engine idling and air-conditioning cooling the interior. Doyle and Alex slid into the rear seats, hearing their luggage being stowed in the trunk. May sat behind the wheel.

"Sorry about this; we may as well put up a flag and say here are the ISS operatives," said May. "I may as well have driven out here in a high commission car."

"Christ," said Doyle, "what happened? How did the high commission and GG find out about our arrival? We were supposed to slip in quietly."

"Yes, I know. Someone at the airport alerted the commission to the arrival of an aircraft outfitted for VIPs. I thought I had all avenues of communication about your arrival blocked. I didn't count on a zealous individual at Jackson's Field calling the commission about a VIP arrival. I heard a kerfuffle and went to see the high commissioner and begged him to keep your arrival under wraps."

"Unsuccessfully, I'm guessing," said Alex. "If it's any consolation, I'm from a colonial family, so I know what it's like when somebody new rolls into town—time to unlock the drinks cabinet."

"I sent a top security telefax to inform Sir Anthony but haven't had a response," said May.

Doyle said, "Use the code word 'Anvil.' That will get top priority. Send him a message anyway, superseding your last, saying we have arrived and that we are being treated as new staff for the high commission."

"I'm still going to look like a bloody beginner," said May.

"How long have you been working for the ISS?" asked Doyle.

"Five years—I was recruited from Special Branch."

"Were you trained in England?" asked Alex.

"No, there's an ISS training facility north of Brisbane. Not much point going all the way to England to train for a New Guinea posting."

Doyle laughed and said, "I only ever did bits and pieces of the training course. I'm an ex-army occasional, so I already knew about hurting and killing people. I did an accelerated course at Chartwell. Ever been to England?"

"No, Australia, some of the Pacific Islands, Singapore, Hong Kong, and Sarawak."

"Sarawak, that's a tough place."

"Yes, I was attached to a squad of special forces. I was still in training, but the ISS wanted me to get field training in jungle operations," said May.

"What were you doing?" asked Alex.

"Conducting cross-border raids into Dutch territory, chasing and assassinating Malay separatists," said May.

"Fun—how many did you kill?" said Doyle.

"All together or me personally?" said May.

"How many did you kill?" asked Doyle.

The atmosphere in the car went quiet. Outside the grubby ugly scenery of suburban Port Moresby flew past. Above the plains were grassy hills on which shantytown settlements were rising up the slopes. At the traffic lights, mad men danced to the sequence of the color changes, children sold newspapers and fruit, and highlanders stood and stared at everything.

"Fifteen, all by hand—usually garrote but a few with a knife. I preferred the garrote because it is almost impossible for the target to escape; you just saw through the neck until you hit the spine, while trying to stay on your feet. It's trickier with the knife. I'm stronger than I look, but it's not all about strength; it's about coordination. You have to grab the target, block the mouth with your left hand, stab the knife in the right place in the neck and then slice it forward in one motion. It should take no more than five seconds, and then you have to hold onto the corpse to make sure there's no noise."

"Straight out of the training manual," said Doyle. He looked at Alex, who was looking at May with a mix of admiration and disquiet. "You're making Alex jealous," said Doyle.

May looked in the mirror at Alex but said nothing.

Doyle broke the silence, "Moresby isn't the jewel in the imperial crown."

"No, it's a dump, but it's got a great sheltered deep water harbor, so the navy loves it. Other than that, you can see that it's barren. The trades blow dry from the southeast for ten months, and then there is a monsoon and it pours for two months around Christmas. The local people are a miserable surly lot. You can see they are descended from Polynesians, but not the nice ones like Cook Islanders—probably village idiots lost on a canoe voyage. We have the squatters from across the country who build the shanties and commit most of the crime. On top of that, every carpetbagger from the empire tries their hand in Moresby after they've failed elsewhere. What can I say? Welcome to paradise; here's your hotel."

Chapter 17

May picked up Doyle and Alex for the reception at the high commission at 5:00 p.m.

"The governor general's residence is up the street behind you, on top of the hill. The high commission was located nearby—all very handy—and then some genius in London decided to relocate the high commission to Waigani, which is nice if you like swamps," said May.

"Ah, but you're a little drop of Irish laughter, so you are, May," said Doyle.

Both May and Alex laughed.

"Sorry, I know, I've not been my usual jolly self. I received a reply from Sir Anthony by the way; Anvil does seem to grease the wheels."

"Anything for us or just happy to hear we'd arrived?" said Doyle.

"Just acknowledging that you'd arrived."

"Who will we meet tonight?" asked Alex.

"Some tame natives, the governor general, the high commissioner, and the staff—the younger ones are terribly earnest."

"I know the type. Any of the locals we should pay special interest to?" said Doyle.

"Not really—they're local worthies, academics, businessmen, and commission staff," said May.

They arrived at the high commission building as the day was ending. May parked the car and then led them into the building, past two native guards at the door. The two men looked smart in High

Commission livery, armed with pistols. Doyle thought they would not present much of a problem to determined attackers.

Doyle heard the sound of merrymaking and people's voices speaking over each other. They entered a large room, and May made the round of introductions to the dignitaries, their wives, and their attendant staff. Doyle shook hands and then made for the nearest drinks waiter. There was no bar, just men and women in uniforms, circulating with trays of hors d'oeuvres and glasses of wine.

Alex was at home in the diplomatic environment and attracted the attentions of all the men in the room, especially the young bachelors. Doyle could see the wives scrutinizing Alex, who was dressed in a simple but well-tailored floral dress cinched at the waist with a belt and adorned with her gold necklace. She wore stiletto heels on what Doyle guessed were very expensive shoes, and she wore minimal makeup, except for her rouged lips.

"Hello, are you one of the new arrivals?" Doyle turned to see a young couple holding glasses of wine in their hands. They were pale, so they were probably new. Both had faces untouched by life and seemed to be all eyes and teeth, with the boisterous, eager-to-please expressions of puppies.

"Yes, I'm Doyle. That's my colleague Alex over there. You can't miss her; she's got men buzzing around her like bees around honey."

He had wanted to say flies around horseshit, but he thought the young woman might burst into tears if he did.

"We saw you came with May. I'm Simon, and this is my wife, Sally."

"Isn't May something rather hush-hush?" said Sally in a quiet voice.

"What?" said Doyle.

"Hush-hush," said Sally.

Doyle looked over at May, who was chatting with a New Guinea woman and who occasionally glanced his way.

"Hush-hush?" said Doyle, deciding to continue being difficult.

"Yes, hush-hush," said Simon, coming to his wife's rescue.

"Oh, you mean intelligence?" said Doyle. "We call it intelligence in the grownup world. What do you two do?"

Simon and Sally blinked at Doyle's insult but decided to press on.

"We're both in the Native Outreach Division," said Simon. "It's our job to ensure that native people understand their rights."

"I didn't think natives had any rights," said Doyle. "That's why there's an empire."

Simon said, "Oh, yes, we know, but there's a lot more enlightened approaches these days, to ensure that even within the empire, native populations should know what entitlements they have: things like local elections, access to schools, healthcare."

Sally said, "And we want to ensure that their lands aren't misappropriated and that they are properly compensated by mining and timber companies, anyone really that's using their land."

Doyle had been listening to this with his eyes on Alex, thinking that she really was a good-looking girl. She had generous curves but was not overweight, and her pale skin was like expensive marble, set off by the rouged lips, copper red hair, and green eyes. *Easy boy,* he thought, *we are on a mission.* Alex flashed a look that was more than just a glance and seemed loaded with possibilities.

Doyle looked over at May and saw no wedding ring on her left hand. She was certainly easy on the eyes. She had less curves than Alex but a face that was sculpted from ebony, with huge dark eyes above her sensual lips. She had placed a frangipani behind her left ear and uncoiled her beautiful shiny hair that hung down her back.

Doyle realized Simon and Sally were still talking to him.

"We think it's a shame that the native kids seem to eat only potato crisps and drink sodas like Fanta. They should be banned or more tightly regulated," said Simon.

"I thought you were working on behalf of native rights? Now you want to take those away or prevent them from having the right to choose? Bit contradictory, don't you think?"

"But there's much wonderful local food here," said Sally. "And fruit grows everywhere. Moresby is full of mango trees."

"I'm Irish—nothing I like more than egg and chips. The spud is Ireland's unofficial national vegetable; I think it's going to be officially recognized as such by the Dublin Assembly. Should I tell them not to go through with it because it's a danger to children?"

"What? No, it's just we've become quite good connoisseurs of kau kau, you know, sweet potatoes." said Simon. "We go every week to Koki market and know the best sellers and the types of kau kau."

"Yes, we don't eat regular potatoes anymore. We also love eating taro," said Sally.

Doyle felt like there was a nest of hornets in his head. He looked over at May and motioned her to join them.

"Do you have a first name, Mr. Doyle?" said Sally as May joined them.

He ignored this and said, "May, these are colleagues of yours."

"Yes, Simon and Sally, from Native Outreach," said May with a smile.

"They were telling me their hatred for potato crisps and Fanta and about their passion for kau kau and taro."

"Yes, we buy them every week," said Simon with enthusiasm.

"Oh, very nice," said May. "Do you grow them yourselves?"

"No," said Sally.

"Kau kau's not too hard to grow, I suppose," said May. "Taro can be grown dry or wet, like rice. It's dreadful work. I help my auntie when I go home to Mussau, but I hate village life."

Simon and Sally looked like churchgoers finding the vicar drunk and exposing himself to schoolchildren.

May continued. "You can't plant and harvest in the daytime. You have to rise at dawn or work in the late afternoon, when you get eaten alive by mosquitos and every other biting fly. I always get malaria or dengue fever when I have been home, and my legs end up rotting away with tropical ulcers. So what's wrong with ordinary potatoes?"

"Oh, they have no taste compared with kau kau or taro," said Simon.

"I read somewhere there are thousands of different potato varieties; some of them must taste nice," said May. "Even rice-growing countries grow loads of potatoes for home consumption."

Doyle tried not to burst out laughing; he plucked two glasses of wine from a waiter and gave one to May. He assumed all kinds of intelligence material flowed across May's desk, including agricultural statistics.

May sipped her wine and said, "Much more nutrition in the spud, especially the skin; and they're frost resistant, so they are good for the highlands where it can freeze at night. Still, nice to hear about your passion for root crops."

"Oh," said Simon and Sally in unison.

May pressed on, saying, "Have you tried sago, sak-sak?"

"Yes, we learned how to make it from the dried powder sold at the market. We like it, though not as much as kau kau," said Sally.

"I think it's like eating wallpaper glue," said May. "It's survival food like swamp taro, when the big droughts come. Have you ever prepared it yourselves?"

Both Simon and Sally shook their heads.

May said, "You have to go into the mangrove swamps to find sago palms, so you get eaten alive again by biting flies. You have to keep an eye out for crocodiles and big pythons. The crocs are the worst because you never see them. After you collect the sago, it has to be mashed and rinsed endlessly. Otherwise, it will kill you; it's full of cyanide."

"I think it is a measure of desperation. All that effort to end up with tasteless glue—it's no wonder native kids like potato crisps and Fanta."

May turned and walked off to talk to one of her New Guinea colleagues. Doyle left the startled Simon and Sally to get a breath of fresh air. He pushed through the crowd and through the French windows, onto a patio. The sky was velvet dark, with the Milky Way splashed across the heavens. Moresby created little light pollution relative to a metropolis like London. Doyle picked out the Southern Cross, Orion, and Scorpio among the stars.

A horrible smell wafted toward Doyle; it was not from a septic tank overflow. The greasy, brassy smell was human. The wine had dulled his wits, so he was fractionally slow. Just as he began to react, six figures emerged on the edge of the halo of light from the windows.

There was a series of twangs, and Doyle felt terrible burning pain. Looking down, he was festooned with long arrows buried into his flesh. He turned, but the shafts of the arrows caught the doors of the French windows and unbalanced him. He fell, striking his head on a table laden with food and then on the marble floor. There was a scream and then darkness.

Chapter 18

The pain came in waves. It seemed to ebb and flow throughout his body. Doyle thought about that and isolated the pain to his torso. He wiggled his toes, and there was no increase in the pain. He tensed muscles of his right arm, and the pain increased. He did the same with the left arm, and the pain stabbed him through the heart. He gasped in response and shuddered from the agony. He realized the periodicity of the pain was a response to breathing.

What had happened? He replayed in his mind what he could remember. The outward journey to Port Moresby was tedious but at least he could sleep. There was a woman: Alex, Alex McCall. He felt he must concentrate on the woman; maybe if he did he could push the pain to the back of his consciousness.

Doyle noticed the pain started to ease. He opened his eyes and took a slight breath that hurt, but not as much as before. His eyes were unfocused. He blinked and saw a white ceiling above his head, and as he shifted his gaze downward, he saw a sheet and a thin blanket. A ceiling fan created currents of air scented with antiseptic and the sickly sweet smell of frangipanis.

He became aware of a woman in the room, sitting by the bed. He had met this woman before; what was her name? Plymouth Rock wandered into his thoughts, and this was enough to remind him— Mayflower Pilgrim, the ISS contact for the British territory of New Guinea.

"May, what happened to me? Why am I in so much pain?"

"You were shot with arrows, six of them, and you and banged your head on a marble floor."

He gingerly raised his right arm to his head, feeling the bandages.

"It was a nasty knock to the head. One of the arrows gave you minor flesh wounds, but five caused serious injuries. You are lucky to be alive.

"Christ, it hurts. Did they tip the arrows with something nasty?"

"No, just ordinary hunting arrows, but they're designed to penetrate very deep and do a great deal of tissue damage. Here take a look."

May held up an arrow. It was fashioned from hardwood and nearly five feet long, without fletching. The black fire-hardened tip was about a foot long, with barbs that decreased in size toward the arrow's tip.

"Who did it? Did they catch them?" Doyle asked.

"A group of Southern Highlanders; they crept into the high commission's garden. The bloody guards didn't spot them, though you could smell them from ten feet away."

"Yes, one of the last things I remember was the stink of unwashed bodies when I stepped out for a moment. I suppose they've been interrogated?"

"Yes, after this debacle, Alex pulled rank on the high commissioner, the governor general, and the whole staff. The local police are effective, thank God. Thankfully, the high commission guards managed to catch two of them as they ran away. They gave up their four mates when I threatened to turn them into eunuchs."

"Remind me not to make you angry."

"The police riot squad was sent into the Paga Hill squatter settlement and went straight to where the Southern Highlanders live. The arrest was easy; the four idiots were drunk from the money they received to attack you. I've questioned all six of them to find out who put them up to this. You made things a little easier for them by stepping outside. They were planning to ambush you, when you came out of the function. They had a photograph of you from the airport after arriving. It turns out they were talent spotted when they first arrived in the city about two weeks ago. Did you study New Guinea for your student days?" May asked.

"Yes, it's a while back though. I know there's a huge difference between coastal populations and people living in the interior. Hell, highlanders weren't even contacted until the 1930s, when the Leahy brothers went in there."

"It's always been a rite of passage for young highland men to make a trek to the coast. That is what made the Leahy brothers curious and why they mounted their expedition into the interior. These days, most of the young highlanders come to Moresby. They can usually find *wantoks*—you're familiar with the term?"

"Yes, people of the same language group or clan."

"It's bit more complicated than that, but wantok also implies a great deal of obligation. The six men that shot you came from a single village in the Southern Highlands region. I've been up there to help release some silly missionaries that nearly ended up in an oven pit."

"What did you do?"

"Crept into the village at night, slit a throat or two, and brought the missionaries out. Sir Anthony wasn't too happy to have the ISS involved, but some of the missionaries were French he didn't want and an excuse for the French to get upset."

"So presumably our smelly six were able to find shelter with other Southern Highlanders?"

"Yes, the wantok system broadens the further you get away

from your origins. So clans that might be at war in their home band together in faraway Moresby. They were ordered to shoot you as you left the reception, but you made it easier for them by walking out onto the patio."

"Who paid them to come and turn me into a pin cushion?"

Chapter 19

"Sampela kongkong man,"[3] said May.

"Eh?"

"A Chinese man," said a voice from the door as Alex entered.

"Good day to you, à colleen," said Doyle. "Have you come to give me a blanket bath?"

Alex was dressed in a tropical white blouse and skirt like May, but she had on some makeup and earrings. Doyle noticed she wore her gold chain again but had replaced this with a gold-ringed ivory cameo. Her face and arms were colored slightly from the sun. There were dark circles and pallor beneath the tan. Her clothes looked a little loose on her, which was not unusual; the body shed unnecessary fat when the temperatures rarely dipped below eighty degrees.

There is a palpable sense of relief in her smile, thought Doyle. *Not surprising after what she has been through in ... God! How many days, weeks even?*

"How long have I been here?" said Doyle. "Where is here?"

Alex said, "The high commission—there's resident doctor and nurse attached to the staff. It's pretty standard for hardship posts like New Guinea. She has a surgery and recuperation room, which is where you are. You've been in a delirium for ten days in all."

"Christ, what a bloody mess, I suppose Sir Anthony wants me

---

[3] A Chinese man.

98

back in England after this fiasco.—so much for Doyle, the knight in shining armor, pulling the empire out of a pickle."

"Well, you can't travel back to England in the shape you're in. Apart from the wounds and biff on the head, you had septicemic poisoning from those arrows; that's what really knocked you out," said Alex.

Doyle looked at the drips feeding into his left and right arms. The pain was still manageable but trying to do the simplest task would be excruciating, and he realized that the arrow wounds had done serious damage to his body. He wondered if his left arm and left leg would be permanently impaired; even the function in the right arm would be dependent on his torso muscles. His head was throbbing from the effort of talking, and he realized that he couldn't lift his head. The effort sent shooting pains through his chest and started a headache.

He took a breath and said, "What about the bombs? Anymore contact from Raptor, or whatever he calls himself?"

"Yes," said May. "I was going to tell you before Alex arrived. He's sent a postcard to the king that the ransom should be paid within 60 days of the date in the postmark, or he will level a city somewhere in the empire."

"Oh, Jesus wept! He might have a bomb on a ship sailing somewhere," said Doyle.

"Possibly," said Alex. "It might be a bluff, but I've heard from Sir Anthony that the bonds are being prepared, but how they're supposed to be delivered is still a mystery."

May said, "Royal Navy and Dominion Navies have been given an order to detain and search any ship they deem to be suspicious. They will use Geiger counters to check for radiation. The bombs are shielded, but they emit some radiation that can be picked up from several yards away."

"It'll be like searching for a needle in a haystack," said Doyle.

"Yes," said May, "There'll be no warning, and one day a major imperial city will vanish in a fireball."

"What was the postmark date?" asked Doyle.

"Two days ago, so we've got about two months," said Alex.

"Any luck with identifying the Chinese man who paid the six assassins?" asked Doyle.

"There's hundreds of Chinese in Moresby," said May. "They pretty much run the city economy, and most other towns in British New Guinea—probably the same across the border in Dutch New Guinea. All we could extract from the stinky six was '*wanpela kongkong*.' Even then, they were approached by an intermediary from Paga Hill. They only met the Chinese man in his car when he gave them an envelope of money and a photograph of you.

"One of them added that the kongkong man said not to go and spend it until the job was done; otherwise he would know. He made them look inside the paper bag with the money, and there was a puri puri charm, so they took it seriously. I examined the photo, and it looks like it was taken when you and Alex were fresh off the plane, probably one of the ground crew making a bit of extra cash. I'll follow up on this later."

Doyle searched his memory for puri puri and the whole belief system of black magic in the Pacific Islands. Every time they had made progress, Raptor anticipated the next step and got it right. Doyle supposed they were lucky that a bomb had not been placed aboard the converted bomber bringing them to Port Moresby.

"Mr. Doyle, Mick, are you all right? You wandered off for a minute," said Alex.

May raised an eyebrow at the concern expressed by Alex, and

though she did not smile, a look of understanding played across her face.

"I think I need to take myself off the table for a while. I'm worse than useless now for the Anvil operation."

"Sir Anthony agrees," said Alex. "That's why May has come up with a solution."

"I'm going to send you to my Auntie Nellie," said May.

Chapter 20

A white-coated doctor entered the room. Doyle thought she looked too young to be a doctor, with long blonde hair, blue eyes, and a slim figure. She was not very tall, maybe a few inches over five feet, but she had the brisk no-nonsense attitude of most of the doctors Doyle knew.

"How's the human pin cushion today? I'm Dr. Delaney. I suppose I should thank you for the chance to practice real medicine instead of popping blisters and dressing tropical ulcers. Do you feel like listening to a roundup of your injuries?"

"Please let me know the worst, Doc," said Doyle.

"If we hadn't been at the high commission and able to get you into and operating theater, you'd be dead. You were shot with six arrows at very close range. One arrow took some of the skin of your right forearm; it carved quite a divot, but it's really just a flesh wound."

Doyle raised his right arm and could see the bandage, above which was a catheter into his vein.

"The other five arrows did the real damage. One shredded the biceps on your left arm, which is why it's hard to move it."

Doyle tried to move his arm but it hurt too much. He looked at the heavy bandaging, and at another catheter into the vein of his left arm. Looking over the side of the bed, he saw a bag filling with urine, so he knew where another catheter was inserted.

"I did some fine work. I'm a good surgeon when I need to be.

I repaired your arm so the muscles will heal, but the left arm will be stiff and will need a lot of exercise to loosen it up. One arrow went through your chest and back. It missed the heart and your spine by millimeters. Another got you in the abdomen and missed your kidneys but pierced your small intestine. It also ripped up your stomach and back muscles. I've stitched you up inside with dissolving sutures. We have to keep you off solids for a month or two. In any case, you'd better eat only mashed food for now."

"And the other two arrows?" asked Doyle

"One went through the right-hand side, through your lateral muscle, ripped that up, but no damage to internal organs. The fifth arrow hit your left leg, another through and through, tearing up muscle. Can you move your left leg?"

Doyle tried but could not make it move.

"Can you wiggle your toes on your left leg?"

Doyle made an effort, and there was a slight movement below the sheet.

"Don't try and lift your left arm, but wiggle your fingers."

Doyle concentrated, and the fingers moved sluggishly.

May and Alex looked on in silence.

"What's your prognosis, Doctor?" said Alex

"Apart from the muscle damage, the nerves have also suffered trauma. If Mr. Doyle is willing to work hard enough, he can come back from this, but it will be a matter of time and constant care."

"I can work hard," said Doyle.

"Good, you'll need to. You're also debilitated from the anesthetic, and though the pain is bad, it's being kept under control by morphine. Normally, I'd be a wary of this constant dosing you up, but the drug's doing its job. I understand from your companions that you are fond of opium, so I am assuming you have a high tolerance to opiates and are either not addicted or a higher-functioning addict."

Doyle grimaced at this assessment; the addict part was probably true.

"So many deep injuries, even treated quickly, were bound to cause infection and septicemia. You had a very bad fever; you were delirious for ten days. We thought we were going to lose you; the antibiotics were only just holding off complete organ failure. I gambled that you had some form of peritonitis, that we had not properly sealed the small intestine," the doctor said.

"I was right, I had May and Alex in the theater along with my nurse. We found the leak and swabbed you out with Eusol, glorified bleach. I added sulfonamide drugs to the cocktail we're giving you. The cumulative effects of all this have rendered you as weak as a kitten."

Doyle assimilated this information. Doctor Delaney was right: he was as weak as a kitten. The injuries were bad and shredded him internally, but the dreadful fever had stripped him of all of his stamina and strength. The bedroom was quiet as Doyle looked at the ceiling, trying to frame all his thoughts coherently.

"Who else knows I'm here?" he said.

May said, "Only the doctor, her nurse, Alex and I, and the high commissioner. We're concocting a series of press and radio releases about your death and the repatriation of your corpse to England."

"Don't worry, Mr. Doyle; we've been sworn to secrecy on pain of death," said Doctor Delaney.

"Where are you from, Doc?" asked Doyle.

"New Zealand, but I trained in England and did some locum work in Jamaica."

"I was trying to figure out your accent. So, nothing else to do; just lie here and be prodded."

"I've a sketchy idea of what's been planned to help you recover. If I were you, I'd enjoy the relaxation here while you can," said the doctor.

Chapter 21

It was still light, two weeks later, when Doyle heard the *Malalangi* engine power down. The vibrations that shook his bunk also dropped, which was a relief, since the pain diminished with them. May came off deck and into his cabin.

"We're here at Emananus, my Auntie Nellie's island. She calls it Mananusa, but the Admiralty mapmakers make their own decisions. How are you feeling? Do you need more morphine?"

"Rough as guts, and better not, if I'm supposed to get better under Auntie Nellie's care," said Doyle.

"Just call her Nellie. She's not your auntie, and she's about your age, I think."

"You don't know?"

"We're beyond the bureaucracy out here. I was born in Kavieng, so I have a birth certificate, but many babies are delivered at home on the island. Remember, she's the younger daughter of a chief and lulawai, a native representative of the regional government. He reports to the kiap or patrol officer who reports to the provincial administrator, Frank Gardiner. She's also a coastwatcher, one of the networks set up by the government to keep an eye out for any humbug from passing vessels."

"What is she, an Amazon?"

May laughed and then broke off into an unintelligible stream of language as someone tapped her shoulder. She went out of the cabin, where there was a great deal of commotion. Doyle guessed that May's auntie and other relatives had come out to the vessel.

The noisy hubbub died down, and May came into the cabin, accompanied by a thin woman who looked very similar to May but older and only just over five feet tall. She was wearing jeans cut off at the knee and a sleeveless top, beneath which she wore a black bra. Doyle could see a strap had slipped slightly down her shoulder. Her arms were slender, with the muscles well defined, and she stood as straight backed as a guardsman. She gave Doyle a huge glowing smile that lit up the cabin.

"Auntie Nellie, em ia dispela Mistah Doyle. Iu must lukautim em gut, mekim strong."[4]

"Hello, nem bilong mi Nellie masta,"[5] said Nellie.

Doyle said, "Just call me Doyle, Nellie."

"Ai! Wanem ia, olgeta manmeri tinktink you mi tupela marit."[6]

Both May and Nellie collapsed into fits of giggles, and he could hear more laughing beyond the door.

Micah put his head around the door and spoke in Mussau, the language of the eponymous archipelago. Three crewmen maneuvered a stretcher into the room. They lifted Doyle off the bed and onto the canvas stretcher. Even though they handled Doyle with care, his torso lit up with pain and his head lolled with the weakness of infirmity.

He was brought on deck and the subject of intense scrutiny by a small crowd that had rowed out to the vessel. The sun slid down to

---

[4] "Auntie Nellie, this is Mr. Doyle. You must take care of him and make him strong."

[5] "Hello, my name is Nellie."

[6] "What! Everyone will think we're a married couple."

the horizon but still gave off intense heat. Doyle felt his skin prickle in the sun's rays.

"Uncle Micah has brought his boat in as far as he dare to the island. There's coral reefs all around Mananusa and Sule point, where Auntie lives, but it's not far. We're going to transfer you to a dugout canoe with some planks over the hull. This is Lumas; she's small and light and will paddle you in."

A girl of about ten peeped out from behind May. She had a shock of black curly hair and huge eyes, which contemplated Doyle solemnly. Before Doyle could respond, Micah barked out commands to his crew, and Doyle's stretcher was lifted over the aft deck rail. Below him was a small flotilla of dugout canoes. If he was dropped in the water, he hoped someone would pull him out. Two men in the canoes stood and gripped the stretcher overhead and then with great skill and balance, they lowered Doyle onto a canoe to their left, which he saw was covered with pieces of driftwood. He felt the uneven wooden surface dig into him, and he gasped with the pain.

What happened next was organized chaos. Goodbyes were said; people scrambled back onto the canoes. Lumas took command of her canoe, and without a sound or backward glance, she paddled into the shore, while darkness descended. On shore, Doyle was manhandled again and the stretcher taken up the beach to a small hut in which there was the glow of a kerosene lantern. There was a camp stretcher cot on one side of the hut, made up with a pillow and sheets. Above the bed was a mosquito net. The two men deposited him on to the camp stretcher.

As he lay still, wondering at the wisdom of this decision, May and Nellie came into the hut.

"I'll stay tonight with Nellie. Our family has another house behind this one, and another in the village where the rest of the family live.

In the morning, I'll come and say goodbye. Lumas will sleep on the floor with you tonight. Just go to sleep. We'll leave the light on; it shouldn't keep you awake," said May.

Doyle contemplated the future; sleep seemed the best option at this point. The pain was subsiding. Lumas brought a tin cup of water for him, while May gave Nellie a box of medications and bandages. May doled out two aspirins for Doyle to drink with the water. He drank, tasting the sweet spring water and wishing it was a strong whiskey and soda. He managed to raise his head and saw his suitcase, briefcase, and grip in the hut.

May followed his gaze and said, "Don't abuse my aunt's hospitality by dipping into your pharmaceutical supplies. Better if you just confine yourself to antimalarial tablets and aspirin."

"Can I get my guns out when I'm strong enough?" Doyle asked.

"Yes, you will need to practice anyway. Auntie Nellie will help you with all of that. Here, go to sleep. You can change into clean clothes tomorrow."

May and Nellie pulled the mosquito net over Doyle, while Lumas unrolled a straw tatami-style mat, cradled her head on her hand, and seemed to go straight to sleep.

"Good night, Mr. Doyle," said May.

"Eloalai,"[7] said Nellie.

---

[7] "Goodnight." (Mussau)

Chapter 22

Doyle slept fitfully, but when he finally awoke around dawn, he felt the cool air blowing off the ocean and heard noises of the world waking up. Lumas was brushing out the hut with a broom made out of the spines of coconut leaves. She heard Doyle stir and looked at him with a smile and then ran out of the hut. Doyle could see more of the hut in the advancing daylight, even though his vision was impaired by the mosquito net.

The hut had a wooden framework over which were attached matted coconut palm panels. The room was a thatch of dried coconut leaves. There was a small table and a chair and a cabinet in the corner, on which was standing a set of shelves. The floor was made of wooden planks. Each upright post of the hut was sunk into the ground.

"Good morning, Mr. Doyle," said May, who knocked and walked in.

"Auntie Nellie will be here in a minute or two with a basin so you can wash, or rather we can help you wash. Here, let me roll back the mossie net."

Doyle was dressed in a white T-shirt and boxer shorts that he had worn on the five-day voyage from Port Moresby, and he realized how ripe he smelled. May lifted Doyle's suitcase onto the table, opening it with a key she had taken from her pocket. She was wearing a pair of jeans and a blue short-sleeved blouse.

"Alex showed me the trick to opening this box of tricks," said May.

"How is Alex? She's been through a lot in a short time."

"I know. We had a proper girls talk while you were fighting off the fever."

"She's been thrown in at the deep end. I don't know what else to say. I've not been a good luck charm for her."

"I think being in Moresby and being your ISS in-country contact is probably the best thing for her. She is realizing that her relationship might well have hit the reef anyway. You're married to the ISS for better or worse."

"Is that how you feel, May?"

"None of your business, cheeky bugger. Come on; you've got to get to your feet, so we can take you down to the sea."

"What about the basin of water?"

"That's to wipe off the saltwater."

Nellie arrived with the basin of water, which she put on the table.

"Aye, kam on, lazy boy, Mr. Dolly," said Nellie as she swished him with the coconut broom.

Doyle tried to get to his feet but felt the weakness in his legs. May came alongside and put his arm around her neck. Nellie supported his other side, and the two of them maneuvered Doyle through the door and down the sloping beach, which was shaded by trees, almost to the waterline. Several dogs followed them and sniffed about Doyle. Nellie was still carrying the broom and swished at the dogs and shouted something in Mussau. The dogs yelped and ran off to sulk.

The two women carried Doyle out into the water until it was about knee high and then let him down. He sat on the sand as the water lapped over him. Lumas came behind with a large bar of soap.

"This is saltwater soap, Mr. Doyle. It doesn't make much of a lather, but it will get you clean. Try to keep it out of your eyes; its stings a lot worse than ordinary soap," said May.

Before he could take the bar, Nellie grabbed it and began vigorously soaping Doyle, commanding him to close his eyes as she washed his hair. She tugged off Doyle's T-shirt and said, "Givim trousers."[8]

"What?" said Doyle.

"Better do as she says, Mr. Doyle. Slip off your undies. Lumas has a towel when you want to get out."

Doyle slipped out of his underwear, which was taken along with his T-shirt by Nellie. She flung the sodden underwear and then began soaping Doyle again, causing him to jump as she ran the bar through his crotch and down his leg. There was a burst of giggles from Lumas and a chatter in Mussau between May and Nellie.

"Nellie said you are just a big baby, Mr. Dolly."

Doyle laughed and relaxed. "Dolly"—he had been called worse. Not everyone could get their tongues around Doyle. The Gaelic spelling of his name was Dubhghaill, which would fox everyone.

He looked out to sea. He saw Micah's coastal steamer anchored beyond the reefs. In the background was a large, mountainous island fronted by several small islets. Doyle saw he was on a point, with land receding to the left and right. To the left the coast emerged beyond the shadow of the point, and he could see there were villages. He could see people were walking down to the shallows and squatting there. Now he understood why schools of fish were swimming around him without any apparent fear.

May had followed his gaze and laughed. She said, "It might be basic here, but it's very hygienic."

---

[8] "Give me your underwear."

"I can think of places in Asia where walking on the beach is like walking in a minefield. Can you help me to my feet? Enough sitting around. I need to get fit, starting now."

"And I've got to get back to Moresby. Micah's going to take me to the provincial capital, Kavieng. There's a daily flight that goes from there to Lae and on to Moresby," May said.

Doyle realized he was naked and took the towel proffered by Lumas, who giggled. Doyle wrapped the towel around him and tried to stand on his own. He felt his legs tremble, but he concentrated on putting one leg in front of the other and found he could actually walk unaided. Nellie shouted out in Mussau, and a boy emerged with a walking stick from the house behind Doyle's hut. A stick would be useless on the sand but would be good to have otherwise, especially if he fell.

The boy put the stick against the hut lintel and watched as Doyle strode one step at a time from the sea and up the sand. The firm wet sand was not too much of a problem, but the powdery white sand above the tideline caused Doyle to stop and take a breather. He stepped forward again, slowly, letting his feet sink in the powdery sand before taking another step. The wounds in his torso were stiff and sore, but the pain was becoming more bearable.

He knew he must be careful of the gut injury, which had pierced his small intestine. He must not reopen the internal wound, which would be fatal this far from a hospital. Sweat was now pouring off him as the seawater dried on his skin. Nellie came alongside and made him lean on her.

"Are you not going to help?" Doyle asked May.

"You'll have to make do with Nellie and her family from now on."

Doyle eased himself up to the hut door and then into the hut itself. Nellie helped him sit on the single chair and handed him a cloth to wipe himself down and clean off the salt. The hut felt cool, but the sun was rising in the sky and the heat was beginning to build. He began the process of cleaning off the saltwater, which also cooled his skin. Mosquitos emerged from the dark recesses under the table and began to bite. Lumas swatted at them with the coconut broom, driving them away.

Chapter 23

May stayed another hour, while Doyle finished cleaning his skin with freshwater, with help from Nellie. He dressed with assistance in a pair of khaki shorts and plain white Indian Kurta tunic. May told him that she and Alex had planted a story on the radio and in the New Guinea newspapers about the attack on Doyle at the high commission.

A British official had said that Michael Doyle, newly arrived in country, was seriously injured in what was described as a burglary gone wrong. A postscript to the story a few days later said that Doyle had died of his wounds and his body would be shipped back to England for burial. There was even a photograph of the coffin being carried onto a cargo vessel in Moresby harbor.

May said, "The first story was front page news, but your repatriation only made a few column inches on the inside pages."

"God, I hope it works. We've been playing cat and mouse with these bastards from the beginning. It would be nice to have some breathing time. Do we have any way of monitoring what's happening on Lihir?"

"No one directly on the island. The island is pretty much self-contained. The mining operation has its own wharf and runway. The main town, Londolovit, has a New Guinea government representation and small police force. Visitors can come by ship or fly from Kavieng or Namatanai. That's the main town in the south of the island."

"What about the coastwatch network? There must be folks along the coast like Nellie?"

"There are, and we've asked for any information on unusual shipping along the east coast of New Ireland and in the east coast channel. We don't want to put too much on the airwaves, even though we use coded messages, Nellie can show you," May said.

May stood up from sitting on Doyle's bed.

"Time to go. Nellie will keep in touch with us; your code name for this mission is Deacon. If someone is reading our messages, Deacon should not arouse any suspicions. It's normal for a place like this to include mention of church visitors to the island, including pastors and deacons. I'll be back in a month, and by then we should be ready to complete our mission. Goodbye, Mr. Doyle."

From his chair Doyle watched as two dugout outrigger canoes pulled up the beach, one for May and one for her luggage. Several people gathered on the beach to see May leave. Lumas rowed one canoe and an older boy paddled the canoe laden with baggage and gifts for May. Nellie stood waving and shouting her farewells to her niece, all the way until the canoes reached the boat. As soon as May and her belongings were taken aboard, Doyle heard the anchor chain rattle and the diesel engine of the *Malalangi* rev up. Nellie watched the vessel pick its way through the reefs, into the open sea, and then southward to Kavieng.

Nellie strolled up the beach. Doyle could see the tracks of tears and was at a loss for what to say. Nellie looked at him, smiled through her tears, and said. "Malalo nau; tomorrow yumi walk."[9]

---

[9] "Rest now; tomorrow we walk."

Chapter 24

The month on Emananus was as tough a time as Doyle could remember. The day after May's departure, Nellie made Doyle follow her along the coastal path. This led first to the church and then the village on the north coast of the island.

Doyle found his feet as he walked behind Nellie, who strode ahead, straight-backed as any fashion model. Several children skipped along with them, including Lumas. The forest of coconuts, casuarinas, and talis trees ended abruptly and ahead of them on the left were extensive gardens of taro, sweet potato, and pumpkins. Doyle noticed that among them were capsicums, tomatoes, and chili peppers. There were banana trees, papaya, and occasionally avocadoes and mangos.

The heat was now intense, and Doyle cursed himself for not bringing a hat. Nellie saw Doyle feel his head and pulled a headscarf from her pocket; she told him to put it on his head, which he tried to do until Nellie said something to Lumas, who pulled Doyle's head down and tied it bandana style for him.

Keeping up was hard work. His left leg dragged because of the deep injury in the thigh and torso. He was soon out of breath and had to stop, leaning on his walking stick. Nellie watched him and waited until his breathing became more regular. The little party pressed on past the church and through the village. Doyle noticed that most of the men and women wore Western-style clothing, not sarongs and mission blouses.

H wanted to ask questions, but all he could think about was walking and not falling over. His shirt was soaked with sweat, and his skin felt slick and slippery. Rivulets of sweat dripped into his eyes, making them prickle. He took in huge gasps of air and croaked a plea to stop again. By this time, they were well into the village, and Doyle knew he was an object of curiosity, but his entire consciousness focused on not falling over. He could feel the relentless tattoo of his pulse in his head, and his breath sawed in and out. He wanted to throw up and felt himself gagging.

Nellie took his hand and led him under a tree to get out of the heat. She spoke to one of the boys, who ran off and returned with water. Doyle was so lacking in strength that his arms shook as he held it to his lips and drank great drafts, which was a mistake. He immediately threw up. Nellie slapped his buttocks, saying, "Drink easy, not like a greedy boy."

In his exhaustion, he heard Nellie was speaking English rather than pidgin. His heart began to slow, and he looked about him at the village. He would have attracted huge crowds by now in the New Guinea Highlands. Villagers here seemed to take him in their stride after initial interest. White men were no rarity in the coastal areas of New Guinea, where there were many settlements and plantations, even in remote islands. The coastal region was also much easier for government officers to patrol, whereas the rugged highlands needed patrols equipped like major expeditions to reach mountain valleys.

Nellie looked at Doyle with an air of satisfaction as he blinked the sweat out of his eyes. "Come, one last short walk. Up there." She pointed to a track off the main village path and to a low wooded peak, perhaps one hundred feet above the surrounding coast.

"Are you serious?" said Doyle.

"Yes, it's not far, and we can rest for an hour at the top. The children will bring us some food when we are up there. We'll have a picnic."

"I don't suppose that I can talk you out of this."

"No."

"I thought you were a devout Christian. Take pity on a poor wretch like me," Doyle said.

"I am. I'm helping you to cleanse your body. May told me you drink, take drugs, and lie with unclean women."

"Bloody hell."

"Please don't curse."

"OK, sorry."

Nellie rattled off a bunch of instructions to the assembled children, who all ran off through the village.

"Where are they going?" asked Doyle.

"To my sister Lucy's house and to my best friend Dunna—they'll make some food and send it with the children up the hill. Come on; let's go."

Doyle shuffled behind Nellie. The rest had returned some strength, but he still felt his legs, particularly his thigh muscles, turning to jelly. He inched along in the full glare of the sun. The sunshine was painful, as bad as anything he had encountered in India or elsewhere in the tropics. Things began to blur: gasping, pain, nausea, the pressure in his head and chest, his left leg creating stabs of pain in his lower torso. Finally, the path left the open gardens and the forest began again, casting a welcome shadow.

"Rest, please, there," he pointed to the entrance of the forest, where he could see a fallen log. Nellie stopped and then took his hand and walked on, squeezing his hand in encouragement. The shady entrance looked farther away as Doyle's breathing trembled in a mix of involuntary gasps as his diaphragm struggled to get enough oxygen into his bloodstream. Doyle thought about just stopping and falling down, but a sense of grit and pride kept him going. He felt rather than saw the shade as they passed through the gardens.

"Wait," said Nellie. She put her foot on the log, which was rotten for about half its length. She rocked it with her foot. A centipede about a foot long emerged and ran over Doyle's sandal-clad foot. He felt the centipede's feet running over his skin; he was glad he was so exhausted that he did not react. A bite from a centipede that size would have been debilitating or even deathly. On the other side of the log, something large moved and slithered into the undergrowth.

"Moran," said Nellie, "Large snake, not poisonous, but they have a bad bite and can kill you by choking you."

Doyle realized Nellie was talking about a python. Some of the largest in the world were found in these islands.

Doyle looked at Nellie, and she nodded for him to sit. He didn't want to waste any air on talking too much. He noticed that Nellie's skin was beaded in sweat, but she was breathing normally. He looked back down the path through the gardens. A few villagers were walking through the gardens but not doing any serious work; this would be done in the early morning or afternoon, when the sun was less savage.

He watched the sweat drops fall onto the powdery sand of the path, razing little puffs of dust as it hit the ground. Near the log were little, perfect round craters. One of his sweat beads fell into it, followed by a fountain of sand grains showered at the crater edge. *Ant lions,* thought Doyle, *beetle larvae feeding on ants.* He looked at his clothes, which were dark with sweat. He realized he had to drink more fluid soon; otherwise, he would suffer from dehydration and salt loss.

"Kam, yumi go, last lap," said Nellie with a laugh.

"Wait, before we go, please tell how May got her lovely name."

Nellie said, "Antap, me tokim stori antap."[10]

Doyle sighed; his gambit for more rest was too transparent.

The slope was steep, but being out of the sun was a huge relief. Doyle put his head down and trudged up the forest patch, which he could see was not used that often, as vines and large blades of grass had to be brushed aside in places. Doyle retreated into himself, looking down at his feet and willing them to move one after the other. He searched his mind to think when he had been in this much pain or as weak as he was now.

The sunlight flashed in his eyes, and he felt the burn of sun again. They were in a little clearing on the hilltop. Behind him, he heard a slap of little feet on the path and the laughter and chatter of children. They carried water, and Lumas and another girl had large bowls on their heads, supported by their hands.

Nellie surveyed the scene with satisfaction as Doyle let himself down onto a bed of soft grass in the shade of a large lime tree on the edge of the clearing. He would take in his surroundings when he stopped gasping like a fish out of water.

Nellie gave a series of instructions to the children, who set out the food and water.

"Come on, big baby. Time for lunch."

"OK, thanks. Now, what's the story about May?"

"May's original name is Inani." Nellie paused to think of the English words. "Her mum was my sister Lucy, who died. Inani was adopted by Lucy's husband's family, but she didn't like them, so she spent a lot of time at our house. She was reading about the history of the Seventh Day Adventist Church, which included the Pilgrims

---

[10] "On top, I'll tell you the story on top."

from the *Mayflower* landing at Plymouth Rock. Inani decided she wanted to be called Mayflower Pilgrim. When the kiap came on patrol, my father told him, and he issued an affidavit. She had no birth certificate, but the affidavit was just as good."

"Thank you, it's a lovely story."

"Enap nau—tok-tok Inglish makim het bilong mi pain. Kai kai, na we go bak haus. Say grace."[11]

---

[11] "Enough—talking English is giving me a headache. Eat, and we'll go back to the house. Say grace."

Chapter 25

Doyle hung suspended in the void. The sunlight streamed through the water and refracted, lighting the depths in shades of color from blue to indigo. The south shore opened up into a bay with two jungle-covered promontories. There were extensive shallows in the bay, but in its center was a large, deep blue lagoon. The mouth of the bay was shallow with reef flats that were a continuation of the fringing reef around the entire island.

Nellie had given Doyle goggles carved from turtle shell, fitted with glass. They were a miniature work of art, but Doyle knew better than to make a fuss about the goggles. To Nellie, they were just functional items. She told him to go swimming every afternoon. At first he had swum from the Sule Point beach, out across the reef, and into deeper water, gaining confidence day by day. He had swum out along a reef wall, as lush and varied with coral as the south shore lagoon. It was a good swim. The reef turned back on itself, leaving about one thousand yards of open water to navigate back to Sule Point.

On his swims, he saw many sharks, usually the smaller black-tips and white-tips. The white-tips would cruise along with him as he passed over their territory. The black-tips would come dashing in from out of the blue haze and then turn away at the last second. Even though he had become familiar with this behavior, it still caused his pulse to race.

Doyle had seen large hammerhead sharks cruising along the bottom, some of which came up to look at him. The eye on the hammer shark stared at him, the protective white membrane flicking across the eye surface. If eyes were the window to the soul, thought Doyle, there was no kinship in that dark pupil like there would be in a monkey or dog.

On one swim, several juvenile turtles swam up alongside Doyle. This was no act of companionship. He backed up onto the reef shallows, the turtles swimming with him. In about three feet of water, he found a sandy place where he could put down his feet without risk from the razor sharp corals. A tiger shark swam by, broaching the surface with its dorsal fin. The turtles swam over the reef crest to deep water on the other side. The shark was at least fifteen feet in length. He turned his head to see the last of his turtle companions swimming away. The shark was unlikely to risk injury or being stuck on the reef crest, but its interest had fixed on Doyle.

The reef crested at about a foot, just enough clearance from him to get over without coral slicing his flesh. Doyle swam backward, sculling the water with his hands, expecting any moment to see a mouthful of teeth twisting in toward him. The reef crest bumped his back, and he felt something scratch his skin. He was able to push against the reef with his hands on the staghorn corals.

He was in water too shallow for the shark to follow. Doyle was still a long way from shore. He swam back along the outer wall of the reef in rougher water. This was preferable than being shark bait.

Doyle swam as close as possible to the reef, but in places, the coral dipped away as deep as ten feet. Apart from the usual reef sharks, Doyle could see no large sharks or threatening shadows in the blue water. He mentally checked himself to be calm and kept up a steady freestyle crawl back to Sule Point.

When he swam toward the beach, he saw two small figures he recognized: Lumas and a boy called Meslee. They were watching him as he swam, the beach not seeming to get any nearer. He continued swimming. Lumas and Meslee began jumping up and down on the sand; Meslee threw a stone into the water that splashed near Doyle. Doyle slowed for a second, as Meslee and Lumas both threw stones into the water. Looking around Doyle saw nothing, but then a large deltoid fin surfaced on the other side of the reef. Doyle felt his heart pound, and he looked at the shore—not so far now. The dark blue water was changing to lighter blue as he crossed the shelving reef. The big shark could easily cross over the reef at deep spots on the reef wall, but Doyle had no option but to press on.

As he swam, he saw the seafloor sloping up no to meet him. He could see Lumas and Meslee still jumping up and down and throwing stones. He was in about six feet of water when something hit his legs. Time stopped; he was struck again, this time on his torso.

Doyle turned to see the grinning face of a dog. Behind the lead dog were three more dogs swimming in a line. Doyle had almost soiled himself but realized that the dogs were protecting him. The four dogs surrounded him and followed him all the way to shallows and up on the sand. They licked his face as he lay panting on the sand.

Lumas and Meslee hunkered down on the sand next to Doyle as he patted the dogs. "Mipela lukim dripela sak, so me tokim dogs i go helpim yu. Mipela trowim stone long sak, mekim go away,"[12] said Lumas.

Doyle sat up, looking out over the placid lagoon where only minutes before he had contemplated his death in the jaws of the tiger shark.

---

[12] "We saw the huge shark, so I told the dogs to go and help you. We threw stones to make the shark go away."

"Tenk yu tru, tupelo,"[13] said Doyle.

The dogs trotted along the beach and then turned into the bush. All the dogs were a gingery yellow color, with sharp foxlike features and big pointy ears. Unlike pet dogs elsewhere, New Guinea village dogs were not arrested into an endless puppyhood. They matured and formed packs with a defined pecking order. They were fiercely territorial. Doyle had learned this running around the island, chased by dogs baying for his blood. The trick was not to run on but to stop, crouch down, hiss, and pick up rocks. The pack would back off, snarling.

In due course all the village dogs were familiarized with him, and some would jog along for a run. Since he had arrived, he knew several dogs lived around Sule Point. Nellie fed them with rice and fish. Lumas and Meslee had told the dogs to go and look after Doyle when the tiger shark was following him. The dogs instantly sensed the danger and swam out to surround Doyle and escort him to shore.

Doyle moved back into the water and continued to float in the southern shore lagoon. Small garfish were swimming around him as though he was a piece of flotsam. He was surprised as always when a large barracuda materialized out of the surrounding blue water, hanging motionless, staring at him. Its jaws were agape, showing the terrifying rows of needlelike teeth that would rip out a chunk of flesh as it hit its prey like a torpedo. Its dark eyes stared at him with watchful concentration. Doyle remembered the stories of divers attacked by big barracudas attracted to the shiny metal of watches or knives. There were other stories of people losing fingers trailed in the sea from boats. Even large Spanish mackerels and giant trevallies could be dangerous if they mistook a watch or a ring for a baitfish.

---

[13] "Thank you, both."

Chapter 26

Doyle walked back to Sule Point. He passed Nellie's hut, where she was operating her radio, using the telegraph key. The hut was lit by two kerosene lanterns, and Lumas was sitting next to her. Doyle looked up and saw the wire stretching from Nellie's hut to high up a coconut tree, where it was fixed via a spring to a loop of metal. As he walked on, he heard the faint bleep of Morse code and Nellie dictating the letters to Lumas. The signals chiefs at the ISS would faint with shock if they knew that Nellie used her niece to help her with her coastwatcher duties. Tough! They were not here and she was, looking after a wounded soldier and keeping this tiny, remote part of the empire safe.

The water used for washing came from a well dug back from the beach and to the side of the two huts, but Nellie had told Doyle not to drink it. It tasted fine to Doyle, but he was not going to ignore her advice. Drinking water came from a small pool below the cliffs of the south shore lagoon, scooped into containers and brought back to the village. It was laborious work, but the water was sweet and delicious. There was a complex traditional story associated with the discovery of the pool. Nellie had told him, but he found it difficult to follow in pidgin.

Nellie came to Doyle's hut after ten minutes, after he had washed off the saltwater and dressed. She had decoded the message.

"Here Mr. Doyle, a message from Moresby."

"Thanks, Nellie."

Doyle read the message: 'Reconnoiter Lihir soonest STOP Military strike planned STOP Need you on island to provide forward intelligence STOP Reinforcements and will arrive soonest STOP.

Doyle absorbed the terse message. He looked out to sea and noticed a light on the horizon.

Nellie followed his gaze and said, "Micah's boat, *Malalangi*."

It took over an hour for the *Malalangi* to come close to Emananus, and it was dark when it was close to the reef pass.

Nellie had given Doyle chicken, taro, and vegetables in a savory broth. He sat at the table while Nellie and Lumas sat on the floor, with their legs stretched out in front of them, their plates balanced on their laps. Doyle had felt awkward at first with this dining arrangement but had given up trying to get Nellie to sit in the chair. Even when he dined at her hut, he ended up being the only one seated, even though there were two chairs.

When the *Malalangi* arrived at the reef pass, the crew used a spotlight on the vessel's roof to spy out the corals while Micah piloted the vessel through the channel. All Doyle could see were the lights of the vessel as it picked its way through the passage in the reef. *People love coral reefs,* thought Doyle. *Pretty rocks and pretty fish, until those pretty rocks rip the bottom out of your boat and the pretty fish nibble on your corpse.*

His thoughts were interrupted by the rattle and splash of the anchor chain. The vessel moored close to Sule Point. Doyle could make out its profile and see activity onboard. A dinghy was lowered over the side of the *Malalangi* and rowed into the shore. Nellie had gone back to her hut and returned with a lantern. The dinghy splashed through the gentle surf and hissed as the aluminum hull slid on the sand. Doyle could see four figures in the dinghy. Two were Micah's crewmembers, who jumped ashore and pulled the vessel higher up the beach.

The other two figures jumped out and walked up to the lantern light. Nellie raised the lantern high to illuminate the newcomers.

"Eloalai,[14] Auntie," said May.

"Hello, Mr. Doyle," said Alex McCall. "You're looking well."

---

[14] "Good evening." (Mussau)

Chapter 27

Micah's two crewmen offloaded luggage and several aluminum boxes used by government officers when on patrol. People were turning up from the village to see what Micah had brought them this time. Nellie ordered several children to take the luggage to her hut, and the patrol boxes were stacked inside Doyle's hut.

May was dressed in jeans and a T-shirt. Alex wore shorts, which came down to her knees, and a light cotton blouse with the sleeves rolled up her forearms. Nellie's dogs fussed around May, pleased to see her, and looked at Alex, who, knowing about dogs, let them sniff her hands. The Emananus villagers were staring at her.

"Don't worry, Alex," said May. "Auntie Nellie will shoo everybody away in a few minutes, now they've had a good look at you. We don't see many white women out here; white men like Mr. Doyle here are relatively common."

"Hey there, missus, who you calling common?" said Doyle in a broad Irish brogue.

"How are the wounds, Mr. Doyle?" said Alex.

"Good, Auntie Nellie won't let me be, except on the Seventh Day Adventist Sabbath—Saturday to you and me," said Doyle.

"Did you manage to keep your hands away from your opium?" asked May.

"Yes, nothing stronger than water has touched my lips, hand on heart. Mind, I could murder a cup of tea, but I gather even that is frowned on."

"It is, but Auntie Nellie likes a cuppa now and again, so we brought teabags with us."

"God, yes, I need a cup of tea to get moving on a morning," said Alex.

"Better not blaspheme, à colleen," said Doyle.

"Oh, Lord, oh sorry, sorry, Auntie Nellie," said Alex.

Nellie smacked Doyle on the arm and said, "No ken praitim youngpela missis."[15]

"Ai, sori, misses, bai mi go silip long kuruk. Ol binatang em i kam kaikai mi."[16]

"Very good, Mr. Doyle, sounds like you have an ear for language," said Alex.

"I know that phrase by heart because Auntie Nellie is always threatening me if I don't do as she says."

Alex looked with interest at the small woman who was now telling the villagers to go home. Nellie called two of them back for a moment and introduced her sister Lucy and best friend Dunna, who smiled at Alex and then wandered off to catch up with the others.

May said, "Alex, you are safe on the island, but ask one or two of Auntie Nellie's kids if you go off wandering. Never walk by yourself in the bush, in the reef shallows, or close to the kuruk, the mangroves.

"Why, snakes?" said Alex.

"Yes, thank God we don't have taipans here, but there are lots of venomous land and tree snakes, and they are very aggressive. Sea

---

[15] "Stop frightening the young white girl."

[16] "Sorry, misses, I'll go and sleep in the mangroves. All the bugs will come and bite me."

snakes nest on land and are the most venomous. They are generally not aggressive but will be if nesting or shedding their skin. Best thing to do is avoid snakes if you see them. There are some very large pythons, not venomous but have a dreadful bite. If you are alone, you might be attacked, crushed to death, and then eaten. Crocodiles or puk puk are the biggest danger; they are mostly confined to the mangroves but can be found in the lagoons. They have no fear of humans and will actively hunt you."

"Blood and sand—I was floating alone in the lagoon this afternoon, not far from the mangroves."

"I doubt you were entirely alone, Mr. Doyle. Remember, some of Auntie Nellie's kids are always keeping an eye on you. But in any case the crocs usually keep to the mangroves during the day and hunt at night."

Doyle now recalled that there were two boys skimming stones from the beach while he swam. Nellie's helpers were so much part of the background that he barely noticed them, unless they walked with him and talked to him.

"Any other nasties I should look out for?" said Alex.

"Plenty, I'm afraid; there are lots of venomous scorpions, centipedes, and spiders, plus some vicious red ants, wasps, and hornets. The corals look pretty, but don't wander barefoot on the reefs. Your feet will get cut and likely get very bad sores that will take forever to heal. Sorry to go on like this, but there are also poisonous plants that sting and leave horrible rashes, so be very careful if you squat to pee.

"Also, you don't want to get stung in the foot by a stone fish or lionfish, which can kill you or may lead to your foot having to be amputated. We generally don't worry too much about jellyfish, but there are some very dangerous stinging jellies; so if you see some, get out of the water. Same for sharks—we have big tigers but bull sharks are the worst," said May.

"You never gave me this speech when I arrived here, and I had a run-in with a tiger shark," said Doyle.

May laughed and said, "You're an old tropical hand. We just expected you knew about the dangerous wildlife. Come on; let's go to Auntie's hut. We need to brief Mr. Doyle on the Anvil operation. Don't look so worried, Alex. We won't let anything hurt you, and if it does, we'll have a remedy."

Nellie made tea while Lumas pulled out straw mats for seating, indicating that Doyle and Alex take the two chairs.

Alex was about to be demure, but Doyle said, "Take the seat, Alex. It's a traditional act of kindness."

In the end, May and Nellie sat on the bed while Lumas doled out tea from a pot on a tray on the floor. May opened a leather map case and unscrolled a detailed map of New Ireland, showing Tabar and the Lihir archipelagos.

May said, "We are not far off from the sixty-day deadline mentioned by Raptor in his last communication."

"Why doesn't Sir Anthony call in a battalion of special forces to take Lihir? All the evidence is pointing there. Even the attack on me in Moresby was likely their work. It also means they have more spies active than we ever imagined."

May said, "Even if there was no doubt about Lihir, charging in with commandos and other elite troops would be no guarantee of success. A bomb could be detonated on Lihir, which would eliminate the island, plus wipe out much of Tabar and the Boang Islands. The east coast of New Ireland would likely miss much of the blast but may be affected by the radiation flash and fallout."

Alex said, "Another problem is that the four other bombs could be detonated, if they have been transported to an imperial city— a radio call and suddenly Hong Kong or Singapore disappears, along with Calcutta and Kuala Lumpur."

"My, you two are cheerful Charlies," said Doyle. "So what's the plan? I assume we have a plan."

"Go to Lihir," said May.

"Presumably to do more than loll around on the beaches," said Doyle.

"Here, take a look at this," said Alex, opening her suitcase.

Nellie and Lumas sighed and giggled when they spied silk underwear.

"Well, you've certainly got the natives all stirred up," said Doyle.

Alex blushed and looked at May for support.

"You'll have to forgive my family, Alex. They're used only to old-fashioned cotton drawers, not silky knickers."

"Well, if we could steer the conversation away from my undergarments for a moment, this is a Geiger counter," said Alex like a starchy schoolteacher. "Let me have your watch, Mr. Doyle."

Doyle did not remove the watch but held his wrist close to the Geiger counter, which burst into sound with a buzz of clicks.

Alex said, "That's from the luminous pigment on the watch, which is harmless but enough to be picked up on the Geiger counter. We have several Geiger counters in the boxes stored in Mr. Doyle's hut. We need to land surreptitiously on Lihir and try to find traces of radioactivity. The bombs or at least one bomb, we think, will be there."

"Think?" said Doyle.

May said, "It's our working hypothesis that at least one bomb will be picked apart so it can be reverse engineered. The others could be used to level a city. The other working scenario is a second bomb might be used as an intermediary step to develop a hydrogen bomb. Nevertheless, that would still leave three active bombs."

"And how do we do all this searching? You and I, Alex, will standout like sore thumbs."

"Not if we pose as government officials making an inspection of native working conditions," Alex said.

"What about you May?" Doyle asked.

"I could come as a colleague, but I think it's better I sneak onto the island with my own little band. There are Mussaus working at the mine. I will contact them, and hopefully they'll help us."

"Us?" said Doyle.

"I'm going with Auntie Nellie and one of her nephews, my cousin Joe Asora. He was an engineer and sapper for three years in the Pacific Islands Regiment."

"Where's Joe now?" asked Doyle.

"Kavieng," said May. "We'll all go to Kavieng in a few days. Micah has to leave to make a patrol out to Emirau and Tench to resupply those islands. The provincial government had hired Uncle Rurusan and his boat, *Totonga*, coming up from Rabaul, which will be here in a day or so to take us to Kavieng."

Alex said, "You and I will take a provincial government charter flight to Lihir. The mine has their own airplanes, but they can't refuse a government plane on a visit. The province administrator, Frank Gardiner, will inform the goldmine that government inspectors are on their way. We can't just drop in unannounced; the aviation authorities would be unhappy. But we can make a visit on short notice."

Chapter 28

May and Alex stayed in Nellie's hut. Alex was embarrassed that Nellie abandoned her bed and slept on the floor with May. Doyle knew that Alex would be like a fish out of water, immersed head-first in a native culture. She would have gotten a small taste of this on the *Malalangi's* voyage from Port Moresby, probably the first time she was in the company of only native people, other than May. All the crew probably spoke some English but not enough to have a serious conversation.

Wait until she sees the sanitary arrangements, thought Doyle. *If she thought the* Malalangi *was primitive, at least it had a toilet.* He had vague memories of being assisted there by the crew while he was in a fog of morphine. He hoped she wasn't too discommoded about squatting in the bushes to urinate. Otherwise, it was into the sea each morning to get a good clear out and a rinse down with well water. He recalled Nellie and Lumas goggling at Alex's delicates and hoped she had packed some more robust tropical wear.

There was a knock on the door. Lumas wandered in carrying a sleeping mat.

"'Allo masta, bigpela meri tok tok bik nait na mi laik silip. Auntie said come na askim yu sapos i'orait me ken silip ia."[17]

---

[17] "Hello, mister, the grownup ladies are going to talk late into the night. Auntie said come and ask you if I can sleep here."

Doyle took a second to translate, his Pidgin was now functional, but he still needed to think about the words. "Yeah, i'orait."[18]

He pulled the table way from the window, so it was immediately to the left of the door. There was a space big enough for a ten-year-old like Lumas between the table and the boxes piled in the corner. The cabinet and shelves were moved to the right-hand side of the door.

Lumas wore a cotton shift for sleeping and had brought a rolled-up mat sarong and small pillow for her head. Doyle could get out of the bed in the night and would not step on the child. He lay back and thought about the mission. It seemed like a desperate throw of the dice to get ashore on a privately run island, not to mention it was a gold mine with an armed security force.

How had the bloody government let this happen? he thought, knowing the answer was, of course, the gold revenues. The islanders had been bought off, or more likely had been coerced or cowed into subservience. The government representation, such as it was, was a single official, either bought off or, just as likely, slumbering toward retirement.

Doyle could imagine the mine owners showing their private security personnel and suggesting that the government need not waste scarce resources on having patrol officers or police permanently stationed on the island. There was probably a well-rehearsed dog and pony show for any visiting officials. Doyle decided to quiz Frank Gardiner about this when they arrived in Kavieng. He'd have to be discreet about showing his face. He wished he had let his beard grow, but he loathed not shaving. He mused that he could adopt a stoop and limp—not that far from reality after being torn up by arrows.

When operation was over, he was going to have a good hot-water

---

[18] "Yes, it's fine."

shave with steamed towels, a long hot bath, and a large whiskey with a laudanum chaser. Moreover, when the operation was over, he was going to reassess his life. He knew that age was catching up with him. Nellie had helped put him back together, but when he was in his twenties, he could have shrugged off the terrible injuries received in Moresby, along with the septicemia.

There was another knock at the door. Alex stood there, looking lost.

"Sorry to disturb you, Mr. Doyle."

"Shhh." Doyle indicated the sleeping child with his head.

"Oh, should I go?"

"No, just keep your voice low. When Pacific Islanders sleep, you'd need Gabriel's trumpet to wake them up. She's just gone off, and so we should let her make her way to the land of Nod. Come on; we can sit on the beach. I'll bring a mat and lantern."

Doyle took an unlit lantern off the shelf and turned the burning lantern down low. He held a straw over the lantern glass, and then when lit, he applied it to the unlit lamp. A cool wind blew off the sea. Down the coast to the west, Doyle could see the lights of the various village settlements of Eruau, Emiok, Talewok, and Emaka. Across the water, lights were flickering on Eloaua Island and in between was the shadow of Nusagila Island, which belonged to Nellie's family. Behind Eloaua there was a faint glow of the mission and government stations at Boliu, which had twenty-four hour power. Eloaua had the only functional airstrip, so all passengers had to be ferried to and from the island, which provided some income to the islanders.

Doyle spread the straw mat on the ground and sat down with Alex.

"You seem very settled here," said Alex.

"I thought you'd be chatting away with Nellie and May."

"I was, but they began lapsing into pidgin, which I could follow a bit, but then they went into Mussau. They'd translate, but I could see it was getting a bit bothersome for May, and she and Nellie wanted to talk freely, probably about family matters."

"Yup, it's a big family. Everybody is related through a tangled network of extended families that is complicated by children being passed to be raised by other relatives."

"Really? Is that common?"

"Happens all the time. Nellie told me one day that her niece and cousin had both given birth within days of each other. The cousin had a girl and the niece a boy. Nellie's cousin had wished for a boy, and though not terribly disappointed—a child is God's bounty after all—was worried her childbearing years would soon be behind her. The niece gave the baby boy to the cousin, which delighted her despite having two children to care for."

"Who keeps track of relatives?"

"They all do. They know who everybody is and how they are related; though God help you if you ask, it takes hours to untangle the family trees. If you are introduced to someone, just go with whatever you are told. Do not try and figure out who is who. I do know from chatting with the kids that Auntie Nellie can't have kids; bel bilong em i nogut.[19] But she had a bunch of children she regards as sons and daughters. So, if Nellie says, 'This is my sonny boy,' don't ask who the dad is."

"Oh, she would be embarrassed."

"No, not at all, but you'd unleash the monster, and it would all have to be explained. If someone says that this kid's mum is Lois and the dad in Donal, don't inquire any further unless you want to

---

[19] "She is barren."

have your patience tested. This is a culture that still relies on oral traditions, even after the missions came in the 1930s."

"Any other conversational tips?"

"Don't get too startled if someone is introduced to you as Alpha-echo or Tin-fish. May told me in the New Guinea Highlands she'd met a Cardboard-box. Most everyone here though has Christian names or traditional Mussau names."

"I thought Port Moresby was exotic, with the sea villages at Koki and Hanuabada, but we could always retreat into the high commission and the GG's residence. Here it's so—"

"Its foreign, and it's not even remotely like England. You'd feel much more at home in Sydney or Auckland, but here there are no cultural reference points."

"You have a knack of summing things up."

"I'm a Paddy who has kissed the Blarney stone and had a bit of education. But I'm just a nomadic Mick with a sociopathic streak that the ISS and the empire have put to good use."

"Just when I think you're quite likeable, you show your feral side," Alex said.

"It's always there. Twenty-odd years of soldiering and being a mercenary is what I'm good at. I'm not a cuddly toy, despite my Irish charm and rugged good looks," Doyle said.

"Oh, now you're being insufferable—ow, something bit me."

Doyle held up the lantern. Mosquitos were buzzing around Alex's legs.

"Wait, I've got something that will help." Doyle crept back into the hut, not wanting to wake Lumas. He returned with a small glass bottle with a cork stopper.

"This looks antique," said Alex. "What is it?"

"Glass by the looks of it."

Alex punched Doyle's arm.

"Okay, its coconut oil with some other things added. Whatever they are, it is a great mosquito repellant and stops bites from itching. Just rub it on to your legs."

"Why aren't they biting you?"

"I didn't do the mossies the favor by shaving my legs, and you're a paleface woman, which they really like."

"Seriously?

"Yes, seen it before in India and other places in the tropics. Mosquitos really like to bite European women, especially redheads. No idea why—probably some scent you give off."

"You never talk much about India, but you were there for nearly twenty years or so."

"I told you about Burma and the Andamans," said Doyle.

"Yes, a couple of incidents, but you hardly ever refer to the place."

"No, I suppose not. It's a common expatriate habit; you open your mouth at a dinner party somewhere civilized and everyone looks at you, wants to ask questions. Usually you can fend these off with a crack about the heat or the rains. Sometimes you meet folks who have holidayed there or maybe been bug hunting and want to show off their Hindi or Urdu, neither of which I speak, other than basic stuff."

"It's a big place, though. I mean look at the size of the ISS South Asian section. Look at all the Indians in the ISS, come to that; it's run by an Indian."

"Yes, it is a big place, huge, the Jewel in the Crown. Sir Anthony is unusual, though, an Anglo-Indian, high-caste Brahmin, and son of a rajah. Have you met his wife, Lady Sonia?"

"There you go, deflecting. I have not met Lady Sonia, as it happens."

"She's a Grosvenor, the Duke of Westminster's family, school chum of Queen Charlotte, and she met Sir Anthony when she was in India on the high commission staff. Of course, she didn't need the money, but you know aristocratic young women no longer just want to just throw balls and give alms to the poor."

"About India," said Alex.

"God, you're as tenacious as a honey badger. We ate a lot of curries, as I recall."

"You mentioned the China–India border war when we were with the king at Sir Anthony's house," Alex said.

"Yes, no one really knows how big a war that really was. Both sides kept the media well away from the front lines. The Chinese caught us napping and deployed near a million troops over abroad from Arunachal Pradesh to Nepal, going through both Bhutan and Nepal. The Chinese occupied a great deal of territory. It looked as if, at best, we could turf them out of India, but they would retain Nepal and Bhutan."

"That didn't happen though," said Alex.

"No, there was a huge surge of national sentiment for the empire, and Indian men and women joined up by the tens of thousands. While we could not fling raw recruits into the battle, it freed up nearly all the full-time and reservist troops to fight. Our biggest advantage was the skill of our artillery and of the air force. People forget that the Indian air force is led by Indian officers and is comprised mostly of Indian pilots. On top of this, we had all the top Indian regiments itching to be let loose, plus the Gurkhas wanted nothing more than to be in a good scrap. I think the Chinese had miscalculated that the North Indian populations would welcome them, as being distinct from the South Asians."

"And you and Sir Anthony were in all of this?"

"Yes, but it's something hard to talk about: ripping apart men at close range with machine guns or skewering them on bayonets; being trapped on a hilltop with no water, ammunition spent, reduced to throwing rocks and seeing your best friends die. We won a great victory over the Chinse, but the dry prose in the history books gives no idea of the horrors of that campaign. Neither side gave quarter. The numbers of prisoners exchanged after we had beaten the Chinese back to their side of the border was tiny."

"Oh, sorry, I'm—"

Nellie appeared, grabbing Alex's arm and saying, "Kam nau; taim bilong silip. No ken sindaun yu tasol wantaim man olsem Masta Doyle. Yu ting u laik mekim guria? Shame. Go bak haus nau."[20]

Alex looked stunned, and Doyle said, "Auntie Nellie's concerned for your virtue. Better go. We don't want to start unnecessary gossip."

Doyle eased himself off the ground. He was healed, but his wounds stiffened and needed stretching to get them supple. He picked up the lamp, took it to the door of his hut, extinguished it, and adjusted the wick of the other lamp. He lay on his bed, not bothering with the mosquito net. He shut his eyes and saw plains of dust and dead men all around him before he fell asleep.

---

[20] "Come now; it's the time for sleep. You can't sit down unchaperoned with a man like Mr. Doyle. Are you thinking of having sex? Shame on you. Go back to the house right away."

Chapter 29

In the morning, everything was business. Nellie and Lumas cooked a breakfast of vegetable omelets. Doyle, Alex, and May went through the patrol boxes to make an inventory of their supplies. Doyle was pleased to see assault rifles, British made but based on a Russian design, which Doyle thought were the most rugged foolproof firearms ever developed. There was also a consignment of Sten submachine guns with silencers wrapped in canvas to protect the operator from the hot barrel. Other boxes contained automatic pistols, grenades, plastic explosives and detonators, and several bush knives. There was also a medical kit, with pressure bandages and morphine injectors.

Doyle wondered whether they should plan to shift everything from the supplies or just cherry pick what they needed. He and May would go to Lihir as government officials investigating labor issues. Doyle worried about being recognized but decided to shave his head; with a moustache, he should be able to carry it off. An army sabotage and subversion instructor advised that the combination of a bald head and moustache was one of the best disguises—no need to rely on prosthetics. He and Alex would insist on staying for several days to see the entire mining operation. At the same time, May, Nellie, and Nellie's nephew Joe, would sail ashore under cover of night.

It would take some time for May, Nellie, and Joe to offload their supplies, even if they only took a fraction of what they had in the patrol boxes. Doyle checked his own kit, which contained a lunar almanac. The moon was on the wane, so if they made a move within the next two weeks, they would be taking advantage of the darkest period of the lunar cycle.

Doyle took a machete and scouted out the ground behind Nellie's hut. This was a small coconut plantation overgrown with secondary rainforest. There was the well-worn path to the bay and the spring, but this was too dangerous for what he had planned. Striking out into the vegetation, he found a natural clearing between the forest and the mangroves. He walked back, still thinking about the Lihir plan.

Several children had shown up and, along with Lumas, were clustered around Nellie's hut. The children were goggling at Alex, who was trying to look nonchalant under their inquisitive stares. May and Nellie were teasing them but in Mussau, so Doyle couldn't understand what they were saying.

"What are you telling them?" asked Doyle.

May and Nellie both laughed. "We said they're acting like they've never see a white woman before. There are white women at Boliu hospital and school, but they've never had someone like Alex come to stay on Emananus," said May.

Nellie said, "Ai, ol lukim leg bilong Missis Alex. I gat planti bite bilong binatang."[21]

Alex looked even more disconcerted and scratched at her legs. Nellie slapped her hand and told her to stop. She brought out her coconut oil and a handful of leaves and a half coconut shell. She made the children chew the leaves and then spit them into the coconut shell. Nellie added the coconut oil and then began rubbing down Alex's blotchy legs before she could protest.

May said, "The leaves have natural anesthetic released by

---

[21] "Look at Miss Alex's legs. They are bitten all over by insects."

saliva. It will kill the itching in your legs. I have a medical kit with antihistamine cream, but believe me, this will work far more effectively."

Doyle explained to Nellie and May what he wanted to do. He brought several bush knives from his hut and handed them out to the children, including Lumas. May spoke to the children in Mussau, and they dashed off into the forest in the direction of the clearing.

"What did you tell them to do?" asked Alex.

"They're going to construct a firing range. We all need target practice with the rifles and Stens, plus I need to get my eye with my pistols. I see there are pistols in the boxes, so we'll add pistol practice too for everyone. I know Joe's not here, but he's got military training, so we'll just have to hope he's a good shot."

"What about stray bullets?" asked Alex.

"We'll keep the kids back behind us, and the bullets should slam into the mangrove trees. All the land here plus the reef belongs to Nellie's family, so no one should be fishing out there beyond the mangroves."

Doyle told May, Alex, and Nellie to follow him to his hut, where they took an empty chest and loaded it with a couple of assault rifles, Sten guns, and pistols, plus ammunition. The chest was heavy, but Doyle and May could manage it between them. They were relieved to reach the clearing, having stopped on route a couple of times to change hands and massage their arms. Alex had volunteered to carry the chest, but Nellie chided her in pidgin.

"Honestly, May, your aunt treats me like a child," said Alex with exasperation.

"Oh, don't worry; she's just worried for you. And, anyway, it's so hot and humid, you might get heat exhaustion," said May.

"What did I tell you about following what Auntie Nellie says?"

said Doyle. "Besides which, she knows English well enough. Eh, tru antap, Auntie?"[22]

Nellie laughed a deep, sonorous guffaw, throwing her head back, revealing her beautiful white teeth. The children had planted fours stakes in the ground and topped them with coconuts scavenged from the forest floor. They had also made a pile of additional coconuts. Nellie and May shouted at the children to go to the edge of the clearing and stand behind them.

"I expect some villagers will come when we start shooting?" asked Doyle.

"Probably. They're still curious about Alex, but they'll approach from behind. The kids will keep an eye out. I'll tell them," said May.

"Okay, come on; we need to load these magazines."

---

[22] "Isn't that true, Auntie?"

Chapter 30

Thirty minutes later, they had assembled sufficient magazine for a couple of hours of target practice. The children had grown bored as the four adults squatted around the chest, engaged in stuffing bullets into magazines. Doyle asked Nellie if they were all still there. He didn't want some kid wandering into the improvised gun range and all the horror that might entail. One boy was missing, and Lumas and the other children shouted out to him. The missing boy, Meslee, wandered back along the path from the lagoon.

"Get them to sit behind the chest. No wandering off again," said Doyle.

Nellie spoke in a strong, commanding voice to the children, so they looked at her with solemn expressions and nodded their heads.

"Who wants to go first?" asked Doyle.

"I'll go first;" said May, "and then Auntie Nellie can follow me. Which weapons?"

"Start with the pistols and then the Stens and then the assault rifles."

May stepped forward, took up the cup and saucer shooter's grip, and loosed off a series of shots at the coconut on the extreme left of the group of four. The pistols were Smith and Wesson nine-millimeter models that held ten rounds, like his Browning Hi-Power.

"Clear," shouted May, holding the gun vertical and with the slide drawn back, exposing and empty chamber.

Doyle walked forward and looked at the coconut. It had a nice grouping of bullets in its center.

"Okay, Auntie, you next. Yu save shootim gun?"[23]

"Ai, yes, but long taim bepo."[24]

Nellie adopted a pose like May, but she was more hesitant. She shot, twitching with each shot but trying to keep her eye on the target. On a shooting range, they would use ear protectors, but here they had no such luxury. Doyle hoped any hearing impairment was temporary. Nellie finished shooting, adopted the same pose as May, with the gun vertical and the slide back. Doyle checked her coconut. It was better than he had expected: over half the bullets had hit the target. Anybody in Nellie's path would be bleeding out or incapacitated.

"Okay, Alex, up you go," said Doyle.

"Why do you get to go last?' asked Alex "So you can show up the women with your marksmanship?"

"Something like that," said Doyle.

Alex adopted the pose and, like May, let fly a stream of shots.

Doyle examined her coconut target—excellent grouping, like May. Stepping back, he loosed off his gun and made a grouping similar to May and Alex.

"Okay, let's have a round of Sten gunfire. May, can you ask the kids to put up new targets?"

The children bounded forward to replace the coconut targets. As they were doing this, Meslee wandered over to the mangrove margin. The firm ground dissolved beyond into a morass of mud and small pools. Doyle picked up a Sten gun, pointing it upward while

---

[23] "Do you know how to shoot?"

[24] "Yes, a long time ago."

the children were in the shooting range. He shouted at them to come back, which was echoed by May and Nellie.

As Meslee turned, something massive erupted from the mud, twisting in midair to grab him around the torso. There was a horrific gasp from the women and children, and Doyle saw May reach for a pistol. He ran toward the mangrove fringe in time to see the crocodile had landed in the pool, with Meslee squirming in its jaws. He fired the Sten gun into the animal's hindquarters, trying to keep away from the head.

The crocodile whipped around to face Doyle, despite having been hit by so many bullets. Meslee was still gripped in the monster's jaws and flailing his arms and legs. Doyle could see that the hits by the Sten were superficial. May joined Doyle and opened up at close range with the pistol as the crocodile lunged at them with the boy still held in its mouth. This additional gunfire did not appear to wound the crocodile.

Doyle began to despair, when Nellie and Alex came alongside. Alex let fly with the assault rifle, which ripped huge rents in the flesh of the crocodile's back. She must have severed the spine, as its hindquarters and tail went still. The wounded beast hissed and roared, and its jaws opened, throwing Meslee across the swamp.

Doyle watched as Nellie and May ran into the mud and pulled the boy away from the thrashing reptile, which though badly wounded, was still dragging itself forward to where Doyle and Alex stood. It reared up on its front legs, and Alex let fly another burst from the assault rifle, which smashed into the beast's jaws. It flopped forward, and Alex fired a short burst between the eyes.

"Well done. I think you passed muster, Miss McCall. These Sten guns are good for close-in fighting but no bloody good against crocs, same with the pistols."

Chapter 31

Doyle shouted out to Nellie as he strode over: "Auntie, olsem wanem? I hurt bikpela or wanem?"[25]

May and Nellie had removed the boy's shirt and pants. Doyle could see the bite marks and puncture wounds on his buttocks and stomach. Meslee was in shock. He was shivering, and his skin was turning grey. Doyle scooped him up and ran for his hut, with everyone trailing after. He laid Meslee on the bed and began emptying the medical supplies on the bed, next to the boy. He grabbed a loaded morphine self-injector and shot about half the contents into Meslee's arm. He found a bottle of medicinal alcohol and began swabbing the bleeding wounds. As he cleaned the stomach and lower belly, he stopped and sniffed at the wound.

"What are you doing?" asked May.

"Smelling for shit—if the boy's intestines were punctured, it's all over. He'll die from septic peritonitis. If not, we can clean and stitch the wound and pump him full of antibiotics. Can one of the villagers go and bring a doctor or a nurse from Boliu? It's better than moving him."

Meslee's shakes had stopped, and his eyes adopted a dreamy expression. Doyle conducted another close examination of Meslee's puncture wounds, and there was still no smell of fecal matter.

---

[25] "How is it, Auntie? Is he seriously injured or what?"

He wondered if there had been any crush injury to other internal organs—kidneys possibly, but they were nestled in a bed of fat, even in a skinny boy like Meslee. There was running feet outside the hut, and a man and woman came in crying when they saw the child.

Nellie rattled out orders to other villagers, who were assembling at Doyle's hut. A fire was built and a large cauldron filled with well water to provide a plentiful supply of hot water. Towels and sheets were brought to make Meslee more comfortable.

Alex found herself numb with shock, and May came and held her, saying, "You saved him, Alex. It was your shooting that stopped that monster."

There was a lot of shouting and gesturing going on outside the hut. Nellie was among the crowd, but May came in and talked to Doyle.

"Nellie said people knew there was a big croc in the mangrove, and it should have been trapped and killed years ago. Some are saying we should not have been shooting near the kuruk, but Nellie has told them if the croc hadn't struck now, it would have later. Someone's child would disappear, as they have in the past."

Many of Meslee's family crowded into the hut, trying to make him comfortable as Doyle shook antibiotic powder on the wounds and, with May's help, stitched up the deepest wounds. Doyle did another sweep of the belly wounds, even risking pressure to see if any fecal matter was seeping out, but only blood emerged. Doyle risked a look up from the boy and could see Alex looking nervous on the periphery of the crowd of villagers.

"Alex, Alex, come here," Doyle said.

"Yes, what?"

"Take Lumas. Go back to the shooting range, disarm the guns, and make sure there are no rounds still in the breeches when you remove the magazines. I don't want to have to deal with a gunshot wound if a kid picks up those unattended weapons. You and Lumas can drag the patrol box between you."

Doyle could see two outrigger canoes paddling out from Emananus, in the direction of Loaua and then to Boliu. It was nearly a twenty-mile round trip, though he hoped that the hospital would have a motorboat that would cut the return trip time. In the meantime, he would have to do what he could for Meslee. He'd become very attached to Auntie Nellie's gaggle of kids, who were always trailing around after him. He knew they were all related to Nellie, but as he'd told Alex, he knew better than to inquire after their genealogy.

Doyle took Meslee's pulse. It was strong, and his skin felt reasonably cool. It was too soon for fever to set it, but it could set in fast nonetheless. The tropics were merciless. Doyle knew you could see someone on a morning looking hale and hearty, and they'd be dead by sundown. Children in particular were greatly at risk from fever, pneumonia, and diarrhea. Doyle looked at the boy; he figured Meslee must be ten or eleven, on the brink of puberty. He was a healthy lad but just skin and bone, no excess fat or water to burn up in a fever. His hair was wavy, like May's, not curly like the majority of villagers on Emananus.

All the wounds were dressed, and Doyle doled out a couple of antibiotic tablets, after checking the dosage on the bottle. He made Meslee drink some water to keep him hydrated as the morning heat turned into the hotter afternoon.

Nellie had shooed several of the relatives out of the hut but let Meslee's parents stay. Meslee was looking relaxed and out of pain, though his eyed betrayed an out-of-focus appearance from the morphine. Doyle checked his watch. They had been shooting at about ten in the morning. Now it was around one o'clock in the afternoon.

He hoped the cleaning of the wounds was thorough; he knew croc teeth were covered with all kinds of filth. *This operation never gets any easier,* he thought.

Doyle looked up again and out of the door. The hubbub had died down. May was clearing up the soiled cotton-wool and other discarded medical equipment.

"Can you inventory the medical kit when you've got a minute?" said Doyle. "Better make sure Alex is on her antimalarial medication. What about you?"

"Native resistance. Never mind me, what about you?"

"Taking my tablets, but I had a few shakes about a week ago. Nellie gave me some quinine. The regular antimalarials do okay, but now and again you need quinine to shift the bug entirely. How are the villagers?"

"Meslee's dad, Jonas, went out and told them to stop bickering. It was his child who was hurt, and it was just a bad accident, he said. We're supposed to be Christians, but the old beliefs in magic and evil spirits are always in the background. And before you ask, I'm no different than they are, despite my education and urban ways."

"Mr. Doyle, we've got the weapons," said Alex from outside the hut. Doyle stepped away from the bed where Meslee's mother, Amy, was still keeping a vigil on her child. Doyle and Alex brought the patrol box into the hut and stacked it with the others in the corner. Doyle returned to the bed and took a thermometer from the medical bag. He shook it and popped it in Meslee's mouth.

"Good, ninety nine point one. He still has no fever." Doyle called out to Nellie to bring a cup of strong sweet tea for the boy, so he could sip it.

"Mama bilong Meslee, mipela makim cup tea for Meslee. Mi save yu no drinkim, but dispel em I marasin, em bai I mekim strong."[26]

"Em nau masta, tenk yu tru, na yu tu misses," said Amy. "Mi harim you kilim puk puk na savim boi bilong mi."[27]

These latter words were directed at Alex, who did not know what was being said but guessed their meaning. Amy held Meslee, who sipped the lukewarm tea.

Doyle stood and gazed out of the window and let his mind empty. He watched the interplay of light and water over the reefs, shifting colors from green and blue to gold and brown.

Meslee stirred on the bed, his face registering pain. Doyle found the morphine syringe and injected the remainder of the drug. Doyle realized how tired he was feeling. He asked May if he could get a cup of tea and a ship's biscuit. The biscuits were thick navy crackers, impervious to the heat and humidity, which most households kept as a fallback in case food was short. Alex was leaning against the wall of the hut, staring across the channel at the other islands. May returned with some strong sweet black tea and the ship's biscuit.

Alex went inside and looked with astonishment at the cracker.

"Is that what our navy used to eat?" she asked.

"Yes, genuine hardtack, as documented by Samuel Pepys. Very popular here because they keep forever and people like them. Do you like them, May?" Doyle asked.

"Yes, but you can't just bite them; you'll shatter your teeth."

Meslee stirred again, and his mother sat on the bed and stroked

---

[26] "Meslee's mum, I'm making a cup of tea for Meslee. I know you don't drink tea, but this is medicine to make him strong."

[27] Okay, mister, thank you, and you too, miss. I heard you killed the crocodile and saved my boy."

his forehead, now covered with a sweat sheen. Doyle placed the thermometer in the boy's mouth. His temperature had spiked to 101 degrees.

"His temperature is up, might be malaria or an infection," said Doyle.

He racked his brains for a way to tell the difference. He placed his hands in the boys groin and felt for any swollen lymphatic glands. There was a grape-sized swelling where the lymph gland was reacting to an infection.

"Damn, damn, damn. Meslee has an infection from the bite. I don't think its peritonitis—his stomach isn't swollen or sensitive—but something's gotten into his bloodstream. I hoped the antibiotic tablets would have taken care of that, but I'm not a doctor."

Meslee coughed and then began gagging. Doyle grabbed him and put his head over the bed. May grabbed one of the bowls on the table and held it so Meslee could be sick.

"We mustn't let him dehydrate," said May. "There's a rehydration mix in the medical supplies. We need to get him to drink this; otherwise he could die, regardless of the infection."

"Alex, call Nellie to bring some spring water."

"Here's the rehydration mix," said May, emptying it into a tin cup. Alex and Nellie showed up at the door, Nellie with a glass bottle of spring water. Doyle poured water into the tin cup and stirred it with a spoon.

"May, tell Meslee's mum to hold him up," said Doyle.

Meslee was like a floppy doll because of the morphine and fever delirium. Amy cradled his head, holding it back so Doyle could spoon the rehydration mix into the boy. May massaged the boy's throat and stomach, letting the medicine slide into the stomach, where it would calm the vomiting reflex and allow liquids to be absorbed. The hut was very hot in the afternoon, with only a slight breeze off the ocean to offset the near 100 percent humidity. Doyle's shirt was dark with sweat. Amy had a colorful blouse and skirt, but sweat ran down her anxious face.

Chapter 32

Meslee's father, Jonas, had returned from the village, and May told him what was happening. The light was beginning to fade, but the heat still throbbed in the afternoon. A wave of utter despair began to wash over Doyle. He wondered what evil gods he had upset to be visited by so much misfortune. He was trying to think what to do next, when there was a shout. Doyle looked out to see a motorized launch pulling up to the beach. Behind it on towropes were the two canoes that had gone to Boliu. A tall, khaki-clad white man and a Melanesian woman in a nurse's uniform jumped from the boat and strode up the beach, carrying a medical kit and canvas bags.

When they reached the hut, the man asked everyone but Amy and his nurse to leave, so he could examine the patient.

Doyle said, "Doctor, don't you want to know what happened, what treatment we've given him?"

"He's been bitten by a croc. You've administered some morphine and antibiotic tablets. He's also been given a rehydration draft."

Doyle followed the doctor's gaze to the table, where there were bottles and packets still sitting there.

"You did the best you could with the wounds. Now, Nurse Karasa and I need to take over. We'll make a thorough examination, redress his wounds, and also hook the poor lad to a drip with saline and powerful antibiotics. I'll give him quinine to keep any malaria at bay. Good enough?"

"Sorry, yes, we'll be outside if you need anything," Doyle said.

Nellie came to the doorway and spoke to the nurse in Mussau. The doctor broke off and turned to Nellie to say hello and then went back to work.

Nellie said to Doyle, "Kam."

Doyle was feeling too punch-drunk to argue, so he followed Nellie, along with Alex and May. Doyle thought back to the briefing with the ISS staff, when Dr. Tambo had said everything in New Guinea would be trying to kill him. So far, the place was testing that proposition.

Nellie led them into her hut. Doyle checked the time. It wasn't very late, about seven o'clock. It felt more like midnight.

"Tupela sindaun. May, kam, yumi mekim kaikai,"[28] said Nellie as she lit the lamps.

Behind the hut was a shelter with a free-standing kerosene stove with twin burners and next to that a clay charcoal pot cooker. Doyle heard the two women working outside, talking in subdued tones in Mussau. Doyle was slumped in a chair, while Alex sat on the bed, her knees drawn up to her chin, her hands clasped in front of her.

"Is it always this bad?" she asked.

"What ... yes, no, I mean this was something that blindsided us," Doyle said.

"May said if Meslee dies, we'd better get off the island. I think she just meant me and you. I don't think the villagers will blame Nellie and May, but we'll get blamed for bringing bad luck."

"Yeah, I know. I'd been thinking about that. It may seem like a peaceful place, but Nellie told me it was only in the 1930s that they stopped killing and eating folks like you and me. We'll have to pay

---

[28] "Both of you sit down. May, come we will make some food."

compensation. I have gold sovereigns. Is there any money in the patrol boxes?"

"Yes, there are more sovereigns and Australian pounds in one of the boxes," said Amy.

"Good, we'll need them anyway."

"Are we still going ahead with the mission?"

"Yes, I know it's awful, but there are bigger things at stake than a little Melanesian boy, much as I like him," said Doyle.

Nellie and May came back in carrying a pot of food, which was placed on the table. It smelled delicious, but Doyle's stomach flip-flopped at the thought of food. Nellie had made a corn beef hash, using leftover rice, tinned beef, onions, and other vegetables. Nellie and May put out plates and dished out the food. Nellie brought a bottle of spring water and poured out measures into tin mugs. May said a quick grace, and then they began to eat.

Seeing Doyle's listless attempts to eat his food, Nellie said, "Ai, kam on, masta. Em i no wrong bilong yu. God bai i helpim yang boi nau. No ken worry tumas. Yu mas kaikai so yu no kisim sik olsem."[29]

They ate in silence, Doyle finding it hard to swallow the food into his knotted stomach. He was aware that Nellie was watching him, so he did his best to clear his plate. After dinner, Nellie began unrolling mats for sleeping. She told Alex to take her bed again, while the three of them would sleep on the floor. Nellie got out her coconut broom and cleaned out under the bed. As she did so, several large, hairy wolf spiders scurried out, making Alex start and leap up from the bed.

May laughed and said, "Don't worry. They won't bite you as long as you leave them alone."

---

[29] "Come on, Mister. It's not your fault. God will the young boy now. Don't worry so much. You must eat so you don't get sick as well."

"What's Auntie Nellie doing?" asked Alex.

"She's going to sleep under the bed to make more room on the hut floor. She wanted to clean it out; I suppose she wasn't keen on company."

"I can sleep there … should sleep there," said Doyle.

"Ai, no kan," said Nellie, looking resolute.

"Hey, where's Lumas? I haven't seen her after this morning," said Doyle.

"Auntie sent her to go and stay with her sister, Lucy."

"Lucy is Lumas's sister?" asked Alex innocently.

"No, Lucy is Nellie's sister. Let's leave it at that," said May.

Nellie chuckled and gently swiped the broom at May's legs. Nellie retrieved old pillows and folded blankets for the mats and directed everyone to go and get ready for bed.

Doyle cast a look at his hut. He wanted to go and see what was happening but knew this was futile.

Everyone settled in for the night, Alex still looking unhappy about sleeping on the only bed. She stripped down to her underclothes and lay beneath the sheet. May, Nellie, and Doyle slept in their clothes. Tomorrow they would wash and clean up.

Doyle lay still, listening to the night sounds. He could hear the regular "crump crump" of breakers on the reef. In daytime this was drowned out by other sounds. He could hear the sounds of the beach and the susurration of the small waves lapping on the shore. There was a permanent screech of cicadas and crickets, which was so loud that individual calls would move in and out of phase. There was a regular "tock tock" call of geckos and an occasional squabble sound as they fought over territory. There were rustles in the roof of the hut and scrabbling sounds outside among the pots and pans. Doyle listened to the noises and slipped off to sleep.

Chapter 33

Doyle was shaken awake in the dawn light by Lumas, who pulled Nellie's big toe protruding from under the bed.

"Kam, dokta i laik tokim yu,"[30] said Lumas with a grave expression on her face.

Bugger, thought Doyle, *it's bad news.* His mind was still foggy from sleep, and his sweat-soaked clothes were chafing his body. They walked to the other hut. Inside was the doctor, looking tired but with a smile. Nurse Karasa was packing up their equipment, while Amy was spooning some mashed banana and papaya into Meslee's mouth.

"God, I thought it was bad news," said Doyle.

Nellie had joined Amy and helped in feeding the weak child.

"How is he, Dr.—"

"Smith, John Smith," said the doctor, who Doyle realized had a refined Cumbrian accent. "It was a bit touch and go; he had a bad infection that needed the intravenous perfusion with some heavy-hitting antibiotics. You were right, though, that his intestines were not punctured. You missed a couple of broken ribs—not your fault—and these are not too serious. His temperature is down, and the wounds no longer look inflamed. I'm still surprised he wasn't bitten in half by the croc. Where is it?"

May had come to the door and said, "It's being skinned. The hide

---

30 "Come, the doctor wants to talk to you."

is worth a lot of money; the villagers will hack up the body and dump the pieces of carcass beyond the reef, for the sharks. I've just come from the kuruk. I had a good look at the croc's mouth. It's missing some teeth in the middle of its skull. It's old after all and has been through a few fights."

"What now, Doc?"

"We'll go back to Boliu and leave behind medicines and instructions. Meslee can be carefully moved back to his home in a day or so. Most villages have some kind of simple aid-post and a stretcher. I'd like to keep the drip in to his arm and maintain the antibiotic. Who's the aid-post orderly?"

"It's the local pastor. There's a stretcher in the church," said May. "But the pastor is away in Moresby at the Adventist College. Auntie, husat I gat key long lotu[31]?"

"Mipela no lockim. Yu ken go insait,"[32] said Nellie from inside the hut.

Lumas appeared, followed by the other children, anxiety on their faces being replaced by huge smiles when Nellie told them that Meslee was going to recover. May rattled out a series of instructions to the children, who ran off, while Lumas stayed. The girl went inside the hut, and Doyle watched as she went and touched Meslee on the shoulder. Amy and Nellie finished feeding him.

Doyle said to May, "The doc recommends we should let him stay here until the intravenous medication is finished. We can take him home tomorrow."

Doyle turned to Nellie and said, "What do you think, Auntie?"

---

[31] "Who has got the key to the church?"

[32] "We didn't lock it. You can go inside."

"Em nau. Larim wan moa day i stap,"[33] she said in Mussau to Amy, who nodded and said something in return.

"What did I miss?" said Alex, appearing in the doorway. "I found myself alone when I woke up, so I thought something must have happened."

"Meslee has pulled through," said Doyle. He was going to say more but was aware of the doctor and nurse and did not want to say anything further.

"I expect you've got things to occupy you," said Dr. Smith.

"Thank you for your help with Meslee. I hope I don't sound too pompous when I say that His Majesty's Government would be grateful if you exercised discretion about what you've seen here."

"I think you can rely on me and Nurse Karasa to maintain quiet about all except the incident with the child and crocodile."

Nurse Karasa was outside, and Nellie and May were talking to her in Mussau while she nodded her head.

"I think I know a military man when I see one. And your companion—"

"Alex will do for now," said Alex.

"I was going to say is very attractive," said the doctor.

Alex had grabbed the first clothing to hand, which were her Spandex gym shorts, showing of her long, shapely legs. Her khaki military blouse was hastily tied, not buttoned, emphasizing her prominent breasts and displaying her toned creamy midriff.

May laughed at the doctor's quip. Nellie came out to see what May

---

[33] "Leave him. He can stay another day."

was laughing about and said in a mock severe voice, "Ai, missis, yu mas karamupim. No ken stand nabout olsem two shilling pumuk."[34]

Alex looked down, blushed, and fastened her blouse. There was another burst of laughter from Doyle, May, and Nellie, which was as much a release of the tension of the past twenty-four hours as Alex's casual dressing.

Three days later, they sailed from Emananus to Kavieng aboard the *Totonga*.

---

[34] "Hey, miss, you must cover yourself up. You can't stand about like a two-shilling prostitute."

Chapter 34

Doyle would have liked more target practice, but after Meslee's ordeal, he decided not to tempt fate. Instead, he, May, and Alex checked and rechecked their gear, making sure all gun magazines were filled and all grenades and explosive charges primed and ready.

The *Totonga* was smaller than the *Malalangi*, with berths in the prow reached from the wheelhouse. Most of the aft deck space and hold was used for cargo. The trip to Kavieng would take most of the day, so Doyle used the time to shave his head and beard, leaving only his moustache. There was a small kitchen area behind the wheelhouse and a sink with running saltwater. Doyle shaved with a straight, along with a shaving mirror. May held the mirror for Doyle, while Alex held a bowl of freshwater used to make a lather for shaving.

Doyle had also retrieved some alcohol from the medical kit, which he used in place of aftershave, not wanting any nicks on his head and face to be infected. When he finished, he looked in the mirror.

"Well, ladies, what do you think?"

"You look like a convict," said Alex.

"Thanks, I hope it's enough of a disguise if Raptor and his gang think I'm dead."

"We've no reason to think otherwise, although the number of operatives and spies they've deployed has got us all worried. Someone in Moresby might have tipped them off about you surviving the attack there."

"Ai, bollo het man,"[35] said Nellie, emerging from the wheelhouse, where she had been chatting with Rurusan.

Everybody laughed. Doyle looked toward the horizon and could see a faint smudge of land, which he reckoned to be New Hanover, about seventy miles from Mussau. Mussau was still visible behind them but was slipping gradually below the horizon. They had set off at dawn to make it easy to pick through the reef passes, and now it was about ten o'clock in the morning.

Nellie grabbed Doyle's arm and pointed to the distant land, saying, "Lavongai."

"Is that the traditional name for New Hanover?" asked Doyle.

"Em nau," said Nellie.

Two of Rurusan's four-man crew stepped to the stern and began unspooling fishing line, on the ends of which were feather lures. They tossed these behind the vessel, throwing them out far enough to avoid the churning propeller.

"Why didn't they start fishing when we left Mussau?" asked Doyle.

May said, "Uncle Rurusan doesn't want the crew fishing in coastal waters. It can be too much of a distraction, and coastal waters are always dangerous—too many reefs, dangerous flotsam, big rollers."

"Fair enough," said Doyle. He spotted a flock of birds ahead, on the port side about a half mile in the distance. He felt the vessel alter course, so that it would run close to where the birds were flocking and diving into the sea. As he watched, Doyle could see fish breaking the

---

[35] "Hello, baldy."

surface, chasing prey. It was too far to distinguish what they were, but he knew that it was likely a tuna school.

Alex stood alongside and asked, "What kind of fish are they?"

Nellie answered her, saying, "Atun."

"Tuna," said May. "Japanese vessels fish out here for bonito. The Japanese pay to catch bait in the Lavongai Islands and catch tuna with pole and lines on the ocean. Look, see on the horizon; you can see a couple of their boats. Here, Alex, take the binoculars. You can see them fishing with poles at the stern and prow. They throw live bait in the water and spray the water's surface to make it look like a feeding frenzy."

As they steamed forward, a school of flying fish took to the air, gliding over the water's surface. Without warning, a large frigate bird swooped out of the sky, catching one of the flying fish. One of the fishing lines went taut, even though they had yet to reach the tuna school. Rurusan's two crewmen manhandled the line into the boat. There was no finesse to their technique, no sporting play with the fish on the line.

Pacific Islanders don't play with their food, thought Doyle, who had been game fishing in the Indian Ocean.

The two crewmen pulled a long slender fish, about forty inches in length, over the stern. It flopped in its gasping death throes. It was aquamarine blue on its dorsal surface, gold and green on its belly. The colors of the fish shimmered and changed shades as it slid and wriggled across the deck. One of the crew retrieved a wooden club and beat the fish across the head until it lay still. As he pulled the lure from the fish's mouth, the other line went taut, and they pulled another similar fish out of the water.

May pointed to the fish and said, "We call these malatu, but they're also known as dolphin or dorado."

Doyle looked out to sea and saw that the vessel was cruising along the edge of the tuna school. He looked into the center of the bird flock and saw a log, almost fully submerged. Small fish were jumping everywhere, trying to escape the tuna, which were causing the ocean surface to fleck and boil. The small fish were no safer jumping, as flocks of seabirds picked them off above the feeding frenzy.

Both fishing lines tightened and were brought in one after the other to avoid tangling. Both had bonito, about two feet in length, with dark dorsal surfaces and striped silver flanks and bellies. These fish did not flop and wriggle like the dorado, but their tails beat in a blur as they skidded across the deck. Blood gushed from their mouths and gills, and they vomited up their stomach contents, a mix of half-digested and freshly consumed small, silvery fish.

Rurusan circled the school while his men threw and pulled tuna on board. Sometimes they would catch larger tunas with the dark-light shading but with yellow fins. Rurusan broke off from the school, and the crew set about gutting and cleaning the fish. One of the holds was opened to reveal that it was an ice chest with fresh food for the crew, which now included the tuna and dorado. Rurusan put his head out of the wheelhouse and shouted to May and Nellie.

"Malatu for lunch," said May. "Hope you're hungry."

Chapter 35

The day was drawing to a close when the *Totonga* motored through the Nusa Channel into Kavieng Harbor. The vessel drew up to a small wharf close to the marketplace. A truck and a car were waiting. A large burly man in a blue cotton military-style shirt stood under a street lamp. Four natives sat on the wharf, smoking and watching the vessel approach.

"That's Frank Gardiner, the provincial administrator," said May as the *Totonga* inched toward the wharf.

One of the crew jumped aboard to secure the bow, while the men sitting on the wharf stood and one caught the stern rope. Gardiner spoke to the men in pidgin, and they stepped aboard, surrounding a pile of luggage and patrol boxes. The luggage and boxes were loaded into the truck while Doyle, Nellie, and May said goodbye to Rurusan. Alex hung back, looking a little lost and unable to speak pidgin. She stepped off the wharf and approached Gardiner.

"You must be Mr. Gardiner. I'm Alex McCall."

"Just call me Frank. That must be Mick Doyle. I know May, so that must be her auntie. I've heard about her but never met her."

"She's quite formidable," Alex said.

"So they say. I got call from Port Moresby yesterday to expect you tonight. A bit of a rigmarole, but I know Nellie is a coastwatcher, so she had to go through her folks to send the message. No bloody good sending it to us and no one to decode it."

Doyle stepped ashore and introduced himself. He had heard the conversation between Gardiner and Alex.

"Hello, Frank, I'm Mick Doyle. Thanks for coming to help us. I heard that you were contacted from Moresby. Was it from the high commission?"

"Yes, bloody people, some Pommy sounding like he had a blocked-up nose. Oh, I shouldn't be rude about the English."

Doyle laughed, "Alex is Scottish, and I'm Irish, so be as rude as you like."

"It had to be a secure line, so I had to go to the phone exchange and take the call."

"Glad you did. I don't want to be too alarmist, but the future of the empire is at stake, so your help is doubly appreciated."

Gardiner took this in his stride and said, "Well, we'll have to do the best we can to make sure you and your folks can get your job done."

May and Nellie joined Doyle and Alex.

"Hello, Mr. Gardiner, we've met before," said May. "This is my auntie Nellie."

"Gutnait Masta," said Nellie.

"Gutnait Nellie, yu stap orait?"[36] said Gardiner.

"Em nau, tasol mi lais long kam longwe long boat."[37]

Behind them, Rurusan was piloting his boat to a mooring near the wharf.

Gardiner said, "Come on, folks, we've got a spare mess house in the government compound that we use for visitors. If you don't mind, we'll squeeze you in there. It's got a couple of bedrooms and

---

[36] "Good evening, Nellie, are you okay?"

[37] "Yes, but I'm tired from the long sea voyage."

some camp beds, plus a bathroom and kitchen. There are ceiling fans and mosquito wire on the windows, so you should be comfortable. We'll put your boxes in the lounge; I expect you want to keep an eye on them."

Alex, May and Nellie huddled on the back seat of Gardiner's car, while Doyle sat next to him. The vehicle was an elderly Holden with official New Ireland Province number plates.

"What's this island called? It must have a name other than New Ireland," said Alex.

May said, "Latangai Island."

"God, do you know I feel a proper chump?" said Gardiner. "I didn't know that, and I've asked a few local people myself, from the mainland and some of the outlying islands."

May said, "It's that not well known, so don't feel bad about not knowing."

Gardiner pulled off the main road onto a road made of crushed coral. At the end of this was a large compound surrounded by a high steel mesh fence topped with barbed wire. The gates of the compound were open but one of the gates had a large padlock, with which the gates could be secured.

"This looks like a bit of a fortress," said Alex, a note of disquiet in her voice.

"We've had a lot of petty crime lately. The plantations economy has been hit by declines in both copra and cocoa prices for a few years. It's not too bad for the big companies, which can weather the bad patch or switch to palm oil or lowland coffee. It's the individual planters who have to retrench workers imported from the Highlands and the Sepik Provinces. They're supposed to send the workers home, but some just let them go with a few bob in their pockets. They end up in either Kavieng or Namatanai."

"Na i ol kamap rascal,"[38] said Nellie.

"Em nau, Auntie[39]," said May.

"Yes, exactly," said Gardiner.

"Turn into criminals, Alex," said Doyle.

Gardiner said, "The local folks hate them. Sometimes there are riots and then all sorts of payback murders. The Highlanders and Sepiks were brought in by the plantations because they're tougher than old boots, so fighting is in their blood. New Irelanders won't work on the plantations, not that I blame them. It's tough work shelling coconuts for a pittance. I've just got permission from the high commission to bring in several of the paramilitary police squads from the Highlands, where things get much rougher than here. We'll bulldoze the squatter settlements and round up the squatters, barge them to Lae on the mainland."

Gardiner had driven between rows of houses made out masonry boards and standing ten feet off the ground to catch the breeze.

"Won't that just transfer the problem to another province?" asked Doyle as they exited the car.

"We're going to ship them home to the Sepik Province or take them in trucks up to the Highlands. It's going to be a hell of a job, but Kavieng is a test case. If it works here, it will be scaled up to the other provincial towns."

The men in the truck arrived, and Gardiner directed them to a house with the lights off. He gave the keys to one of the men, who organized the transportation of boxes and luggage up by the external staircase. The lights came on, and Gardiner led them up to the mess

---

[38] "And they all become criminals."

[39] "Yes that's true Auntie."

house. The boxes had been neatly stacked against one wall, while the luggage was sitting on a sofa.

Doyle said, "We need to meet tomorrow, as soon as your office is opened."

"How about seven? Our caretaker Robson opens the provincial administration compound an hour before folks begin to arrive. I'm usually there a little after seven. His daughter is my secretary, and she comes in early to put on the coffee percolator and bring fresh morning rolls from the bakery. But if it's that urgent, we can meet now or early morning."

"We're trying to not draw too much attention to ourselves," said May. "We've been dogged by bad luck in this operation. We'll tell you tomorrow, but we're hoping, praying really, that we've shaken off the devil and his legions."

"If we keep to normal routines, it means we won't stand out," said Doyle. "Though I'm still worrying about our arrival this evening."

"Well, if it's any consolation, you don't look like your photo. After I talked with the high commission, they sent pictures of you and Miss McCall to the telefax in the exchange—again the same concerns about security, as we've got a machine in the office."

"That's reassuring," said Alex.

"Very," said Doyle. "Could you send your car for us after it drops you at the office? Even if the government offices are nearby, I'd rather we didn't stroll down the street."

"Yup, no problem. Belinda, my secretary, will come for you shortly after seven. My wife did some shopping this afternoon, and there is some bread, butter, milk, eggs, and bacon in the fridge and some tins of bully beef in one of the cupboards. There are some bananas, limes, and pawpaw in there also."

Doyle looked at his watch; it was eight o'clock. It felt a lot later. "I think we're going to get cleaned up and then hit the hay," said Doyle.

"Bugger, forgot about soap," said Gardiner.

"I have a bar in my luggage," said Alex. "Imperial Leather, very appropriate for our little band."

"Right enough," said Gardiner.

Nellie had been quiet throughout, sitting on the sofa while the others stood in the lounge. As Gardiner readied to leave, she stood and said, "Tenk you, tru masta. Mipela amamas tru yu kam alivim olgeta."[40]

"Tenk yu olsem, Nellie," said Gardiner. "Long taim igo quiet gen mi laik sindaun, tokim yu long Mussau."[41]

"Em nau," said Nellie.

"Who's going first in the shower?" said Alex, pulling the soap from her bag.

---

[40] "Thank you, mister. We're happy you came to help."

[41] "Thank you as well, Nellie. When things have settled down, I'd like to talk to you about Mussau."

Chapter 36

They took showers, one after the other. The showerhead had a water heater, common in the tropics where water was usually only a little below the air temperature. Doyle was surprised how much he'd missed the simple pleasure of a hot shower. He had shaved on the vessel, so his jaw was still smooth, and using the bathroom mirror, he could see that his moustache was growing out well. He would need to shave his head every two or three days, but he was pleased to recall Gardiner's comment that he didn't resemble his photo.

Doyle looked at his body in the mirror. The time in Mussau had melted any excess fat from his already lean body. His arrow scars looked like copper pennies on his skin, though the one on his belly showed where the doctors had opened him up to repair internal damage. He was as brown as a nut except for the shocking white of his upper thighs and groin area.

I'm really going to have to do more than just thank Auntie Nellie for restoring my fitness, he thought. Nellie would be embarrassed and offended if he offered her money, but there had to be something he could do for her; he would check with May.

As he expected, Nellie had told Alex to take one bedroom and Doyle the other. He didn't bother arguing, but he could see it still grated a little on Alex, that she was always being privileged over the two native women. There were some very stormy times ahead, and right now the last thing they needed to be thinking about were sleeping arrangements.

Dawn came, as it did in the tropics, in a blinding rush after first light, accompanied by a chattering dawn chorus of birds. Doyle got up and joined the bathroom queue as Nellie was organizing breakfast in the kitchen. She was chopping fruit, making tea and toast, and frying eggs and bacon. Hands were joined and Nellie made Alex say grace. Both Doyle and Alex had now become fluent with Catholic and Anglican grace before meals, dredged up from childhood memories.

May broke the silence. "Can you cook, Mr. Doyle?"

"Aye, I can, the Indian army requires an officer to know the dietary restrictions of all his men and to be able to forage and help cook for them in the field. Mind, being Irish I'm good at stews and steaks. Never really got the hang of pastry. Nellie, can I cook something?"

"No."

"Well, I tried."

Everyone laughed. Shortly after seven o'clock Gardiner's old Holden pulled up and a well-dressed Melanesian lady stepped out, introduced herself, and beckoned them to get in. As they drove through town, Belinda gave them a guided tour.

"I'll take you the long way around," said Belinda, giving Mr. Gardiner a chance to have his cup of coffee. Belinda drove down a rutted coral road with native housing on either side, between patches of secondary jungle growth. They emerged onto a tar-sealed road with a wide expanse in front of them.

"That's the runway, with the airport at the far end," said Belinda. "We're turning onto the last part of the Bulominski Highway, which runs from here to Namatanai."

"Who was Bulominski?" asked Alex.

May and Nellie looked out of the window, and Doyle listened to Belinda for her answer.

"He was the last German governor of New Ireland. His grave is down by the beach in Bagail. He was a real brute. If villagers did not keep the coral road through their village smooth, he would uncouple his horses and make them pull his carriage back and forth between the village boundaries for a couple of hours. There are photos of villagers carrying little bags of crushed coral with them, just to fill in holes in the road."

"Sounds like a good man," said Doyle, which earned him a slap on the shoulder from Alex and gleeful laughs from Nellie and May. Belinda smiled.

"It's the longest roadway in the Pacific Islands, connecting two major urban centers, Kavieng and Namatanai," said Belinda. "We are on Coronation Drive, the main road in the town. On your right is the Seventh Day Church."

"Ai, lukim bik lotu,"[42] said Nellie.

"And here on the left is the hotel. Across the road is WestPac Bank, and then the road to the right goes to Chinatown and the main business area. There is the Kavieng Planters and Social Club on the left. Across the street is the local supermarket, New Ireland Traders, followed by the Bank of the South Pacific." They drove on, down a steep, curving hill to a Y-shaped junction, where Coronation Drive was joined by another road.

"This is Marine Parade," said Belinda.

Even for a jaded old traveler like Doyle, the view was breathtaking. The road ran long and straight without much deviation, with houses to the left and to the right the shoreline and sea. The coral reefs were

---

[42] "Look, big church."

extensive and golden at this time in the morning. The water of the Nusa Channel was a deep blue, and on the opposite shore, more golden reefs ascended to the shoreline of the Nusa Islands.

"Those are Nusa and Nusalik, and further across the passage is Nago. Small boats can navigate the passage between Nusalik and Nago," said Belinda. "But large vessels have to use the southern route into the harbor. Here's the wharf you came to last night, just down from the market."

"Anything interesting in the market?" asked Alex.

"Tupela buai na wanpela daca,"[43] said May, which made Belinda laugh and Nellie playfully slap her niece's arm.

Doyle translated and saw the allusion, two betel nuts and the pepper-vine inflorescence. "The ladies are having a little joke at your expense. The daca is a betel plant catkin, and buai are the betel nuts. Do you I need me to spell it out?"

"Oh," was all Alex could say, and Doyle saw in the mirror that she blushed. She was sitting between Nellie and May. Nellie took her hand and said, "No ken wari. May emi hambag girl."[44]

They turned left off Marine Parade and onto a short link road, to the left of which was a wire-enclosed compound flying the British flag and a British New Guinea flag with a Union Jack in the left corner and a splendid bird of paradise in the flag's center. As the car passed, a tall young man in khaki pants and shirt, with a blue beret on his head, stepped out of the shade across the road. The car pulled in, and the young man followed them, coming to where they parked.

"Belinda, this is my cousin brother, Joe, Nellie's nephew. He's going to be coming with us."

---

[43] "Two betel nuts and pepper vine flower."

[44] "Don't worry. May is a naughty girl."

179

"OK, let me take you up to Mr. Gardiner's room. Anybody need the bathroom or want some coffee? No? Okay let's go."

"I gather your father is the caretaker Belinda?" said Doyle.

"Yes, he and my mum are from Kavieng. Dad saved every penny he earned, and mum too, to put me through the Catholic Mission School and secretarial college in Moresby. Mum grows veggies and catches fish. She sells them to the expats, to the hotel and club—makes more that way."

"You must be very proud of them," said Alex.

"Not half as much as they are of me. Dad's going to ask a huge bride price when I get married."

Doyle said to Alex, "May and Nellie can explain bride price later. Let's focus on the mission."

Gardiner stood on a veranda surrounding the office complex's second floor.

"Hello, folks, let's go into my little conference room." He turned and disappeared through a doorway.

Belinda led the way up and into the conference room. Gardiner sat at the head of the table.

"Take a seat. Who's this strapping young lad?" Gardiner said.

"My sonny boy Joe," said Nellie.

"Good morning, sir, I'm Joe Asora. I've just completed a three-year tour in the Pacific Islands regiment."

There were badges on Joe's beret. Gardiner looked at them and said, "Engineer and sapper—very impressive, son. What are your plans?"

"First to help out Auntie Nellie and May, and then look for work," said Joe.

"Come and see me when all this fuss has died down. I'm sure we can find something for a useful lad like you," said Gardiner. "Where are you staying?"

"In Rawal, and thank you, sir," said Joe with a big smile.

"Now, what's all the flap about?" said Gardiner as he sat at the head of the table. Doyle sat to his left, with Alex to his left. Across the table was May on Gardiner's right, with Nellie next to her and Joe next to Nellie.

Chapter 37

"Do you mind if we close the windows?" said Doyle. "It'll get warm, but I want to try and keep as much of this as confidential as possible. Please can you ask Belinda not to disturb us?"

Gardiner called out to Belinda and asked for a "do not disturb" sign to be posted on the conference room door.

Doyle asked Nellie for the map she carried. He spread out the map on the table and gestured with his forefinger. "Here's New Ireland," said Doyle. "Here's Lihir, which we know is a massive gold mine. Nothing you don't already know. What you don't know is that we suspect that five atomic bombs stolen from the Royal Airforce in England are being kept there and ransomed for one hundred million quid."

"God help us," said Gardiner. "What evidence do you have that leads to Lihir?"

Doyle outlined the events and evidence that had pointed to New Guinea and the Lihir gold mine, staring with his call back to the ISS and the ambush at Windsor.

When he had finished, Gardiner said, "I've never been fully comfortable with the German company left in control of the mine, but they pay their taxes, lots of money. I'm sure you know it keeps the province pretty much autonomous from Moresby, which is why the arrangement is tolerated."

"The evidence is all circumstantial, but there's no other place that looks as likely as Lihir. Did you know this Elaine Chan?"

"Did I ever—nice mixed-race girl, lovely as you like. Goes off to university in Italy of all places, and comes back with all of this anti-imperial rhetoric. Tried to organize a rally against the empire—unsuccessfully I might add. It's hard enough to get the buggers to work—begging your pardon, ladies—never mind march around town with anti-imperial banners." He looked at Nellie and May, who laughed.

"I went and saw her dad—nice bloke, owns a big store in Chinatown. I think he read the riot act at her, and next thing I knew she had gone to work for the mine. Who was the other Chinese lady?" said Gardiner.

"Still no idea, but she must have grown up in New Guinea. She mutters pidgin in a delirium. Seems like she has not been in trouble; we have no fingerprints on file. Alex, was there any update on who she might be? I know her photo was telefaxed to our governments and police forces worldwide."

"Nothing, I mean, she's a young Chinese girl; looks like a million Chinese girls. We were lucky with Elaine Chan, since she's mixed race and had very distinctive features."

"There are thousands of Chinese in New Guinea. The economy is built off their backs," said Gardiner.

Alex asked, "Why were they brought here, plantation labor?"

"No," said Gardiner, "they were brought in to manage the plantations. But they were too smart for that, and soon figured that the real money lay in trading and commerce. In theory we should have shipped them home if they left their jobs or completed contracts, but they often married into the local communities and didn't cause trouble, far from it. They made our part of New Guinea a commercial success. But, anyway, what are your plans?"

"Make it up as we go along," said Doyle.

"It's not that far from the truth," said May. "But London wants us on the island, providing forward intelligence. There's going to be a military operation soon, and they want us in place to advise."

"Also, we need to snoop about for the bombs ahead of time. We have Geiger counters to sniff out radioactivity. The bombs are well shielded, so humans can handle them, but they still give off radiation," said Doyle. "We think one bomb will be picked apart to reverse engineer it, but the other? There's one school of thought that it will be deployed, somewhere really populous, like Sydney, Hong Kong, or the big cities along the west coast of the Confederated States."

"And what's the other school of thought?" asked Gardiner.

"Compound the knowledge from the first bomb and use the other four to construct a hydrogen bomb. Atom bombs are city killers; hydrogen bombs are nation killers."

"Do we have hydrogen bombs?" asked Gardiner.

"Yes, but someone else wants them as well, and it looks like they want to jump past developing atom bombs," Doyle said.

"Who do you suspect?" asked Gardiner.

"Germany, it's been itching to get even for the three times in the last century we knocked the stuffing out of them. It's not well known, but if the Germans hadn't surrendered after the devastation of two coastal cities, some in government would have atom bombed Berlin and just kept going."

"Is it just Germany?" asked Gardiner.

"No, there's another actor at work here. I'd bet my bottom dollar that China is involved. China has been flexing its muscles since it threw Japan out of Manchuria and Korea. Might be Russia, but they're a land empire; get them on water, and they're a joke. China is still smarting from the drubbing it took from various powers over the past two hundred years. It hates the Hong Kong territory, and Macau come to that, but the Portuguese seem to rub along with the Chinese authorities better than the empire."

"Kongkong man i smat,"[45] said Nellie, indicating that she was following the conversation even if in English.

"What makes you think that Anvil is a Chinese-supported operation?" asked Gardiner.

"Germany's military was reduced to a nominal defense force under the 1966 treaty. France was all for punishing the Germans by ploughing the country into one giant farm to feed the French. We weren't having any of that and told the French if they didn't play nicely, we'd annex their colonies as well. The other European states and Russia fell into line, and Germany was stripped of its colonies and most of its military. France wanted gold as well, but we shut that demand down."

"Tell Frank what else makes you think it's China," said May.

"Elaine Chan and our mysterious Chinese girl in England. Frank, is there any way of knowing which Chinese family might have sent their daughter to be educated in China?" Doyle asked.

"Don't know; it's not something we'd typically keep tabs on. Tell you what though; we could ask the immigration authorities in Moresby for all entries into British New Guinea with an Aussie passport and China visa. All BNG citizens are eligible for Aussie passports for travel, so it should show up in our records. What's your angle?" said Gardiner.

---

[45] "The Chinese are clever."

"I think the Chinese girl went to China, was recruited by Chinese intelligence, and in turn recruited Elaine Chan. She came back from Italy, where their academics still revere socialism, even though it's not caught on with the general public or elsewhere in Europe. We've just laughed it off as a bizarre phenomenon, the rediscovery and fervor for dead bankrupt philosophers like Karl Marx and Ilyich Ulyanov. Looks like we might have to get the Italian government to do some dirty work," said Doyle.

"China's an imperial power too," said Alex. "How does that fit in with the Chan girl?"

"Imagine you're young and impressionable and back from college, full of ideas that are contrary to the prevailing circumstances in the empire? It would be easy for a skilled operative to drip poison in her ear, especially if they both have Chinese heritage. China is the motherland; yes, it has an empire but the emperor is just a figurehead from a Confucianist society, which is far superior to the British Empire, where foreigners are sidelined by arrogant white barbarians," said Doyle.

Gardiner laughed uncomfortably and said, "You make a great argument."

"London and the big imperial cities are different. People of different races mix more easily, and people's career paths are defined by ability, not skin color or ethnicity. There are more mixed marriages than ever before, including my boss in the ISS. Out here on the margins of the empire, it still seems things are stuck in the early 1900s, not the 2000s. That's why we are staying in the provincial government mess, not the club or hotel, which wouldn't admit natives."

"We're getting that fixed," said Gardiner with discomfort.

"Sorry to put you on the spot, Frank, but it's the same in the other remote areas of empire. The notions of egalitarianism are a hard sell."

"To be honest, I'd rather be staying where we are," said May. "We've become an odd little family, and we're going into battle soon, so I'd rather be with my wantoks. But if I was refused service because of my skin color or who I am, someone is going to get hurt."

"Ha!" said Nellie, banging the flat of her palm on the table.

Joe remained silent, but Doyle could see he was grinning at his cousin, sister, and aunt.

"Now that we've all joined hands and sung 'Abide with Me,' have you got an operational plan?" said Gardiner.

Doyle said, "Nellie, Joe, and May will go on the *Totonga* close to Lihir and row in on a dinghy at night. They'll take most of our supplies. It's going to be tough. They'll have to navigate into a bay near Londolovit. It's got a narrow reef and black sand, and then there's forest almost down to the high tide mark. If they go at high tide at night, Rurusan's crew can get them over the reef and help unload the boxes. Nellie, May, and Joe can then set up a camp in the forest. The mining barracks are close by, so we're relying on Joe to infiltrate these and find the Mussaus."

"You've no guarantees that the other Mussaus will help," said Gardiner.

"No, true, but all we want Joe to do is bring a message to their head man or bossboi to meet with her and May," said Doyle.

"How will you make a camp in the dark in the jungle?" asked Alex.

May, Nellie, and Joe all looked at her. "Oh, sorry, silly me," said Alex.

"Frank, Alex, and I hoped you'd send us on a plane to Lihir as government labor inspectors, so we can snoop around and eventually make contact with Nellie and co."

Chapter 38

"I can do better than that," said Gardiner. "Lihir mining is shipping out a load of bullion. We don't have much presence on the island; another thing I'm determined to change. We fly in immigration and customs officers to oversee the ship loading and fulfil customs formalities."

"Who is your man there?" asked Doyle.

"Bloke called Mike Kasakov. The locals call him 'giaman grass' because he has a wig. A bad-fitting one at that—it looks like a dead squirrel on his head. He's just treading water until retirement. He has a couple of local constables, not regular police but two local fellows who help keep the peace. Most of that is slinging drunks into the cells for a few hours.

"I'll have to radio Lihir management to expect government personnel for the shipment. I'll tell them to expect a couple of employment inspectors. It's not unusual for foreign employers to be inspected now and again to make sure the buggers are compliant with territory labor laws. Come to think of it; I don't think Lihir Gold have ever been inspected, at least not while I've been the PA," said Gardiner.

"When does the flight leave?" asked Doyle.

"Day after tomorrow—that should give Nellie, May, and Joe a head start on the *Totonga*, if you leave today.

"May, Nellie, Joe, you okay with this?" asked Doyle.

"Yes, Mr. Doyle, we'll tell Rurusan to leave today. Nellie will go down to the vessel to see Rurusan. Me and Joe will go to New Ireland Trading to buy supplies. We've plenty of guns but nothing to eat, and I'm not foraging in the forest," said May.

"Frank, can we commandeer your car and Belinda to shuffle folks about today? I don't want anyone getting hurt carrying heavy loads or getting too hot in the sun," Doyle said.

"Sure, glad to help. Why don't the three of you take off now and start your errands? I want to talk to Mick some more."

"Alex, go with Nellie, Joe, and May. It will give you a chance to see Kavieng. It's one of the most famous towns in the South Pacific. Errol Flynn lived in and around here, so did Queen Emma, the plantation queen."

Alex's eyes opened in surprise, but Doyle could see she had mixed feelings about leaving. Nellie made her mind up for her, taking her hand and saying, "Kam, mipela showim you Kavieng. Maski sit bik mornin talk olsem lapun."[46]

"Bloody nice-looking girl that Alex, so's May. I know Mussaus tend to be photogenic, but she's got the height and the straight hair too. They both could be doing fashion plates," Gardiner said after everyone but Doyle left.

"Yeah, they are nice, but you don't fish off the company pier, and especially not in the middle of an operation. Besides which, Alex is on the rebound from a broken engagement, so she's strictly verboten."

Gardiner laughed and said, "If China is helping the Germans, it makes sense militarily. Germany's got a tiny army, only a coastal navy and a few military transport airplanes. If they developed nuclear

---

[46] "Come, we'll show you Kavieng. Never mind sitting about all morning talking like old men."

bombs, then the whole game changes. Even here in the back of Woop Woop, we're not totally cut off from news."

"The last thing Europe or the empire needs is a militarily resurgent Germany," said Doyle.

"The China connection is still speculative," said Gardiner.

"We have the physical evidence of Chan, and that ties her back to Lihir. The unknown Chinese I helped capture spoke pidgin when in delirious fugues and what may be ples-tok. The shrinks said that this would happen if she was reliving childhood memories. Learning the language later in life would not evince such behavior. Also, we have a man matching Chan's partner going aboard a steamer in Batavia and listed as a mining engineer; he exited the vessel in Port Moresby. Besides, a gold mine is a great place to hide atom bombs; from what I've read, it's better than lead for shielding radiation."

"How much time is left until the deadline to respond and deliver the ransom?" asked Gardiner.

"Not that long, the original demand was sixty days, and that's getting on for a month or so. I'll check with Alex; she'll know exactly. The instructions will likely be last minute, but give time for transport. My guess is the Raptor mob will want it dropped on an uninhabited oceanic island. My other guess is that the pickup will be by a submarine. We know the Chinese have submarines; they've been building up their navy with new vessels, including subs, and are building an aircraft carrier," said Doyle.

"What's really in it for the Chinese, creating this ruckus? They don't need the money, so I'm guessing is about reinforcing their position in East Asia. We've got thousands of Chinese in New Guinea, probably a lot over the border in Dutch New Guinea. There's been Chinese here since the mid-nineteenth century, but most of them here now came relatively recently."

"I think you're right. They're keen to reassert themselves in what they see as their rightful sphere of influence, since they threw out the Japanese occupiers. The real power in China stems from the imperial bureaucracy and the prime minister. The current PM is Mao Xinyu, who is from a very powerful family in China. He has strong connections to the military, which he's reinforced by throwing money at them."

"I thought you were an ISS occasional. Where did you learn all this about China? I thought India was where you were most at home," said Gardiner.

"Most of it you can read in the papers. Plus I've always been on a leash from the ISS, so I tend to know the resident spooks wherever I am and have a beer or two with them and catch up on what's making London nervous," said Doyle.

"If you all get in place, what then?"

"We'll send as much intelligence to the ISS before Lihir is invaded. I suspect imperial special forces units are converging somewhere in Australia. There are probably a couple of imperial aircraft carrier groups steaming this way. Alex and I will try and find the bombs."

"Make sure you check the freighter. They could ship one or all bombs off the island with the gold. Didn't you say gold is as effective as lead in shielding radiation?" Gardiner asked.

"Yeah, I'd thought of that. There'll be hell to pay if there's a full-scale assault and all we end up with is a bunch of aggrieved German miners. The ISS will be a laughing stock; Sir Anthony would have to resign; and Alex, if she isn't sacked, would end up with the deadbeats at a place called Cambridge Circus," said Doyle.

"What about the local crew?" asked Gardiner.

"Christ, May would be let go at a minimum. Nellie and Joe might end up in jail, so might May. Do me a favor: if everything goes belly-up, please can you do your best for Nellie, May, and Joe, even if it's as little as having them transferred to the local jail."

"What about you?"

"I'll survive—plenty of legal thuggery out there. But I doubt I'll ever be allowed to return to Britain, not even Ireland," said Doyle.

"Well, let's hope and pray for the best. You know how we Aussies are: hate the Poms most of the time, especially at cricket, but first to put our hands up when the mother country calls," said Gardiner.

"Thanks, Frank. God I hope everything goes as planned or we can improvise our way out of the way before shit hits the fan. Anyway, I thought it was the Kiwis who had a special place in Aussie hearts?"

"Oh, yeah the South Pacific Poms—they do have a way with them that ruffles our feathers. Still, I'll do what I can to make sure I help. I'll have New Ireland Provincial Government ID cards made for you and Miss McCall. Thankfully, we've got a Polaroid camera that's still working; everything falls apart in this bloody heat and humidity. Come by tomorrow, and I'll also have your tickets for the flight. We'll charter a plane from Territory Airlines."

"Do you know how many expatriate staff there at the mine?"

Gardiner consulted a folder he had brought with him to the briefing. "There's the director, Gustave Jäger, and under him he has a staff, including an assistant manager, secretaries, ten engineers, a personnel officer, and an assistant. There's a laboratory with a chief scientist and a staff of five other scientists and a couple of metallurgists. There's a small hospital with several doctors and nurses and a mess with a chef and five other cooks. Besides what I'd call civilian staff, there's a chief of security, who has thirty men under his control."

"Christ, that's a bloody army! No one objected to this?"

"There are compelling reasons for a lot of security. When the mine is ready to ship bullion, there's millions of dollars of gold. It's a tempting target. A well-organized, armed raiding party could come ashore, guns blazing, and commandeer a bullion ship or steal the gold directly. We're only a stone's throw from Indonesia and the Philippines, which have some notorious pirate lairs in the ungoverned parts of the country."

"Yeah, okay, but our little group is going up against a platoon-strength squad, who are all armed, not mention about forty other expatriate staff. Are they all German?"

Gardiner shuffled in his chair and looked uncomfortable.

"Yeah, I believe so, German or German-speaking people from Australia and New Zealand. The working visas are issued by the customs and immigration service in Moresby, so we don't know much about them other than what I've told you. Here, take these files. I copied them for you. I don't think they'll add much more to what you know and what we've talked about today."

"What aren't you telling me?" Doyle asked.

"There's been a suspicion for some time that palms are being greased to look the other way from Lihir mining, both Australian and local New Guinea civil servants and politicians."

"Great, now I'm even more buoyed up with enthusiasm."

Chapter 39

Doyle let Gardiner get on with administering to New Ireland and hung out in the library until Belinda returned to give him a lift home. He reckoned he could have walked the mile or so, but it was blisteringly hot with no breeze, and it was not Mussau, where he could just cool off in the sea. He half expected the library to be a dark, moldy collection of books and magazines and old government papers. He was pleasantly surprised to find a light, airy room of tidy shelves, overseen by a small, neat, young native woman.

"Hello, I'm Mick Doyle. Can I look around?"

"Help yourself. I'm Mary Asua."

"Where are you from?"

"Central Province, Tubusereia. It's a sea village, like Hanuabada. It's across from Bootless Bay."

"What brings you up here, to New Ireland?"

"A job, and it's nice here—better than some freezing highland town and being stared at by chimpanzees."

"Ha, Mary, that's not very appropriate."

"I don't care. My sister was raped by highlanders in Moresby, and she was lucky to survive. It took a long time to care for her and help her get her confidence back. Luckily, we have family in Cairns, who took her in and found work for her. She's still a bit nervous around black fellows, but she's okay."

"Did she see a psychiatrist?" Doyle asked.

"Yes, but family care was really important. I took six months off work from the library at the university in Moresby to care for her. She'll probably never marry, and her bride price would be next to nothing," Mary said.

"God, Mary, I didn't mean to stir up bad memories."

"It's okay, and you didn't. What are you doing here?"

"I'm on a mission for the government; that's all I can tell you."

"Like a policeman?"

"Something like that."

"I saw you come in with some Mussaus and a pretty white lady."

"How did you know they were Mussaus?" Doyle asked.

"Lots of people in New Guinea have distinctive features. You can't always explain why, you just know," Mary said.

"Do you have anything about Lihir?"

"Yes, lots of government reports, some anthropological theses, and a couple of books."

"Anything like a synopsis I could read?"

"Here's a guide to New Ireland for public servants. There's a section on Lihir. That's the best I can do, unless you just want a general overview."

"Thanks. Is it okay if I read it here?"

"It's what the library is for; help yourself."

Doyle read the paragraphs on Lihir, which were dry and prosaic, including geography, climate, population, traditions, and of course the mine, which was the largest open-cast mine in the world. Doyle shuddered when he thought about the South African gold mines where men labored over twelve thousand feet underground. At least in Lihir you could see the sun.

What would happen to the mine, Doyle thought, *if there was a Sino-German plot with the stolen atom bombs? We might save the empire, but we can't shut the mine down, throw thousands out of work, cut off the lucrative taxes, which allow the province a high degree of autonomy.*

Doyle's first task was to locate the bombs and ensure they could not be detonated and that nuclear material did not pose a danger to the environment. Doyle thought about the opposition. If all went according to plan, he and Alex would confirm the bombs were within the Lihir mine complex. He would then contact Nellie and May, via Joe, who would join the Mussaus employed by the mine. He would confirm the find to Joe, who would slip into the jungle and have Nellie and May send a radio message to coastwatcher HQ in Moresby and on to the ISS, which he assumed would trigger the command for an all-out raid on Lihir. *God*, he thought, *should "ifs" and "ands" be pots and pans, then what a tinker I would make.*

Doyle looked out of the window, its view out onto Kavieng Harbor. It was a glorious view. The harbor was oriented on a north–south axis, bounded by mainland New Ireland on the east and coral islands on the west. Doyle had a good view of the gap between Nusalik and Nago. The harbor water was calm, but massive rollers crashed on to the fringing reefs of Nago and Nusalik. The breakers came through the Nago Channel and dissipated in the harbor. Doyle mused on the idyllic view, thinking people paid big money to visit places like this.

The Caribbean was already spoiled. Its proximity to the Confederated States and Canada meant that hoteliers and tour operators were taking advantage of plentiful cheap flights and package tours to bring more and more tourists to Bermuda, the Bahamas, and Jamaica. Even islands further afield, like the lesser Antilles and Trinidad, were increasingly affordable.

In Europe, sunseekers were crowding the beaches of Spain, southern France, Italy, and Greece. North Africa, once a destination for aesthetes, artists, and homosexuals was now on the tourist trail. Egypt was a tourist destination for two centuries, and East Africa was experiencing more safari traffic, even for people who were not interested in bagging big game but just photographing them.

Maybe a few judicious atom bombs might make the Earth a better place, thought Doyle. *Clean up horrible tourist resorts with their cheap, ugly hotels, trinket shops, and lobster pink northern Europeans overeating and drinking too much cheap booze.* Favorite haunts that Doyle knew from his army days and subsequent skullduggery were descending into gewgaw-ridden kitsch nightmares.

His mood darkened further. *What are we saving the world for?* he asked himself. He did not want to contemplate Nellie, May, Alex, or Joe bleeding to death, half their faces blow away or their guts spilling out into the red tropical earth. *If the bastards have gotten the five bombs, our bloody fault for making them in the first place and then losing them. Why should the people I've grown close to have to risk their lives for countless others they don't know?*

Why haven't special forces just gone in boots and all to Lihir? So what if it is a fiasco; it's what they are paid to do. Yeah there would be a big song and dance, the Germans would be up in arms, but so what. They are always complaining about something. They lost three wars with the British Empire in the twentieth century and are lucky that London kept France on a leash when the peace terms were dictated, thought Doyle.

He cursed himself for letting people get too close to him. Now the damage was done, and he was compromised, and as he saw it, less effective. He closed his eyes again and tried to drive out images of Alex's pretty face scarred or mashed up by heavy caliber bullets. Joe had seen active service, putting down local rebellions in the Solomon Islands and the New Hebrides, but Auntie Nellie wasn't a soldier, just

Paul Dalzell

a tough nut. So was May, who had experienced serious fieldwork and getting her hands dirty. But this was going to be bigger than anything she had encountered in the past. The images of their faces played through his mind. He felt stupid for letting his mind relax and wander. He needed to be doing something, anything to unclutter his mind.

"Fuck it!" said Doyle.

"What?" said Mary with astonishment.

"Oh, hell, sorry, I do apologize, Mary. Things have been a bit rough of late. I was just brooding about them."

"Don't worry. I've heard worse when its pay night and the drunks fall out of the local bars. I live in a woman's hostel in town, and we have to fend off drunken men. Luckily the doors have strong locks, and there are iron bars on the windows."

Doyle smiled, liking Mary, so typical of many people in New Guinea: warm, open, and capable.

"You've come across betel nut on your travels?" said Mary.

"Yes, though not used as much as here, well not as messily."

"I don't chew myself. Our church discourages it. However, it's a problem with drunks. They don't fall down and sleep; they just keep going. Can you imagine energetic drunks? It's a big problem in New Guinea. In the new Hebrides and Fiji, people drink kava, so they fall over when they combine it with alcohol."

"I assume, like most places in the empire, that alcohol sales to natives are restricted."

"Yes, it used to be banned, but people made their own home brews from bananas and coconut toddy. Worse was the people drinking methylated spirits. All the men and many of the women in a village in the Highlands went blind on a meth binge. Someone stole several barrels of methylated spirits from a store compound, which they drank over a weekend. Apart from blindness, there were deaths and insanity. News got around about free alcohol, so other villages came, and no one stopped them; they were all too drunk. The churches were the driving force for the native sales ban, but it was the lesser of two evils: let people buy safe alcohol or risk more catastrophes—no choice really."

"Forgive me for asking, but the men who raped your sister—"

"It's all right, but yes, drunk out of their minds and high on betel nut. After their trial, they and their village had to pay a huge compensation to my family. One of the men committed suicide with weed killer; it took a week for him to die. 'Vengeance is mine,' says the Lord. Still, I felt no pity for him, and I wished they had all done the same." Mary broke off and turned away, wiping her eyes with a handkerchief.

Jesus Christ, thought Doyle, *I am worse than bloody Jonah.*

There was a knock at the door. Joe stood there with a broad smile. He waved a greeting to Mary, and said, "Mr. Doyle, sir, we've come to take you back to the compound."

Chapter 40

Belinda drove the five of them back to the mess in the government compound. The morning heat was building, but the house caught the breeze, and with the overhead fan, it felt comfortable. They sat around the dining table, updating the mission plans, with a map of Lihir on the tabletop.

May told Doyle that boxes of food had been dropped down to the *Totonga*, both for the crew and for the Lihir scouting party. The vessel had also been refueled and additional diesel fuel loaded in forty-four gallon drums.

"Belinda's going to come for us this afternoon, along with the truck. We'll take the weapons we need and some empty boxes to store our supplies," said May. "If we leave this afternoon, we should be at Lihir tomorrow midafternoon. It's about two hundred miles. If we make good time, and it's still light, we can hang off the coast until it gets dark."

"You'll have most of the weapons and explosives. We'll have to go in with just handguns," said Doyle. "I've got my Browning and shoulder harness rig. That's thirty rounds, but I'll have to wear my tropical linen jacket, otherwise it's going to seem bloody odd for a labor officer to be so well tooled up."

"I'll take a Smith and Wesson, which I can put in my purse. I'll also wear the thigh holster with a Beretta. It's only six rounds but better than nothing," said Alex.

"Joe, I need you to plant explosives around the mine—not to kill people but as a distraction, especially if we get captured."

"Yes sir," said Joe. "I can make a lot of small bombs with the plastic explosive. I went through the explosives equipment. There are a bunch of radio detonators there, very sophisticated. I've not seen stuff like that before. The detonator control has twenty separate channels, but I can double up the bombs so I can set forty or so, firing off two at a time."

"How's your marksmanship?" asked Doyle.

"Pistol, machine gun, rifle, I've used them all. I qualified as a sniper scout in training."

"Great, you've seen what we've got in the boxes. I like the silenced Stens, but they're useful only up to about one hundred yards. The assault rifles have a better range and more punching power. You've heard about the croc attack?"

"Yes, Stens and pistols would not do much to a full-grown puk puk[47]. They've got boney plates in their hide."

"I'm also going to bring my Mauser nine millimeter," Doyle said.

"Won't you need a trailer for that antique?" asked Alex.

"Don't start. I've heard all the jibes before. All I know is it's gotten me out of more scrapes that I can count. I have a Chinese model that has twenty and thirty round magazines and full automatic fire. That's a lot of fire power with a couple of spare magazines."

"You can't fire it on full auto. It just sprays everything like a watering can," said Alex.

"Ah, but the trick is to turn it sideways, so it spraying horizontally. It can do a lot of damage."

---

[47] Crocodile.

"What did you do this morning after we'd gone?" May asked Doyle.

"I talked a bit more with Frank Gardiner and then spent time in the library. The librarian's a nice lady from near Bootless Bay in Central Province. Didn't find much more about Lihir."

May said, "I've met the librarian. Her sister was horribly gang raped in Moresby. It was in the papers. It caused a huge uproar. People marched on the National Assembly, demanded the death penalty and castration."

"Yeah, her sister lives in Cairns now. Mary, that's the librarian, said her sister had no prospects for marriage, said she'd not get a decent bride price."

"What's a bride price?" asked Alex.

"A reverse dowry," said May. "If someone wants to marry me, they'd have to offer my family a decent bride price. In some places its cash and traditional items, like shell money and bird-of-paradise plumes. But I'd marry you for nothing, Mr. Doyle." May batted her eyelids seductively.

Alex looked shocked and shot a malicious glance at May.

Doyle, Nellie, and Joe laughed. Doyle said, "And this is why you don't fish off the company pier, especially in the middle of an operation."

Nellie took Alex's hand and said, "No ken wori, yungpela missis. May emi making stori tasol. Kam, yumi go mekim kai kai."[48]

Alex was mollified by Nellie but still turned back to give a pouting glance at Doyle.

"Good job. We're going to split up I think. Thank you, May!"

---

[48] "Don't worry, young Miss. May is just playing games. Come, we'll go and cook food."

"You're welcome. So do we have all the wrinkles sorted out?"

"When you've set up a camp on Lihir, make sure you've got the radio up and functioning. Put up an aerial, and just listen to radio traffic. We'll assume that if the radio can receive, it will also transmit, but we'd better not risk trying it out. Joe, you get into the mine and find the Mussau workers. There'll be a bossboi,[49] so let him know what's going on. We are probably going to need their help when the shit hits the fan. They should at least know of Auntie Nellie, so hopefully that will carry some weight."

"You'll arrive sometime in the morning of the day after tomorrow?" May asked.

"Yes, I haven't got our tickets yet so I can't give an exact time. We'll do the rounds of the mine, as good public servants, and see if we can get a reading on our Geiger counters. Thankfully the ISS boffins have reduced these to the size of a pack of playing cards, so we won't look so obvious. In the nighttime, we'll check out anywhere we've not looked or been steered away from," Doyle said. "If we find the bombs, we'll need to get a message to you and Nellie to call in the cavalry. It's going to be tricky. I can't just run down to the native workers' quarters in the middle of the night, so, Joe, we should aim for a rendezvous, say before dawn."

"Yes, sir, once I've found the Mussau workers, I'll try and persuade them to lay the explosive charges."

"Yes, that might be challenging. If this goes according to plan, the mine is going to be closed for a while, the prospect of which might not get a great reception from the Mussaus or the other mine workers," Doyle said.

"Just be honest with them," said May. "If they know that these

---

[49] Native overseer.

are bad men and that Auntie Nellie is fighting with us, that might be enough. You can mention me, but I'm young and spent most of my life away from Mussau, so I don't think they'll know who I am. You should ask Auntie Nellie to pray for the success of the mission, if she isn't already doing so."

"Really?" said Doyle.

"Yes, she's quite well known in southern Mussau as a person who will offer prayers on your behalf. It can't hurt, can it?" asked May.

Chapter 41

Belinda picked up the little party at around 3:00 p.m., driving Gardiner's car, which was followed by the provincial government truck. The luggage for May, Joe, and Nellie was loaded, along with the patrol boxes of equipment. Rurusan smiled, looking big and confident in his brown sailcloth sarong held up with a large brown leather belt under his belly.

"See you in a couple of days," said Doyle, feeling his throat constrict. Joe shook his hand and gave him a big smile, while May and Nellie hugged him and Alex. Ropes were cast off, the *Totonga's* engine revved up, and the prow facing south swung around to the north and the vessel maneuvered to the middle of the Nusa Channel. It motored through the North Channel, past Cape Nuan, and slowly around the North Cape. The vessel was now under the influence of the great Pacific Ocean rollers and bobbed side to side, settling into the voyage.

Belinda had remained by the car, and Doyle and Alex rejoined her as the truck lumbered off to the provincial government compound.

"God, I could do with a drink," said Doyle.

"I can drop you at the club if you like. You get five visits before they ask for membership."

"I heard it wasn't open to natives," said Alex.

"Technically, no, but it wouldn't survive without local custom, so the movie nights and dances are open to all. I sometimes go in with Frank after work for a drink. He signs me in."

Doyle turned to look at Belinda, who was a very good-looking New Ireland girl, possibly from Lavongai, given the velvet dark chocolate–colored skin.

"That doesn't, um, create a bit of tension with Mrs. Frank?" Doyle said.

Belinda laughed and said, "Well it might, except Mrs. Gardiner is the club president and one of my best friends. We play golf together."

They drove into the club carpark. Along one side of the compound was a row of club bedrooms. Next to this, though not physically connected, was a concrete structure with open sides, in which was a full-sized billiards table. The club proper was reached by a set of steps from the carpark. Immediately before this was a noticeboard listing prospective memberships, club events, and people banned for infractions of the rules, which meant starting fights, being hopelessly drunk, or not settling bar bills.

Sprawled across the board was a foot-long insect. Alex looked at it in consternation and said, "Is it real?"

Doyle touched the insect, and it instantly curled its tail over its back like a scorpion. Alex jumped back, and Belinda laughed.

Doyle said, "It's a giant phasmid, a relative of the stick insect. That tail reflex looks dangerous, but it is utterly harmless. I have an uncle who is a naturalist and collects beasts from this part of the world. He used to breed these things in his hothouse in Bantry."

They went up the steps and approached the bar, over which was a sign saying, "Keep your hat on and it's your shout." Gathered there were a collection of mostly men, probably plantation managers and civil servants, nursing their drinks. Below them to their left was the billiard room, where there were the occasional clicks of the ivory balls. Most of the men looked up and ran their eyes over the newcomers. Most eyes lingered on Alex.

"Who's the new Sheila?" said one of the barflies.

"Enough of that," said a tall, buxom, blonde-haired woman, who had stepped into this part of the bar from the next-door lounge. The bar drinkers looked chastened and returned to cursory chatting or staring at their drinks.

"Hello, Belinda, who are your new friends?" said the woman.

"Hello, Charlene, this is Mick Doyle and his colleague, Alex McCall."

"Doyle, eh, another bloody Irishman, and you Miss McCall, Scottish, I suppose," said Charlene with disapproval.

"Mrs. Gardiner, I presume," said Doyle.

"You presume correct. Are you the folks keeping my husband busy at the moment?"

"Guilty as charged," said Doyle, though he winced inside at being exposed in public.

Charlene's attitude softened, and she said, "Let me get you a drink. What'll you have?"

They gave their drink orders.

"Come on into the lounge. This place looks like an old folks' home with these old soaks," said Charlene. In the lounge there was a couple no younger than those at the bar, but whose complexions were a muddy green color under the fluorescent lights.

"Don't mind the Browns. We call them the green people. Their skin looks all right in daylight, but they go this weird green color under the fluorescents. It's what happens after you've taken antimalarial pills all your life. Most of us stop taking them; we become immune, like the locals. The Browns though live on Djaul, which has a ton of mossies and very bad malaria."

The couple waved a hand at Charlene and then went back to sitting in companionable silence. Charlene led them to a coffee table with four armchairs. Doyle looked around; it could be any club anywhere in the confines of the empire, especially the tropics. Bigger clubs had reading rooms with airmail editions of the English papers and monthly magazines, others had sporting facilities, but all had a bar and a lounge like this, and uniformed local club staff. Charlene was the club president and somewhere there would be a manager, but his or her power would flow from Charlene.

Doyle liked her, a no-nonsense Australian, probably from Queensland or the Northern Territory. Her skin was pale but not alabaster white like Alex. Her eyes were a vivid blue, and though she was carrying some middle-age weight, she still had a good figure surmounted by an impressive décolletage.

"You're a bit of a looker, Miss Alex. What are you doing out here in the back of beyond with this unsavory looking character?" She nodded at Doyle.

"Er … I'm with the high commission. I'm accompanying Mr. Doyle on an inspection of the Lihir goldmine and its labor conditions."

"Hmm, you don't look like the typical civil servant the mother country sends out here."

"Well, you have start somewhere. I wanted to travel, so I applied for a high commission post and was accepted," said Alex, trying to sound unruffled.

"And you Mr. Doyle—"

"Please, Mick."

"Very well, Mick, you look like labor conditions are the last thing you'd be inspecting."

"It's just a job. I'm not with the government full time, and I do a lot of freelance work in labor relations. I'm contracted to look at the mining industry in British New Guinea. I did a lot of work in the petroleum industry in other places, like Burma. It's very similar, labor intensive, dangerous, dirty, large reliance on native labor, which has a high turnover, and not always harmonious relationships with employers."

This seemed to put Charlene off the scent, or at least blunt her inquisitiveness. *Just being a bloody woman,* thought Doyle. Though she was right: Alex looked too good to be swanning about in the outer edge of a remote imperial territory.

Drinks were brought. Doyle reached for his wallet, but Charlene waved him off, saying, "Let me get these. Tommy, put this on the president's account. Perk of the job—I get drinks at cost."

"Are you from here, Charlene?" asked Alex.

"No, I'm originally from far north Queensland, outside of Cairns, in the Atherton Tablelands, little hamlet called Tolga."

Doyle mentally awarded himself a point for guessing right about Charlene.

"Frank's folks are actually from here in New Ireland. They moved to New Guinea from India. They came gold prospecting initially, and when that didn't work out, they got into plantation management. Frank's great grandmother is reputed to have had a fling with Errol Flynn. Not sure that's true, but he was a regular at the club here and was a real larrikin."

"Oh, we know all about Errol Flynn, Charlene. My pupu, my granny, said that as a little girl she was warned to keep clear of him when he ran the Lavongai plantations near my village, Narimlaua. Apparently, he had a reputation for liking young girls, very young girls."

"Dirty bugger, he'd end up in the kalabus[50], now," said Charlene.

---

[50] Jail.

Alex looked both shocked and disgusted.

"There's a lot of blokes come here thinking this is like the Deep South in the nineteenth century," said Charlene. "There was a case recently where Frank had to deport a plantation manager on Lemus Island. He was sleeping with underage girls on the islands and boasting about it right here. He hurt one of the girls, and her sister had a policeman boyfriend. She swore out a complaint against him. Frank talked with the magistrate and worked out a deal, a year in Brisbane jail and a banning order preventing him from setting foot in New Guinea."

"That was remarkably lenient," said Doyle.

"Not really—in Brisbane he'll be locked up as sex offender, even if only for a year. His criminal record will never be wiped clean. He'll end up in places nobody wants to go in the backend of nowhere, drinking himself into an early grave."

"Serves him right," said Alex.

"I see we're all getting along then?" said Frank Gardiner, who had strolled into the club and joined them at the bar.

"Here, Mr. Gardiner, take my chair. I have to go home," said Belinda.

"I can drop you home and then come back here," said Gardiner.

"No, it's evening. There's plenty of PMVs, and I want to go to the Kop Kop market and store. I'll see you tomorrow morning. Thanks for the drink, Charlene. See you tomorrow afternoon at the golf club."

Belinda strode away behind Doyle and out onto the sidewalk by the club. Doyle could see the evening traffic was streaming past, including many minibuses, which plied for passengers.

Gardiner said, "See you've met the wife. These folks are going to Lihir the day after tomorrow, with customs and immigration."

"So I gather. We were just talking about Errol Flynn, and I mentioned Tony van der Hoff."

"Oh God! Don't remind me of the creep. Do you remember I told you that Mike Kasakov was the government representative on Lihir? His best mate was van der Hoff. Kasakov's wife runs the Kop Kop store, bloody little goldmine," said Gardiner.

"Why's that?" asked Alex.

"It's on the main road and has a huge hinterland of villages that stretch from Kop Kop to the airstrip. It just sells the basics, but that's enough for a village store. Van der Hoff used to be married to a lady called Maria Kop Kop. I think she was named after the place, but she runs a big local brothel out there."

Alex laughed and said, "Oh my goodness, this place is like a soap opera."

"Just small-town life, dear," said Charlene.

Gardiner said, "I gave a lift to a white girl, who was walking into town on a hot day. She was an innocent little thing attached to the Catholic mission, came from England like yourselves. She used to go out to Kop Kop on weekends to have a cuppa with Maria. I didn't have the heart to tell her that Maria is a brothel madam. I don't know; Jesus loved sinners, so perhaps she knew, but in any case, she was invalided home, had some form of nervous breakdown."

"Happens more than you'd think," said Charlene. "The endless heat, the strangeness of a foreign place, no familiar faces, and home is thousands of miles away. Some folks don't even make it more than a few months. Most at least recognize that they're getting into deep water and go home, but this poor girl tried to shoulder on through her depression and then just lost it."

"Well, this is cheerful," said Gardiner. "Have you two got any dinner plans? How about eating here? They do a reasonable steak.

It's either here or the hotel right now. There was the Malangan Lodge, but that's closed right now; a new owner is renovating the place."

"OK with you, Alex? Sure, let's eat here," said Doyle.

Chapter 42

Dinner lasted an hour, punctuated by chitchat, until it was 11:00 p.m. and time to up the shutters and call it a night. The Gardiners lived in the government compound, so they dropped Alex and Doyle off at their temporary accommodation. Doyle followed Alex up the external wooden, stairs, mesmerized by the beautiful swaying curve of her buttocks. *Too many drinks after a long dry period,* he thought. He had to get a grip. Fun was fun, but this was a prelude to a major operation.

Still, they had a virtual free day tomorrow. There were the plane tickets and photographs to be taken for the government ID cards, and then in the evening, they had the final packing and equipment and weapon checks.

"Fancy a nightcap?" said Doyle, retrieving a bottle of Johnny Walker Black Label from his suitcase. He retrieved ice from the freezer cabinet and poured out two generous measures.

"Did you really stay abstemious on Emananus?" asked Alex.

"Had to. May said not to indulge myself out of respect for her auntie."

"Must have been hard."

"I'd been juiced up on morphine for a couple of weeks, so actually, it was quite nice to be compos mentis for a change. Besides, Nellie worked me half to death each day, so I was grateful to collapse into bed each evening."

"What'll you do when all this is over?" Alex asked.

"Dunno to be honest. I hate to admit it, but I'm not getting any younger. There's old soldiers and bold soldiers but no old, bold soldiers," Doyle said.

"That's a bit bleak."

"Truthful though—plus do I want to be cracking skulls and creating orphans forever?"

"Now you're being feral again." Alex drained her glass. "Fancy one more?"

"You must have a hollow leg. Sure, I'll have another, but then definitely bed."

Alex poured them each another large scotch on the rocks and settled back on her seat, folding her legs underneath her.

"How do women sit like that? Do you have to be double jointed?"

Alex laughed and then said, "Tell me more about Auntie Nellie. Is it true she's not married … never married?"

"Yes, though I think she's not a pious virgin, but you'd have to ask May about that. She's sharp as a tack, conscientious, and tough, and she has natural leadership qualities. I could mount a very effective guerrilla campaign with her and a few like her."

"Hmm, sound like she's found a little place in your heart."

"Don't be cheeky, à colleen. I'm match fit because of her hard work. Anyway, Miss Pilgrim has already made her intentions known."

"Oooh, beast," said Alex, who stuck her tongue out at Doyle.

Doyle just smiled, enjoying the scotch.

"Are New Guinea women always so … brazen?"

"Brazen, who the hell do you think you are, John Bunyan?"

"Well, you know what I mean," Alex said.

"I think you'll find that island women across the Pacific aren't shy about making their feelings known to blokes they like. It's not

England, with its more restrained mating conventions, like all the fan waving and eye contact in Jane Austen novels. Anyway, all this scotch has gone to my head—bedtime. You can have first dibs on the bathroom," Doyle said.

Fifteen minutes later, Doyle checked the locks on the doors and windows and retired, shoving his Browning under his pillow. He lay in the dark, listening to the night sounds for anything untoward. They were too far inland to get more than a muffled wump from the surf. Crickets made their high-pitched calls, while flying foxes flapped and yelped, fighting over ripe custard apples in a tree close to the house.

The town was nosier than Emananus. Drunks weaved their way home, singing, while dogs yelped and barked, some howling like wolves. There were chickens in nearby yards, which were sleeping, but the occasional cock sounded off, staking out his territory. The air was full of little clicks from geckos, sometimes scampering over the mosquito wire. Fights would break out, with the loser landing on the polished wooden floor with a wet slap. The quiet night air carried the sounds of couples fighting, probably wives berating drunken men who had pissed away the housekeeping on beer. Babies cried and mewled, and little children cried out in the night. Doyle slipped away into sleep.

His eyes flew open, and his hand reached for his gun. Someone had come into his room. Outside the rain was pounding down, and there were livid flashes of lightening and great crashes of thunder. A lightening flash lit Doyle's room in an eerie blue color to reveal Alex standing there.

"Alex, what the hell … I could have shot you."

"Sorry, the storm woke me. I was having a bad dream and was afraid. I didn't know where I was … I didn't want to be alone."

Doyle sighed and said, "Sit on the bed, and get your breath back.

It's blowing a good one out there. Do you want a nip of scotch to help you go back to sleep?"

"Can't I stay with you?" Alex asked.

Doyle was going to say no, but he could see she was upset. *Probably a combination of all the recent events,* he thought, *surfacing in a bad dream in a strange land.*

"Here get in."

Doyle moved over to the far side of the bed, against the wall. Alex was wearing a thin cotton nightdress, with only her panties beneath. She slid in and fitted her body into his, like a spoon. Doyle passed his right arm under her right armpit, so her arm would be free, and did the same with his left arm.

His face was pressed into the back of her head and buried in the soft, sweet-smelling hair. He had tried to put his hands neutrally on her body, but they came to rest on her breasts, which were big and firm. He felt himself stiffen, with all this wonderful fragrant womanhood pressed up against him. He was beginning to suggest they sleep, when Alex spun in his arms and kissed him long and languorously on the lips, slipping her tongue in his mouth. At the same time, she reached down and took hold of his penis, which brought him to full tumescence. He ached for this woman. It had been a long time to be celibate, and despite his good intentions, the mission could go hang for the night.

He brought his hands up the insides of her legs, finding her panties, which Alex obligingly slipped off, while pulling off her nightie. Doyle's hand penetrated between her legs, which was deliciously smooth and hairless, and his middle finger stroked the hot wetness as her vaginal lips parted. She moaned and arched her back instinctively. Doyle took a breast in each hand, sucking and nibbling at the nipples in turn. He couldn't come to terms with the size of her breasts, which were not only large but firm and ripe with the elasticity of youth.

216

Doyle maneuvered Alex onto her back and then slid his penis into the wet, welcoming mouth of her vagina. She gasped out aloud when he thrust deep and wrapped her hand around his buttocks, urging him on with cries of wanting. He kissed her neck and gently bit her ear lobes, licking the velvet soft skin behind each ear. Alex now let out a low, wild, and continuous moan, reaching toward a climactic shudder. Doyle could feel the wetness squirting out of her, and his penis seemed enveloped in hot liquid silk.

He continued thrusting into that delicious, sweet wetness, while Alex began a throaty moan again that built to a series of gasps as she orgasmed again, accompanied by vaginal squirts and this time intense waves of contractions that Doyle felt along the shaft of his penis. The vaginal muscles held him in their grip, but he could still move because of all of the fluid Alex had ejaculated.

Doyle wished this would never end. Alex was kissing him with absolute abandon, growling in his ear. He thought by now she would be spent, but she seemed to gather more strength, and he could feel her build again to another shattering orgasm, complete with the vaginal pulsing and fresh ejaculation. Doyle felt his own orgasm building, and in his head he could see could see colors and stars. It felt like his whole groin contracted repeatedly as he shot hot semen into her.

Like runners spent after a marathon, they both collapsed breathing heavily, aware of the heat and sweat cooling on their bodies. Doyle slipped off Alex and drew in great gulps of air. The air was charged with pheromones and the unique musky sex smell. Doyle wondered if their neighbors had been unwilling witnesses to their congress.

"God that was good," was all Doyle could think of to say.

"Yes," said Alex. "Let's do it again."

Chapter 43

They found the strength to repeat another four times. Doyle doubted he would have the stamina or seminal fluid for the last bout, but Alex was relentless and irresistible. Dawn was showing as a dirty smudge when they finally slept.

The heat and light of equatorial morning woke them. Doyle thought Alex might have crept back to her bed, but she was happily wrapped around him, her hair a riotous mess of waves and curls, her marble skin showing the red wheels and marks of Doyle's kissing and love bites.

"Thank you for a pleasant evening, Miss McCall," said Doyle.

"You are most welcome," said Alex. "I suppose we must be getting up. Is Belinda going to pick us up?"

"Christ, yes, eleven o'clock—what time is it?"

"Relax, it's only nine thirty," said Alex.

Doyle surveyed the wreckage of his bed and said, "Come on; we'd better get moving anyway."

Alex was unfazed about being naked, so Doyle let his eyes linger over her body as she bent down to pick up her clothes. When she stood, she faced him, a flame-topped Venus with a beautiful ogival figure. He looked at her magnificent breasts, which despite their size and weight did not sag but were proud and prominent; her legs were slender and long, culminating in her hairless vulva.

"You like what you see?"

"What's not to like? Do you deliberately downplay your boobs?"

"Yes, with old fashioned brassieres designed to flatten not accentuate. I don't want to be known as the redhead with the big tits. I get enough flack as it is about my bum."

"It's a very nice bum."

"Yes, but I'm more than tits and arse, though others in the ISS only see my physical attributes," said Alex.

"And your hairless … pussy?"

"I had a Brazilian wax. One of my girlfriends who'd worked in the tropics said it was good for hygiene, and I'm a redhead, so can get a little … piquant."

"Nice way of putting it."

Doyle looked at the sheets, noticing for the first time there was a smattering of blood on the bottom sheet. He looked quickly at his penis, and then he realized where the blood had come from.

"You were a virgin," Doyle said.

Alex looked both pleased and proud of herself. "Yes, I was, but I'm a maid no more. I can't think of a better man to take my maidenhood."

"You mean you and what's his name—"

"Never consummated our relationship?"

"Er … yes."

"No, another tension between us. We would get all hot and passionate, but he was a traditionalist. He wanted to wait until our wedding night."

"I—" Doyle realized he was at a loss for words.

"So we English girls can be just as forward as these island girls," Alex said.

"Evidently, and clearly you liked the experience."

"It was, was ... I don't know, bloody marvelous. I had my first fuck."

"Not like you to be so crude," Doyle said.

"We use 'work bonk' and 'bonking in the office,' but occasionally we like to say it to shock the middle-class girls."

"What about the working-class girls?" Doyle asked.

Alex laughed and then realized Doyle was serious. "Oh my God, there are no working class girls in the ISS, except those cleaning the offices and making tea."

"Not very egalitarian."

"Lady Jane would never permit it."

"I didn't think her responsibilities ran to personnel management."

"Lady Jane is about as high up in the English aristocracy as it's possible to be other than being a Howard, and she works for a high-caste Brahmin."

"That explains all the pearls and twin sets," Doyle said.

"I believe MI5 has less exacting standards. They recruit from the grammar schools and redbrick universities," said Alex.

"God, no wonder I'm kept at arm's length as an occasional."

"You, an Oxford and Harvard graduate, with connections to gentry, all be it rather bog Irish."

"God bless yer ladyship," said Doyle in his best Irish peasant voice.

Doyle stood, and Alexa flung her arms around his neck to kiss him.

"Your body is so scarred, like a roadmap of violence. It's rather exciting for a girl."

"My God, I think I've created a monster, an upper-class Messalina."

"Typical man—I think I had something to do with it."

"That you did, and it was bloody marvelous, bloody, bloody marvelous. Now I can go into battle a happy man." He kissed her hard on her full lips.

"And I won't die a virgin."

Talk of death and fighting broke the playful air, and both Doyle and Alex showered, breakfasted, and waited for Belinda.

Chapter 44

The day seemed interminable, the lull before battle. Belinda collected Alex and Doyle before lunch. They were photographed and presented with their New Ireland government passes. These described them as employment and labor officers, Malcom Donaldson and Alison Grose. Frank Gardiner gave them an envelope with tickets, saying that Territory Airlines would fly them and the other government personnel to Lihir at 11:00 a.m.

It was usual to arrive after eleven, so the mine could give them lunch. Since they would be staying for a few days, they would stay at the mine hostel and take their meals there or in the mine canteen. Gardiner offhandedly mentioned that the hostel restaurant and mine canteen were first class, with great food cooked by French-trained New Guinea chefs.

Doyle said if they found nothing, they would return with the customs and immigration staff. However, if they did find evidence of the atom bombs, Gardiner's world would turn upside down as imperial troops descended on Lihir. Doyle and Alex would retreat into the bush and link up with Nellie, Joe, and May to get the word out and then take cover as the empire forces invaded.

Doyle said, "Any communication from us will come via the coastwatcher network from Moresby. You might hear Nellie's transmission, but it will all be in code. If someone gets in touch directly, it will be some innocuous message about a deacon. That was the code word used with the coastwatcher network, so we might as well continue to use it. If something happens, you'll get a message with 'deacon' in it."

"What should I do if that happens?" Gardiner asked.

"Get on the phone to the high commission, and tell them to send in the cavalry. They may already be planning that anyway, but they may need to advance their schedule. Five lives might be at stake."

That night Belinda dropped them off at the Kavieng Hotel, where Doyle and Alex dined on spiny lobster, a local delicacy, which was prepared along with juicy river prawns. They walked back to the government compound. Doyle insisted on a rigorous run-through of the mission and stripping firearms and checking ammunition. He poured a nightcap of scotch before they fell into bed for another torrid night, stopping a little earlier than the previous evening to get some sleep.

The following morning Belinda collected Doyle and Alex a little before 10:00 a.m. She made some remarks about the blotches on Alex's skin, saying it looked like mosquitos had bitten her. Doyle stared out of the car to hide his smile. Redheads had such delicate skin.

Kavieng was a modest town by British New Guinea standards, but the airport was large, as the town was a major entry point into northern New Guinea. They joined a small line of passengers at the Territory Airlines check-in. There was a smartly dressed receptionist registering the passengers, weighing their luggage and the passengers.

There were seven passengers, including Alex and Doyle. Two native men were dressed in blue immigration service uniforms, and a native man and woman wore the green outfits of the New Guinea Customs Service. The fifth person, a European, wore civilian clothes.

They all turned to look at Doyle and Alex as they joined the line. Doyle nodded to the other passengers. Alex looked remote, wearing sunglasses, even in the cool airport interior. The European man introduced himself as Chris Hawkins, a government health officer going to conduct an inspection on the crew of the bullion vessel. Doyle feigned interest as his stomach tightened.

After check-in, they were shepherded out to a two-engine plane with seating for twelve passengers. Doyle saw the check-in luggage being stowed by a couple of local men in Territory Airlines overalls. The receptionist walked out to the plane and handed the manifest to the pilot, a European, accompanied by a native copilot. Before they took off, the receptionist climbed aboard and carried out the preflight announcements. Doyle realized that with such a shoestring operation, staff had to fill multiple roles.

One of the two ground staff pulled away the wooden chocks from the wheels, and the propeller engines started one after the other. Doyle looked at Alex, who gave him a smile. He patted her hand and looked at his feet, where their hand luggage was stored. Both had handguns and their Geiger counters in their carry-on bags. The plane taxied to the eastern end of the runway, which was fully sealed, unlike many Pacific Island coral airstrips.

The plane was quickly aloft, flying over the town and out across Kavieng Harbor. Below, the calm sea was turquoise in the shallows, with the coral shimmering in gold. The water became darker blue as the channel deepened, with patches of reef studding the waters. Over Nusa, the plane began a turn, first to the north and then to the east. Doyle could see the New Ireland eastern coast and the unbroken fringing reef stretching to the horizon. The plane passed over a succession of plantations and villages through which ran the Bulominski Highway.

There was an announcement from the pilot, rendered almost unintelligible by the engine noise. Doyle caught the name of the town of Konos. They headed out to sea to cross to Lihir. The flight would take about forty-five minutes, and it was now thirty minutes since departing Kavieng. They were over deep ocean, with the Tabar Islands on the left of the plane. The engines throttled back, and the plane began to descend. Doyle could see only water out of his window and then a coastline appeared, and they began to track across green jungle.

The plane passed over a huge terraced hole in the earth, around which Doyle could see trucks maneuvering. After the hole, the plane tracked along the east coast of Lihir, toward Londolovit. The plane turned east out to the sea and then turned west to line up with the runway. The plane was buffeted by thermals of hot air as it crossed the coast. The pilots revved the engines to gain a measure of stability and control and then committed to a glide path, skimming over treetops.

The wheels touched down with a screech and puff of smoke, and then the propeller pitch reversed. The plane taxied back up the airstrip and then turned right into the airport, a large building with "Welcome to Lihir" emblazoned across the front.

Doyle willed himself to be calm while the flight attendant gave the welcome message as the plane taxied to a stop. The engines were switched off. Ground grew emerged into the noonday sun to fix the chocks and unload the small amount of baggage. As the door of the aircraft opened, the heat blew in like a blast from a hair dryer. The passengers walked down the steps deployed by the aircraft and made their way across the airport apron to the terminal building.

Chapter 45

As they entered the building, a white uniformed guard asked for identification. Doyle noted the man was wearing a sidearm. The ground crew brought in their luggage, which included Alex's suitcase and Doyle's suitcase and leather grip.

The guard who had checked their identification looked at Doyle and said in a thick German accent, "That's quite a lot of luggage for a short visit."

"Is it causing you any discomfort?" said Doyle.

The man looked bewildered by Doyle's response. "What, no," he said with a waver on uncertainty in his voice.

"Then I shouldn't worry about it," said Doyle. "Where's our transport?"

The guard was caught off-balance again but rallied and said, "Ja transport outside. Please follow me."

Alex looked at Doyle with a smile as the other passengers studied Doyle and walked behind the guard.

"That was nicely done, mate," said Hawkins. "These bloody Krauts strut about like they own the place, not just on lease."

"Thanks. I thought the government rep, Mike Kasakov, would be here to meet us," said Doyle.

"Old Giaman Grass[51]—probably been in conference with Captain Morgan this morning. Look out here he comes."

---

[51] Man with a wig.

A stocky man with a huge belly hanging out over his shorts puffed his way to meet the government party. His face was bearded and florid. His hair looked as if he had picked up roadkill and slapped it on his head.

Alex put her hand to her mouth and laughed. Hawkins nudged Doyle, while the four native officers maintained stoic expressions as Kasakov drew near.

"Sorry, sorry, I'm late," he all but bellowed in a voice carrying the fruity aroma of rum. "Here's your transport to the accommodation. We'll drop you there and then take you to the mine administration to begin your work."

Doyle spoke softly to Alex. Let's make these aliases work for us. Just call me sir, and I'll call you 'Ali,' okay?"

"Em nau, masta," said Alex.

A large people carrier was waiting in the air terminal forecourt. Two uniformed local officers, more smartly dressed that Kasakov, were leaning on the carrier.

Kasakov knew the five officials in the party, with the exception of Alex and Doyle. Doyle made the introductions.

"I'm Malcom Donaldson of the Ministry of Labor and Employment, seconded to the New Ireland Province. This is my assistant, Alison Grose, also with the MLE but also on attachment from the University of Wollongong, where she's doing her PhD."

Alex had completely changed her character, protruding her upper teeth and looking all fingers and thumbs, accentuating her voice to sound naïve.

"Hello, Mr. Kasakov, I'm so pleased to meet you. Gosh, it's so hot. I thought Australia was warm but not like this. Golly, I do blab on, sorry."

"No worries, miss. Since it's the first time for a while for a labor inspection, I thought I'd take you to the mining director, Gustave Jäger, and his deputy, Erich Koenig."

The bus was now motoring from the airport. Doyle was glad that Kasakov wasn't driving; this task been delegated to his subordinate. Kasakov took some surreptitious nips from a hip flask and soon had the carrier smelling like a Jamaican rum bar.

"I was surprised just how big the place is. Still, it is the largest open-cast goldmine in the world. Any complaints?" said Doyle.

"What, me? No, I mean it's no secret I'm working out my remaining years and will retire in a year or so. This is not plantation labor with men living in barracks, eating the cheapest food going. People come with families. We have schools. We have supermarkets, a post office, banks, a hospital, a social club. It's better here than Kavieng or Namatanai. The pay's good; my government pay is a bit meager by comparison."

"You sound like a company man," said Doyle. "Could you work for Lihir Gold if you retired?"

"Not for two years," said Kasakov. "Government rules are strict about post-retirement employment."

"But will you end up working for them? You've got your shop to tide you over in the interim," said Doyle.

"You've been busy in a short time."

"Oh, we're very conscientious," said Alex in a gush.

"Fair enough, and yeah, if they offered me a position in a couple of years' time, I might take it. Right now though, I'm going to take the customs, immigration, and health folks where they need to go. They've been here before, so they know what they're doing here. I can't recall when we had a visit by the Department of Labor."

"You haven't had one since the mine reopened after the 1966

war. I think a forty-year gap is reason enough for the government to poke about. What are you up to now, taking us to our appointment?"

"Yes, I'll drop you at the LG hostel. You can check in. I'll drive these guys where they need to be. When I get back, I'll take you over the street to introduce you to Jäger and Koenig."

"It's a hell of a big place, the mine and the gold extraction process," said Doyle.

"There's a scale model of the mine in Jäger's office," said Kasakov. "He can describe the whole process of how the ore is turned into gold."

The LG hostel was a well-appointed hotel in all but name. After being assigned rooms, Doyle changed into his tropical linen suit and slipped on his shoulder holster beneath his jacket. He put the Geiger counter in his briefcase, along with a notebook.

Doyle waited in the foyer for Kasakov, who returned with his wig looking even more askew.

Doyle said, "Mr. Kasakov, would you care to visit the bathroom so your wig is at least halfway straight?"

"What, aww, yeah, thanks—bit of a rush this morning. Thanks for the consideration, and call me Mike."

Alex arrived. She hadn't changed, but Doyle knew she would be carrying weapons in her purse and strapped to her thigh. She was also carrying a clipboard, which was a nice touch.

"Where's Kasakov?" asked Alex.

"Gone to fix that flattened squirrel on his head."

"My God, why does he bother? I bet he bought it through mail order."

"Male vanity, something that rarely troubles me."

Alex punched him lightly and laughed. He was blessed with dark Irish good looks and the blood of Spaniards cast ashore from the ill-fated Armada. He rarely exercised but had a tough, wiry physique, which was now leaner, thanks to Auntie Nellie, and burned brown as a nut, emphasizing his blue eyes.

"I like your giddy schoolgirl, by the way."

"Not much of an act—I was pretty much like that a few years ago. My younger sister still is."

"Where did you go to school?" Doyle asked.

"Roedean and then the sixth form at Charterhouse. I was going to a Swiss finishing school but was recruited by the ISS. They sent me to Cambridge while I trained in my spare time. There's an ISS facility in the town, actually within one of the colleges."

"What did you read?"

"Politics, philosophy, and economics—PPE—and spying on anti-imperialist students and groups for the ISS. They want their pound of flesh, even from a student."

"Did you unmask any conspiracies?"

"Most of the student activists were harmless, but I found a nest of vipers that were advancing anti-Empire sentiments under the guise of communitarianism."

"Oh God, Marxians?"

"Yes, they were all rounded up and locked away in the St. Kilda penal colony."

"Well done. Look out; here's Kasakov."

Chapter 46

Kasakov bumbled up, his wig looking a little neater but not much of an improvement. Doyle guessed that Kasakov had refreshed himself from his hip flask while he was in the bathroom. Doyle felt a wave of disgust. He was putting his life and that of his team on the line to protect bumbling oafs like Kasakov. Why the hell had the New Ireland administration left him in place? Frank Gardiner seemed like a competent individual, but like any bureaucrat, the preferred option in decision-making was the path of least resistance, so Kasakov hung on.

Kasakov led them to the people carrier that was still driven by his staff.

"Peter's helping out Dr. Hawkins," said Kasakov as if he felt the need to explain the absence of his staff member.

"How far is it to the LG headquarters?"

"Not far, you could walk, but it's so hot.

They drove about four hundred yards and pulled up to a large, impressive building on the main road through Londolovit. Over the building's front door was a sign that said" Lihir Gold Mining Company," and underneath in smaller print, it said "Lihir Goldbergwerksgesellschaft."

In the building foyer it was blissfully dry and cool. There was a reception counter with two uniformed men: one European, the other from New Guinea. On one wall was a large aerial photograph of the mine and processing plant. On the other was a directory to the personnel in the building.

Kasakov approached the reception counter and said, "Hello, I have two visitors to see Mr. Jäger, from the New Ireland Government."

The native reception officer said, "Good morning, please can we see your identification, and will you please sign in." He pushed a ledger book toward them, with columns for name, affiliation, location they were staying on Lihir, and a contact phone number.

The European officer said, "If you're staying at the hostel, just put 'hostel' for phone contact. Here, please put on these visitor badges. Mike, you can leave them with me; I'll take them up. Is Mr. Jäger expecting them? He is? Good."

Kasakov turned to go but Doyle spoke. "Mike, I need a government vehicle, doesn't matter if it's a car, truck, or minibus. Please have one sent to the hostel and the keys left at reception. Thanks."

Kasakov blinked and said, "Anything else?"

"Not right now."

Doyle said goodbye, while Alex smiled and waved as the European guard took them to an elevator. He pushed the button, and after about ten seconds, the elevator door opened. Doyle noted that both reception officers carried side arms. They also carried handcuffs and what looked like telescoping batons. *Nice*, thought Doyle, *not designed to put people at ease.*

The elevator reached the top floor and opened onto a large workspace separated by cubicle dividers. Doyle felt his clothes unsticking from his skin in the cool, dry air. All the staff, European and native, were immaculately dressed. The company staff paid Doyle and Alex scant attention; everybody looked busy and occupied. They proceeded into a conference room, at the end of which was a door with two names on it: Gustave Jäger and Erich Koenig.

The reception officer knocked and walked in. Beyond the door was a severe, middle-aged, European woman sitting behind a typewriter. Her nameplate said "Lisle Dorfmann." There was a jacket that matched her skirt hanging off her chair. To the right was a striking native woman with the darkest skin Doyle had ever seen in his travels; her nameplate said "Margaret Richards."

The reception officer, who Doyle guessed from his accent had been recruited from New Zealand, said, "Here's two government folks for Mr. Jäger." Doyle looked at the clock on the wall behind Miss Dorfmann. It was now a little after noon. He looked down at Dorfmann, who was looking at him and Alex with a neutral expression. He looked at her hands folded in front of her and saw no wedding ring. She punched a button on her phone intercom box and said something in German. There was a metallic voice response, and she rose from behind her desk.

"Please follow me." Doyle would have thought the offices would be behind the two secretaries, but there was a small conference room, followed by a kitchen area, and then a small foyer with tables and chairs, where visitors could wait. In this instance, Dorfmann showed them right into Jäger's office.

The office was a big room, with another aerial shot of the mine on the left-hand wall, beneath which was a scale model of the mine and its surroundings. Behind the desk was a man Doyle guessed to be in his fifties. He had severely cropped hair, which was going silver at his temples. He was clean-shaven and deeply tanned. He rose from behind his desk. He wore a check waistcoat, jodhpurs, and riding boots. He caught Doyle and Alex staring at his outfit.

"I like to ride to and from work, Mr. ... Donaldson, and this is your colleague Miss Grose."

"Mr. Jäger, pleased to make your acquaintance," said Alex, sounding as if she had just come off a netball court.

Doyle noticed the man had impressive facial scars on his head and cheeks, and said, "A graduate of Heidelberg, Mr. Jäger?"

"Ah, very observant, Mr. Donaldson. Not often that anyone is familiar with the traditions of the University of Heidelberg or of Schläger fencing.

"Oh, what is that?" asked Alex.

"Another time perhaps," said Jäger. "I'm sure, like me, you are busy people. I understand that you are here to conduct a review of our employment practices?"

"Yes, I'm sure it's a wonderful place to work. Mr. Kasakov was assuring us on the run in from the airport. However, an onsite inspection hasn't been conducted since your company was granted the concession to keep mining after 1966. Being good bureaucrats, we felt we should at least take a look and tick a few boxes."

"You English are so droll," said Jäger, letting out a quick laugh. "Do you mind if I ask my colleague to join us?"

"Please go ahead."

Jäger punched an intercom button and spoke a few words of German. A connecting door from the next office opened, and a tall, slender man joined them. Doyle saw he was younger than Jäger. He was very tall, with a boyish face and intense blue eyes. Doyle thought the lack of any suggestion of a smile and his height made him especially sinister. Despite the German name, he wondered if Koenig might be of Russian ancestry, maybe a descendent of Germans who went east when Catherine the Great was on the Russian throne.

"This is Erich Koenig. May I introduce Miss Alison Grose and Mr. Malcolm Donaldson. They are here to make sure we are not making the natives work too hard. Erich is our chief mining engineer, as well as deputy director of the mine."

Jäger had maintained an air of bonhomie, but Koenig preserved his glacial manner. "Pleased to meet you and to be of service. Has Gustave explained to you our mining operation?

"I was going to call on you to do that, Erich," said Jäger.

"Indeed, please if you would take a look at our scale model and photograph over by the wall. I can explain the operation and also answer any questions. The process of mining is straightforward: We blast the ore out of the ground. The ore is taken out of the mine by our trucks, which run twenty-four hours a day, carrying about 140 tons per load.

"The mined rock is taken by conveyor to a stockpile, from where it goes through a series of grinding circuits. The ore is then added to pre-oxidation tanks and through to the autoclaves. We use cyanide to extract the gold from solution and absorb it onto activated carbon, essentially charcoal. This we smelt to extract the gold and cast it into bars."

Jäger turned to his desk and walked back. "This is the first gold block we produced after 1966," he said.

"It's not like how I imagined a gold ingot," said Alex.

"I know the type you mean, pretty but not functional. These are simple, rectangular blocks, easy to stack," said Jäger.

"How often do the bullion ships come to take the gold? What about security in these pirate-infested seas?" asked Doyle.

Koenig answered, "At the moment we have a bullion ship come every two months for the gold, and we aim to increase this to a monthly shipment. We do not advertise the bullion vessels, and the ship's voyage is kept secret. The crew includes a permanent detachment of our armed security guards. Pirate ships in this part of the world are usually motorized canoes or dinghies operating from a mothership. They are used to soft targets. Our vessels blow them out of the water. If it's convenient for us, we'll blow up the mothership; otherwise we pass on the information to the New Guinea Coast Guard and British Navy."

"That's very public spirited of you. I have got no time for this nonsense that people are driven to piracy through necessity," said Doyle.

"Ja, we agree; don't we, Erich?" said Jäger.

Koenig nodded and said, "So, how can we be of assistance?"

"I think the logical way to proceed is start at the beginning and move like the gold through the processing plant," said Doyle.

"Very sensible," said Jäger.

Alex's eye was caught by a road on the map that branched off the main road that ran from the mine through Londolovit and out to the airport. The road branched to the west, passed through a few villages, and ended at a few buildings.

"What's this place all the way in the jungle?" asked Alex.

"What? Where?" said Jäger, in what Doyle took to be feigned astonishment.

"She means the jungle testing workshop," said Koenig.

"Ah, yes, we have a facility out where our scientists and other technical staff research mining methodologies that may be dangerous. So we isolate them to minimize danger," said Jäger.

"We'll include it in our tour once the personnel at the mine proper have been interviewed," said Alex.

"Oh, please, there's no need to drive all the way out there. The roads are atrocious. We try our best to smooth them, but they are always getting torn up after the rains. We can bring the workshop people in for you to interview," said Jäger.

"That's kind of you to offer, but our modus operandi is to interview in situ," said Doyle.

"Well, if you're sure," said Jäger with reluctance in his voice. "I'm sure it would be easier and less stressful to not go out there, especially for a delicate bloom like Miss Grose."

Alex gushed and said, "Thank you for the complement, but rules are rules." She wagged her finger like a young schoolteacher.

"Do you have a blast scheduled in the morning?" said Doyle,

Koenig said, "There will be a blast at ten in the morning, so if you set off shortly before, you can witness this and then pick up the trail of the gold ore from there."

"We'll have our own transport. Who should we check in with when we get to the mine site?"

"The pit coordinator is Franz Linderhalt. He'll be on the mine rim supervising the blast. I'll call him to expect you tomorrow," said Koenig.

"Fine, many thanks, gentlemen. We'll try to make this as unobtrusive as possible and be out your hair as soon as we can," said Doyle.

"Can we have a look at the gold on the bullion ship?" asked Alex. "I've never seen a lot of pure gold in one place."

Jäger said, "If it was up to me, I would say go ahead. However, there are strict orders from our company and the New Guinea government that restrict access to the vessel. Apart from a limited number of the company personnel, access is restricted to authorized customs, immigration, and health inspectors. I am sure you understand. I'm allowed onboard, but poor Koenig is not!"

"Oh, well, not to worry," said Doyle. "There you go, Alison. You'll have to buy your wedding ring the old-fashioned way."

Jäger gave a brief laugh. Even Koenig looked less forbidding.

Jäger said, "I'll have a car take you back to your hotel. Lisle, Miss Dorfmann, will escort you to the elevator." He spoke into his intercom in German.

They walked back through the executive suite to the elevator, following Lisle Dorfmann. Alex was going to speak inside the elevator car, but Doyle cut her off, indicating with his eyes that the car might be bugged. They stepped out of the cool quiet calm of the mine building on the Londolovit main street, which though hot and humid, was bustling with activity.

"I was surreptitiously checking my Geiger counter in my purse. Nothing out of the ordinary. I was a little surprised you didn't push back on access to the bullion ship," said Alex.

"It's probably a blind alley. Gold mine security is more stringent than a high-security jail. Everything is weighed and reweighed and inspected going onto the ship. Those customs and immigration officials probably have to sign off on every load that goes onboard. Hiding a large atom bomb in among gold bars is not impossible but probably not worth the difficulty. I'll ask the navy to board the ship once it has steamed off."

Doyle paused to wipe the sweat from his face with a handkerchief. Despite the crushing heat and humidity, Alex looked cool and poised.

Doyle said, "Fancy a jungle mystery trip tonight? They certainly don't want us poking about that place they have out in the jungle."

"Yes, I noticed that. They became very jumpy about their jungle testing facility. I wonder if the bombs are being kept out there."

"Maybe, but it's a bit too obvious, don't you think? Something did catch my eye though. Their model was a work of art. All the terrain around the mine was modeled as if the military had put it together. It's like something we would use in the army for mounting an attack. Most of the rest of Lihir was not included. But there was a small path through the jungle, just before their testing facility. Did you notice that? Why do that? Why mark something so insignificant that just ends at the river?"

"You think there's something across the river, maybe something more concealed?" Alex asked.

"That would be my guess. Look out; here's the car," Doyle said.

Chapter 47

A Mercedes-Benz sedan drew up to the curve, and the driver stepped out to open the rear door for Alex and Doyle. They sat in silence as they were driven back to the hotel. Parked by the curb outside the hotel was a Land Rover with the New Ireland Provincial Government seal on the doors. Doyle looked inside and saw that the keys were still in the ignition. He showed them to Alex.

"Car theft must be a rare crime here," he said with a laugh. They stopped at the hostel reception desk, and Doyle asked about places to eat. The receptionist passed him a photostat page, which listed bars and restaurants, including the hostel dining room and the mining canteen.

"Is this the only one you've got?" Doyle asked the receptionist.

"Yes, sir, we need to print a batch more."

"Okay, we'll look at it later, thanks."

Doyle and Alex had rooms on the first floor but separated from each other by several other guest rooms.

"I think the accommodation could be improved somewhat," said Alex in a low, sultry voice.

"Hmm, I agree Miss McCall, but we're on duty now—best not taking any chances or get distracted. Its four o'clock now; fancy meeting at five to get a drink and eat?"

"Yes, see you in the lobby at five." She reached up and kissed him on the cheek.

Doyle unlocked his door and threw his briefcase on the bed. He rubbed his scalp and noticed it needed a shave. He would do this in the shower and shave his face as well, though he was pleased his moustache had now increased in thickness.

As he showered and cleaned himself up, his thoughts took stock of their situation. He needed to contact Joe, Nellie, and May; although he expected they had seen him and Alex arrive, so they would likely be in contact soon. He dried off and slipped on his underwear and a pair of cotton shorts.

There was a knock at the door, and a female voice said, "Housekeeping."

Doyle shouted out, "It's okay. I just checked in."

"Housekeeping."

Bugger, thought Doyle, *is the bloody woman deaf?*

He opened his door. Two Melanesian women were standing there smiling at him.

"Turn down your bed for you, Mr. Doyle."

"May, Nellie, what the hell are you doing here?"

"Hee hee," said Nellie, beaming at him with a smile like a searchlight.

"Can we come in?" said May.

"Yeah, come in, come in," said Doyle.

Both women were dressed in the hostel housekeeping uniforms: blue dresses with white deep-pocketed aprons and starched caps on their heads, with hair drawn back. May smiled broadly while Nellie laughed and clapped her hands, saying, "Surprise!"

"What the hell?" said Doyle, a grin spreading across his face.

May was about to explain, when there was a knock at the door. Doyle put his finger to his lips and gestured to the two women to get out of sight. He opened the door to find Alex standing there in a short

241

dressing gown and a towel on her head. She was keeping the dressing gown closed with her hand.

"I was hoping you might help me dry my hair," she said.

Doyle took her hand and yanked her into the room. Her robe flashed open to reveal she was naked. Alex gasped when she saw May and Nellie. May gave Alex a withering look, and Nellie laughed. Alex pulled her robe tight around her, while Doyle looked up and down the corridor.

Taking a deep breath, he closed the door and said, "Look who's showed up."

"How—," said Alex trying to regain some poise and composure.

"Hello, Miss McCall, I see you are no longer devastated by your cancelled engagement," said May.

'What ... oh ... yes, err, I was just coming to ask Mick, I mean Mr. Doyle, if he'd heard from you or Joe."

"Thank you for your concern. Auntie Nellie, Joe, and I have been busy. I see you've been busy too," May said.

"Why don't we all sit down?" said Doyle, trying to defuse the tension in the air. Alex and May continued to stare daggers at each other, while Nellie looked like she was trying her hardest not laugh.

"May, how long can you and Nellie linger here without attracting attention?" said Doyle.

May said, "Ten minutes maybe. If someone comes looking for us, they'll see the service trolley outside and may knock on your door. In any case, we finish our shift at six o'clock or when we've done our room quotient."

Doyle stood and indicated to Alex to sit in the room's armchair. He retrieved a chair from under the bedroom's desk, and May and Nellie sat on the bed.

"OK, great to see you. How the hell did you get here?" said Doyle.

May said, "Everything went as planned. We were dropped off by Rurusan, and we set up a camp in the forest. We realized the place is so big that we didn't need to hide out; we could hide in plain sight. We were walking around Londolovit when we met our cousin sister, Kathy. She's a senior nursing sister at the hospital."

Both Doyle and Alex stared at May and Nellie in astonishment.

"She hadn't been appointed all that long ago. I wasn't aware she was here."

Nellie said, "Sorri, mi porget."[52]

Alex was about to say something but then discretion took over.

May said, "Big family—we know who everybody is and how they are related but not what everyone is up to."

"So you saw who, again?" said Doyle.

"Sister Kathy—she asked what we were doing on Lihir, so I said we'd come by boat and were looking for work. We said we didn't know she was now at Londolovit Hospital. She took us to the native recruitment office, and we were signed up right away. They might be suspicious of unfamiliar white skins but not of Melanesians. Joe got a job in one of the machine workshops when he said he was an ex-army engineer. Mussau women are well to be among the best domestic workers in New Guinea, so we were signed up for the hostel."

Doyle shook his head. He had been plagued by visions of his native comrades living in the jungle or being caught and killed. The latter was still possible, but this was far better than he had expected.

"Are you staying with Sister Kathy?"

"No, Joe's in the men's barracks. We share a room in native quarters for hostel workers behind the main building. The working conditions are very good," said May with a rueful smile. "We get fed.

---

[52] "Sorry, I forget."

The meals are docked from our pay, but it's only a small contribution. The meals are all subsidized, same for Joe."

"Have you found out anything? We're going to check something suspicious out in the jungle that the mine management would rather we didn't see."

"We can't stay much longer, but we should meet later. What are you planning to do, apart from dry your hair?" said May, glaring at Alex, who glared back.

"We're going to meet up at five and go for a drink and then dinner. Where can we meet you when we get back?" Doyle said.

"There's a balcony all along this floor. You see that door beside the window? It opens on to this. It's a fire escape. We'll keep an eye on your room. If you put your lights on when you've got back, we'll come up. It should be quiet, but the management is going to be unhappy with staff sneaking about, so we'll need to be careful. Joe is planning to walk over from the barracks, so we should all be able to come up to your room."

"Okay, let's do that. If anybody gives you a hard time, I can say I know you from Kavieng, or some other crap."

May and Nellie rose to leave. Doyle indicated with a nod of his head that Alex should follow them, saying, "Thanks, ladies. Alex, I'll see you as planned at five in the lobby."

Doyle watched, staying in the doorway, to make sure there was no unpleasantness in the corridor. May and Nellie walked off to the right, wheeling the trolley to a service room at the end of the corridor, while Alex turned left and walked back to her room.

Doyle shut the door and breathed out a long sigh. On the one hand, they had fantastic good luck with advancing the mission; on the other, he had to keep Alex and May from combusting, which he thought would be more deadly than any atomic blast. He looked at the time: five minutes to five. He donned a clean shirt, over which he wore his shoulder harness with the holster and spare magazines. He made sure his New Ireland Provincial ID was in his breast pocket, his moleskin notebook in another. He poured a quick nip of scotch from his suitcase supply and made ready to take on the now-combustible Alex McCall.

Chapter 48

Doyle arrived at the foyer on time, but Alex was still not there. He studied the restaurant list and then the reception girl. She had blonde, curly hair, an elongated skull, and facial features common to many Lihir natives. The girl smiled at him when she saw he was looking at her. Alex showed up looking delightful, but she was being remote, hiding behind her sunglasses. Doyle lost his appetite but soldiered on.

"The list or restaurants includes the DukDuk Bar and Lounge on the coast, practically within the mine and a great view out to sea."

"Let's go there then," said Alex without any enthusiasm.

"Unless you have another suggestion."

"No, it sounds fine to me. Let's go."

Christ, this is going to be fun, thought Doyle.

They drove in silence to the restaurant in a cove by the seas, backed by the gigantic machinery for processing the ore. They ordered drinks and then surveyed the menus, both ordering grass-fed New Ireland steaks and locally grown fresh vegetables.

The drink thawed Alex. "Sorry if I'm being a bitch this evening, but May really got my goat earlier."

"You'll forgive me if I suggest coming to my room practically naked was going to set tongues wagging, regardless if May and Nellie were there or not."

"I … I just wanted to see you."

"You'd just seen me."

"Not like that."

"You and May better make you peace. We cannot mount an effective operation with you two fighting."

"It's not just that. Am I just another piece of skirt, another score on your notching post?"

"No, Alex, I have been giving my life a bit of thought, and it occurs to me that you might be the right sort of girl with whom to settle down."

Alex brightened but remained cautious and said, "You're not just saying that?"

"No, most definitely not—we've more in common than you might think."

"Oh, what?"

"Both Anglo-Celts, son and daughter of the landed gentry, both committed to the ISS. Look, Alex, I'm in my midforties. I've been knocking heads together and bloodletting for the ISS or other paymasters for over half my time on Earth. I've never been hurt as badly as the Moresby attack. Apart from recuperation, it gave me time to think. God knows I don't think I'm a great catch, a nomadic sociopathic Paddy, but I can't go on as I have. I was going to ask Sir Anthony for a London post or consultancy, something close by, Bletchley or Chartwell perhaps. Settling down to a more sedate existence would be easier with the right partner, and that makes you the front runner at the moment."

"Oh, my, that's taken my breath away. Do you mean it?"

"Yes, but's let's be realistic. You are on the rebound from your broken engagement, and you only know me slightly, when all is said and done. We might end up being a lousy couple. I am almost twice your age, so I have all kinds of bad habits you don't know about. One

247

of which is consuming a lot of whiskey, sometimes laced with opium, and being a Paddy, I'm overly fond of pig and weed."

"Pig and—"

"Bacon and cabbage, not as bad as it sounds."

"All couples have to find their way without a roadmap—that's what my mother says. I think my father would like you, being an ex-military man himself."

"I'm nominally Catholic, not Church of Scotland. I suspect that might wrinkle a bit. But we should learn to walk before we run. Now, one other of my bad habits: I like to eat in silence, especially a good steak."

He picked up his glass of scotch and knocked against Alex's wine glass, saying, "Sláinte mhaith."

After finishing their food, Alex asked about Schläger fencing.

"It's a form of German college sword fighting, where the head is not protected from a blade strike. Goggles are worn to protect the eyes and nose, and the rest of the body is protected in a padded suit. Some fencers use a sword with a large bell-shaped guard, which they call the 'soup plate of honor.' The fencers can get some nasty head and cheek cuts, which leave prominent scars. It's practiced at several German universities, but Heidelberg is where it's most popular."

"Sounds bizarre."

"It's a student fraternity thing. It's like anything else that young men do to pull girls, like playing the guitar—"

"Or boxing?"

"Well, yeah, but in my case, it's also a family tradition."

"Can you fence?"

"Yes, it's still mandatory in the Indian Army for officers and men to do sword drill. There are plenty of places where swords are commonly used and where fencing skills come in handy, especially in close quarters."

"I can't imagine you fencing—boxing, yes, but not fencing."

"I'll give you a lesson when we get back to England," Doyle said.

Alex laughed, and they ordered more drinks. After lingering over a nightcap, they went back to the hostel. Alex drove as Doyle felt muzzy-headed from several large whiskeys.

I'm out of training, he thought. *Auntie Nellie and her clean living was a bad influence.*

Back at the hotel, they picked up their keys, and there was a note for Doyle along with the key in the pigeonhole. It was on New Guinea Airlines notepaper and simply said, "Please contact room 330."

"Who delivered this?" he asked the receptionist.

"A pilot for New Guinea Airlines. They stay here overnight when they fly the evening flight into Lihir from Kavieng. The one that wrote that note is in the restaurant."

"Thanks. Alex, can you wait here a second?" Doyle strode off to the restaurant through a glass door and returned shortly thereafter carrying an envelope.

"It's not nine o'clock yet, but we can go to my room and put the light on. I want to read this; it's from Frank."

They bounded up the stairs and into Doyle's room. Just for the hell of it, he flashed the room lights on and off three times, which he thought would likely catch the eyes of May, Nellie, and Joe.

He opened the letter, which was handwritten, and read it aloud.

Hi Mick, I know writing to you is a risk, but I didn't want to use the phone, and the NGA pilot is a buddy of mine and ex-military. I asked him to deliver it to you at the Lihir Hostel, person to person.

I had the immigration folks do the search you requested. I know our librarian Mary has some wantoks working there, so she asked them to make it a priority. Anyway, it turns out that two years ago an Irene Fong entered the territory from Australia. She had a Chinese student visa so was questioned about this; its routine for folks to be questioned about travel to exotic places like China.

According to the interview records, she had gone to study in Canton, working on the history of the Chinese diaspora to the Pacific Islands, with a focus on New Guinea and Melanesia. She came back from her studies just over two years ago and took up a post at Lihir Gold in the same department that later employed Elaine Chan.

Luckily, for us, she got all lippy with the immigration blokes in Moresby, who were just following the rules when they spot visas of interest. Typically, they would have just asked few questions, but when she began to get stroppy, they followed the rules exactly and took her fingerprints. These were filed away and did not raise any red flags when the Anvil case blew up.

However, some further digging in the Moresby registrar's office by Mary's wantoks turned up that she was originally from New Guinea, born on a plantation on the New Ireland West Coast, and so grew up speaking pidgin like a native, probably the local ples-tok.

I know most out-of-town births are not registered, but the Fongs were smart, since life is a lot easier if you have a birth certificate for passports and employment by territory or Aussie government—or in Irene's case, student bursaries to study at the Universities of Queensland and Canton. They just drove over to Konos and did it there, with copies sent up to Kavieng and Moresby.

I know that more and more records are being transferred to computers these days, but old paper records like the fingerprints of a Chinese girl from the territory are about as low on the totem pole as it gets.

I asked the immigration chief to personally hand deliver the fingerprint card to the high commission head of security, with instructions to send this by telefax secure line to the ISS HQ. You Poms can be on the ball when you want to be—pity not at cricket! I was dragged out of the office a couple of hours later to the telephone exchange building to take a secure call. I'm to let you know the prints were a match for Irene Fong, so you've closed that loop, and now it looks like the balloon is going up.

I am to ask you to get Nellie to contact coastwatcher HQ ASAP. I think that you can expect a lot of fireworks soon. All the best, Frank

Chapter 49

There was a gentle knock on the veranda door, and Joe, Nellie, and May filed in, May looking back over her shoulder to see if anyone was watching. They sat in a line on the end of the bed.

Doyle saw Nellie nudge May, who said, "Alex, I'm sorry I was a bit of a cow earlier. We're in the most important operation of my life, and I behaved like a jealous bush kanaka meri."[53]

Alex said, "Me too. I'm glad we're friends again. I couldn't … wouldn't have coped with this operation without you. You've been like a sister to me."

They both started crying and stood and embraced. Joe and Nellie looked on, smiling, while Doyle sighed and said, "Okay folks, this is going to be a briefing where I want to hear everyone's views. Here—read this, better still. May, read it so we don't have to wait for Joe and Nellie."

May complied, and both Joe and Nellie looked grave.

Nellie said, "Mi save Fong. Emi gat plantation long West Coast, na stoa long Kavieng. Stoa gat haus mek bread. Mi bin woking long ples i mekim meri blaus na laplap[54]."

"Did you know Irene?" asked Doyle.

---

[53] Native woman.

[54] "I know the Fongs. They have a plantation on the West Coast and store in Kavieng. The store has a bakery. I worked there making blouses and sarongs.

"Yes, mi save em, tasol no tumas,[55]" said Nellie.

"So we have two New Guinea women of Chinese origin, both working at the gold mine here, turning into psychopathic killers and being part of the organization to steal five atom bombs. I suspect Raptor is the nom du guerre for Gustave Jäger, or at least he's in charge of Raptor on Lihir. But there's something else at work here, and I think that's the Chinese government, who are lending their assistance to Raptor so both China and Germany can fast-track nuclear bomb development. Does that sound logical?"

Alex said nothing.

May said, "It sounds logical to us. Did you understand all that, Auntie?"

Nellie nodded.

"Have you folks seen or heard anything unusual? I know you've only been here a couple of days longer than we have."

Joe said, "Nothing I've seen, but there's rumors of something that sounds like a submarine that's been seen by Lihir villagers that's made its way into the mine."

"In broad daylight?" asked Doyle.

"No, dawn and dusk. It's been spotted by fishermen out before dawn or out when it's getting dark. Among the Mussaus, the Lihirs are a bit of a joke. They jump if they see a shadow. They are very superstitious, which is saying something for Melanesians—eh, May?"

May giggled, and so did Nellie.

"We shouldn't be so superior; in the middle of the night we all get scared of masalai[56] and people making papait.[57] Still, the old beliefs

---

[55] Yes I know about them as well but not that much."

[56] Ghosts and demons.

[57] Magic and sorcery.

are much closer to the surface than on Mussau, even though we were just as isolated," said May.

"So what did the villagers think—it was some kind of sea monster?" said Alex.

"Something like that," said Joe.

"This may be good news," said Doyle. "A sub can't carry many troops, maybe a squad or two of marines, probably hotboxing with the crew."

Joe said, "They could have built up a platoon over time."

Doyle said, "By sub? That would take forever. Then they have to be housed, fed etc."

"Em nau," said Joe. "A squad is usually self-sufficient, and they'll have support from the submarine."

"Yeah, that's my thought. So our adversary's forces are not that big, though big enough without soldiers to oppose them. May, is all your kit still in the jungle?" asked Doyle.

"No, Kathy took us into the bush in her pickup truck, and we retrieved everything. Nobody's going to be suspicious of local people taking patrol boxes into a house; everyone uses them. Anyway, our weapons are with Sister Kathy. Nellie has her radio. We put up a cable saying it was an additional washing line for our clothes, and now have an antenna. Nellie received some communications from Moresby this evening. I think more or less that the military will soon be here in force," said May, looking to Nellie for confirmation.

Nellie nodded her head and said, "Lukim, me raitim message. Mi waitim yu tokim i orait long mekim ansa."[58]

Doyle took the proffered piece of paper and read the message.

"'Please indicate soonest when you are in position STOP Troops

---

[58] "Look, I wrote the message. I am waiting to say it's okay to answer."

assembling in Australia and Moresby for operation STOP Ask Deacon if bombs located STOP Go decision on your signal.'"

May said, "We haven't responded. We wanted to get your okay to go ahead. See, we were paying attention to your orders, masta."

"Have you had a chance to plant any explosives?" said Doyle to Joe.

"About fifteen so far, small charges, mostly diversionary, like you said. We don't want to kill anyone."

"No, good. One thing that this operation should strive to do is minimize any damage to the mine. We don't want to put folks out of work or bugger things up for the Lihirs. The government will likely appoint another mining company to run the place, once the Germans are cleared out, and then auction the mining rights."

"You're like a social worker not a hooligan," said Alex.

"I've found to my cost that just shooting bad guys and blowing things up is the easy part. This is not the movies. There are peoples' livelihoods at stake. Every man in this mine probably has a family, same for all the women workers. You can do the arithmetic and figure out how many lives this place supports; and that's just the mine itself, never mind what smart folks called the expanded economy," said Doyle.

"I keep forgetting you're a smart man with degrees," said May.

"Me too," said Alex.

"Now you know what kind of responsibility sits on Sir Anthony's shoulders. It's not just spies and espionage; preserving the empire is ultimately about people."

"Baravae tuegi!"[59] said Joe with a laugh.

"OK, that's enough bollocks from me. We've still got a job

---

[59] "Preach brother." (Mussau)

to do. Here's what I propose: Nellie, send a message to Moresby coastwatcher HQ. Keep it brief; I'm still paranoid about you being captured if, as I suspect, there's someone keeping a watch on radio traffic. Tell Moresby that there are about thirty to forty armed guards here. Say submarine spotted and that Alex and I have gone out tonight to check out a suspicious place on the island."

"What else should we do?" asked Joe.

"Tonight, do nothing other than the radio message, but keep a look out for Alex and me tomorrow. What's the phone service like?"

"It's good," said May. "But I thought we were trying to keep away from unsecured communications."

"We are, but I think you could call the provincial government and ask for Mary Asua, the librarian, or Belinda. Mary and Belinda don't know the whole Anvil operation, but they know you and that we all met with Frank Gardiner. If we don't show up in our rooms tomorrow morning by 6:00 a.m., especially if our vehicle is not parked in front of the hotel, call the provincial government after eight. Belinda will likely be there earlier, but the switchboard won't be open. If anyone is nosy, you can make up a story about church business. I doubt the precision of the folks here extends to briefing on local provincial government employees and the churches to which they belong. Say that you are worried that the new Seventh Day Deacon appears to have gone missing and please let Mr. Gardiner know so he can inform the Kavieng church and the appropriate authorities."

Joe asked, "How much time before the ransom has to be paid? How will it be paid?"

Alex said, "Ten more days. The imperial bearer bonds are to be delivered to a Swiss bank, the Zug Kantonalbank. That's it. The bank will take possession and hold them for their client, presumably some commercial enterprise established by Raptor."

"Wea dispela Swit za land?"[60] asked Nellie.

"Bihain, Auntie, me tokim yu long en.[61] Em nau masta. We'd better leave you to get on with the mission. Take care," said May.

"Thanks," said Doyle, thinking this was bloody inadequate. He shook hands with Joe and embraced Nellie and May. Alex embraced everybody.

Nellie said, "Mipela pre strong tunait kam bek safe."[62]

---

[60] "Where is this Switzerland?"

[61] "Later, Auntie, I'll tell you about it."

[62] "I'll pray hard tonight for your safety."

Chapter 50

Doyle changed into dark overalls and tough canvas jungle boots for nighttime fieldwork. Under the overalls was his shoulder holster with the Browning. Doyle mentally checked the arithmetic; thirty rounds in all for the Browning. He would ask Alex what weapons she was carrying and how many spare magazines. They did not have any other ordinance; that was now all stored at Sister Kathy's house, but they were only going out to reconnoiter the jungle facility.

He emptied his leather grip and threw in the Mauser, fitting it with the thirty-round magazine and adding the three twenty and ten round magazines for spares. He also threw in a battery-powered flashlight and a standard issue ISS dynamo torch. He added the map of Lihir and night makeup for when they reached their destination. He recalled the army instructions about application of night camouflage: "Don't forget your eyelids." These flashed like stars to eyes conditioned to darkness.

Alex knocked on Doyle's door. She was dressed in overalls and jungle boots as well.

"What are you carrying for weapons?" asked Doyle.

"Smith & Wesson, with a shoulder rig like yours, two spare magazines and silencer. I've got the Berretta Pico in my thigh holster. Are you bringing your museum blunderbuss?"

"Cheeky bitch, yes, it's in the grip, along with flashlights, camouflage makeup, and the map. I wish we had some grenades, but we can't drive up to Sister Kathy and ask her to lob us a few grenades. Have you brought your flashlight?"

"Yes, oh damn, I forgot my dynamo torch. Should I go back and get it?"

"No, I've got mine. Hopefully we don't have to use it. Here, you take it."

They walked downstairs past the receptionist. They were getting into the Land Rover when a uniformed man walked up to them and said, "Papers."

Alex started to retrieve her identification, but Doyle looked the man up and down and said, "Papers, papers; where the fuck do you think you are Herman, Berlin? This island is the sovereign territory of the British Empire, which kindly allows your company to mine here for gold. Miss Grose and I are representatives of the imperial government. Moreover, we are labor officers—which means, Herman, I might ask for your passport tomorrow and cancel your working visa. Now fuck off."

The German mine guard beat a hasty retreat, and Doyle settled himself into the vehicle. Alex got into the passenger seat.

"How do you do that?" said Alex.

"Do what?" asked Doyle

"Standing up to the guard. It's silly, I know, but I was terrified. I thought we were going to be arrested. You did it at the airport too."

"That's where you need to embrace your inner imperialist. No point in having an empire if you do not use that power. He was probably within his rights though, with a bullion ship in town, but I hate the hectoring manner of Germans."

"God, Doyle, I know this is entirely inappropriate, but it's very sexy."

He laughed and then said, "Yeah, sexy now, but not very loveable if I stumble home half cut and wanting my dinner."

Alex laughed again and said, "Pig."

Doyle passed Alex the map and said, "Come on; you navigate. Let's go and see what the Germans are hiding in the jungle."

They drove west through the center of Londolovit, passing shops, offices, and churches of various denominations. All the churches were signposted, but Doyle noted the Seventh Day Adventist Church out of the corner of his eye. The town main street joined a main road that was signposted; to the right was the airport and to left the mine, various mining offices, and the processing plants. Alex was holding a Lihir map with the roads marked, which was already outdated as the mine grew.

Alex said, "Take a left. In a few minutes we should come a T-junction and take a right; this is the jungle road to what they told us was the mining test facility."

Doyle grunted and drove on. As they left the town, they left the streetlights behind, and now the headlights provided the only illumination. Doyle could see the road was well maintained, with distance markers and concrete posts supporting power lines. In the dark he could see the silhouettes of coconut and other forest trees. The coconut trees looked fearsome at night, with their spiked pinnate leaves. It was easy to imagine all manner of horrible things lurked in the dark.

There was no sign at the T-junction, just a blazon of bleached coral road. As they drove, plants slapped the windscreen; the road was bumpy but still drivable. They were startled by a flying fox looming out of the dark and flapping over the Land Rover. Doyle could see bats flitting out of the dark, pursuing insects, which beat a regular tattoo splatting on the windscreen. Something monstrous flew out of the dark and made a clunk against the windscreen, startling them both. Doyle saw that it was a coconut beetle. It slid about on the hood of the Land Rover and then fell off.

They pressed on into the dark until they broke out of the tunnel-like road and into a clearing. Doyle slowed down to a crawl and completed a circuit of the clearing. On two sides were buildings, but this was not a village and the buildings were unlit. Doyle kept the engine on idle as they turned back the way they had come. The headlights lit a wall of jungle straight ahead, and there were building to the left and right. Doyle turned off the engine and sat, letting his eyes adjust to the darkness. He could sense Alex wanting to speak, but she was a professional and knew Doyle was looking and listening.

The night was alive with jungle sounds, mainly crickets, with an occasional distant dog bark and rooster crow.

"I feel like saying it's too quiet, but you know what? It is too quiet," said Doyle.

"Not much of a moon tonight," said Alex.

"No, still on the wane. Can you hear if anyone followed us? I don't think they did. I can't see any lights."

"I'm pretty sure we weren't followed. I can't hear anything, and there are no lights back along the road that I can make out."

"As I recall, in Jäger's office the hill's to the north of us, not on this road. Are you up to a little jungle stroll? There's not much out in the bush that can hurt us, except for someone with a gun."

"I think I saw a small path about fifty yards back," Alex said.

"Let's have a poke around. These buildings look harmless. Are you showing anything on your Geiger counter?" Doyle asked.

"No, just the usual background radiation. I'm up for a night patrol if you are."

Doyle retrieved his leather grip and rummaged about, taking out the battery-powered flashlight and the dynamo torch. He put on the flashlight and kept it on the seat to minimize its glow. He pulled out his Mauser and what looked like some form of camera accessory. With a few twists and turns, this extended into a skeleton shoulder stock; it slipped onto the Mauser handle.

"Now we have a machine gun if we need one, and it's accurate up to two hundred yards."

Alex smiled in the dark and said, "Okay, I'm convinced."

Doyle passed a tube of nighttime camouflage to Alex, who applied it to her face as Doyle did the same. He was pleased to see she blackened her eyelids without having to be told.

Doyle retrieved the twenty- and ten-round magazines for the Mauser. He pointed his flashlight to the ground as they set off back along the road. Alex kept her flashlight off, so they had a fully charged torch for the walk back. After a few minutes, they came to the path branching off into the bush. It was not as wide as the road they stood on, but Doyle noticed that it would accommodate vehicles. There were crushed stalks and white streaks on the foliage that indicated a vehicle had passed this way, splashing through the many puddles.

The night was hot, and there was no breeze on the road deep within the shelter of the forest. The humidity was nearly 100 percent, and sweat streaked down their faces and bodies. The sweat ran over the camouflage that was waterproof, but this soon became streaked as they wiped the sweat out of their eyes. Doyle watched the path, seeing the eyes of toads and frogs as they jumped out of the way; they encountered a huge python crossing the path. Doyle stopped; Alex bumped into him and then grasped him when she saw the huge snake. Doyle took a breath and then stepped over it, looking at Alex to do the same thing.

As they pressed on, Doyle began to feel a slight drop in temperature and the riffle and gurgle of flowing water. They broke out of the jungle and into a clearing beside a small river. At first Doyle thought the river was running over rapids, but then he looked more closely.

Alex said, "It's a ford, and whatever drove down this path crossed over there."

Doyle said, "Come on; I doubt it's very deep. Watch out for loose rocks and slippery rocks."

They stepped out, easily at first, but with more difficulty in the middle of the river as the water came up to their knees and the current kept trying to sweep them away. Doyle had his left hand directing the torch while keeping the Mauser held pointing at the sky to avoid the water. They moved beyond the middle of the river and made it to the other bank.

Alex said, "The model didn't show the path on this side of the river. Can you see anything?"

Doyle shined the torch up and down the bank. He looked for vehicle tracks, but the ground looked as if pigs had been foraging along the bank and in what looked like an abandoned garden. He took a guess and turned up river, thinking this might be it could be a wild-goose chase. Perhaps the collection of buildings behind them really was the mine test facility. Maybe he was reading too much into a simple path—and then he saw an opening in the jungle, with crushed vegetation and splash marks.

"Lead on Macduff," said Alex at his shoulder.

"I'm game if you are, but this may yet be a fool's errand," Doyle said.

They walked into another clearing. At first, he thought they were opposite a rock face, perhaps an old coral quarry. They walked up to the vertical face and saw that this was not rock but two huge iron doors at the base of the hill.

Doyle turned to Alex when there was a crackle of gunfire from out of the jungle to their right. The shooter was firing an automatic weapon. They ducked immediately to the ground, and the flashlight rolled away from Doyle's hand. This saved them, since the shooter fired at the flashlight, eventually hitting it. Doyle and Alex remained still. There were footsteps in the bush; someone was walking toward them but in the dark. Doyle doubted the person was wearing night goggles, or they would have been them off while they were prone on the ground.

Doyle picked out two voices murmuring as they walked forward. They did not put on a flashlight to present a target for shooting. Doyle could hear the two sets of footsteps emerge into the clearing. He flicked the Mauser to full automatic, aimed at the sound, and squeezed off a long burst. The muzzle flashes revealed two armed, uniformed men reacting to the hail of fire. There were howls of pain and cursing in German. Doyle fired another short burst, expecting return fire. He realized he must have inflicted serious wounds on both gunmen. The muzzle flashes showed them retreating in the dark and then heard them stumbling and crashing in the forest.

"Were you hit?" Doyle said to Alex.

"No. God that was bloody close."

"Too bloody close—there must be more than one way in and out of this hill. We're lucky they forgot to bring grenades. Have you got your flashlight?"

Alex retrieved it from a pocket, but she could not make it work.

"It was working in my room. Something must have been damaged when we fell to the ground."

"Have you got the dynamo torch?"

"Yes, let's get out of here."

"Wait, check the Geiger counter."

Doyle heard the little dynamo torch wheeze and cast its feeble glow. Alex gasped.

"There's something emitting a lot of radiation behind those doors."

Chapter 51

The retreat back through the jungle was arduous and fraught with the possibility of being followed or attacked. The dynamo flashlight produced only a dim glow, so they had to move slowly, especially crossing the river. Sweat continued to course down them. Doyle's overalls were damp with perspiration, and he thought that Alex was probably just as soaked.

He knew mosquitos would be feasting on her exposed skin. He could feel the occasional bite, but he knew it would be worse for Alex. Alex pressed on, depressing the dynamo torch continuously to generate the beam. It seemed they were sleepwalking when they emerged onto the forest road leading to the buildings. They trudged down this before Doyle took Alex's arm and pulled her head close to his. There were noises in the bushes. Suddenly, a herd of pigs crashed through the dark in front of them, the dynamo torch picking out an eye in the dark.

"Christ, I nearly had a heart attack. Take out your gun. I don't want us wandering into a real ambush when we come to the Land Rover."

Alex took out her Smith and Wesson, while Doyle kept the Mauser at the ready. Alex put the dynamo torch back in her pocket. They were now walking by starlight, under which the road was visible as a dirty white scar. The buildings loomed out of the dark, and Doyle could see the reassuring outline of the Land Rover in the center of the clearing. They moved cautiously toward it, Alex holding her gun in two hands, pointing downward but ready to shoot. They stopped and listened for any odd sounds in the dark, the rattle of a magazine or the snick of a safety catch.

Nothing.

They approached the Land Rover, Doyle blowing a sigh of relief. Doyle thought the shooting in the jungle had not been well planned nor well executed. It might just have been someone trying to scare them off, but there was deadly intent in those shots. They reached the Land Rover and were about to get in when Doyle paused.

"Let's check that no one has left us a souvenir. This is a mine with tons of explosives and plenty of people who knew how to use them," said Doyle.

Alex gave him the dynamo flashlight, and Doyle checked the doors were not wired to anything, though it was difficult with the feeble glow. He moved on, feeling under the vehicle, starting and cursing when he burnt his hand on the still hot exhaust. He gingerly undid the hood restraints, feeling for any wires that might trigger a bomb. He looked at the alternator and the electrical circuits for the ignition.

He almost missed it: a small, neat block of plastic explosive wrapped in black cloth as camouflage, with wires attaching themselves to the starter motor. Doyle asked Alex to come and look as he kept the dynamo flashlight beam lit. As a new ISS operative, Doyle reckoned her knowledge of bombs and bomb circuitry was better and more up to date.

"As far as I can see, it's pretty straightforward. There's a detonator under the explosive, with wires taking power from the starter motor circuit." Alex gently moved the wires apart and buzzed the dynamo torch for a continuous beam.

"Hmm, nasty."

"What is it?" Doyle asked.

"Tamper circuit—crude one, but if we had just pulled the wires away, it would blow."

She reached in and delicately removed and pulled the blasting cap from explosive. Once the cap was clear, Alex yanked the wiring out of the Land Dover.

Doyle thought that the black cloth was a clever move. Thank God his eyes were still sharp, and thank God Alex remembered her explosives training. They sat in the Land Rover, and Alex put her gun away and stashed the bomb components in Doyle's grip.

Doyle dismantled the Mauser stock and put it in the grip. He inserted the key in the ignition and then, taking a deep breath, started the Land Rover. The engine roared to life without any fireworks. They drove back to Londolovit in silence, both of them exhausted from the nights trek and their bodies calming down from an adrenaline high. More wild pigs dashed across the road before they came to the main road and retraced their way back to the hotel.

Chapter 52

At the hostel, Doyle and Alex strolled in, with Doyle checking his watch. It was just after 2:00 a.m. The receptionists had changed and behind the desk was a man seated and dozing. Doyle woke him to get their keys and to check there were no messages. He guessed Nellie and May would be asleep, but he would flicker his lights to see if one of them realized they had returned. They walked upstairs and stopped at his door.

"I'm going to flash my lights and see if Auntie Nellie or May is awake. Why don't you take off and get some sleep? Jäger said there was a blast scheduled at ten. I think we should keep up this charade, but we have enough evidence to call in the cavalry."

"What about the attempted shooting and bomb?" asked Alex.

"Oh, don't worry, I want to see what Jäger and that stiff icicle Koenig say when we confront them."

"Should I wait with you to see if Nellie or May comes to your room?"

Doyle decided this was probably not wise; he might be tempted to take a shower with Alex. That was not a wise move at this point, he decided.

"No, I'll wait five minutes and then shower and turn in. You get some sleep. Check you have no cuts or scrapes, especially below the knee. How are your feet? Did your boots rub and chafe? Mine bloody did."

"A bit. I'll pop any blisters and rub them with alcohol. What time shall we rendezvous in the morning?"

"Nine, in the lobby—we'll grab some breakfast and then head to the mine and work our way back to Jäger's office. If I don't see the ladies this evening, we need to find them first thing and get Nellie to send a message to coastwatcher HQ. If they can do it tonight, so much better."

"How long will it take for our forces to get here?" Alex asked.

"At least a day—I'm guessing they'll send in native paratroopers from Moresby in case the runway is blocked. If the airport is secure, then more troops can land. I expect there's a carrier group on the way already."

"Is our job done?"

"We know where the bombs are. Let's hope both of them are there, but at least one must be. The only major worry I have now is if there are additional military personnel on the island. They could be concealed in that cave we found. It might contain a Chinese infantry battalion, which means anywhere from three hundred to eight hundred troops, in addition to the thirty or so security personnel. So, no, I do not think our job is done until Lihir Island is fully under our control. Go on now. I'll let you know if I talk to May or Nellie."

Alex reached up and kissed Doyle on the cheek and then went to her room. Doyle slipped into his bedroom and gave his lights a series of on–off flashes. He sat on the bed, waiting, and took off his boots to make himself more comfortable. He was about to give up on May and Nellie when there was a quiet knock at the balcony door. Doyle turned off the room light and looked out of the window. May was standing outside his door.

"Come in. I'll keep the lights off while you are here."

"I was sleeping but got up for a glass of water. I wasn't looking at your room directly, but the flashes caught my eye. I didn't want to wake Auntie Nellie, and I have another message for you—but what did you find?" said May.

"More than we bargained for. There's a large cave in the jungle, with huge metal doors. We took a Geiger counter reading that showed radiation leaking out. I think there's a dismantled bomb inside the cave, so its shielding has been reduced. What was the message you received?"

"There has been another communication from Raptor. When the bearer bonds are deposited, the bombs will be left at Belmonte Island, Saints Peter and Paul's Rocks.

"Where is that?" Doyle asked.

"Mid-Atlantic, it's an uninhabited Brazilian territory, midway from Brazil and West Africa, a long way from here. I bet it is just a feint. The Germans are not going to surrender the bombs but will go through the motions. The ransom payment will just buy them more time."

"What do we do now? It all feels a bit surreal," May said.

"Surreal, big word for a native girl," said Doyle.

May slapped his arm.

"When we were in the jungle, someone took a potshot at us, and this." He opened his grip and extracted the plastic explosive wrapped in black cloth. "This was hidden in the Land Rover engine, close to the starter motor. The wiring and blasting cap are in the bag. So, yes, it is surreal. I think our disguise has been penetrated, but there hasn't been any move against us. I'm more concerned for your safety and Joe's. But, please, wake Nellie and send this message."

He took out his notebook from his overall chest pocket and wrote, "Bombs located STOP Thirty security guards maybe more in jungle

STOP No other opposition spotted STOP Take Lihir soonest STOP Have navy intercept bullion ship STOP."

"We're going to continue to play at being labor officers, so we are going to see the mine and processing plant tomorrow morning. Go now. I'll watch as you go back to your room."

May nodded and then reached up and kissed Doyle full on the lips, her tongue writhing about in his mouth. She broke off with a smile and said, "Yes masta."

Doyle smiled as May slipped out of the room, sliding along the wall, making her way back to the staff native quarters by sticking to the shadows. Doyle watched to see if there was anyone following her. He had enjoyed his goodnight kiss and felt his body responding. He left the room light off but went to the bathroom, where he took a cold shower.

Chapter 53

Doyle slept with his Berretta under his pillow. He knew he would wake with the dawn, only about three hours away. As a precaution, Doyle had placed the armchair against the room door and the desk chair under the handle of the balcony door.

He rose at about 8:00 a.m., shaved his face but not his head, which was still slick and hairless. He donned his tropical linen suit, which was looking a little rumpled. Under his suit, he wore his shoulder holster, and his Beretta was stuck again in his waistband, behind his back.

Walking down to the lobby at a few minutes to nine, he found Alex waiting for him. She was a trained professional and would have taken precautions, but he was glad that his anxiety could ratchet down. While they had breakfast, he spotted Nellie and May cleaning the downstairs corridor, presumably as a prelude to cleaning the rooms.

"May came up last night. She gave me a message, and I told her to have Nellie send one saying bombs found, send in the troops."

"Oh, how long did she stay?" said Alex in a neutral tone.

"Five minutes, ten at most."

"Hmm, what did she tell you?"

"The drop point for the bombs is a remote uninhabited archipelago in the Atlantic, Belmonte Island, Saints Peter and Paul's Rocks."

"Never heard of it. What do we do now? Keep up the pretense?"

"Yes, though I would like to toss that lump of plastic explosive and blasting cap on Jäger's desk. But that would give the game away, and I'd like to see our lads' boots on the ground first."

They finished breakfast and went to the reception desk to drop their keys. As they did so, Nellie and May walked past carrying brooms and mops to take upstairs. Nellie smiled, as she did at everyone. May raised an eyebrow, by which Doyle knew that his message had been delivered.

Outside, Londolovit was bustling. Women made the rounds of the stores for the day's shopping. Parties of school kids drove by in school buses on field outings. Mining personnel drove back and forth between offices and the huge mine facilities stretching over five miles and occupying twenty square miles of the island.

Doyle drove the Land Rover to the mine, following the signs to the onsite management office, perched above the lip of the mine pit. Doyle and Alex could see that there were two pits: one was to the south and no longer used, while the northern pit was a hive of activity. Huge, empty dump trucks descended into the mine, and loaded trucks crawled slowly up the mine road to the surface.

It was a gross understatement to call the mine a hole in the ground. The excavation was a vast, terraced construction. At first Doyle thought that the terraces were roadways, but the road itself was a simple circuit of the pit that descended to the bottom. Springs from the surface and out of the earth cascaded into a dirty green lake at the base of the pit.

Volcanic vents blew plumes of steam. The place looked like the pit of hell imagined in the most outlandish creations of Dante or the Apocrypha. Everywhere, men bent to their tasks. No body loitered or sat about smoking. In the pit, diggers gathered up the loose rock freed by previous explosions. Men were already preparing the next blast. On the surface, the dump trucks unloaded their ore onto a pile that was scooped onto a long conveyor belt heading down the coast to the processing plant

Alex pointed along the conveyor and said, "That must be where the rock is crushed and the gold extracted."

"Yeah, just make some notes about the place looking professional and run well. We'll head down there in a minute."

"Good morning," said a voice behind them. "I'm Linderhalt, Franz Linderhalt, the manager of pit operations. I heard you would be coming down here today. We'll be blasting in about five minutes."

The man was German but spoke with strong inflections of Australian in his voice.

Doyle and Alex turned to look at the newcomer.

"I'm Alison Grose, and this is Malcolm Donaldson," said Alex.

"Here, please put on the helmets and high-viz jackets. It's company policy."

"Thanks," said Doyle, "we were admiring your operation."

A siren began screeching, and men rode up from the pit on a series of trucks. Doyle saw a native explosives engineer prepare an electronic detonator box. A recorded message was blasted out of loud speakers on the management office in English, German, and pidgin. A miner jumped from a truck and gave a thumbs-up to the explosives engineer.

"Come," said Linderhalt, and he took them to the lip of the pit.

There was an eerie silence and then a series of booms accompanied by fountains of rock debris.

"There wasn't much of a tremor," said Alex.

"It's the depth and the downward blast," said Linderhalt. "Do you want to go down in the pit?"

"Fancy a ride into hell, Ali?" said Doyle.

"Why not?"

Linderhalt waved and a Mercedes-Benz, four-wheel drive vehicle, similar to a Land Rover, drove over to where they stood. They piled in. The Mercedes was driven by native mine worker.

"We've already abandoned one pit; you saw it from on top. The gold petered out. This pit is going to last longer. The gold concentration gets higher as we dig down."

"We've heard that the whole island is one giant gold nugget," said Alex.

"Bit of an exaggeration, but not that far from the truth. Not like Pogera, where there are gold nuggets strewn around the surface. You can see now as we enter the pit what we have to contend with. See the streams from the surface and pouring out of the rock. We get on average three to four meters of rain a year; that's 120 to 160 inches. The bloody island is like a giant sponge. The steam comes out of volcanic vents. We tap the steam back toward the town and use it to generate electricity."

The Mercedes-Benz stopped at the bottom of the pit. Doyle, Alex, and Linderhalt got out of the vehicle.

"Don't go too far to the edge of the lake. The ground gives way, and the lake water is unpleasant," said Linderhalt.

"Is it toxic?" asked Doyle.

"Everything just drains in there, plus there's sulfuric acid from the mixing of the springs and the gasses from the volcanic vents. It won't kill you, but its nasty stuff and can make you sick and hurt your eyes."

Mine workers were entering the pit and doing their various tasks. A team of drillers and explosives men were setting the next blast. Two mechanical diggers were loading huge dump trucks, the wheels of which were taller than Doyle.

"Miracles of modern technology," said Linderhalt.

"Why's that?" asked Alex.

"Diesel-powered but the engine doesn't drive the wheels. It powers a generator that provides independent electrical power to the wheels. Gives a lot more control on these steep slopes and rough terrain. The trucks have a whole team dedicated to them, working around the clock. They're like surgeons; they extract oil to check for metallic fragments, so they know how the engine is wearing."

Doyle looked up to the rim of the pit. This deep in the earth there was no breeze and the heat and humidity were worse than the jungle. He noticed in the deep hole that some of the brighter stars were visible in daylight, shaded from the sun's overpowering glow.

"Seen enough?" asked Linderhalt.

"Yes, thanks. Alex, anything more to do here?"

"No, thank you. I assume just from looking around that your workers are happy here?"

"Go ask them if you want, but they won't like being interrupted. Lihir pays well and has one of the highest standards of living in New Guinea, but don't take my word for it. Hey, David!" Linderhalt shouted to the driver of the Mercedes-Benz and beckoned him to come over.

"David, where are you from?" asked Linderhalt.

David looked surprised but said, "Morobe, boss. I used to work at the Wau goldfield."

"Do you like it here?" asked Linderhalt.

"Eh, yes, great job, big pay, cheap meals, free hospital, soccer and rugby on the weekend—"

"Thanks, David. Let's go back to the top," said Linderhalt to Doyle and Alex.

They piled back into the Mercedes-Benz and began the ascent

to the surface. David drove in low gear and four-wheel drive on the muddy road, which was much more navigable by the huge dump trucks. At the surface, Alex made a show of drafting some notes on her clipboard.

"Here, walk with me. You can see what happens to the ore. It's only a minute or so," said Linderhalt.

"Has anyone fallen in the lake?" asked Doyle.

"Happens now and again," said Linderhalt. "They climb out, and we send to them to the hospital. They usually pump out the stomach to be on the safe side. Here, this is where the ore gets unloaded. We can climb up on this platform." Linderhalt pointed to a staircase to a viewing platform.

Doyle followed Linderhalt up the steps. From the platform they could see a long, continuous conveyor belt disappearing into the horizon. A dump truck was parked close by, and a digger was unloading the ore onto the conveyor belt.

"The ore goes up there into the processing facility. There's another facility behind us, but the main one is at the end of this conveyor."

"Why build it so far away?" asked Alex. "Why not site it much closer to the mine itself?"

"Because all this ground will be dug up, eventually. The processing plant sits on ground with low gold deposits. There's a road that runs alongside that will take you into the processing circuits. I assume that you'll want to see those and talk to the native workers?"

"Yes, thanks," said Doyle. "Much appreciate the guided tour."

Linderhalt nodded then looked north to the horizon. "That's not good," he said, almost to himself.

"What is it?" said Doyle, looking out to the horizon. There was a thin black line where the blue sky met the sea.

"Big storm—see the dark line? It's a long way off way off yet, but it'll be here soon enough."

"A hurricane?" asked Alex.

"They call them cyclones down here. No, we're too near the equator to get proper cyclones. They clip the south of the territory and the Solomons get pounded. It's the end of the north–west monsoon season. Sometimes we get a really big blow before it's all over and the southeast trade winds come back."

"How long will it last?" asked Doyle.

"Hard to say—sometimes a day or two, but they can settle in for a week before they blow themselves out."

Doyle and Alex settled back into the Land Rover and set off traveling parallel to the conveyor belt.

Chapter 54

"Is it serious, the storm?" asked Alex, seeing the stony set of Doyle's face.

"Yes, you're not a tropical hand. That's not a criticism, just the facts of the matter. What's the worst rain you've ever seen?"

Alex thought about it and said, "Persistence-wise I suppose Scotland, when it's drizzling and we call it a 'fine soft day.'"

"Good for the complexion. What about downpour?"

Alex thought again and said, "Once at Wimbledon, there was a summer storm where the rain bounced up a foot from the ground."

"That's what it can be like for a week, with occasional breaks. I won't quiz you about winds; you know what westerly gales are like. Well, that's the kind of blow we're in for. Would you mount a military operation in weather like that?"

"Oh, my God, no."

"Precisely. The military won't risk a parachute drop or amphibious landing. Aircraft will be grounded. We're on our own until this filthy weather blows over."

"Better keep up the pretense."

"How many more days until the ransom deadline expires?"

"Eight days, not long. What if the empire pays the ransom? Isn't it all over?"

"No, it'll buy time, but if it's paid, we'll never get it back once its squirreled away in a Swiss bank. There is no account number; all the government has to do is turn up at the Zug Kantonalbank with a bundle of bearer bonds. The manager will wish them a brisk good day and then put the bonds into whichever account or deposit he's been told to put them in."

"Bloody hell," said Alex, "we're the empire, for God's sake. Couldn't we kidnap the manager and demand the account number?"

"Rule Britannia," said Doyle. "Yes, we could, but there is probably a password, probably several, most likely negotiated with the account holder and each one known to an individual bank employee. I'm probably overcomplicating it, but you covered Swiss banking law in your training; you know what the Zurich gnomes are like. There are billions in those banks from unclaimed accounts, where people have died without passing on their wealth. The banks just continue to charge fees and draw interest."

"Still, I think it's worth a thought," said Alex.

"Oh, aye, I agree, but then the imperial government would have kittens messing with Swiss banks, too many overextended clients in the empire at the mercy of the Swiss calling time on loans. They would put enormous pressure on the government. Every time a big enterprise like South African goldmining, Middle East oil, or Indian steel wants to expand or just recapitalize, they go to merchant banks that spread the loan risk, which includes the Swiss banks. Just calling in 10 percent of a loan on a cash-strapped enterprise could be a disaster."

They had been driving along the straight road parallel to the ore conveyor. To the right and left were mine facilities, but the road passed a bay converted into part of a larger port facility. They came to the end of the line, where the conveyor rose upward, so the ore cascaded into a massive heap of rock. Wheel loaders shoveled ore onto another conveyor that took it into the extraction circuit. This conveyor went underground, so that it did not interfere with traffic.

"I think I've learned all I ever wanted to know about gold mining," said Alex.

"Would you say that if it was a lipstick mine?"

Alex punched Doyle on the shoulder.

"Come on. Let's park the Land Rover and walk about. I find it interesting," said Doyle. "Just bear with me. We might even run into Joe."

They followed a signposted path that told them this was the crushing circuit. Native workers walked by, while others were working on the rigging and scaffolds, which supported the huge rotating drums grinding up the gold ore. A group of six men approached, all of them wearing orange high-visibility overalls, rubber boots, and hard hats. One of the men said hello; it was Joe.

"Hello, Joe," said Doyle, "thought we might find you in here. Can you stay for a moment? We won't keep you long."

Joe rattled out something in pidgin, too fast for Doyle to translate completely, but he caught some of it.

"Have May and Nellie told you what we found?"

"Yeah, something out in the bush, registering on the Geiger counter. I heard you had a run-in with a gunman and someone put a bomb in your car," said Joe.

"Here's the explosive," said Doyle, taking it from his pocket.

"Looks like the stuff used in the mine. The stuff I'm using to rig the bombs is probably the same stuff, but it's dyed a different color."

Alex said, "There's a big storm coming."

"Em nau, mi save, matbung I kam[63]," said Joe.

---

[63] "Yes, I understand a big storm was coming."

"Matbung, sounds dark enough for a bad storm," said Doyle.

"It means no military operations, according to Mr. Doyle," said Alex.

"How many bombs have you planted?" asked Doyle.

"Thirty, that's the entire explosive I had," said Joe.

"Do you have any guns handy?"

"A pistol and box of ammo in my locker, along with the unused blasting caps and the remote control detonator for the bombs."

"I think Jäger and company are just toying with us. It's hard though to figure out if the whole mine is in on this Raptor business or just Jäger, Koenig, and the security guards."

"The mine supervisors are all gutpela masta na missus as far as I can see."

"They all seem German, though, even if with Aussie and New Zealand accents, but maybe they're miners not terrorists. Still, I want you to disappear into the jungle at the first sign of trouble or if anyone is asking for you. Keep your gun with you at all times from now on," Doyle said.

Joe looked understandably concerned and said, "What about Auntie Nellie and May or Sister Kathy?'

"I'm as worried as you are. May's a professional, like Alex and Me and you. Your aunt is a tough customer, but we're all vulnerable to a bullet. I think Sister Kathy will be left alone, but still, good to remember we've more to think about than just us five. If we go missing and you're still here, take off. Find out where we are being held. Use your wantoks, anybody you can trust, to find where we are being held, and see if you can get to us, but don't do anything suicidal."

There was a shout from Joe's coworkers, who were waiting for him.

"Got to go. We've got a big job on changing out a major valve, and I'm the one who knows how to do it without getting us all killed." He grinned at Doyle and Alex and then jogged down between the machines to the other workers.

"OK, list that we've interviewed more workers at the mine. When we head back to town, let's drop by the hospital. I'll ask for some antifungal cream and try to give Sister Kathy a little toksave[64]."

"Toksave?" said Alex.

"You'll figure it out," said Doyle.

---

[64] Announcement or alert.

Chapter 55

Clouds appeared out of nowhere, changing from white to gray to dark blue. Storm demons leered down out of the great mass as lightning flashed, thunder rumbled, and the cumulonimbus split open. Columns of water splashed down.

Doyle and Alex ran back to the car, both soaked by the time they scrambled into the front seats. Doyle started the vehicle, and driving slowly, he retraced the route back along the mine conveyor. They passed the gaping pit of the mine, where huge waterfalls were streaming over the edge. Water was flooding out of the jungle, and streams turned into torrents, though not yet overrunning their banks.

Doyle wanted to fly along the road to Londolovit, but he forced himself to be patient and drive safely. The windscreen wipers barely coped with the drenching rain, and the lights disappeared into the whiteout. Cars and trucks traveling in the opposite direction loomed out of the murk. Once Doyle had to swerve to avoid a head-on collision with a truck. He almost drove into the jungle but recovered at the last moment, scrambling back on the road.

Doyle remembered that the hospital was just past the turn off for Londolovit. The Land Rover windscreen fogged up, and Alex leaned over Doyle to wipe it with a handkerchief. The dark and rain were not letting up. Overhead the sky was the color of bruised skin, and lightning bolts were flashing all around them. Lightning struck a tree

285

in front of them on the right-hand side of the road, sending the tree crashing to the highway but leaving enough of a gap to drive around.

Doyle held his breath, hoping that no other vehicle was in his path, as he maneuvered around the fallen tree. Just as he did so, car headlights pierced the rain, making Doyle turn hard right and then back to the left, causing the Land Rover to fishtail. He dropped his speed and steered into the skid and then powered up as the Land Rover straightened.

The Londolovit turnoff flashed past. Doyle slowed and looked into the gloom for the hospital sign. Within a few seconds, a road sign appeared, indicating the hospital was fifty yards ahead. Doyle slowed, looking in his mirror for any lights behind him. He signaled but stopped for a second to see if anybody might be coming in the other direction. There was no gleam of headlights, so he held his breath and turned left across the road. He slowed down and drove into the hospital car park. All the best parking spots were under a broad, sheltered walkway. One space was available, but it was for handicapped reserved parking. Doyle drove in and jumped out of the vehicle. Without looking back, he heard Alex slam her door.

The hospital comprised three large buildings. There were signs everywhere, but none indicated where he thought he would find Sister Kathy. He cursed himself for not asking Joe. A woman pushing a trolley dressed in an orderly's blue smock came toward him.

Doyle said, "Do you know Sister Kathy?"

"Wanem?"[65] said the woman.

"Sister Kathy?" Doyle wanted to pick the woman up and shake her, when Alex walked up behind him,

"Ask her in pidgin," said Alex.

---

[65] "What?"

"Ai, yu save Sistah Kathy?"[66]

"Em nau, mi save em."[67]

Doyle mentally counted to three in his head and said, "Em is stap we?"[68]

"Ah, go long front, na askim long re-cep-tion,"[69] she said with a smile.

"Tenk yu tru."[70]

Doyle walked as fast as he could. Rain was leaking through part of the roof and making a puddle. Doyle stepped on this, and his legs shot out in front of him. He would have cracked his head on the concrete if Alex hadn't caught him.

"Hi, handsome, is Heaven missing an angel?" said Alex in a corny American voice.

"Thanks, my poor noggin has had too many knocks of late," said Doyle.

He counted to five and walked normally to the hospital entrance and to the reception desk. Two receptionists were answering phones and directing inquiries. There were two rows of people opposite on benches. Some people were standing, as the benches were full. There was a ticket dispenser with the instructions to take a ticket and wait for a receptionist to call your number.

"Oh, sweet Jesus, we'll start a riot if we try to jump the queue," said Doyle.

'What did you expect?" said Alex.

---

[66] "Do you know Sister Kathy?"

[67] "Yes, I know her."

[68] "Where is she?"

[69] "Go to the front and ask at reception."

[70] "Thank you."

"Not this! Not a Turn-O-Matic machine," said Doyle, reading the brand name of the dispenser. He noticed that he and Alex were attracting less than sympathetic stares from the waiting patients, including a heavily pregnant woman who looked like she could go into labor at any second.

Alex said, "Look, up the corridor."

Doyle looked and saw a sign that said "Gifts and Pharmacy" on the right-hand side of the corridor.

Doyle and Alex walked up the corridor and turned into the shop. There was one customer concluding a transaction, while a few native people were browsing the items on display.

As the customer walked away, Doyle asked the shop clerk if he knew Sister Kathy.

"Yes, I know Kathy, tall lady from Mussau. Why do you want to see her?" said the woman who looked mixed-race, with pale skin, long blonde hair, and New Guinea facial features.

"We have a message from her cousin-brother, Joe," said Doyle.

The clerk looked at Alex and said, "Ooh, I like your blouse. It looks really nice. Where did you get it?"

"London, before I was posted to New Guinea. Tell you what; I've got a few like it at home in Kavieng. I can send you one if you can do us a favor."

"Thanks, what do you need?"

"Can you call Sister Kathy and just say Joe's relatives are here? I know we're not his relations, but we do need to see her."

"Yes, okay, here's my business card. I own the shop—well, actually my dad and dum do, but I run it. I have a ton of business cards; we're always going to Asia for our stores."

Doyle felt blood might start leaking out of his ears and nose, but the clerk picked up the phone and chattered away in pidgin.

"Okay, she's on her way."

"Your name's Daphne. That's very pretty," said Alex.

"Is it? I never really liked it. No one is called Daphne anymore."

"Ah, but in Ancient Greece Daphne was renowned for her beauty and chased so much by the gods that she begged to be turned into a tree."

"Really, wow, thank you."

Chapter 56

"Hello, mi Sister Kathy. Husat I laik tokim mi,"[71] said a tall Mussau woman from the door. She was dressed in a white smock and pants, with a nurse's cap on her head. Like many Mussau women, she had razor sharp cheekbones and large eyes, long loose limbs with well-defined muscles, and slender fingers.

"Go and talk to Sister Kathy. I'll chat with Daphne," said Alex.

They stepped out into the corridor, and Doyle said, "I'm Doyle; that's Alex in the gift shop. We're with May, Nellie, and Joe. Did they tell you about our mission when they stored their boxes at your house?"

Doyle could see Kathy mentally shift gears to talk in English. He knew to be a senior nurse she would be fluent but would speak pidgin most of the time.

"They said it was a big national security samtink,"[72] said Kathy.

"Yes, it is. Do you know what's in the boxes?"

"Yes, weapons and other things. Nellie and May came and took a couple of boxes after they got jobs as housemaids at the hostel."

"Look, we think the whole situation is about to turn very nasty. Mine security may connect you to Joe, May, and Nellie. You brought

---

71 "I'm Sister Kathy. Who wants to talk to me?"

72 Issue.

them to the mine employment office and spoke up for them as I recall."

"Yes, but all I said was they were three wantoks looking for a job. I said Joe was an ex-army engineer and May and Nellie were looking for housekeeping jobs, either for the company or private. They put cards up at the office from folks looking for private housekeepers. Mussaus are very much sought after. But why would they be searching for them?"

"Because if Alex and I are captured, they'll know instinctively that we couldn't be the only people involved in flushing out this … this … conspiracy. White people are much easier to spot and track, especially coming by plane. The mine security will look at the employment logs for the last month or so. They'll see three people hired two days before we arrived. They'll ask the employment office who these new people are. The employment folks will say a nursing sister brought them in. Even if they don't remember your name, they'll look at the names. Pilgrim will throw them, but Saupa, Asora, someone will likely recognize these as Mussau names. Okay, how many senior Mussau nursing sisters are there at the hospital? Problem solved."

"Oh Lord, what should I do?" said Kathy.

"Nothing, just act normally. If mine security apprehend you and search your house, plead innocent. Say you didn't know what was in their patrol boxes. Repeat the story that they were dropped off from a canoe, that they appeared, and that they told you they were looking for work. You helped them retrieve their belongings. I know you're afraid—"

"Mi no prait. Mi askim Lord Jesus i protectim mi,"[73] said Kathy.

---

[73] "I'm not afraid. Lord Jesus protects me."

Doyle realized that further instructions would be useless. Hopefully the mine security would not get to Kathy too quickly. She was one of the most senior nurses in the hospital, Doyle had noted from a plaque in reception, which was a New Ireland Provincial Government hospital, no doubt with supplemental funding from Lihir Gold. In a crowded hospital, it would be difficult to storm in and frog-march Sister Kathy away, given that she was a government employee.

Alex stepped out of the store and said, "Are you all done with Sister Kathy?"

"Ai, smart missus, May na Nellie tokim mi you wanpela pretty white lady. Em I tok stret,"[74] said Kathy.

Doyle saw Alex beam at this complement. He grabbed her hand and said, "Thanks, Kathy, we'd better go. Yu lukaut[75], okay?"

"Em nau, lukim yu bihain,"[76] said Kathy.

"Come on; the rain is easing off," said Doyle.

They walked to the Land Rover. Doyle noticed a mine truck with a canvas awning over its rear. It was parked at an angle across the car park, and he tensed as he realized the truck's tailgate was hanging open. Doyle could not make out if there was anyone in the cab. The rainstorm was passing, but it was still raining heavily.

Alex said, "That wasn't here before."

"No, it wasn't."

As the words left Doyle's mouth, khaki-clad soldiers jumped out of the rear of the truck and raced across the carpark. It was too late for Doyle and Alex to run as the soldiers fanned out to block any

---

[74] "Smart lady, May and Nellie told me you were one pretty white lady. They were right."

[75] "Be careful."

[76] "Yes, see you later."

vehicles exiting the hospital. Four soldiers were close now, and Doyle could see they were Asian, with a dragon insignia on the pockets of their uniforms.

"Put your hands up," Doyle hissed to Alex.

As they did so, the four soldiers split into two pairs. The ones on the other side of the Land Rover reached Alex, who stood in the surrender position, hands in the air. The soldiers came to a halt and then slammed their rifle butts into her head and face. Doyle began to shout, but as he turned to move, two rifle butts slammed into his head.

He did not pass out immediately and staggered away from the Land Rover, trying to reach his pistol. The last thing he saw were puddles on the ground as the rifle butts repeatedly slammed into him.

Chapter 57

Doyle surfaced from a dark pit as his head was yanked up. He opened his eyes to take in his surroundings. He tried to flex his limbs but found he was restrained. He could flex his fingers and wiggle his toes, so he knew he was not paralyzed. His head hurt, and the last thing he recalled was a rifle butt slamming his head into the ground.

Doyle could feel blood caked on his face, and it had run down his chin and splattered onto his clothes. He was sitting bound to a chair. Looking to his right, he saw May, Alex, and Nellie. All looked bloody and disheveled. Alex's lips were bloody and swollen. She also had a large knot on her forehead. Nellie had an eye almost closed, and May sported both a black eye and bloody face, with a swollen lip.

"Ah, good, Mr. Doyle, you are awake. I think we can now forgo the shallow pretense," said Jäger.

"Oh yeah, and what would that be?" said Doyle, taking a chance to look around. They were in a volcanic cavern. There were lights everywhere and the scurrying of activity, as Jäger's men and Chinese troops looked like they were readying for a rapid departure. Doyle looked further down the cavern, and what he thought was the dark back wall resolved itself into a submarine with a conning tower emblazoned with a Chinese imperial dragon.

"That you are a harmless labor inspector. I must admit, your subterfuge, and your simple disguise, initially took us in. We thought the noble Doyle had been killed in Port Moresby. However, your midnight excursion alerted us that you were more than a harmless busybody—isn't that the correct English expression?"

"I've always liked the Aussie expression of 'stickybeak,'" said Doyle.

"Stickybeak, ja, I like that, stickybeak. So no more stickybeak—we realized who you were."

"I suppose you're going to kill us, but first you want to do your 'madman taking over the world' monologue." Doyle could see the three women were all beginning to recover from their beatings

"I like you, Mr. Doyle. It is an English characteristic, to stare down death with humor—what is it, gallows humor?"

Jäger was perched on a table, still in his riding outfit, his riding crop in his leather-gloved hands.

"With the culmination of this operation, we will avenge Germany's humiliation by the English. Three wars in the last century. Each time our country reduced to penury, our national borders reduced and overseas territories were seized. At last, Germany will redress the balance of power."

"Oh, please, I've got an almighty headache from your Chinese friends," said Doyle, now seeing a Chinese soldier in an officer's uniform, standing on the other side of the table from Jäger. He had not been there when Doyle came awake. He must have walked up while Jäger was speaking. Doyle saw he had three stars on his uniform collar, signifying the rank of colonel.

Shaking his head to clear some more cobwebs, Doyle adopted a thick Irish accent, sounding like a sheep farmer from Tipperary.

"Oy ... Fu Manchu, what der feck are ye doin' with this wee manky eejit? Oi tort you'd be a bit wiser, youse bein a Chinee an' all."

Jäger held his superior Teutonic smile, while the Chinese soldier was impassive.

295

Doyle continued. "I smelled a rat when the bomb recovery site was revealed. I mean, really, Saints Peter and Paul's Rocks? How would you get five atom bombs onto those windswept crags?"

"Yes, Mr. Doyle, another of our subterfuges. We need more time to study the bomb due to the ravages of the last war and the restrictions placed on our military. However, once we have all the secrets, we plan to deliver two bombs to London and Philadelphia to begin with. The empire will be plunged into chaos and confusion. Our Chinese allies are not so bound by the handcuffs you have placed on us."

"Do you honestly think that wiping out London and Philadelphia will be the end of the empire? Really?" said Doyle with withering scorn.

"You could not—"

"Oh, please, you believe that?"

For the first time, the Chinese soldier looked at Jäger, a flicker of concern in his otherwise poker-faced countenance.

"London extends down further than it does up, same in Philadelphia. We don't just keep the office supplies down there. Yes, it would be a hammer blow but nothing from which we could not recover. You'd need to carpet-bomb Britain with atomic weapons to do the job properly."

"That can be arranged," said Jäger curtly.

"Sorry, Gustave, but no. You've got five bombs: one dismantled, four throws of the dice to bring down the greatest empire ever established. Sorry, Colonel Chop-Suey, but the Germans are once again military idiots. If I were you, I'd get out of here as soon as possible and leave Jäger and his troop of mental dwarves," Doyle said.

Jäger stepped forward and lashed the riding crop across Doyle's face. It stung like an electric shock, but weeks of pain and toughening under Nellie's care had hardened Doyle like a piece of rawhide.

"Touched a nerve, did I? The ransom was another clue to cluelessness. Ten billion pounds is lot of money but not an insurmountable sum for the empire. That and the payment in bearer bonds—gold would have been better, but I can see much less wieldy."

"You're bluffing, but very commendable," said Jäger.

"Actually, I'm not. You know what, ladies? Let's forget this operation. Jäger, just go; take your bombs. Go! I really don't care anymore; just let us go. We'll take a canoe and paddle to New Ireland. I don't see why we have to die for the conceited antics of Germany and China. I certainly don't want to see good and faithful servants of the Crown killed to satisfy what must count as the maddest plan I've ever heard. If you have a shred of decency kill me, but let the women live; they're no danger to you."

"So gallant, Mr. Doyle," said Jäger, who had now been joined by Koenig.

"I see your reptilian pal's shown up. I think you have what passes for brains in this outfit. Let me guess—you are an officer in the Abteilung?[77] I don't know how much you've overheard, but do I sound like a raving idiot? You must have thought this through. I suppose your Chinese pal is from the Jinyiwei?"[78]

Jäger looked rattled as he watched the piercing green-blue eyes of his colleague, who was matching the Chinese officer for imperturbability.

Doyle could sense rather than see the fine cracks in the demeanor of Jäger, Koenig, and the Chinese officer. He felt the adrenaline surge

---

[77] German Secret Service.

[78] Chinese Secret Service.

in response to the riding crop blow and the heedless courage of the condemned.

"The Stewarts have been providing brides and bridegrooms to every royal house in Europe, and some beyond, for centuries. Sure they're constitutional monarchies for the most part, but don't you think the demise of Uncle James might be upsetting? They would add their voices to those seeking revenge. Russia will certainly declare war and invade. Austria-Hungary might take Germany's side, as in the past, but the mass destruction of London alone would likely make them sit on the sidelines. Only France no longer has an active monarchy, but they will still join in. Hell, even Lichtenstein and Monaco will line up to give Germany a kicking," Doyle said.

"You forget our Chinese allies. You've seen the techniques they have developed to instill devotion to our cause. Half a million Chinese invading Siberia would likely neutralize the Russian threat. We have been building up our military in secret in China, away from prying eyes. For thirty years, Germany has been expanding its army and air force in China, deep in the heart of the country, away from the gaze of the British Empire. In return, our naval architects have built the Chinese navy, in places closed to foreigners like Hainan and the Penghu Islands, on the coast of the Bohai Sea and deep in the Chinese interior. Our rivers are so vast and navigable that—"

Chapter 58

"Our rivers? Our rivers?! You forget yourself," the Chinese officer barked at Jäger.

"Colonel Sung, my sincerest apologies. I was becoming carried away at the creative genius of the alliance forged by our two nations."

"This is not an alliance of equals, Jäger," said Colonel Sung.

Koenig's face now looked much less detached. The Chinese soldiers had all stopped in their tracks and were looking at their superior. Jäger's men, who had been standing at ease with submachine guns held across their chests, now gripped them tighter, looking for an order from Jäger and Koenig.

Doyle took his eyes off Jäger and looked at the three women. They looked at him for a lead. "Feel free to join in, girls," said Doyle, "This isn't a boy's only conversation."

"Get out of my country," spat May.

"I thought you would have no love for the empire, especially the English," said Jäger.

"Mr. Doyle's Irish, so his country is as much of a colonial outpost as mine, just nearer to England. Do you think you are the first white man who has ever questioned my loyalty to king and country? Of course the bloody empire's not perfect: racist, elitist, and merciless with dissenters. But a barefoot bush kanaka meri like me still rose to the challenge. Auntie Nellie is a coastwatcher, devoted to the empire. She has a portrait of the king on her hut wall."

May looked at Doyle. "Can you get her a personally signed portrait of the King and Queen Charlotte when we get out of this mess?"

"Oh, he'll just forget May. Don't worry, I'll ensure Nellie receives signed portraits of King James and the royal family," said Alex.

Nellie laughed and said, "Mistah King, Mistah King, Missus Kwin[79], Missus Kwin." She then spat some unintelligible invective at Jäger.

Jäger lashed Doyle about the head again with his riding crop and then turned to the women with loathing in his eyes. Doyle guessed his intent and toppled his chair forward, falling into Jäger and distracting him. Jäger threw him sideways, and his arm and shoulder broke the fall.

"Where is your other companion—the native man?" said Koenig.

Doyle gazed up from the floor and said, "Lot of men here. You need to be more specific."

Koenig turned and shouted out an inquiry in German. Lisle Dorfmann walked up, dressed in much the same office clothes but with an open jacket perched on her shoulders. She responded in German, but Doyle heard Dorfmann say "Asora, Joseph."

Jäger said, "We would prefer you reveal that information without causing unnecessary distress to the ladies."

Doyle looked at Dorfmann, thinking that she was probably another Abteilung officer.

"Couldn't get more distressing than this, could it?" said Doyle. "Could someone lift me up? If I'm going to die, I'd prefer to be upright."

---

[79] Queen.

Koenig shouted a command in German. A soldier detached himself and came over and pulled Doyle's chair back into position.

May said, "Joe's out in the jungle. Good luck finding him."

"It's true," said Doyle. "I gave him orders to make himself scarce at the first sign of trouble."

"Do we believe them?" Jäger said.

"It is not important. Shoot them and be done with it. I tire of these infantile games you Europeans like to play. The Middle Kingdom will assume its rightful place as the lord of worlds," said Colonel Sung.

"Did you hear that, Jäger? Think of that when your children are on guard duty in Harbin, freezing their bollocks off."

After that, there was mayhem.

Chapter 59

A huge blast shuddered though the cavern. Doyle was knocked back in his chair, hitting his head on the concrete floor. His eyes went dark for a few seconds; he recovered his wits and knew by instinct what was happening.

"Alex, Nellie, May, get down."

Alex, Nellie, and May toppled their chairs sideways. Doyle's chair had been in the path of the explosion, but the three others were not. Machine gun fire lit up the cavern. Doyle watched as dark figures ran in through the gap in the metal doors. Doyle could see Joe and other native men directing the armed mineworkers to make up a skirmish line, advancing in ragged units, while being covered by their comrades behind. They leapfrogged into the cavern and, when close to the captors, began throwing grenades to rip gaps in their ranks.

More men continued pouring into the cavern, some armed only with bush knives. They soon outnumbered the German and Chinese troops. The rain of hand grenades continued, and Doyle prayed they would not drop nearby. Joe was yelling instructions to the mineworkers and pointing to where Doyle and the three women lay. Other individual mine workers were also yelling commands and directing the improvised army.

NCOs, thought Doyle. *Of course, there are other ex-soldiers at the mine.*

The mineworkers reached Doyle and the women, loosening the rope that bound them to the chairs. Several others stood over them to protect them from enemy fire. Doyle shouted to the women to stay down. He scrambled on the floor across to the table where Koenig and Colonel Sung had stood. Doyle took a sweep around the cavern.

Behind him, stragglers were still coming through the metal doors. Doyle saw that the blast had blown a gap between the doors, bending one of the doors so the corner folded back like a piece of cardboard. All the resistance was now coming in front of Doyle. May, Alex, and Nellie crawled over to the table to take in the firefight. The cavern was bifurcated into two separate hollows. The submarine was moored in the left-hand grotto of the cavern. The right was living quarters for the Chinese troops and a workshop.

Doyle could see a mass of metal on a table, which he recognized from the schematics as the innards of an atomic bomb. The main feature of the bomb was a sphere, a plutonium core, surrounded by high explosives. The explosive would compress the plutonium metal to supercriticality through a focused blast. Doyle noticed that the sphere housing was still there, but the shielded plutonium sphere was missing.

The mineworkers occupied the entire cavern except the grotto with the submarine. The German and Chinese troops had been surprised but were professionals so soon recovered. But it was too late. The mine workforce outnumbered them. The miners lay down withering volleys of gunfire and hurled grenades. The Chinese armory had been reached, and more men were taking up guns and grenades.

Joe slipped back to ensure his auntie and friends were not mortally wounded. Other native men were yelling commands and directing the mineworkers to keep the Germans and Chinese in retreat.

"Auntie, yu orait?"[80] said Joe.

"Em nau, olgeta I no gat pain. Go tokim bikman, Doyle."[81]

"Hi, Mr. Doyle. We overran the Lihir Gold Mining office and found their arsenal. We already had plenty of explosives. I'll tell you the details later. What do you want us to do?"

"Get weapons for us, pistols if there are no machine guns, and then try to stop the submarine from leaving," Doyle said.

Joe shouted out something in pidgin, and two men dodged through the hail of bullets to hunker down next to Joe. They had scavenged two German machine guns and two Chinese pistols. May and Alex took the machine guns, while Nellie and Doyle grabbed the two pistols. Joe ran back to where the mineworkers were pouring fire on the retreating Chinese and Germans. They were scurrying to a hatch door in the side of the conning tower. Chinese sailors on the top of the conning tower had set up a heavy machine gun that raked the miners.

Doyle watched as Nellie, Alex, and May began blasting away. May and Alex fired short bursts with deadly accuracy, flooring German and Chinese troops. Nellie was picking off wounded soldiers with her pistol. There was so much gunfire and smoke that Doyle only shot if he was being menaced, preferring to watch the progress of the battle in the cavern.

Nellie ran out of bullets and found a bush knife. A wounded German rose off the floor and pushed her, trying to get to the submarine. Nellie fell on her back but held on tight to the bush knife. She swung with deadly force at the retreating soldier's leg, slashing through skin and tendons. Hobbled, he collapsed to one knee, allowing Nellie to make a backhanded stroke along the man's

---

[80] "Auntie, are you okay?"

[81] "Yes, we're all okay. Go and talk to our leader, Mr. Doyle."

neck, causing blood to gush from his carotid artery. He fell forward twitching as blood streamed out of him. Nellie pulled a pistol from the dying man's belt holster and began picking off the wounded again. May saw what had happened and moved next to Nellie, while Alex stayed with Doyle.

Joe directed fire at troops running into the hatch door on the side of the conning tower. The door was soon blocked with piled-up bodies. Doyle saw the sailors deploy a rope ladder on the far side of the conning tower.

Grenades thrown at the submarine had little success. Some bounced off the submarine and exploded in the water. Those that did explode on the submarine caused no damage to its steel plates.

The fusillades were slowly dying away. Fewer German or Chinese troops were running to the submarine, and the sailors dismounted the heavy machine gun.

In all the frenzied action, Doyle almost missed Jäger and Koenig run around the narrow shore and into a tunnel at the back of the cavern.

Chapter 60

Joe yelled, "Cease fire, cease fire." The other ex-soldiers took up the cry, and the shooting died away.

The cavern was abruptly quiet. The submarine sat floating in the cavern pool. Doyle noticed that the vessel was now untethered. Mine workers milled around, looking at the men who had been issuing commands. Others wandered around the cavern, helping themselves to anything that lay at hand. A couple of men lifted a box on to the table and pulled out Doyle's shoulder harness and holster.

"Hey, that's mine; bilong mi!" yelled Doyle.

He ran over to the men with the box. It contained all the firearms taken from him and Alex. The two men looked reluctant to surrender these treasures. One of the men, who had led the mineworkers, barked something in pidgin. The two men backed off. Doyle took the box and handed Alex her guns.

"Nellie, please lukautim dispela musket,"[82] said Doyle, handing her the Mauser. He then looked at all of his team members. "I saw Jäger and Koenig; they didn't get into the submarine. They went into a tunnel on the other side of the lake cavern. I am going after them."

"Someone should go with you," said Alex.

"Take Joe," said May.

"Joe is needed here. So are you two. Do not let anybody take

---

[82] "Nellie, please look after this gun."

souvenirs from the bomb, especially the core. I will be careful. If I don't come back within a few minutes, one of you come and find me," said Doyle.

Doyle ran to the lake cavern, stooping to pick up the long bush knife used by Nellie. He flexed his arms into his shoulder harness and took out his Browning Hi-Power from the holster. He pulled the magazine out and saw it was fully loaded. He pumped the slide and ejected a round, which he pocketed. Doyle passed the nose of the submarine, water was churning up from below as it readied for departure.

Doyle stepped nearer to the tunnel, lit like the rest of the cavern by fluorescent roof lights. The tunnel curved upward on a steep gradient for about twenty yards. Doyle pressed himself to the inner side of the curve to minimize his visibility.

He rounded the bend, which opened into another well-lit cavern. It looked as if Jäger and Koenig were gathering documents from a filing cabinet prior to departure. This smaller cavern also had a lake. An outboard-powered speedboat was moored to a small wharf. There was an exit tunnel, which, Doyle guessed, opened to the sea surface. Doyle figured the two Germans were fleeing separately. He wondered if they had a prearranged rendezvous with the submarine or other naval vessel.

Doyle stayed hidden and looked around the room, realizing it was a mess facility. The German security force must have wanted a place to eat pork knuckles and sauerkraut and relax away from the Chinese. The filing cabinet stood alone against a left-hand wall. Next to the filing cabinet were a fridge and gas stove. The main feature of this part of the cavern was a long table with dining chairs scattered around. Behind the table were rapiers hanging on the wall.

Doyle looked to his right and saw Schläger fencing suits and goggles hanging on pegs. He strode out of the tunnel and into cavern.

"Gentlemen, hands on heads please," said Doyle.

The two Germans froze; Doyle could only see their backs, but he assumed they were armed.

Doyle said, "Did you come here to relive the happy days in Heidelberg, clouting each other around the head with these cocktail sticks?"

Koenig whirled, pulling a pistol from his belt. His gun boomed, and Doyle felt the bullet pass his cheek. Doyle fired, and his bullet caught Koenig in the chest, who landed on his back. Doyle put another round into Koenig's torso and then aimed his gun at Jäger, who raised his hands.

Doyle directed Jäger to step away from the filing cabinet and walk to the far end of the mess table. Doyle walked over to examine Koenig, who was still alive and groaned loudly. Doyle was distracted long enough for Jäger to go for his gun. His shot was wide, but he kept firing. Doyle threw himself under the mess table and returned fire, aiming to hit Jäger's legs. His gun jammed after two shots.

Doyle heard Jäger's gun clicking on empty. Clearing the jam in the Browning would take a matter of seconds, but time was a luxury in a cave with swords and a desperate man. Jäger jumped to the wall and wrenched a rapier from the display. Doyle scrambled out from under the table but wished he had stayed there. Jäger advanced on Doyle, making slashing cuts in the air. He could not reach the sword display so drew his bush knife.

Jäger guffawed. "You are going to defend yourself with that? This will be easy."

Doyle's bush knife had a curved three-foot blade like a saber, but all resemblance stopped there. Though it was sharp, the knife's weight was all in a blade designed for slashing vegetation. The only advantage that Doyle could see was his hours of training with a havildar master at arms. This included not only formal fencing but also a range of dirty tricks.

Jäger came in, making Doyle fight for his life with the clumsy blade. Jäger's rapier was everywhere, darting at Doyle's face and then chest, back to the head and slashing at his flanks. Doyle knew he could never win with a knife that was little more than a sickle. As Jäger advanced on him again, Doyle parried a blow, grabbed a handful of knives and forks from a cutlery tray, and threw them at Jäger.

It was a desperation move but it worked. Jäger had to put his arm up to protect his head from the volley of silverware. There was not enough advantage for Doyle to land a killing blow. Instead, he rolled over the table and grabbed another rapier from the display.

He was just fast enough to elude Jäger's sword, which slammed the table behind him, nicking his shoulder.

Jäger's eyes narrowed.

"I congratulate you, Mr. Doyle, but I doubt you are my equal, even with a real sword."

"Aye, right enough, Gustave, I'm much better."

Doyle came out from behind the table and went on the attack. Jäger parried Doyle's thrust, but circumstances had reversed. Doyle could gauge the strength of Jäger's weaker wrist. Schläger fencing was static, limited to taking cuts and blows at a head. This was fencing, as Doyle knew from India, where there were bandits armed with knives and daggers as well as swords, some of them dipped in poison.

Doyle advanced, his blade a blur, slashing and sweeping at Jäger.

Jäger threw a plate from the table like a discus. Doyle dodged this like a boxer rolling with a punch.

They paused. Sweat was beading on Jäger's forehead, and there was fear in his eyes. He looked right and left for a way out. If he moved to one side or the other, Doyle easily countered and kept Jäger at bay.

"Hey Gustave, did I ever tell you about my uncle, Father Bernard? He runs a boxing gym in Derry—Londonderry if you want to be Protestant. He says you have to get the Holy Trinity to work together: head, hands and feet. It's the same in fencing."

Jäger made a desperate rush at Doyle, slashing for all he was worth. Doyle parried each slash and thrust until they were hilt to hilt. Both were breathing heavily, and Doyle could smell the garlic and mustard on Jäger's breath. Doyle could see desperation in Jäger's eyes. Jäger spit, hitting Doyle's right eye. He stepped back to run him through.

Doyle's reflexes were all that saved him. He anticipated a thrust, backed, and turned side on. Nonetheless, he received a deep cut along his chest. One eye was closed, stinging from the saliva; the other was watering in sympathy. The tears refracted his sight, so he was fighting in a blur. He saw multitudes of blades and felt Jäger land another cut on his arm.

Doyle cursed his stupid overconfidence. He jumped back as far as he could and kicked a chair at Jäger. If Jäger had been fresh, he would have dodged it. Jäger staggered as the chair hit him but held onto his rapier. It was only a few seconds respite, but enough for Doyle to wipe his closed eye. Both eyes were still watering, but his sight began to improve. Jäger's legs looked weaker, and his chest was heaving.

Doyle needed some more distractions.

"Thank you, Auntie Nellie," said Doyle.

"What?" said Jäger, making another slashing attack on Doyle.

"Auntie Nellie, the best trainer money can buy."

"What is this nonsense?"

Doyle took another leap backward and rubbed his eyes again with his sleeve.

"Thank you, Havildar Singh Das."

"Again with the names?"

"Ah, Gustave, no more spit left? It's time to end this nonsense."

Doyle made a ferocious slashing attack on Jäger, driving him where he wanted by the skill of his swordplay. He backed Jäger against the cave wall. Doyle made several blurring slashes that inflicted deep cuts on Jäger's arms and chest.

"That's for being a clever shit and spitting in my eye, though by rights I should have kicked you in the bollocks." Doyle punched the hilt of his rapier against the forte of Jäger's blade, an old trick Havildar Singh Das had taught him. It spun from Jäger's hand and clattered to the floor. Doyle's sword was now at Jäger's throat.

"Come on now; be a good lad and know when you're beat."

"Congratulations, Mr. Doyle, I do keep underestimating you."

Jäger's eyes flicked right. Doyle was aware of movement in the entrance to the tunnel.

"Who's there?" said Doyle, not dropping his guard on Jäger.

"It's Alex and May," said Alex. "We saw you fencing ... I ... am lost for words."

"Makes a change," said Doyle. "Get some rope or handcuffs."

"Man, u save faitim gut wantaim cutlass,"[83] said May.

All the while, Doyle's blade pressed hard against Jäger throat. Doyle was feeling the strain and relaxed to get his breathing under

---

[83] "Wow, you fight so well with a sword."

control. Jäger grabbed the rapier blade in his right hand. Before Doyle could wrest back control of the sword, Jäger impaled his eye on the sword tip and thrust forward, bearing all of his weight on the blade. His other eye flickered and went blank, and his arms fell slack to his sides. Jäger continued to stand while Doyle ripped the sword out of his skull. Jäger's knees buckled and he fell.

"Shit, shit shit shit!"

Doyle lashed the bloodied sword on the mess table, cutting linen and scattering plates and cutlery.

"He's still breathing," said May, who was using napkins for a pressure bandage on Jäger's bloody eye socket.

Alex joined May and said, "He's still alive, Doyle. We could have the medics stabilize him. Brain wounds are funny things. If he had slashed his jugular, he might have bled out by now."

Chapter 61

Doyle picked up Jäger and slung him over his shoulder. He felt Jäger's pulse. It was still strong, but he could be brain dead with body still functioning. He had seen weirder things in war.

Back in the main cavern, the miners were standing around the periphery of the cavern lake. The water welling up from under the sub was increasing, and its propeller was turning.

"They're leaving," said May.

"The other bombs, can anyone see them?" said Alex.

"They must be in the submarine," said Doyle.

He laid Jäger on the cavern floor next to Lisle Dorfmann.

"Here's someone to keep you company," said Doyle.

"What have you done to him?" said Dorfmann.

"He got something in his eye."

Doyle looked across at the partially dismantled bomb. He looked into the box used to store his weapons and saw two Geiger counters. He activated one and saw the readings were high, not yet past the danger mark but close to it. He turned back to the submerging submarine. He was tempted to lob a load of grenades into the water, but he knew these would do no damage to the vessel.

"Masta Doyle, dispela man i save where bot i kam out long bik solwara,"[84] said Nellie.

---

[84] "Mister Doyle, this man knows where the boat comes out in the open sea."

Nellie was holding the arm of one of the mine crew, a Lihir man, judging by his appearance and head shape.

"Em nau, mi save, em I gat bik maus underneat solawara long Suein."[85]

"Suein, where is that?" asked Doyle.

"North coast," said the Lihir man.

"Must be the tunnel that connects the cavern to the sea. We could blow it up, but we'd better hurry. Can we improvise a bomb?"

"Yes," said Joe, "but we'll need to fire it by wire. Someone will need to go down and place the bomb on top of the tunnel, and we don't have any diving equipment."

"I can do it," said a wiry, bushy-haired man with skin the color of butter.

"Manus man," said May.

"Okay, what does that mean?" said Doyle.

"It means they are among the best free divers in the world," said May.

---

[85] "Yes, I know that there's a big cave underneath sea at Suein."

Chapter 62

Doyle rattled out instructions to his ragtag army. He wanted two trucks, one loaded with armed miners, the other with the explosives crew, to fashion a large explosive charge with several hundred yards of wire cable to a surface electronic detonator. Scattered around the cavern were wounded men, some dying and some crying out in a mix of languages. Some men were trying to staunch wounds, while others were ministering the last rites to the dying.

Alex had been scouting around the cavern floor, looking at the dead and wounded. She dragged Lisle Dorfmann to her feet. She had lost her jacket and one arm hung limp from a bullet wound.

"We'll have to interrogate her later," said Doyle.

"I can make her speak," said May.

Doyle was about to argue, but May dragged the woman to a table and shouted out some instructions in pidgin. Two men threw the woman on to her back with her legs in the air. May took a bush knife and sliced off the woman's skirt. Dorfmann gasped in pain, yelling in German about her injured arm. The men now pulled back on her legs, so her belly and crotch were exposed. May grabbed the woman's panties and sliced these off in a fluid motion. Dorfmann gasped and protested in German and English about being brutally disrobed.

One of the men handed May a crow bar. She looked at the woman, whose vagina and anus were now pointed upward. Many of the native

315

miners stared with fascination at a white woman's vagina. Doyle heard a lot of murmuring of surprise and admiration.

Dorfmann fell into sullen silence, punctured only by cries when her injured arm was disturbed.

"Are you going to tell me where the submarine is taking the bomb?" said May.

Dorfmann remained silent.

May showed her the crowbar, which was about an inch across and had a blunt point. May placed it on Dorfmann's anal opening and began to work it past the sphincter. Dorfmann screamed.

"China, China!"

"What else?" said May.

"I don't know anything else," shouted Dorfmann.

May worked the crowbar's tip. Some of the men laughed.

"The bomb, the bomb ... it will be copied ... they have the schematics."

"Do they know how to make a core?" said Doyle. "I'd answer if I were you; I am not going to stop her."

May kept up her probing with the crowbar.

"No, they can't make a core; they have to dismantle it somewhere safe. That's all I know."

May pulled the crowbar back. She had not penetrated far up the woman's anus, and there was not even a trickle of blood.

"Very effective, May, though she's German, so I was afraid she might enjoy it," said Doyle.

May gave an evil laugh and said, "I've never met anyone who didn't break with the crowbar."

Doyle responded, "She's German intelligence, so an extremely valuable prisoner. If she had a poison tooth, she would have bitten it by now. Nevertheless, she is likely to have a poison pill somewhere.

Get the men to tie her up. Put her arm in a splint and tie her to a stretcher. Please can you ask Nellie to stay and look after her and Jäger? Have her do what she can to bandage his head. God knows how long he'll live without proper medical treatment.

May turned to Nellie and talked in Mussau. Nellie nodded and talked back in the same language. Several Mussau men in the mine workforce went and stood with her. Joe got on a table with the other miners, who had led the fighting. He spoke in pidgin, outlining the plan. Doyle could follow though Joe spoke very quickly. He understood the need to get to Suein and also to save the mine, since everyone worked there. There were a few questions but no serious opposition.

"Christ, can we get going?" said Doyle.

"Sorry, Mr. Doyle," said Joe, "but we don't want to have a tribal war on our hands. Everybody knows what is happening, and all have agreed what has to be done. New Guinea is very democratic."

They raced out of the cavern to the vehicles. Doyle knew the submarine must be reversing down the underground tunnel. The vessel was probably navigating by periscope and lights. It would be moving slowly and on limited battery power. The convoy set out on the same road Doyle had driven a few nights previously.

This time the vehicles had driven up to the cavern doors, so there was no treacherous walk over the river ford and along the jungle path. Doyle was in the lead vehicle with Alex. In the back were Joe and the other explosive experts constructing an improvised bomb. Behind came another truck with armed miners. Doyle thought it unlikely there would be anymore resistance, but he did not want to be outgunned.

The trucks rattled and jolted until they hit the smooth coral surface of the main road and were able to speed up. They thundered up the road past the Londolovit turn off and then the airport road. They followed the road as it turned west and shortly thereafter were in Suein. The Lihir man was in their vehicle; he clambered down onto the running board and told Doyle to follow the road down to the beach.

The road descended down into a small inlet, with cliffs on one side and relatively flat land on the other. A few ragged mangrove trees fringed the cove. *There must be a freshwater outlet,* thought Doyle, seeing the dark water where there was a break in the reef.

There were small canoes pulled up on the shore. Joe shouted instructions, and two canoes were put into the water. The Lihir man paddled one canoe and Joe the other. The Manus man picked a big boulder from the shore and put it into the canoe with him and the Lihir man.

"What are your names?" said Doyle to the Lihir man and Manus man.

"I'm Lamilla," said the Lihir man.

"I'm Molean," said the Manus man.

"OK, you know what you are doing? Who's going with Joe?"

"I am," said May.

"Alex, come with me. I can paddle a dugout, learned on Emananus."

The little flotilla of canoes slid through the water, following the dark blue of the cleft within the reef. On either side Doyle saw flashes of color as fish darted along the reef. Below in the dark blue there were silvery flashes of small baitfish and the occasional flash of a larger fish like a jack.

After a few hundred yards, Lamilla pointed to the sea and signaled to stop. The three canoes came together. Molean slid over the side between the canoes. Lamilla handed him the bomb, a sack of plastic explosives. Doyle slipped into the water to help Molean. Outside the bag was a neat coil of wire, which Molean would bring back to the surface once the bomb was planted. Doyle used a section of rope to tie the bomb to Molean's back, using a quick release knot. Lamilla leaned over and tied a long rope around Molean's waist. Joe handed Molean the large rock, and he was gone.

Chapter 63

There was a set of handmade goggles in the bottom of the canoe taken by Doyle and Alex. They looked old and worn, but Doyle slipped these on and dove down as far as he could. He could see the reef slope and a figure getting smaller and smaller, trailing bubbles. Doyle had to surface for air and ducked below the surface again. He had lost contact with Molean. He could see the rope connecting Molean with the surface, but it just faded into the twilight of the deep reef.

Alex tapped him on the shoulder, pointing behind him. A large tiger shark had cruised in, attracted by the commotion. It swam past with cold distain as it examined Doyle and the canoes. It swam off into the open ocean. Doyle put his head below the surface again, checking his watch; one minute, two minutes, three minutes ticked past, and Molean remained submerged. Doyle imagined Molean in trouble on the seabed, seized by a giant clam or a large octopus, attacked by sharks or blacking out from the rapid descent.

Doyle was about to look at his watch again when he saw the rope twitch. He must have been underwater for close to five minutes thought Doyle. May and Joe began to pull up the rope as fast as they could. Doyle watched as a figure emerged from the blue murk. Molean was voiding his breath in great silver clouds of bubbles to avoid an embolism. The thin black detonation wire in his hand, Molean saw Doyle in the water and gave a thumbs-up.

Doyle climbed back onto the canoe. Once Molean was back onboard with Lamilla, Joe attached the wires to the electronic detonator, primed the batteries, and pressed the button. The surface of the water shuddered, and a cascade of seawater reared up and overturned the canoes.

Doyle surfaced and counted five heads bobbing on the sea. Despite the explosive cascade, no one was hurt. The canoes were close by, so they swam to these and righted each one in turn. Molean and Lamilla swam after the paddles. Lamilla located two paddles and swam back to his canoe. Molean swam about and found the other paddle, but he did not return to the canoe.

The water surface was the color of milk from the explosion debris. Dead and stunned fish littered the surface. Large jacks and red snapper circled about, making dashes into the cloudy water to hunt. Molean swam farther out to sea, where there was clear water. Doyle hissed with impatience and fear. Large triangular fins were slicing through the water.

Sharks bumped and scraped against the canoes in pursuit of fish. Alex let out an involuntary yelp. Doyle was grim faced, but the islanders seemed indifferent to the feeding frenzy going on around them. Molean pressed on, looking below the surface. Doyle saw him cup a hand to his eye, making a lens by blowing air from his nostril into the cupped hand. Once he was satisfied, he swam back to Lamilla's canoe, carrying the paddle. Twice he stopped to fend off sharks with the paddle, but not aggressively, just pushing them away with the paddle tip. He climbed back into Lamilla's canoe.

Alex said, "My goodness, Molean, you were very brave, I mean those sharks—"

Lamilla, May, and Joe laughed. Molean blushed and said, "Emi sak tasol, misses."[86]

The men in the second truck had been on the shore all this time and were joined by the Suein villagers. The three canoes paddled in. Doyle told Alex to gather the dead and stunned fish, like the other two canoes.

"We've got to pay the rent," said Doyle.

Several villagers went to the shore to retrieve their canoes. Lamilla exchanged a few words with the Suein villagers, who looked amazed when he told them the story. They were happy with the piles of reef fish in the canoes. Doyle, Molean, Joe, Alex, and May came up the beach, dripping wet but none the worse from their drenching.

"What now?" said May.

"Back to the cavern," said Doyle. "I'm assuming the submarine will go back there. They might detonate the atom bombs, but they would just leave a hole in Lihir. Most likely the blast would flow out of the tunnel, so another big fish harvest."

He looked out to sea, where the blue color was slowly returning. The Suein villagers were at the shoreline and a few had gone out to gather more of the unexpected fish bounty. Increasing numbers of shark fins slashed through the water as they competed for the dead fish.

"Any crocs here, Lamilla?" asked Doyle.

"No, not enough kuruk, you know, mangroves," said Lamilla.

"Come on; let's get back to Auntie Nellie, said Doyle.

The ground shook, and there was a muffled roar. The water turned milky again as coral and sand were put into suspension. Some sharks surfaced, writhing and splashing on the water with their fins.

---

[86] "They were just sharks, miss."

Doyle knew that underwater blasts were most effective against fish with swim bladders. Nevertheless, sharks close to the blast would be damaged through the pummeling of their internal organs.

"Bloody hell, was that the atom bomb?" asked Alex.

Everyone was chattering excitedly about what may have happened. Doyle raised his voice and said, "May, Joe, translate for me; my pidgin's not good enough." He continued. "That was not the atom bomb. My guess is that the submarine fired her aft torpedo tubes in order to try to clear the blockage we created in the tunnel." He heard May and Joe explaining to the crowd of miners. These were men used to technology, not tribesmen praying to passing aircraft or who believed a white man wore long trousers to cover up his huge penis.

He saw the looks of comprehension on their faces. May and Joe explained that the submarine had probably been destroyed, but they should get back to the cavern in case they came back. The miners quickly jumped on both trucks. Doyle could not see who drove the lead truck, but now all he could think about was making sure there was not a second firefight back at the cavern. Some of the Germans and Chinese wounded might even join in. Doyle recalled that guns and magazines were scattered about the cavern floor

It seemed as if all of Lihir had turned out to see the two trucks drive past. There were vehicles streaming in and out of Londolovit as mayhem had descended on the mine.

"Christ, I hope the military get here soon," said Doyle. "These are good fellows to have in a scrap. But now that this is drawing to a close, it could get nasty if folks start turning on each other, easily done after a few beers."

Alex and May were with Doyle in the truck, and May nodded in agreement. "We'll need to disarm everyone as soon as possible. The best thing would be to get everyone back to work and cleaning up after today."

Doyle could see the miners in the lead truck being jolted about and slapped by the overhanging vegetation. He saw how the men were all talking animatedly, their eyes bright and hands making extravagant gestures. These were men still in the grip of battle fever; this needed to be nipped in the bud as soon as possible. The women would be particularly vulnerable if a spark unleashed an orgy of violence.

They reached the cavern. Nellie was sitting outside, Mauser in her hand and a bush knife on her lap. She sat next to Lisle Dorfmann. She had wrapped a blanket around Dorfmann to preserve her modesty and folded another on which to rest her shattered arm. Jäger lay close by, still alive but inert, and with a proper pressure bandage over his eye and a blanket folded under his head.

The other Mussaus and remaining miners were dragging out the dead and wounded onto the grass. A plume of dust was making a lazy spiral into the air from the cave mouth. Doyle said nothing but joined other miners running into the cave.

He yelled back at May and Alex, "Stay here. Make sure the Dorfmann woman is left alone."

He ran into the cavern, noticing for the first time how the tunnel mouth sloped down into the cavern itself. His fears about the submarine and the other atom bombs evaporated. Doyle looked down into the clear waters of the lake. He could see a submerged tunnel large enough to allow the passage of the submersible. This was now full of debris. No submarine could pass the huge boulders strewn in the tunnel mouth.

Doyle guessed the tunnel roof had collapsed, crushing the submarine. He tried not to linger on the alternative if the submarine was intact. The tide was coming in carried and diesel oil that made rainbow patterns on the water surface.

Doyle looked around the cavern. There were still corpses strewn around, and he could not see anyone who looked alive. He trod on bullet casings and on metal and stone. Great gouts of blood were splashed on the floor and walls. Human body fragments were scattered everywhere, hands, fingers parts of skull and jaw. In the movies, bullets leave a neat round hole. In reality, Doyle knew a heavy-caliber pistol bullet could blow off limbs or vaporize a head.

Doyle glanced up at the ceiling. The lights were still running. He wondered if there was a generator somewhere or if there was a connection to main's power. He walked with other miners back to the entrance, seeing Joe, who had been at his side when he ran into the cavern. He realized that Joe had been guarding him as Nellie was guarding the Dorfmann woman.

"Thanks, Joe," said Doyle. "That's very mealy mouthed, but I don't know how to express my thanks. The king and emperor, England, New Guinea, me—we all thank you. They should make you join up again and promote you to general."

Joe gave a deep resonating laugh and slapped Doyle on the back, almost driving him off his feet. *God, everyone in this country is Mr. Muscles,* Doyle thought, *even the women.*

"I see you found other soldiers," said Doyle.

"Em nau, there's a few in the mining crew. Some of them were NCOs like me, so it made things a little easier."

"I need the names of all those men and of the dead men. The empire should recognize them all. We can't hand out gongs, medals, to everyone, but I can see that a few get awarded to the most deserving."

They emerged from the cavern entrance. Nellie sat with Lisle Dorfmann; May and Alex looked at Jäger's bandage. Several men were talking to the miners and making them put their weapons into neat stacks; joshing them when it was clear some were hiding pistols or bullets for souvenirs.

Doyle could see a stream of men walking down the path back to the main road, not wanting to wait for the trucks. Most of the men remaining were those from the trucks that went to Suein. They all seemed very pleased to have been in a fight, which Doyle found unsurprising, given that New Guinea was famous for warlike tribes.

There was a faint buzzing. Alex shouted to Doyle to look up. Planes were flying overhead and hundreds of parachutes blossomed in the afternoon sun. He walked over with Joe to where May, Alex, and Nellie sat with the scowling Lisle Dorfmann.

He looked at them and said, "I've learned one thing about Miss Dorfmann. I'll bet she doesn't wear a bikini when she goes to the beach."

Chapter 64

Dorfmann let out a harsh laugh.

"You think you have won, Englander. There is another bomb on the island, which will be detonated."

Doyle's sense of victory evaporated, replaced by an acid sensation in the gut.

"Tell me what you know. Where is it? When's it due to detonate?"

Dorfmann stared back at Doyle, silent.

Doyle did not hesitate. He grabbed Dorfmann's broken arm and began twisting it back and forth. There was an audible click and rasp of broken bones moving over one another. Dorfmann screamed and then swayed, nearly fainting with the terrible pain. Sweat beaded her upper lip and trickled down the sides of her face.

Doyle made as if to begin working her broken arm again, but she cried out, and he stopped.

Slowly, in halting breaths, Dorfmann related what she knew. "It is not an atomic bomb. It is what you English call a dirty bomb. This is a weapon of last resort, in case our plans were discovered. It will blow up and make the island of Lihir uninhabitable for thousands of years. The dismantled bomb you saw in the cave was sacrificed for the dirty bomb. As I recall, the weapon's warhead is now in a canister packed with high explosive and will be fragmented on detonation."

"Where's the bomb? Is it guarded?" said May, picking up a bush knife.

"Here somewhere, I think. Believe me, I wasn't told everything about all aspects of the operation. I do know that there is a detachment guarding the bomb, and they will fight to the death to protect it."

Doyle looked skyward at the parachutes. He wondered if he should wait until there was a squad or platoon to conduct the search. But where would he look? He hoped that the dirty bomb was not hidden elsewhere on the island.

"Nellie, lukautim Miss Dorfmann.[87] Joe, May, Alex, with me, we need to look in the cavern for a door, probably hidden well, so look carefully. Nellie, tokim soldiers long taim I kamap. Tokim em weah mipela go[88]."

Nellie told Dorfmann to lie down. She put Dorfmann's broken arm under a folded blanket on her chest to give it support. She also took Doyle's Mauser and tapped Dorfmann on the shoulder with the barrel, to reinforce that she was still armed and quite capable of blowing off Dorfmann's head.

The four headed into the cave. Alex and May took the left-hand grotto, while Joe searched the walls around the cavern lake. On a hunch, Doyle went up in the chamber where he had fought Koenig and Jäger. The room was how they had left it. Koenig was lifeless on the floor, though the blood had stopped seeping out of him. The two Schläger rapiers lay on the floor, both blooded from the swordplay. Doyle stood in the room and looked intently at everything in sight. There was the next cave with the smaller lake and speedboat, which they had not explored, but he sensed there was something he was missing.

He cast his mind back to when he had seen Koenig and Jäger at

---

[87] "Nellie, look after Miss Dorfmann."

[88] "Tell them where we've gone."

the filing cabinet and decided to check it out. He had assumed they were gathering documents from its drawers. There were some folders and papers on the floor, but not much considering the cabinet. It was of a modern design with five lateral drawers, five and a half feet tall and three feet wide. He went over to the cabinet and rocked it back and forth to move it forward. It took about a minute to get the heavy cabinet away from the wall and allow Doyle access to the rock face. The strip of rock behind the cabinet was no different as far as he could see. He put his hand on the rock wall and detected remote vibrations.

Doyle put his ear to the wall and heard a low thrumming drone. As he continued to look at the wall, he was joined by Joe, May, and Alex.

"Mr. Doyle, do you think there's something behind that wall?" said Joe. Doyle had given up telling him to call him Mick; Joe's military training was still ingrained.

"I don't know. Did any of you find anything in the other caves?"

May said, "We found a door in the barracks room and workshop. It wasn't hidden and led to a generator room and other corridors. We checked the generator. It's running off a huge diesel reservoir, so it'll run for hours yet. There's an exhaust tube that disappears into the ceiling that must come out on the surface."

"Alex, put your ear to the wall, next to my hand," said Doyle.

Alex complied and said, "Something buzzing back there. I don't think it's from the generator room. Besides, that thing is mounted on large rubber washers to minimize vibration. I imagine vibration isn't a great thing if you're doing technical work like dismantling atom bombs."

Alex stepped back into the main cavern and returned a few moments later with an ISS Geiger counter, brought to the cave along with their other kit when they were captured. Alex turned it on and the needle flew to the right, just bordering on the safe cutoff and the red danger zone.

"The radiation is probably higher inside," said Alex.

May and Joe stepped up to join Doyle and Alex. They all stared at the rock face in silent contemplation. Joe put his hand out as if he were opening an ordinary door in room, but instead of turning a handle, he pushed hard on the rock. Nothing happened for a second and then there was a creak as a two-foot wide sliver of rock opened inward. The door was the same height as the filing cabinet, so Doyle and the others had to duck to look inside the concealed passage.

"Who wants to go first?" said Doyle with a grin, pulling out his pistol and ducking under the lintel. Once through the door, he was able to straighten up. There was a short corridor, which ended at the foot of a spiral staircase. The tunnel and the staircase were lit by low-wattage bulbs, designed, thought Doyle, to make it difficult to see properly. He stepped back, and ducking his head, he put a finger to his lips.

"There's a corridor, about ten feet long, ending in a spiral staircase. It's lit but with low-intensity light bulbs. My guess is there are two or more of Jäger's men with the dirty bomb up there. If they contaminate Lihir, it will have devastating consequences for New Ireland and New Guinea. The mine will be out of action forever. The plutonium will be broadcast on the winds and affect all the neighboring islands, including mainland New Guinea and Australia. I don't think this was a fallback plan as Dorfmann said. I think it's all part of the attack on the empire."

"Do you think whoever is up that staircase knows we've discovered them?" said Alex.

Joe looked at the door and ceiling of the corridor. "Look, there's wiring leading to the door."

There was a clatter as something tumbled down the spiral steps. Even in the gloom, they all saw it was a German potato masher hand grenade. Doyle grabbed May, and Joe pulled Alex out of the passage. They all flattened themselves against the outer wall, with the two men shielding the women from the blast. There was a large bang and rock splinters and dust flew into the cavern. The filing cabinet was flung across the cave, its drawers falling open, spilling paper and file folders on the floor. The gloomy interior of the passage and steps was obscured with a dust cloud. A beam of light from a powerful torch pierced the cloud, and Doyle realized there must be a German on the stairs but out of sight, behind the bend of the spiral stairs.

"May, get me one of those sauce pans—quickly!" said Doyle, indicating the pile of pans around the cooking range.

May grabbed the pan and handed it to Doyle, who threw it into the passage. There was a burst of machine gun fire, which rattled the pan and threw up more dust. Doyle waved his hand across his throat for all of them to be quiet. He gently pushed May down until she was on one knee, as if genuflecting in church. Joe and Alex cottoned on quickly and arranged themselves similarly, so that there were four pistols pointing into passage. As Doyle had hoped, a figure edged around the curve of the staircase.

At first, there were just the tips of his boots, but slowly he emerged, dressed like his comrades in the Lihir Mine security uniform. The low lighting was an aid to the occupants of this secret niche, but the glare of the bright cavern lights was blinding to eyes attuned to the gloom. The man carried a Schmeisser MP 40, which he held out in front of him. A voice shouted something in German from the top of the staircase. The man shouted back without taking his eyes off the door. As he left the cover of the staircase, he was hit by four bullets.

The man pitched back to the bottom of the staircase, his MP40 rattling to the ground. The shouting from up above was much more urgent. The shot man lay on his back, moaning in pain. He had been hit in both legs and his abdomen.

Doyle made another signal to move into the passage and begin the assault on the upper chamber. Alex knelt next to the moaning trooper.

She whispered, "I speak German, Doyle."

"Ask him how many more of his pals are upstairs. Say we'll get him to safety and treat his wounds."

Alex spoke softly into the man's ear, while the other three kept looking up the spiral staircase in case anybody else emerged or another grenade was tossed down. The unseen voice shouted out another anxiety-laden inquiry in German.

Alex looked up and said, "There are four of them. They were left behind to set the bomb timer and then escape through the jungle to the coast, where they have an outboard-powered dinghy to take them to Lyra Reef, to rendezvous with a submarine."

"Lyra Reef?" said May. "That's at least a hundred miles from here, across open ocean."

"But possible with enough fuel?" asked Doyle in a low voice.

May looked at Joe, who said, "Yes, just about. You'd need six tanks of petrol. It's also straight north of here, so easy to navigate."

Another voice shouted down from above.

Doyle turned to May and said, "Can you do the honors?"

May gently tugged Alex away from the wounded man. She pulled a Commando dagger from the waistband of her underwear, knelt, and with one fluid motion, jabbed the knife up under the man's chin and into the brain. She pulled the knife out and wiped it on the man's uniform.

"Right, I've had quite enough of these bastards. Alex, take the MP40. We can't sling grenades into the room, given there's a bomb up there. We need to create a flash that will blind the other three Germans," Doyle said.

"We might blind ourselves," said Alex.

May stepped back out of the passage and into the cavern. Doyle saw her rummaging through Koenig's pocket. She came back and did the same with the other dead German. Doyle understood; May was going to make an improvised flash grenade from two butane cigarette lighters. Doyle could vaguely remember how this was done, but Alex knew and helped May, grabbing some tools and a roll of adhesive tape. While the two worked on converting the lighters into a flash grenade, there were more shouts from above.

Doyle and Joe watched the staircase, listening for any footfalls that would betray someone descending. May tapped Doyle on the shoulder.

"It's got to be thrown into the room to ignite. I'll have to go up the stairs until I can see the opening. I hope it doesn't disturb the bomb, but it's really just a firework," said May.

"OK, I'll cover you. Christ, I hope they don't lob another grenade."

May flattened herself against the inner wall of the spiral and began to climb. It was hard to gauge how far above the chamber was, since sounds echoed off the walls of the spiral staircase. Sweat was beading off both Doyle and May as they continued their slow climb. May stopped, signaling to Doyle that she thought the room lay just beyond the next curve on the staircase. May moved with all the stealth and patience of a praying mantis, aware that three sets of eyes would also be looking at the staircase with weapons poised. May risked a peep around the stair, which was met by a volley of bullets and muzzle flashes that were blinding. Doyle realized that the security guards had done themselves no favors by firing their weapons, as did

May, who took advantage of the temporary blindness of the three Germans to emerge and throw the improvised flash grenade.

Doyle and May shut their eyes tight and huddled against the wall as there was a loud bang and a brilliant flare of light. There was a startled chorus of curses by the Germans. Doyle and May ran into the room, firing at anything that moved.

Chapter 65

Doyle looked at the three men and started to conduct a triage to see who was the least wounded. He heard Joe and Alex enter the room behind him.

"Which of these men are still alive?" said Doyle.

Joe, May, and Alex checked one man each. Two were dead, but one of the security guards was alive, though with several bullet wounds. Doyle looked at the man's injuries and reckoned he might be saved with proper treatment. For now, May and Alex found a first-aid box and staunched the man's wounds.

Doyle looked around the room. It was relatively spartan, but with all the resources for a few days. There was a small gasoline generator to provide independent power. The exhaust hose disappeared behind sleeping bags rolled up and pushed to the edge of the room. There was a large carboy of freshwater, a chemical commode, and a gas-powered double-ring burner.

On its own on a table was a cylindrical object, which had to be the dirty bomb. It was secured in a shallow cradle with a crescentic support at each end. The cylinder was about as big as one of the sleeping bags. Its surface was smooth and unmarked except for a plate held down with four screws. Doyle touched it, realizing that the bomb controls lay behind the plate.

"What's the name of the wounded man?" said Doyle.

Alex asked him and received the reply, Werner.

"Can he speak English?"

Doyle heard a faint, "Ja."

"Werner, I'm going to ask you questions, and you're going to tell me the answers," said Doyle. "If not, then I'll ask May to persuade you, and believe me you don't want that. She broke your colleague Lisle Dorfmann in less than a minute. If you tell us the truth, we will save you. I can't promise a glittering future, you'll spend some time as a guest of His Majesty, but I suspect with some words from me, things will go well for you. Now, do you understand?"

"Ja ja, yes yes," said Werner.

"Has the bomb been set to explode?" Doyle asked.

"Yes, in … about an hour, at five o'clock. It would blow open the side of this chamber and shoot the plutonium over Lihir."

"Is there a tamper switch?"

"Yes, it will blow if anyone tries to open the control hatch."

"What about if it is moved?"

"I don't know, but probably not."

"How were you supposed to get out of here?"

Werner raised a weak arm and pointed at the cave wall. "Move the sleeping bags."

Joe and Alex pulled these away from the wall to reveal a small opening a man could crawl through and where the generator exhaust fumes were vented.

"It opens onto the side of the hill. From there we could emerge and run down to our dinghy."

"To take you to Lyra Reef, where you'll be picked up by a submarine. Your colleague told us about that. Do you actually believe that there will be submarine there?"

"Ja, yes, it's what we were told."

"There's not the slightest shred of doubt?" Doyle asked.

Werner was silent and then said, "Perhaps, the four of us talked about it, but we are Germans; we obey orders."

"Why hadn't you left?"

"We were set to leave when you discovered us. Our orders were to fight to the last man if we were found.

Joe said, "We've got an hour. What are we going to do?"

"How heavy is that thing?" Doyle asked.

Joe tried lifting one end. The bomb casing rose but with considerable effort.

May said, "Even four of us would have a hard time getting that out of here, and then what are we going to do with it?"

"Sink it; the waters here are some of the deepest in the world. If the water gets in, it might damage the circuitry. If it explodes underwater, the plutonium fragments will be scattered but will sink down to the abyssal plain or into a trench."

"Hello, anyone up there?" said a voice at the foot of the staircase.

"Yes, please come up," said Alex.

An English officer ran up and introduced himself. "Hello, I'm Lieutenant Norton, with the Gurkha Rifles." Despite the circumstances, Norton let his eyes linger on Alex and May.

"I'm Doyle. This is Joe, Alex, and May; we're ISS operatives. You'll have to take that on trust; we don't have our identity cards with us. Are your men close by?" asked Doyle.

"Yes, what do you need?"

"A party of men to manhandle that cylinder to the speedboat below. It's bloody heavy, so it might be best to put it into a blanket and take it down that way. The spiral staircase will be difficult, but I know Gurkhas never shrink from challenge."

"Is it an atom bomb?" asked Norton.

"No, it's what's called a dirty bomb. There is a bloody great charge of high explosives wrapped around a canister of plutonium. It will blow this chamber wall open and scatter plutonium to render the Lihir Mine inoperable for thousands of years."

Norton went to the staircase and rattled out a series of commands in Nepali. A flurry of action began, with a Gurkha sergeant major leading troopers into the room to assess the task. They took one of the sleeping bags and gently removed the bomb from its cradle. They lay the bomb on top of the sleeping bag.

Doyle looked at his watch. It was 4:20 p.m.

Doyle said, "Joe, go ahead of these fellows, and get the speedboat started. We'll have to carry this on the back seat."

Joe ran down the stairs while Doyle, May, and Alex followed the slow procession of the bomb.

Doyle said to Norton, "Get some of your other men to pull the dead man below out of the way." Just for bounce he added, "I suppose we might have saved him, but I let May keep her assassin skills sharp."

Norton looked suitably impressed.

Doyle continued. "I was tempted to turn her loose on the German up there; his name's Werner. He was helpful; save him if you can. We've carried out some first aid, and I think he can recover. We may get some more useful intelligence out of him."

Chapter 66

The tough, wiry Gurkhas got the bomb down the stairs in a nonstop chatter of Nepali, joshing and cursing each other, heedless of the danger. This was, thought Doyle, why they were the most admired and feared soldiers in the world. Resistance would fade away when Gurkhas joined the fight. He'd seen Gurkhas charging into battle in the Indio-China War and was astonished that many threw their guns down at the last minute and went in using their famed kukri knives.

Once clear of the passage, Doyle ran ahead to find Joe. He was sitting in the driving seat of the speedboat with the engine bubbling away and exhaust smoke bursting from the bubbles. The key had been in the ignition, so no hotwiring was required. Doyle looked at his watch. It was 4:40 p.m.

The Gurkhas, Joe, and Doyle put the dirty bomb on the back seat of the speedboat, causing the vessel to sink lower in the water, but not dangerously so. Joe had found a large flashlight, which he handed to Doyle.

"You can drive one of these things, right?" said Doyle.

"Em nau masta, mi save gut."[89] Doyle laughed and took the sarcastic putdown with grace.

Joe motored to the passage off the lake. Doyle pointed the flashlight into the cyclopean black eye of the opening to the sea. The

---

[89] "Yes, sir, I know how."

speedboat only just fit in the passage and banged against the rock walls. Doyle checked his watch. It was fifteen minutes to 5:00 p.m. There was still no sign of the opening, but the water now began to roughen and waves slapped the boat. A tense minute passed, and a spot of light in the far distance showed the entrance. Joe gunned the engine to speed up but not enough to damage the speedboat.

As they came nearer to the entrance, Doyle realized the high surf was pounding against the cliff. They would have to pick the right moment to ride over the surf. Doyle knew surf came in sets, usually seven or so waves and then a calm interval. At the entrance, the waves were surging into the tunnel, making it difficult for Joe to keep the speedboat steady and pointed to shoot out of the cave.

There was a lull in the waves, and Joe gunned the throttles fully open. They emerged into slack water, but a towering wave rolled toward them. Joe rode up the face of the wave, while Doyle threw himself forward to prevent the speedboat toppling backward. There was a moment of terror on the peak of the wave, and then they flew over and into the trough between waves. They did this three more times, but the final time, their momentum stalled and the speedboat slipped back and overturned.

Doyle was plunged into the roiling surf. He lost his bearings and had to pause and watch bubbles to know which way was up. He swam to the surface and emerged in a sea of foam. He feared he would not be able to breathe, but a wave picked him up and he was able to take several deep breaths. He could hear his name being shouted above the roar of the surf. He looked around the crazy sea with waves bearing down on the island and waves reflecting off the cliffs. Finally, he saw Joe and the upturned speedboat.

Joe had held onto the boats wheel and climbed on the hull. The water was in another lull between wave sets but with white water all around them. Doyle checked his watch. It was two minutes to 5:00 p.m.

"Mr. Doyle, here—get out of the water before the bomb blows," Joe said.

Joe hauled Doyle onto the hull, which didn't appear to be sinking due to foam built into the body of the boat. They sat side by side, looking down into the water. Doyle glanced at the coast and thought he recognized Suein, which made sense since the two cavern lakes were part of a larger system on the north side of Lihir. Doyle knew the bomb sank in relatively shallow coastal water, around five hundred feet, not the abyssal plain but the plutonium would sink or be dispersed in the sea and not over the island.

It was five minutes past five. Doyle began to slowly relax and think the bomb would not explode. Suddenly, a shock wave from the depths created a fountain of water and rocked the boat.

"Shall we swim to shore, Joe? I think we're drifting out to sea," Doyle said.

"We could try, but there are rip currents here and a lot of sharks. Look, there are several vessels heading this way."

Doyle shaded his eyes and saw a variety of vessels speeding to where Joe and Doyle were. *God,* Doyle thought, *that was a narrow victory; we will have to set up monitoring to make sure the plutonium is not contaminating fish and seafood. Royston Rogers and Professor Sykes will have their hands full dealing with the outcome of Operation Anvil.*

"I'd buy you a beer, Joe, but you're a Seventh Day."

"I'm flexible on some Seventh Day restrictions, beer being one of them—just as long as Auntie Nellie doesn't find out."

Chapter 67

A victory is twice itself when the achiever brings home full numbers.[90] Doyle said the quote to himself over and over. *Did I bring home full numbers?*

There were many dead miners piled up outside the cavern. A lot of fathers, brothers, and sons would not be going home. Many New Guinea families will be grieving. Meslee might have been another statistic, along with Kemal and his family. We all got off with cuts and bruises. He inhaled and enjoyed the scent.

"What are you thinking about?" asked Alex as she lay in Doyle's arms in a Port Moresby hotel room.

"How sex with you always makes me wish I still smoked."

"Liar, you had that dark look about you."

"What dark look?"

"When you're brooding on things. We've all seen it. Your eyes look as if you are staring into infinity; you clench your jaw and your fists."

"No wonder I never win at poker. I was thinking about the dead."

"Oh."

"Sorry, very gloomy of me. I should rejoice that this bloody mission was a success. I wasn't a great stalking horse after all. Too many innocent lives were lost, not just the miners who helped us

---

[90] *Much Ado about Nothing,* act 1, sc. 1, l. [8].

out, but also all those ISS personnel who were killed for knowing too much or because they could be manipulated. Looking back, I can't believe we made it. The Anvil conspiracy was the best-planned stab at the heart of empire I have encountered. Chinese and German efficiency and ruthlessness are unmatched. Thank God they were prey to incompetence."

"That's a bit rich. I thought the British were world leaders in incompetence," Alex said.

"Oh, God, don't get me started. Do you know why Scotland united with England?"

"I know the Act of Union was in 1707 but not much else."

"The entire country, and I do mean the entire bloody country, invested in a scheme in Darien, in Panama, to build New Scotland in Central America—for Darien just substitute New Guinea. Darien is probably worse, more venomous snakes, more diseases, and like New Guinea, an equatorial latitude—about the worst place you could send Scots. Scotland was driven to its knees by a 'get rich quick' scheme, not by an invading army of English," Doyle said.

"Are you picking on Scotland for my benefit?"

"No, just the first one that popped into my head. There was the Dublin property bubble in Ireland just before the 1800 Act of Union. The Dublin property market collapsed pretty much after an Irish rebellion attempt a couple of years before. Many of my ancestors, both Protestant and Catholic, were executed or deported after that little episode. There was the South Sea Bubble fiasco at about the same time in England, people buying shares in a company whose assets were greatly inflated and with no prospect of profit. People never learn. When there's a smooth talking fellow promising easy cash, check your strongbox and lock your daughter in her bedroom."

Alex laughed and said, "You are such a conundrum. Are you

still serious about trying to make a go of things when we are back in London?"

"Sure, a new life, back in the bosom of the mother country," he said as he grabbed Alex's large breasts.

There was a knock at the door and a slight swishing noise as a piece of paper slipped under the door.

"Looks like the world won't leave us alone." Doyle untangled himself from Alex and picked up the paper.

"Hullo, it's from May. She's downstairs, asking we would grace her with our presence."

They both dressed quickly. Alex was in the next room to Doyle, but there were connecting doors, so she slipped away to make herself presentable. They descended together and saw that May was with Nellie and Joe.

May said, "I would have phoned, but I was unsure which room to call."

Alex gave a sour smile while Doyle laughed aloud and then embraced Nellie and Joe. Alex did the same.

"I paid for them to come down on today's flight from Kavieng. They'll stay with me for a few days. I just wanted to have us together again, so did Joe and Nellie," said May.

"How about a cup of tea?" said Alex.

"Em nau, mi laikim tea,"[91] said Nellie.

They went through from the lobby onto a verandah that served as the hotel's tearoom and coffee shop. May ordered tea and scones for the five of them.

"I put it on Alex's account," said May.

"Thank you very much," said Alex.

---

[91] "Yes, let's have tea."

"Well, we are all here again—," began Doyle

"Ai, bikman, yu loose ting ting yumi mas pray befoa mipela kaikai,"[92] said Nellie.

"Ah, yes, please go ahead," said Doyle.

Nellie made everyone join hands and close their eyes while she thanked God for their safe deliverance and for the food and drink.

Nellie poured tea, telling Joe, "No kan shame, kai kai[93]."

"No change in your auntie then?" said Doyle.

"No, I still feel like a pikinini," said Joe.

"Did Frank Gardiner offer you any work?" Alex asked Joe.

"Yes, when I go back, I'll start in the Lands Office. You know how difficult land ownership and tenure is in New Guinea. Mr. Gardiner reckoned I would work well in helping sort out disputes. He said I had good leadership qualities so could expect to rise up in public service."

"Plus he's a big, strong lad and a bit of a hero after Lihir, so Frank likes having him around in case there's any 'mek noise,"[94] said May.

"How's Meslee?" asked Doyle.

"We haven't been back to Emananus, but someone came down yesterday on the boat. Meslee's fine. A few nightmares but he is better from his injuries. They breed us tough in New Guinea," said May.

"And you, Nellie, you good?" asked Doyle.

"Ai, so good to see you all, but me laik go back haus, long Sule Point[95]."

"Is Sister Kathy all right?" asked Alex.

"No worries," said Joe

---

[92] "Hey chief, you've forgotten we must pray before eating."

[93] "Don't be shy, eat"

[94] Trouble.

[95] "I want to go back to my house at Sule Point."

They chatted and reminisced into the late afternoon, and then May drove them to a seafood restaurant in Boroko, where they feasted on locally caught barramundi, prawns, crayfish, and lobsters. Nellie passed Doyle a photograph for him to keep. It showed Lumas, Meslee, and Micah's daughter Rellin. They were dressed in their Sabbath clothes, smiling at the camera. Meslee wore long pants and a shirt, the girls in pretty frocks, and all three wore shoes. Lumas's hair had been brushed out into a great shimmering cloud.

May took them back to the hotel, saying she expected travel orders for Doyle and Alex in the morning. Doyle had a lump in his throat, Alex was sobbing, Nellie cried and held onto Doyle, and Joe had tears in his eyes. Nobody wanted to break up the goodbyes, but Doyle knew that this was the end of this road. May and Alex embraced, Alex saying she would miss her so much and thanking her for being a rock when Doyle was wounded. May said she could be in England soon; she had heard rumors at the commission of promotion and possible additional training.

May kissed Doyle hard on the lips and slipped her tongue down his throat. She told him that he knew where she was if he ever got tired of gingerbread girls. Alex's smile became lopsided.

Finally, everyone stood back. Joe gave a smart military salute and then led Nellie back to May's car. May jumped in behind the driving wheel. They drove off with a volley of goodnights and waves.

Chapter 68

Sir Anthony had insisted that Doyle stay with him at his Windsor home. There had been a brutal week of meetings and debriefings, and there were further meetings coming in the following days, with other government departments and ministers of state.

Doyle had hoped that he could stay on his own at the Union Jack club and sneak Alex in up to his room, but she was in Tunbridge Wells with her parents, who wanted to hear about her adventures in the South Seas.

Gurung gave Doyle a salute and took his luggage up to the guest room.

Sir Anthony said, "Let's go through to the study. I know we both want to relax, but it's a better place to talk about work. We can have a serious drink, nonetheless."

"Where's Lady Sonia?" asked Doyle.

"At the palace—she's got lady-in-waiting duties. There is an official visit by the Swedish monarchs, so it's all hands on deck for the week."

Sir Anthony poured them both a generous measure of Irish single malt. He put the bottle on the table. *Must be digging in for the night,* thought Doyle.

"I gather you would like to come home," said Sir Anthony.

"My Ulster grandmother would say it's the talk of the steamie."

"Are you serious about coming back to England?"

"Yes, this mission reminded me I'm not immortal. I'm not the Wild Colonial Boy anymore."

"And I suppose Miss McCall also plays into your plans?" Sir Anthony asked.

"Tongues have been wagging, but yes, I think I'd like to make a stab at domestic bliss, and Alex is probably my best chance of doing that."

"There's a bit of an age difference, but I would say yes, give it a try."

"Thanks. I'd better get a place to live. I'm not sure I can sneak Alex into the Union Jack Club."

"I'll let you have the use of an apartment in a safe house. Stay as long as you like; gives you time to look for a decent place. Now, what do you want to do?"

"I was thinking of a post at either at Bletchley Park or Chartwell, or somewhere in the Home Counties."

"Why don't you take over the Circus?"

"What, really?" Doyle said.

"Yes, it's underutilized. I know you use it as a private reference source. I have a notion to use the Circus as a vetting agency. We would send cases and operations over for a second opinion. We need to be constantly on our toes, as the Anvil incident has shown. People become too comfortable without challenge. We have a tendency to interpret information in a way that confirms our preexisting beliefs."

Doyle said, "Confirmation bias, it's a big thing in the scientific world. I came across it at university. Academics interpreted new data as confirmation of their theories and assumptions. It cannot be avoided entirely. We are human therefore fallible, even the Pope, despite dogma to the contrary."

Sir Anthony smiled and poured another measure for them both. Doyle took a sip and looked with admiration at the drink.

"What shall we do with Miss Pilgrim?" said Sir Anthony.

"I heard rumors of promotion."

"Yes, but to do what? She's a first-class intelligence officer."

"You must have other local officers in training."

"Yes, and we must allow for promotion. We have several native people in training in the Brisbane facility."

"Get them in place and promote May to overall chief for the Melanesian Islands. Base her in Fiji, so she is also close to Polynesia and Micronesia. She can understudy the South Pacific ISS chief and be prepped to take over. By the way, Nellie has a niece, Lumas. She's ten now but should be schooled to take over Nell's coastwatcher duties," Doyle said.

"I gather she already helps her aunt. It is not unusual; it is a good thing in many ways, even if our cypher section gets upset at the thought. Here, this is for ... Auntie Nellie."

Sir Anthony passed over an envelope. Inside was a color photograph of the royal family, with their signatures.

"King James had it laminated; he knows equatorial climates are so destructive. It will go in the diplomatic bag to Moresby, and I have asked Miss Pilgrim to deliver it in person to Nellie. Does she have another name? I can't keep referring to her Auntie Nellie."

"It's Saupa. It's in our report footnotes. Here, I'll write it down." Doyle printed out Nellie's second name on a notepad on Sir Anthony's desk.

"The king wanted to pass out gongs to everyone, but you know we don't accept them for active service ISS staff," said Sir Anthony.

"Yeah, guessed as much. I have enough fruit salad on my army jacket. I am just glad we won, without too many losses. What about

349

the miners who were killed in the fight at the cavern and the two lads who helped with the bomb, Lamilla and Molean?"

"Miss Pilgrim has advised that a financial emolument should be paid to the families of the dead miners. I am also advised that it might create unnecessary tensions if those two men were singled out in particular," Sir Anthony said.

"Yeah, New Guinea is a bad place for jealousy and grudges. What about the mine?"

"Returning to normal under government supervision. There was no damage to the mine itself and the processing plant, though the bombs had to be removed. Most of the mine personnel are blameless. We checked their backgrounds very thoroughly. They were hired, among other things, because they could speak German. I hear you gave quite the speech about seeing the operation through without creating mass unemployment."

Doyle shifted uneasily in his chair. "Yeah, well, we don't have an empire just to create widows and social misery. We leave that to the French and the Belgians."

Sir Anthony laughed—something Doyle could not recall him doing, even as a young man.

Doyle said, "The ISS and New Guinea Special Branch need to look into what Frank Gardiner told me, that Lihir Gold had been greasing the palms of local politicians and public servants, to keep away any scrutiny. I would guess that's how they avoided employment inspections."

"I have already telefaxed instructions to Miss Pilgrim to begin that investigation. I suspect there will be a great deal of bloodletting, hopefully only in the metaphorical sense. Speaking of which, what about your pistol? Why did the Browning jam?"

"Dud round—even the best ammunition can be affected by

the awful humidity and jungle conditions. He's demanding the manufacturers up their standards."

"Quite right. I don't want ISS personnel being shot because their guns fail."

"Has the volcanic cavern been explored?" Doyle asked.

"Yes, we have divers ready to begin looking for the submarine and the other four bombs. The place is riddled with tunnels, several to the outside with hidden doors. That is how you were ambushed on your first foray. I think it was as you said in your report, all hastily improvised when your Land Rover was seen heading into the bush. Another team must have gone to your Land Rover to plant the bomb. Again, it had all the hallmarks of improvisation, although wrapping the bomb in black cloth was a damned clever idea."

Doyle said, "Did Dr. Hilborn ever crack Irene Fong?"

"Yes, funnily enough with cups of tea. He had conversations about her early life in New Guinea and subsequent education in Australia and China. Just by keeping her comfortable and not under pressure, he was able to help her break the conditioning. Hilborn says it's not a new idea, simply treat the patient with kindness and be prepared to listen if they want to talk."

"That was some fiendish psychological conditioning," said Doyle.

"Yes, we have encountered it before though. Some of the prisoners exchanged after the Indo-China War were programmed, if that is the right word, to be assassins. Luckily, the Chinese conditioning techniques were in their early development. The men started exhibiting strange behaviors resulting from inner conflicts."

"Well they must have ironed out the kinks. We need to find out more about how they did it. Has Fong talked about it?"

"Yes, it's a mix of hypnotic drugs and therapy, though Fong

was already susceptible. She will have to serve time in prison for complicity, though we will ask for leniency."

"Stupid idea, but she might be a useful asset when released," Doyle said.

"Not so stupid, and we'll think about it. At least we could try her out on a probationary contract under Miss Pilgrim."

"We need to develop methods to screen for people who have been conditioned."

"Already underway—you can imagine if the Chinese or Germans could place these people within the ISS, what this would do. All leave is cancelled while we conduct screening. It's not very popular, but I would rather be unpopular than assassinated."

"We also have the woman, Dorfmann, who can probably fill in any gaps, with a little persuasion. I'm assuming that the Germans who came to England with Chan and Fong were conditioned the same way. I expect they were Abteilung volunteers."

"Yes, Dorfmann is under twenty-four-hour watch and secured as Fong was. It's not often we get our hand on a senior Abteilung operative. The man you shot at Kemal's shop was an Abteilung operative called Hans Küng. The Finnish police recognized his fingerprints. He was caught burgling the house of a Finnish military officer in Helsinki."

"I know Koenig was from the Abteilung; what about Jäger?" Doyle asked.

"Also Abteilung, but a sleeper agent, who was activated when he became the Lihir mine director ten years ago. We think the Abteilung cleared his path to the directorship, probably with help from the Jinyiwei. Like many Germans, he had a strong grievance with the empire for killing relatives in the 1966 war. We are looking to see if Jäger and Koenig traveled to China."

"I'd say it was a foregone conclusion. Is Jäger still comatose?"

"Yes, the sword penetrated through to his brain junction, the corpus callosum, partially severing it," Sir Anthony said.

"I'm still kicking myself for taking my eye off the ball for a second."

"Don't, you were battered to within an inch of your life and concussed. He was determined to commit suicide and not be taken prisoner. That is why he did what he did. If he had slashed his neck, you might have saved him. In any case, the ISS operatives parachuted in with the troops and took photographs, fingerprints, and blood from all the Germans and Chinese, dead and alive, so we now have a wealth of information."

"What do Tambo and Hilborn think about Jäger regaining consciousness?"

"They are pessimistic, but they will conduct some experiments with his brain."

"Do I want to know?" Doyle asked.

"No."

"What about the security guard we left in the chamber above the spiral staircase?"

"Recruited from the German military by the Abteilung, as were all the other security guards. He survived, and we'll question him, but I suspect he was just a functionary, obeying the orders given to him."

Doyle shrugged and took another drink.

Sir Anthony said, "The Chinese soldiers and sailors, both captured and killed, are regular military. Colonel Sung, though, as you said in your report, was likely an officer of the Jinyiwei. That's where we need to concentrate in the future. I'm putting more people and funding into the ISS facilities in Hong Kong, Singapore, and our embassy in Peking.

"I would boost them everywhere in East and Southeast Asia."

"We will over time."

"Speaking of China, I don't suppose the fellow who put the black spot on me in Moresby has been identified?" Doyle said.

"Miss Pilgrim is looking into this, but it's unlikely he will be identified. He was probably a Jinyiwei operative. Incidentally, Miss Pilgrim's last communication indicated there had been a development on the intermediary who recruited the men to kill you. He was found dead in a Port Moresby flood channel with two bullets in his head."

"Double tap, I like the classics."

"He was from the Southern Highlands and worked as a gardener at the Chinese embassy in the capitol," Sir Anthony said.

Chapter 69

Doyle sat on a park bench at Riverside Gardens, a small green space four hundred yards from Vauxhall Cross. It was turning into midsummer, a few days when temperatures exceeded eighty degrees and the English went mad.

There would be the outrageous headlines in the tabloids about the temperatures being higher than Athens. Hospital emergency rooms would be swamped with heatstroke victims. Newsreels would show clips of the English flocking en masse to the beaches, with men and women in deck chairs, acres of white pasty skin broiling to lobster red, the occasional young woman with a plump curvy body splashing in the shallows, and other attendant horrors of the seaside in summer.

And then it would all be over for another year. Temperatures would fall below seventy degrees. The sunburned suffered in agony for a week, until their skin and swollen lips recovered. The English could go back to dressing properly again and scanning the skies for rain.

Doyle stared across the Thames, looking north, where he could see the towers of the Houses of Parliament on the skyline. The empire could rest safe, unaware that the fate of millions, perhaps billions, had rested on a desperate little squad that Doyle called Auntie Nellie's Army. This wasn't just himself, Alex, Joe, May, and Nellie, but also the others who had helped so much. This included the gaggle of kids like Meslee, Resllin, and Lumas, Dr. Smith, Nurse Karasa, Frank

Gardiner, Micah and Rurusan, Belinda, Mary Asua, and the ex-NCOs, who had steered a riot into a rescue mission.

There were critical questions requiring answers. Sir Anthony agreed with Doyle that neither Jäger nor Koenig were likely to have been the head of Raptor. So who was it? The Chinese government was set on a vigorous expansionist program. It had conspired with the Germans, helping them secretly rebuild their military. How had that escaped the notice of the ISS? He had a whole project outlined in his head for the queen bees and old China hands at the Circus. They would burrow into the files to find missed clues, and if items were suppressed, who was doing the suppression.

The other atom bombs had to be recovered. That amount of plutonium could not be allowed to leak out and contaminate the water table or flow into the sea. It would require a monumental project and expert divers to get to the crushed submarine. And then the divers would have to gain entrance to the vessel.

Little was known by the ISS about Chinese submarine interiors. The working assumption was that the bomb would likely be stored in a forward compartment, lowered into the vessel through an escape hatch. Once the divers were inside, the bombs would be dismantled to remove the plutonium core. This was supposing that the bombs were intact and that the cores could be removed. Doyle figured there would be many folks spending a long time on Lihir and improvising.

Someone sat down next to Doyle.

"You're in your dark place again."

Doyle flashed out of his reverie and said, "Hello, à colleen. Good to see you. Give me a salacious kiss."

They embraced and kissed as though it was the last kiss on Earth and the world crumbled on Judgement Day. They parted and stared at each other, both reveling in the other and the intensity of being together again.

"Hungry boy," said Alex, flicking her hair back.

"Hungry girl. I'd better put my jacket on my lap, or I'll shock the folks out for a walk along the river."

"God, it's good to see you again. I've been closeted in so many meetings and debriefings since I came back from Tunbridge."

"I was hoping to debrief you myself."

"Rude beast!"

"You look great; you're still tanned. I was worried you'd be one of these redheads who just burns."

"I still have to be careful until the skin darkens."

"You've been gossiping in the ladies lavatory," Doyle said.

"How ... oh, Sir Anthony—I told Jane to be discreet."

"I can't imagine that you would expect to stay secret."

"No, no, I suppose not." Alex laughed.

"Have you heard that Sir Anthony wants me to take over the Circus?"

"Will you accept?"

"Already have, although Sir Anthony retains the right to deploy me in the field if he needs an old hand to put some stick about."

"I hope you don't expect me to join you there."

"Christ, no—if we're going to make this relationship work, we need some boundaries, work being one of them. Have you told your mother and father about me?"

"I had a quiet word with mother," Alex said.

"And? Don't keep me in suspense."

"A cautious nod of approval. She says we should be settled and then come and visit her and papa."

"What about Lady Jane?"

"She still thinks you're a grubby Irish hooligan, but that I should grab you with both hands and hang on."

"Oh, good, in that case Alexandra McCall, will you marry me?"

"What, really?"

"Yes, really. I thought I should allay any anxious thoughts. I wish I had an engagement ring, but I thought it would be more fun to shop together and find something you like and I can afford."

"In that case, I accept—yes, I will marry you, but let's just live together first, so we can find out more about whether we are a match made in heaven or hell."

"Faith and begorrah, à colleen. You've made me a happy man, so you have," said Doyle in his peasant Irish brogue.

They kissed again for a long time, Doyle thinking that he wished they were in a bedroom.

"Sir Anthony has let us have an apartment in a safe house. I have the key. We'll have to get our own place, but there's no rush apparently," Doyle said.

Alex hugged Doyle again and then laid her head on his shoulder. She said, "I forgot to mention, I'm pregnant."

Printed in the United States
by Baker & Taylor

Printed in the United States
By Bookmasters